HE SWORE TO PROTECT HER.
BUT AT CAMP BLACKSHEAR, EVERYONE IS A PREDATOR.

A SHATTER IN THE WOODS SERIES

BLACKSHEAR

M.E. MASON

For all the good girls who dreamed of being pinned to a tree by their childhood crush, but were too shy to say anything.

This one is for you.

PLAYLIST

Creep - Radiohead
Bury A Friend - Billie Eilish
Sabotage - Beastie Boys
11 a.m. - Incubus
Passenger - Deftones
Pet - A Perfect Circle
Closer - Nine Inch Nails
1979 - The Smashing Pumpkins
Magnetic - Wage War
Chokehold - Sleep Token
Rooster - Alice in Chains
The Red - Chevelle
Schism - TOOL
Black Hole Sun - Soundgarden
Dreams - Fleetwood Mac
Just Pretend - Bad Omens

The full Blackshear playlist is available on Spotify.

WELCOME TO CAMP BLACKSHEAR

BEFORE YOU ENTER

This story is not safe.

If you're searching for soft edges and easy happily-ever-afters, turn back now. *Blackshear* might feel like a summer fling at first touch, but the deeper you sink into these pages, the darker it gets. What starts as a slow burn becomes a descent.

In the words of Max McKinnon:

"You good, baby?"

This is a dark romance. It is not gentle. It is not kind. It does not ask for your permission before it hurts. Please read with care.

This book contains, but is not limited to: psychological trauma; complex PTSD responses; coercion; power imbalances and control dynamics; obsessive and possessive behavior; stalking; emotional abuse and gaslighting; explicit sexual content including scenes with dubious or pressured consent; loss of bodily autonomy; non-consensual or legally questionable decisions made on a character's behalf; graphic violence including stabbing and blood loss; threats of sexual violence; and substance use.

Lines are crossed. Boundaries are blurred. Consent is complicated.

This book ends on a cliffhanger and is part of a continuing story that does have a happy ending.

1

MACKENZIE

AGE 11

Ashbourne, New York
2012

I was eleven the night the FBI came for me.

My house had always smelled wrong at night. For years, it had always smelled rotten.

But the night they came for us, the smell was worse.

My eyes snapped open as soon as I heard the sirens wailing outside.

Blue and red lights pulsed across my bedroom walls.

The air from the window unit buzzed against my face—too cold, and too normal for a night like this. I clutched Clover to my chest, burying my nose in his matted fur. I had him since I was five. He was my good luck charm.

Boom.

Boom.

BOOM.

Heavy boots stomped, the sound echoing through the house like gunfire. I could almost see the thuds in the walls.

I squeezed my eyes shut and pressed my hands over my ears.

"Mackenzie," a whispery voice called. "Mackenzie. Wake up."

Two hands gripped my shoulders. They shook me until the room fractured into focus.

A man in black sat beside me.

He was so still. Dark hair slicked back like a soldier in a movie. Bold letters stretched across his chest.

F.B.I.

I sounded them out in my head, one by one, like I was learning to read again. I was eleven. I knew how to read. But these letters didn't make sense.

Fear curled in my stomach, crawling up into my throat.

Then he looked at me, and everything stopped.

I shouldn't feel safe. He's a stranger in my room. There was something sweet about his eyes.

He seems nice, I think.

A calmness slid through me. The same feeling I got when I smelled cookies baking in December or stuck my hands in warm laundry straight from the dryer.

"I'm sorry to wake you, little one," he said, his voice thick and sweet, like honey poured over ice cream. "But we've got to go. *Now.*"

My fingers tightened around Clover.

"Where's my Mommy?"

"I'm here. I'm right here, baby."

She stepped from the shadows, eyes wide, face pale. Her shaking hands grabbed mine.

Then I saw the blood.

It streaked across her cheek and forehead, sharp and red, turning her into a monster.

I jerked back. "What's that?"

My voice sounded sharp and strange.

"We don't have time for that, honey," she whispered, her eyes flicking to the man. "This is Agent West. He's here to help us."

She glanced over her shoulder, just for a second. The hair on my arms rose like they were listening to something I couldn't hear.

"Where's Daddy?"

"That's not important, sweetheart," she said gently, brushing her bloody hand over mine as she lifted me out of bed. "Listen to me; we're going to a warm place, somewhere you've never been before. It'll be fun, okay? A new adventure."

Her voice was soft, like lullabies and nighttime prayers, but I could hear the fear in it.

I glanced around my room. "But what about all my stuff?" I asked.

Mommy smiled, but it didn't reach her eyes. "You'll have a new room," she said softly. "With new toys. Even better ones."

Agent West leaned forward, arms out. "Want to go for a walk?"

His voice was kind.

I shook my head. "No."

I didn't want him to hold me. I didn't like not understanding. I didn't know what was happening, and I hated it.

He lifted me anyway.

My body locked up, stiff as a board. Clover was crushed tight against my chest. Mommy trailed beside us, her hand clamped on his sleeve. I could feel the muscle in his arm flex beneath her grip.

Then—

a shout.

It ripped through the house like lightning. Agent West flinched. He let go.

I slipped.

There was nothing to catch. No railing, no floor, no air. I just fell.

My body twisted in the air before I smashed into the steps.

Once.

Twice.

CRACK.

The back of my head slammed into the bottom step. White-hot pain burst through my skull like fireworks gone wrong. I saw them behind my eyelids.

Red, white, blue.

Sound stretched thin, like I was underwater. Everything faded. A faint ringing nestled into my ears, climbing higher, higher, until I wanted to scream just to break it.

Someone was screaming.

Not me.

Mommy.

Her voice cut through the ringing. She sounded wild.

"Mackenzie. Mackenzie!"

She scrambled down the stairs, hands slipping in my blood as she tried to cradle my head. Her fingers shook. She lifted me, stared for a heartbeat, then dragged me against her chest with a sob that sounded like begging.

"No, no—baby, please—please!"

Agent West's voice broke somewhere above us. "Mackenzie! Oh my God!" He fumbled with a walkie-talkie, shouting into it, "Bobby! I need med now."

The basement door swung open, and a man in a black cap appeared, rushing toward us with a bag clutched in one hand.

"What happened?" the man in the black cap asked.

Black spots swam around the room like lazy bugs in sunlight. A small white moth buzzed near my ear, landing on the wall. I watched it, waiting for the ringing to stop.

"I dropped her. God, I dropped her!" Agent West shouted. "She hit her head."

The man knelt beside me, holding up two fingers. "Can you tell me how many fingers I'm holding up, sweetheart?"

His voice was thick, round, and warm. The kind of voice that always sounds like it's smiling, even when it isn't. He had a mustache. It looked silly. I felt woozy. My thoughts bounced around my skull.

Something on the floor beside me caught the light. It was dark and slick, shining like a puddle after rain.

"Two," I mumbled, barely moving my lips. My stomach churned. My head burned.

He leaned in, gloved fingers gently brushing behind my head. When he pulled his hand back, it was soaked in red.

Agent West's face went as white as a ghost.

"Does your head hurt?" the black-capped man asked.

His question pinned me to the floor more than his hand did.

"Yes," I whispered.

A flashlight flashed across my eyes. I blinked but didn't turn away.

"Concussion. She probably needs stitches." His voice was steady, but worry edged it. He turned to Agent West. "You've got two minutes before the Butcher's back. You're out of time. We got most of the bodies out, but there's one… It's going to take us some time to clean up."

The air had that sharp, coppery smell again. The one that never went away, no matter how hard Daddy tried to clean up his mess.

"I know," Agent West snapped. "Do you have something? Wrap her up."

The man nodded. He pulled a towel from his waistband and quickly wrapped it around my head, tying it tight. Blood stained the white like spilled paint.

"Keep pressure on it," he said to Mommy. "Don't take it off until you get to the safehouse."

My eyes fluttered. I really wanted to sleep.

"Okay." Mommy's hands shook as she pressed the towel down on my head.

Agent West lifted me again. His hand clamped around my legs so hard it burned. I wanted to cry out, but my voice was gone.

When we reached the car, he set me in the seat. The buckle snapped shut around my waist, the click jolting me awake. I hugged Clover to my chest.

Mommy slid in beside me, pressing the towel to my head. Her arm wrapped around me, pulling me in.

Agent West climbed into the driver's seat and turned the key. The engine growled.

"Don't worry, Mackenzie," Mommy whispered. "You're going to be okay. We'll set up your new room exactly how you want."

My eyes sagged. "Can I have butterflies on my wall…" I was so tired, "…with glitter?"

"Yes. Whatever you want." Her breath shook when she said it.

I blinked, and the world outside was orange. Flames licked the sky. The snow glowed red. Our house was burning. I tried to speak, but my eyes fell shut.

When I woke, we were still moving. The sky was pale blue. The sun stretched its fingers over the horizon. My head felt heavy.

"I have to go to the bathroom," I whispered.

Mommy checked the towel. "The bleeding's stopped," she told Agent West. "But I'm worried about her walking."

He flicked the blinker on. "I'll take her."

We pulled into a gas station. I reached for the buckle, but Mommy's hand stopped me.

"Wait. Agent West has to check first."

Her eyes were everywhere—windows, mirrors, corners.

Outside, Agent West circled the car, one hand inside his jacket. He glanced at the empty pump beside us and nodded.

"Okay," Mommy said. "I'm getting out first."

She lifted me, struggling, and passed me into Agent West's strong hands. He held the towel tight as we moved inside. The bell over the gas station door jingled. A slow country song floated through the air.

He carried me to the girls' bathroom and set me on my feet, steadying me. "Make it fast. I'll be right here."

I noticed the blood on my pajamas.

Mommy glanced down, then back at me. She took my hands and made me look at her. "You're so beautiful, you know that? I love you so much. You don't have to be scared. We're safe now."

When we finished, Agent West scooped me up again. The smell of coffee wrapped around us. My stomach growled.

"I'm hungry," I murmured.

"We'll get something in a bit," Mommy said.

Back in the car, Mommy tucked me close. Agent West returned with donuts. I bit into a chocolate one. It tasted warm and too sweet.

His walkie-talkie crackled, making me jump.

He turned away from us, shoulders stiffening. "We just stopped," he said. Then, quieter: "Yeah. I see him. I don't know how they found us so fast."

Out of the corner of my eye, I saw him.

The man Agent West was talking about.

My shadow.

He stood by the pumps, still as a statue, watching us.

My chest thumped.

Ba-dump.

Ba-dump.

His face looked like Daddy's, but I knew it wasn't him. Boots. Black vest. Hat pulled low.

Ba-dump.

Ba-dump.

Ba-dump.

He stepped closer. Something long and dark glinted in his hands.

CRACK.

The windshield bloomed with white fractures, spider legs racing across the glass.

CRACK.

Another blow.

CRACK.

Three times, and the warm, safe world inside the car shattered.

2

MACKENZIE

AGE 12

Camp Blackshear
Blackshear, Georgia
Six Months Later

The shrill buzz of cicadas drilled through the trees. Their clicking scraped against the dusty cabin windows like fingernails.

It was almost eleven p.m., and I still couldn't sleep. Every creak of the bunk sounded like a footstep.

Shadows crawled up the cabin walls, pooling in the corners, stretching thin like hands reaching for me.

I'd been at Camp Blackshear for two weeks, and I already knew every exit. The front door stuck if you pulled too hard. The side door by the laundry room, in case I needed a quick escape. The path behind the cabins that cut straight to the woods. I told myself it was just in case. But what was I running from? My Daddy? I still didn't know.

Everyone said a new town would help. New state, new school, new camp. Like you could drive away from the bad stuff if you went far enough.

9

But it didn't matter how far we drove. Some nights, it still felt like the blood was on my hands.

When I got here, I already felt broken in ways I didn't have words for. I wasn't really looking for a fresh start. I just wanted the old stuff to stop chasing me.

Sometimes it felt like there were cracks inside me that nobody could see. Like if I moved the wrong way, I might fall apart.

The silence didn't feel like freedom. It felt like being dropped into the deep end of the lake. My lungs squeezed tight as I closed my eyes, putting my hands over my ears. I could hear the screams even when they weren't here.

I kicked my feet against the mattress like I could keep myself from floating into the nightmares. My shadows swam underneath me, bumping against my legs. The loneliness chewed at my insides, fluttering against my skin like a moth stuck too close to a candle.

A tiny ping tapped the window. I jerked upright.

Ping.

Ping.

PING.

The last one was loud enough to make me flinch. I sat up too fast and cracked my head on the low wooden beam.

"Ow," I hissed, rubbing the knot behind my ear. My fingers brushed my scar. The one that reminded me he was always watching.

I carefully peeked through the warped glass. Max stood there in the bushes, freckles dusted across his sunburned face, smiling like we shared a secret.

Max was my first friend here. On day one, a counselor had pushed me toward him. "Mackenzie, this is your camp buddy. You'll like him."

"Hi," I'd said, trying to sound casual. I could be casual. Right? Or did I say, "Hi, I'm Mackenzie. My Daddy is a killer, and I'm in witness protection. Did you know this camp is being watched?"

But I couldn't say any of that.

"Hi!" He'd grinned and offered a Fruit Roll-Up like it was a peace treaty. I'd taken it, unrolled the paper, and popped the end of the strawberry tail into my mouth. His smile was… comforting. There was something about him, about his voice. It felt familiar in a way that made my chest ache and relax at the same time.

We had nothing in common. He loved baseball, bugs, and country music. I hated Star Wars, and he quoted it daily. But he was funny, and when he laughed, it made me forget the sound of my daddy's voice.

When Max looked at me, I was just Mackenzie from Marigold, Georgia. But I still wondered if that other girl—the scared one who'd seen her dad covered in blood more times than she could count—was still hiding inside me.

I looked at Max's beaming face through the window. He motioned for me to come outside.

I slid into my worn tennis shoes and crept past the sleeping girls, tiptoeing between their beds. Someone snored. Someone mumbled in her sleep. The cabin's screen door pushed back as I nudged it open, letting out a soft whine that made me hold my breath.

The night smelled sharp. Smoke and citronella bit at my lungs in a way that now felt almost like home.

"Max?" I whispered.

"Right here!" he hissed. Hands clamped down on my shoulders. "Boo!"

I yelped and socked him in the gut.

"OOMPH! Trouble… you just rearranged my organs alphabetically," he wheezed.

I couldn't help laughing. He was the only person who called me Trouble. He said it was because I didn't bring trouble; I was trouble. I hadn't liked the nickname at first, but it was growing on me.

Our shoes crunched on the rocks as we walked down the gravel path.

Crunch, crunch, crunch.

The black night pooled at the edges of the trees, and I got that crawling feeling that something was following us. I got it a lot in the dark.

Almost like he could sense it, Max handed me a flashlight. The bright beam bit through the darkness.

"Why didn't you bring yours?" he asked.

"I didn't know I'd need it." My voice came out small.

"It's kayak night. How could you forget?"

But I had forgotten. My brain had been skipping over things lately.

And honestly, I was a little terrified to go out on the water.

We were kayaking to a part of the lake that glowed at night, or so they said. The counselors said it was because of bioluminescent microorganisms, little things called dinoflagellates, that made the water shimmer with this weird, magic-looking glow.

I peeked over at Max. We moved together, our footsteps echoing softly in the stillness. He knew I was scared of the dark, and he stepped closer, like a quiet shadow, always watching, always ready to protect me from something I couldn't see.

As we walked, a memory from two days ago flashed through my head.

"That's good," he'd said, looking over my shoulder while I drew in my journal. Then he'd pointed at a shadow in the trees. "What's that?"

"That's my shadow," I'd told him.

"But you're in the water." He was always so matter-of-fact, so literal.

"It's the one that watches," I'd admitted.

He'd looked at me, his blue eyes full of questions, but he never pressed.

I'd fingered the scar on the back of my neck, just below my hairline.

"Okay," he'd said. "But you need to draw me in next time. I'll be your new shadow." Then he'd nudged my shoulder with his.

"Come on." He'd jumped up. "They're bringing out the archery bows. I feel like shooting something."

His smile was contagious, and I'd closed the journal and followed him out to the fields.

Now, on the trail, he reached for my hand. It was sweaty, and I wanted to tease him about it. But I knew he wouldn't even care. I didn't let go.

By the time we reached the dock, Counselor Graham was waving us over. We slid our kayak into the water, and the glow sticks snapped to life. Max's glow stick was a deep electric blue like his eyes, and mine was a pale yellow.

The same color as the flowers I used to hide in.

I sank down into my seat in the kayak, getting my oars ready. The whole thing nearly flipped when Max climbed in.

"Max!" I yelped. "You almost capsized us!"

He laughed, grabbing his oars.

"Too bad those lake monsters didn't show up tonight. I was gonna help your mom plan a nice funeral," he joked.

I scanned the water around us, staring straight down into the dark lake, and he giggled.

"Relax. You ready?"

The dark swallowed us quickly. I tried to match Max's paddling.

Left, right, left.

But my pulse was already racing ahead.

And then, out of nowhere, my Daddy's voice cracked through the night.

"Mackenzie! You can never go into my basement. Never. YOU HEAR ME?"

I froze. My chest locked up. I only heard my Daddy's voice in the shadows.

I let out a little squeak, trying to push his voice out of my ears. A warm hand on my leg stopped me. A different voice cut through the memory.

"Trouble. It's okay. We're almost there."

Max was my anchor, always pulling me back to safety.

I was about to say thanks when the water beneath us bloomed into glowing aquamarine, every ripple like liquid stars.

"Wow," I breathed. It looked just like Max's eyes.

He was smiling at the water, but I could still feel his hand resting against my leg.

For the first time in weeks, the fear loosened its grip.

But it never really left.

It waited in the shadows.

At Blackshear, even the wind was a predator.

3

MACKENZIE

AGE 18

Summer 2019
Present Day

I was eighteen the summer everything changed. And, like always, it started at Camp Blackshear. The only place that felt like mine. A refuge. A world untouched by the chaos I was born into.

And it was the only place I saw Max.

He'd be there waiting like he always was. Same crooked smile, same laugh that could crack through my worst days. We never needed to catch up. We just picked up where we'd left off, as if the rest of the year was just one long pause.

We lived three hours apart and had our own lives outside of camp. But at Blackshear, it was just *us*.

I counted down the days like I was in prison. Agent West and my mom had locked me out of the normal teenage world, and isolation became my default state. I still didn't have a cell phone or social media.

"Digital thumbprint remains confidential," West would say, like I was a classified file, not a girl.

15

My father was still out there, somewhere in the darkness. I hadn't seen him since the night of the fire, but I could feel him lurking, like a shadow pressing cold and heavy against the back of my neck. I knew nothing about that night. My mom refused to tell me. It was all a black, shifting fog in my mind, a part of my life erased, forgotten.

The only sign it was real was the nightmares—haunting visions of the things he used to do—things he forced me to do. The FBI still watched us, like silent, black-vested shadows in the corners of my room. It was unsettling, nerve-wracking, and every time I asked my mom about it, she only shook her head and whispered, 'Not now.'

They'd been stitched into our lives for so long, I barely remembered a time without them.

Agent West was always there, hovering at the edges like he belonged to us, like he was our family. In a way, he was. I sometimes saw him as a dad. His son, Jeremy, also became part of our lives. He slept over and ate at our table. More like a brother than a friend. It was normal in the way that only things you never question can be normal.

But I knew it wasn't. Not really. My story had changed. I lived by rules no one my age had to live by. And even though I pretended not to notice, I did. Especially when Jeremy would flaunt his iPhone in my face.

"You're a loser," he had said, texting his girlfriend. He was five years older than me and liked to remind me about it.

"Shut up," I had said back, trying to kick him in the balls. "I'm going to punch you in the face."

"I'd like to see you try, little sis," he had laughed, flipping his black hair back and walking off.

I wanted to know why I was the only teenager in my entire fucking town that wasn't normal.

But with Max, the feeling of the unknown faded. He made me forget I was a 'federally protected asset', as West said. With him, I was just Mackenzie. My life hadn't really started until I came to Blackshear and met him.

We talked almost every night on my stupid landline. We talked about everything. He told me about his high school baseball championship game. He was a good player, and his dad made him practice with a coach who had played in the MLB.

"You think you're going to become a professional baseball player? Am I going to get front row tickets?" I had asked him.

"You know it. I'll sign my jersey for you."

He had sounded so confident. I tried to replicate his confidence, but I had more of a crippling anxiety disorder.

When we didn't talk, we wrote letters as if it were 1995. Max's letters were filled with doodles and dumb jokes, while mine were filled with random pictures I thought he'd like. He swore he kept them all, saying I was his favorite artist. I wasn't sure if I believed him, but he'd pinky promised. And Max didn't break those.

We even had friendship bracelets. Our tether to a summer filled with friendship.

But as camp crept closer, I couldn't shake the ache of knowing this would be our last summer together. College was waiting, pulling us toward different paths.

One night, while painting my nails and listening to *Creep* on my stereo, we talked about everything and nothing. Vanderbilt came up; his dad was pushing for it. Max pretended he didn't care. Then, out of nowhere, he said:

"What are you thinking about?" His voice was deep now, really deep. But it still held that same aloofness: funny, goofy, just *Max.*

"How I can't wait to see you in a few days."

I heard his smile over the phone before he spoke.

"Me too. I can't believe we get to be in the same counselor group this year."

We had been counselors since we had turned sixteen, but had

never been placed together. I loved that we would finally get to lead a group together for our last summer at camp.

"I know," I laughed. "Whoever decided that hasn't met us yet."

I was met with complete silence on his end. In my defense, I wasn't a comedian, but he usually would at least entertain me with a small laugh. He seemed pensive; I could tell that he was deep in thought.

"Do you think it's weird to think we're leaving soon?" I asked to cut the silence.

"Every day."

A pain clutched my heart when he said that, and I bit my lip to stop myself from crying. I couldn't imagine a life or a summer without him.

"Do you think your mom would let you apply out of state?" he asked. "I know you already got into GCU, but maybe?"

I laughed bitterly. "Hell, no. Georgia only. You know that."

What I didn't say was that I needed FBI clearance to leave the state. Max had no idea about my life. It was a secret I had kept from him throughout our entire friendship.

"I'd be cool to see you every day." Max's voice broke me out of my thoughts.

Something in his voice, soft, almost hesitant, made my chest tighten.

"You got into GCU, too, you know. You could always come."

"I know," he said softly. And then, "You know, the guys give me such a hard time at school about you."

I could almost see him rolling his eyes.

"Why? Because they know I can beat you up?"

"That was one time." He paused for a beat. "You haven't seen me in a year. I've changed." He got quieter and said, "I've dated a few girls this year. I'm cool now."

I could hear the laughter under his words, but that news landed like a splinter under my skin. I told myself it was fine. I'd dated too. But hearing him talk about them made something cold and unfamiliar curl inside me.

Max had dark, tangled hair that he wore under an Atlanta Braves baseball cap. The light sprinkling of freckles covered his cheeks and the tip of his nose. His blue eyes were constantly hidden by a bright red sunburn that reddened whenever he smiled or laughed. He was tall now, maybe 6'3", and his body was lean, like a baseball player.

The girls had been eying him more at camp, but he always ignored them. Too focused on kayaking, hiking, or just being Max. It was always just him and me. Bonnie and Clyde, we always said.

I couldn't imagine him being any different.

But apparently, he *was* different. And girls were noticing. It shouldn't have been a surprise, given that he was always so funny and kind. But I didn't like that he had kept his dating details from me. I tried to keep my jealousy at bay. But I was jealous.

Because he was dating someone. Because he hadn't told me.

"Look at you. Guess I'll have to start training if I'm going to keep up with Max McKinnon, thirst trap in the making."

"Careful, Trouble." I could hear his mouth tilting into a half-grin. "You'll be lucky if you get to see me in one."

"Oh, so you're admitting it?"

"Please. I'm fucking hot as hell."

"Oh, sure. Who lied to you? You've dated the entire senior class, now, right? Those girls must be blind."

"I'm selective, Trouble. I only pick girls who can keep up with me. And trust me, they aren't blind."

"So, what happened? Did they tap out or realize how big a nerd you are?"

"Maybe I'm just waiting for someone who can actually challenge me," he said. His tone sharpened just a touch. "Someone who doesn't get bored the second things stop being easy."

I raised a brow.

"Someone who will make me beg," he added. I could almost hear the smirk in his voice. "I like being on my knees."

I blinked; once, twice, three times.

"Wow. Cocky much? I hope those aren't the one-liners you're using on those girls because it sucked."

Heat crept up my cheeks. This was the first time he'd ever made a sexual joke like that.

He scoffed. "Please. I don't talk to them like that."

"Why not?"

"Because they don't get it," he said quickly. Then, quieter: "They're not you."

I laughed. "Max—"

"Don't laugh at me, Trouble." His voice lost the teasing edge. "They seriously make fun of me. They lose interest immediately. Like I'm something they tried on and decided didn't fit."

He paused, then added, almost too casually, "You don't do that."

I shook my head, ignoring that comment, but my pulse skyrocketed. Was I... actually *nervous* around Max McKinnon?

"Why? You have a tick?"

He laughed.

"No, I tell them I have a girl best friend from summer camp, and they think I'm lame."

I could hear him saving his video game, the familiar click that meant he was getting ready to turn in for the night.

I didn't like him talking about those girls. The feeling surprised me. I'd never felt territorial over him before, but now it sat heavy in my chest. It wasn't that I wanted to claim him—just that the idea of anyone else having him made my stomach twist, and that realization unsettled me.

I was starting to feel a bit... possessive.

And the worst part? It sounded like I wasn't alone in that feeling.

"That's because they don't get it," I said. "I'm awesome."

"Yeah, you are," he laughed. Then, softer like he hadn't meant to say it out loud, "You're my favorite person."

Something in my chest tightened. I wanted to say, *'You're mine too.'* But the words hovered there. Saying them would change something, and I wasn't ready to know what.

So I laughed instead.

"Five more days," he said.

"Can't wait."

I glanced at the calendar.

June 2nd. Camp day.

Five days later, Mom's car rolled to a stop in front of Camp Blackshear's gates, and for the first time in weeks, I smiled.

"When does Max get here?" Mom asked, pulling the keys from the ignition.

"Three o'clock," I said, glancing at my watch.

She popped the trunk, and I stepped into the gravel. My Converse shoes sunk into the familiar dust. That's when she handed me a small pink gift bag, her face lit with secret excitement.

Inside, there was a brand-new silver iPhone.

"What?!" I gasped, clutching it like it might vanish.

"You're an adult now," she said, grinning.

I gave her a look. I'd been an adult for a whole year already. I was only a few months shy of turning nineteen.

She lifted her hands in surrender. "I know. I know. It's over-due. Don't shoot the messenger."

"Mom! I can't believe you got me a cell phone!" I

exclaimed, looking at the shiny new screen. I hugged her, breathing in her floral scent. "Did West say it was all right?"

"Yes, he said it was time. It'll be monitored—calls and texts only. No internet. You can't download any apps. But at least now, we can text every day."

West would see everything, but I didn't care.

"I love you," I said.

"I love you, too. And maybe this year, I'll finally meet Max."

She'd said that before. Every year, she left before he arrived. She never made it to Parents' Weekend, and when she came to pick me up, he had already left. He was always leaving early for baseball camp.

There was a strange tug at my heart when I thought about the two of them meeting. For some reason, I didn't want her and Max in the same room. Part of me knew that worlds like mine and his shouldn't touch outside of Camp Blackshear. It felt like it could explode.

Just as I thought it, I sensed him, like my body had tuned itself to his presence.

The hair on the back of my neck prickled, and I lightly touched my scar, turning towards the parking lot. When I turned, Max stepped out of his dark blue Chevy truck, and my entire world stuttered to a halt.

He stood just beyond the knot of counselors and older campers, taller than I remembered, moving with a maddening calm that made everyone else look like they were trying too hard. His dark hair had grown past the neat boyish cut he used to keep, curling at the ends like he hadn't bothered with a haircut in weeks. I wanted to run my hands through it, feel its weight between my fingers.

I immediately bit my lower lip and shifted my weight, silently scolding myself for thinking that way about him.

He took off his sunglasses and tucked them into the collar of his white cutoff shirt. The frayed sleeve edges revealed his strong, tanned forearms—evidence of his baseball training and outdoor lifestyle. His physique wasn't merely muscular; it seemed designed for movement, as if he'd forget how to breathe if he stayed still too long.

The sun had deepened his skin to a golden-brown, but the crooked smirk tucked into the corner of his mouth hadn't faded. Only… it wasn't boyish anymore. There was nothing innocent about it now.

When he reached for his duffel, his shirt lifted just enough to flash lean, toned abs where there had once been a soft belly. He had on scuffed-up combat boots under jeans, and when I dragged my gaze back up to his face, I hit the full force of his eyes.

God, those eyes. Had they always been that blue? Not sky blue, too pale. Not ocean blue, too blue. They were the impossible, glowing blue of water lit from within.

And just like that, I was back on the lake at sixteen, knees knocking in a kayak, both of us staring at the aquamarine shimmer beneath us.

"This is so cool," he had said, leaning closer. "I had forgotten how blue it was. It looks like you."

"Huh?"

"Nothing," he'd muttered, then whispered so softly I almost missed it. "So pretty."

I'd pretended I didn't hear him.

But this Max McKinnon, the one I was staring at, wasn't the boy from my childhood. He was a man.

And he looked *dangerous*.

"Mackenzie." My mom's voice was far away, like she was calling me from the bottom of a tunnel. She jabbed me in the ribs, and I nearly jumped out of my skin.

"What?" I yelped, too loud, heart racing like I'd just been caught doing something I shouldn't. She followed my gaze and raised her brows. "Is that him?"

I tried to sound normal but failed. "Uh… yeah. Yes. That's him."

Fuck. I was stuttering.

Her lips curved knowingly. "Oh, I see. I *get* it now."

"It's not like that," I blurted. "He's just my friend." I was already looking anywhere but his arms.

"Mmhmm," she said, amused. "So not future son-in-law material? Because if he were, I wouldn't complain. He's *super* cute."

Jesus Christ.

"Oh my God, Mom." My cheeks were on fire.

I watched him grab his Atlanta Braves cap from the truck bed and quickly flip it backwards on his head. His eyes scanned the parking lot, stopping briefly before moving on.

"He's looking for you," Mom whispered. "Let's go."

I trailed behind her, stomach flipping, as Max swung his duffel bag onto his shoulder, locked the truck, and spotted me. In an instant, he was moving toward me, all warmth and confidence, arms wide. He wrapped me in a hug so tight I could barely breathe.

"Max!" I protested. "You're going to break my spine!"

He set me down slowly, his hands skimming my waist a fraction longer than necessary, and gave me a smile that made my knees threaten mutiny.

My pulse was a drum in my throat. He smelled like summer, a mixture of salt and sun, and I wanted to drown in it.

When he turned to my mom, recognition sparked in his eyes. "Wow, is this your mom?"

"Yes, I'm her mom," she said, stretching out a hand.

"I'm a hugger, Ms. Hamill," he grinned, pulling her in.

I wanted the ground to swallow me whole. My mother giggled.

Giggled.

I yanked him back.

"Okay, that's enough." My fingers curled around his arm, warmed by the muscle there.

Mom whispered as she hugged me goodbye.

"Make the most of this summer." Then, tighter, her lips brushing my ear: "He likes you."

I pulled back, flustered. "Mom—No."

"Okay," she laughed. "What do I know?"

But her eyes said something else as she walked away. She briefly looked around her, staring a long time at some of the senior counselors before walking off to her car.

It was weird. Her behavior was off. But I didn't think much about it because Max was crowding my space.

"Wait… no way. You got a cell phone?" Max's voice was rough, almost amused, as he grabbed my hand and lifted it like a trophy, eyes gleaming with something unreadable. "Look at you. Finally, one of us."

I scoffed, snatching my hand back like it burned.

"Says the imposter who's taken over Max," I shot back, already moving toward the check-in. He slid beside me, shadowing my pace.

"When did this happen?" I asked, twisting my hand on his bicep, feeling the muscle tense under my fingers.

His grin split his face, part cocky, part dangerous.

"Told you I had to bulk up for the scouts. Worked like a charm." He lowered his voice, lips curling into a playful smile. "Jealous?"

"Jealous of your fake muscles? Hardly." I grinned, challenging him. "I could still make you eat dirt."

His eyes flickered, sharp and calculating. He leaned in, breath hot and low.

"Careful, *friend*. Keep talking like that, and I might have to make you eat dirt."

The word 'friend' rolled off his tongue differently this time, a warning disguised in a casual tone. We were talking like child-hood friends.

But we both knew we were holding back. His tone was different. It wasn't entirely playful; it was *flirtatious*. My breath caught before I recovered.

"Please," I shot back, stepping closer, voice dropping with something reckless. "Too bad for you, I've been living danger-ously since day one. I don't care that you're a fucking giant, standing there at six-foot-three, or whatever. I'll beat your ass."

He chuckled low, a growl deep in his chest that scraped something raw inside me.

"Six-four, Trouble. I had a growth spurt."

I leaned in too close, standing up on my tiptoes. His eyes immediately went to my lips.

"Six-four? Huh? Guess I'll need a step stool to smack that cocky smirk off your face."

What the hell was I doing? I was flirting back with him.

He opened his mouth to say more, but I spun away, heart pounding too loud. "I'm going to check in." My voice was shak-ing, betraying me.

At the check-in, we split lines. I could hear his rich voice carry as he told the staff he was glad to be back.

"Great to see you again, Mackenzie," Graham greeted. He was older now, in his late twenties, but still as eager as ever. He was now full-time staff.

"Great to see you, Graham," I said, rifling through my folder. "Am I in Cabin 5 again with the girls?"

He glanced up, fingers tapping keys.

"Didn't get the email? We had to adjust cabins this year. Renovations."

"You sent the email to my mom?" I blinked, confused.

"Yeah. Needed her okay on this. Some junior counselors are bunking together. You're technically an adult, but since we've mixed your cabin with boys, we needed her consent."

My stomach dropped.

"Your mom said it was all good. She approved it."

I blinked. My brain did not compute. I was staying in the cabin with the boys. That meant…

"Hey, roomie!" Max's voice cut through, his hands gripping my shoulders like I was his prize.

"Um… yeah." My mind was screaming chaos.

Shit.

I wasn't going to survive the summer.

4

———

MAX

She was acting off. Way off. I looked different, sure, but Mackenzie? She was the type who didn't give a damn about appearances. Or so I thought.

The second our eyes met, she couldn't hold my gaze. It was making me feel insecure. We'd never had problems communicating or hanging out together. I didn't know why that had suddenly changed. It was like she was nervous about being around me, or something.

We hit the cabin. The air was thick between us. Bunk beds lined the walls, each tagged with names. When we reached the back, I saw it before she did. A private alcove: one bunk bed in the middle corner of the room, a window on the far left, and a tiny bathroom off to the side.

My brain spun, trying to make sense of what I was seeing.

We had our own room for the entire summer.

Private. *Really* private.

Of fucking course.

We had a bedroom door. We could close it if we wanted to. I started to panic a bit. She was already acting weird around me, and this was going to set her over the edge.

I nervously watched her as she slung her bag onto the bottom bunk, walked in behind me, and put her hands on her hips, observing our new sleeping quarters.

"I can't believe my mom agreed to this," she muttered under her breath.

I felt her stiffen as she gazed at the beds. We both knew what this meant. They'd put us together on purpose. Nearly nineteen, we were the oldest counselors here. But still, we were *barely* adults. Mackenzie and I were close, but not *that* close.

Or *were* we? Did they think we were?

I tossed my bag onto the top bunk without hesitation, breaking the ice.

"I call the top bunk."

She smiled, that spark lighting her eyes like a dare. "We should flip for it. Don't want you breaking through the mattress and crushing me."

"Checking me out already, Trouble? That's two comments about my new body in a span of one hour."

Shit.

Was I… flirting? Did she think I was flirting? Did she like it? I had never flirted with her before, but now I couldn't stop myself. Her cheeks flamed scarlet, and she snapped her head away as if she had just been caught stealing.

"No!" she squeaked, but the flush said otherwise.

I swallowed the sudden rush inside me, that electric flare that always came with her. She played untouchable, but I'd just cracked that armor with a look. And she definitely liked it.

That blush? It lit a fuse deep in my gut, something feral and hungry I didn't want to fight. She didn't roll her eyes. She didn't punch me in the arm and call me a perv like she used to. She blushed. She fucking *blushed.*

It was dangerous how fast I could get addicted to it, this feeling.

I ripped open my duffel, tossing clothes onto the bed while

sneaking glances at her. Dark curls framed her face, half-tied up in two messy buns, the rest cascading down her back. Her Van Halen shirt hugged curves I'd spent years guiltily memorizing. Black cutoff shorts left little to the imagination, and I had to stop myself from staring at her legs.

Had they always been that long? That tan?

She had laughed at one of my stupid jokes, scrunched her nose, and stuck her tongue out in that way that made my stupid grin grow wider.

She was cute as fuck.

I wasn't shy about the crush I'd carried for years. Hell, it felt like it'd been carved into my skin, sharpened every summer I spent too close to her. I'd learned where to put my hands, what thoughts to bury, which lines not to cross. Was I crossing them now? I kind of wanted to, but I was a mess waiting to happen. I didn't want to drag her down with me.

Not yet.

But our room was a trap. I was a red-blooded male for crying out loud, and they put me in close proximity with literally the girl of my dreams. I needed to behave myself.

She's your best friend. I kept telling myself.

But she was one of the prettiest girls I'd ever seen, and I was already chasing her in my mind.

Fuck.

"Think I made room for your stuff in this drawer," she said, glancing up with a smirk.

I grabbed my pile, but she stopped me, eyes narrowing. "You're putting those in the drawer like that?"

"Yeah?" I shrugged, catching the judgment. "Problem?"

"How will you find anything in that mess?"

Her fingers played with her hair, curling it around her pinky like a siren's spell. My eyes drifted down to follow the motion, more than once. A weight settled low and sharp in my gut. Heat spread through my body.

I was drunk on her, already.

"Do it yourself, then." I handed her the mess and tried not to look at her. I looked away.

"I love you, Max. But I'm not your damn maid." She dropped the clothes on the floor, frustration etched on her face.

I leaned back on the bottom bunk, arms behind my head, hearing her words echo inside me: *I love you, Max.*

God, how many times was I going to replay that in my head? Her voice was so soft, warm, a tether I never wanted to break.

"Guess it's someone else's problem now," I said, smug. I left the pile where it was.

She exhaled sharply but started folding. I got up and joined her. I was clumsy, but I made her laugh, and the tension eased a bit.

"That's the saddest fold I've ever seen," she teased.

"It's modern art," I shot back.

"What is its title? Crumpled mess?" She grinned and then showed me how it was done.

Five minutes later, our stuff was sorted, mixed up, and somehow… right.

"Unfair," I muttered. "You're just naturally good at this."

"Nah, you're just bad," she said, eyes sparkling.

"Ouch. Remind me why I stick around you?"

"Because you love me?" she said, licking her lips and leaning in a little too close.

I froze, caught in her gaze. She held her breath.

"Do I?" I teased, and I let the question hang there. I was daring her to flirt back.

She smiled, turning away.

"Yeah, it's okay. I love you, too. *Platonically*. Don't get too cocky."

"Too late. Head's already swollen."

We stared at our intertwined clothes, and a rare calm settled over me. This made sense to me. Always had. Always would.

I WAS HALF-ASLEEP, SUNK INTO THE BOTTOM BUNK, WHEN A TINY alarm crackled through the old PA system. My eyes were gritty, my head foggy. I shifted, and that's when I felt her.

Mackenzie was sitting at the foot of the bed, a book open on her lap, our legs tangled like they used to when we were kids. Back then, it had been innocent. Now, it wasn't. Not for me. Not with the heat of her skin brushing mine. Not with my blood running too hot for this to be nothing.

Her eyes flicked down to where we touched, lingered for half a heartbeat too long, then she pulled away. She was too gentle. She knew exactly what she was doing to me.

She shut the book, stood, and something unspoken coiled in the space between us. It was heavier than friendship. We were being pulled towards each other by an invisible string.

She had to feel it, too, right? I *knew* she did. There was a faint flush on her neck, and her eyes dragged up my body more than once. She was choosing to ignore what was building between us.

"Counselors! Report to the dining hall for your assignments!" The megaphone screamed through the static.

I rubbed my face, trying to focus on something else, anything else. Anything other than her.

"You'd think after all the years we've been coming to this hellhole, they'd stick us in one of the renovated cabins." My tone was lazy, but my pulse wasn't.

"I don't know… I'm kind of into this little room back here," she said, smiling as if it were a private joke.

Yeah. Fuck yeah. Me too. I liked it a lot.

My grin broke through before I could stop it, and she caught me with those green eyes. I could fall into them and not bother coming up for air.

"Come on, let's go," she said, looking away. I let out a breath I didn't know I'd been holding. My chest was tight in a way that had nothing to do with the lack of oxygen.

We barely made it ten steps toward the dining hall before some guy slammed into my shoulder hard enough to jolt me.

"Excuse you?" My voice came out low, sharp. I sized him up. He was maybe 5'11", lean build. But I had both height and weight over him. I found myself straightening my spine to hover.

His badge read **JACKSON KENSWICK,** written in black Sharpie. I had never seen him before. He was new.

His eyes shifted to Mackenzie, his gaze traveling over her body. He didn't just look at her; he assessed her as if he'd already had her once and was deciding whether he wanted seconds.

Mackenzie froze. The color drained from her face, eyes going wide—too wide—like she'd stepped into something out of a nightmare.

Her hand drifted to her neck, fingers curling around it, thumb pressing into the side. She thought no one had noticed.

But I did.

I didn't like it. I didn't like it one fucking bit.

"You're excused," he said, before walking off like I was nothing.

I stared at him, fists tight.

"What a dick," I muttered, turning to her. She still hadn't shaken that look; her face looked somewhere between fear and fight-or-flight.

"You, okay?" I reached out and put my hand on her shoulder. She flinched, as if my touch burned, and stepped back.

"Yeah. Fine. Totally fine." Her voice was too high. She took off toward the dining hall, and I had to lengthen my stride to catch her.

When I finally did, I grabbed her shoulders and turned her toward me.

"You're not fine. What's going on?"

She stepped in close to me. Her breath touched my lips.

"You don't have to worry about me, Max. I can take care of myself."

She smelled like oranges and coconut, and for one split second, all I could think about was dragging her face to mine and tasting her. I clenched my jaw so hard it hurt.

She broke the moment first, turning away. My gaze dropped. I couldn't help it. I tracked the lines of her legs, the smooth skin, the way her shorts hugged her.

I wanted to touch her. To claim her. I shook my head to clear it in defeat. I'd ruin everything if I did.

She was making me insane. I couldn't hold a straight thought around her. What the fuck was wrong with me?

I fiddled with my friendship bracelet on my wrist and forced my eyes up, calling after her.

"Trouble! You know what? Forget it. It's orientation night, let's have fun."

We shuffled into the main dining hall, were handed our orientation packets, and endured the same stale safety drill we'd been hearing since we were kids. The big reveal this year? First-grade day campers.

"Great," I muttered, rolling my eyes.

"This is so exciting! I love the babies," Mackenzie beamed, her whole face lighting up.

"Yeah, we're glorified babysitters," I groaned.

She bumped my arm. "Come on, Max. Bugs, fishing, their cute little giggles. It's going to be fun." She sniggered just thinking about it, and I felt it—that dangerous pull.

God, she was beautiful.

Max, stop, I told myself. I was losing it around her. My brain was a fucking rollercoaster of hormonal thoughts.

"Fine," I said. "But you're on bathroom duty."

"Okay," she agreed too easily.

Orientation dragged on for fucking forever—until, finally, freedom. We grabbed dinner and slid into a seat at a table in the corner, eating in companionable silence.

Peanut butter and jelly sandwiches and pretzel sticks. A classic camp staple. The familiarity of it made us smile at each other, like this place had never stopped being ours.

And then that dick arrived.

Jackson.

He set his tray down softly, as if he belonged here, right across from us.

"Hey, Mackenzie. You okay with me joining you and…" His gaze flicked to my counselor badge. "Max?" The smile he gave me was all teeth.

I already wanted to put my fist through his face.

Mackenzie was mid-bite, swallowing quickly, but before she could respond, I cut in. "Hey, dude. What's your problem?"

His expression didn't even twitch. That calmness made my skin crawl. "No problem. Just wanted to say hi to Mackenzie."

I leaned back, studying the way they looked at each other. The hair on her arms stood up, and she wouldn't quite meet his eyes. But when she did, something unspoken passed between them.

Recognition. History.

"How do you know each other?" I asked casually, tearing my sandwich in half, my arm sliding over the back of Mackenzie's chair until my thumb hovered just above her shoulder. Close enough for him to notice.

His eyes narrowed. He didn't like it when I touched her.

Interesting.

"Oh, how do we know each other?" Jackson scoffed. "You want to tell him, Mackenzie, or should I?"

My fist curled under the table. I forced myself to breathe,

three slow counts, because I could feel the urge to hurt him like it was a living thing.

"I … uh …" Mackenzie stammered. "Jackson and I … We went to school together. We … uh …"

Her cheeks flushed. It didn't take a rocket scientist to figure out they had hooked up.

He smirked, and it landed like a blade between my ribs.

My jealousy ripped through me, and I couldn't stop the image that followed. His hands were on her body, where they didn't belong.

The thought alone made me want to tear him away from the table, put him against the wall, and see what he looked like afraid.

I blinked.

Wow. This was new. Raging psychopath wasn't a personality trait I generally harbored. I didn't know how to handle these feelings swirling inside me.

He finished his food. "See you later, Mackenzie," he said, standing and walking off like he owned the room.

I pulled my arm back, folding my hands in my lap to keep from doing something stupid. I'd known her for years, talked to her almost every day, but suddenly I realized there were entire chapters of her life I'd never read.

I got up and dumped my tray without touching the rest of my food. My appetite was gone. My humor was gone. And the last thing I felt like doing was pretending otherwise.

She came up behind me, tray in hand, her presence soft but impossible to ignore.

"Hey… what's up?" she asked quietly. There was a hitch in her voice. It was hesitant, like she already knew I wouldn't like the answer.

"Nothing," I muttered eventually, my eyes fixed on anything that wasn't her. The trees, the gravel path, my shoes.

Her hand caught my arm. I looked down into those green eyes that had always been my undoing.

"Forget him, please." Her voice was pleading, earnest.

My chest felt like it was closing in.

"Who *is* that guy?" The jealousy in my voice was unmistakable. I didn't even bother to hide it. But I wanted her to tell me that he was no one, and that my suspicions were just paranoia.

"Uh…" She averted her gaze. "We used to date."

I'd always known she had boyfriends. But hearing it now, seeing her say it, was something else entirely. The unfair part? I'd dated plenty of girls back home. Never serious. Never long. Always disposable. But *this*? This wasn't disposable to her.

"How long?" The irritation leaked out before I could rein it in. "He's a dick. I can't believe you dated that guy."

We stopped under the shade of a big oak outside the cabin. I hooked my arm around a low branch, holding her gaze. She wouldn't hold mine back. She was looking everywhere but at me.

"Not very long," she said, voice clipped. "We dated for eight months."

Eight months?!

"Not very long? Jesus, Trouble. That's a long fucking time," I muttered, kicking at a loose rock.

Eight months. While I was at home, cutting things off before they got serious. I was always circling back to her. Meanwhile, she'd been in something real. Something I hadn't even known about.

Maybe we didn't tell each other everything after all. Perhaps I didn't know her as well as I thought I did.

"Why's he here then? You still seeing him?"

"No," she said quickly, glancing over her shoulder like the guy might appear. "I don't know why he's here. Honestly, I'm just… surprised." Her voice was softer now, restrained at the edges.

I didn't need to push anymore. I'd gotten my answer, but I hated it.

"Hey," I softly said this time, threading my fingers through hers and tugging her into me. She let me pull her close, and I leaned down a bit, so her chin fit into the crook of my neck like it always had. "Let's drop it."

She nodded. The scent of her hair, faintly citrus, pulled me straight back to when we were sixteen.

"Trouble, you're my best friend," I had told her, after seeing the drawings she left out. Shadows stood behind her in every single drawing. I knew something was wrong then, that she was hiding something she hadn't told me.

"You're mine, too," she had said, smiling like she meant it.

"Don't ever forget that," I had whispered.

What I really meant was: I know you're scared. But I won't let anyone hurt you.

✳

BACK AT THE CABIN, SHE SAT CROSS-LEGGED ON THE BED, frowning at her new iPhone.

"You want me to set that up for you?" I asked, holding out a hand.

"I think I've got it. It's simple, right?"

Five minutes later, she was sighing, muttering about iCloud and face recognition. "This is too much. I just want to text my mom."

I laughed. "Give it here. I can help you. You know I'm great with tech."

"Yeah, I know. Too good," she said, rolling her eyes. "Fine."

She didn't know how good I actually was. I'd reset locked accounts, recovered fried hard drives, and even bypassed password encryption. Systems made sense to me. People didn't.

She handed me her phone and then said, "Here you go— secret agent."

Immediate turn-on.

I almost grabbed her, but my fists curled at my sides. I bit back a response. I'd behave, for now.

A few quick taps, and it was done. I added my number to her contacts as

MAX 🩶

and sent her a text.

Hey

Her head snapped up. "Oh, come on. You really think I'm letting you put a heart next to your name?"

"I mean, I just rescued you from the hell of setup screens," I said, fishing my swimsuit from the dresser. "Plus, the way you've been eye-fucking me all day, it seemed fitting."

Her eyes went wide.

Yeah, maybe I'd pushed *too* far, but the truth was, it wasn't entirely a joke. Her eyes had been eating me up, and I really fucking dug it.

"It's just an emoji, Trouble. Keep up, chill," I added, trying to lighten the mood.

"Whatever. I'm changing it as soon as I figure out how." She disappeared into the bathroom, shutting the door behind her.

From the front of the cabin came the muffled sounds of arriving counselors. The first-day lake visit was tonight, just like every summer.

When she emerged, she was wearing a white swimsuit cover-up, a towel in one hand, and a flashlight in the other. "You ready?"

"Hell yeah, just need to change. Grab my towel from my bag,

pretty please?" I held up my hands in a praying motion and stuck out my bottom lip.

"Yeah," she said softly, giving me the fucking cutest smile ever, and turning her back to me. She grabbed the towel and threw it at me.

I caught it one-handed and gave her one last glance as she turned towards the window.

She pulled her cover-up off and threw it onto the floor, rubbing sunscreen onto her bare stomach.

I averted my gaze at first, but then, unable to resist, I let my eyes drift back her way. Her right leg was now up on the bedpost, and she was leaning over so far that she left little to the imagination.

Uh, she knew I could see her, right?

Her dark green bikini barely covered her fucking ass.

My eyes traced the curve of her waist, the rise of her hips, the long line of her legs. Her hair tumbled down her back in a lazy wave, and fuck me, heat was burning through my entire body.

She was *perfect*.

She looked back over her shoulder at me and gave me a soft smile.

Was she fucking with me?

It was like my pulse couldn't decide whether to race or stop entirely. Every nerve in my body lit up, every cell wired to her. Looking away would've been the decent thing to do—but decency didn't stand a chance with the way I felt right now. For whatever reason, Camp Blackshear made the best of us a little bit mad.

The obsession I had for her always returned as soon as I stepped through the camp gates. An obsession I had kept bottled up for seven summers.

She was a slow-burning fever I'd never recover from. The

kind that seeped into your bones and rotted you from the inside out.

I didn't just want her. I wanted to be the one she looked back for. The one she chose without realizing she'd already decided.

The one she chose outside of Camp Blackshear.

And maybe that was sick. Perhaps it was wrong.

But I had never felt like this about anyone. The feelings surprised me. I had been so good at suppressing them over the years. But now? I was losing it, and I didn't trust myself.

I rushed into the bathroom, pressing my back to the bathroom door, and forcing a deep breath into my lungs. We'd been friends forever, but now I couldn't stop imagining her naked. I wanted her in that tiny bunk bed, under me, tangled in sheets.

My desire for her was so strong that it was a little overwhelming.

You're a gentleman, Max. She's your best friend. Please don't do it. Don't fuck this up.

But the thoughts of her in that swimsuit overpowered me, and Max, her best friend, was a goner.

5

MACKENZIE

The lake shimmered in the gold of late afternoon, the sun hanging low, turning every ripple into liquid light. I exhaled slowly, the knot I'd carried for a year loosening in my chest. For the first time in months, I felt still, exactly where I was supposed to be.

I spread my towel across the dry grass at the bank, and Max came up beside me, his shadow falling over mine. It usually would've scared me to see a shadow looming like that, but a quick poke to my ribs made me yelp. And he laughed, low and easy. The type of laugh that made my heart swell.

"He's so hot," one of the girls murmured behind me.

My stomach turned.

"He's fucking *fiiine*."

"What do you think he's like in bed? Like, he can't possibly be a virgin, right? He's so tall, he's got to be huge. Like he'd probably rip me apart."

Their voices were grit in my ears. I didn't need to look to know all eyes were on him, tracking the casual power of movements, drinking in the broad-shouldered, sun-browned version of him.

A strange possessiveness fell over me. I wanted to throw a towel over him and protect him from their greedy eyes. But he was a grown man now and could take care of himself.

He dropped his towel beside mine, oblivious to their commentary, and leaned back on his palms, legs stretched out. I mirrored him, tilting my face toward the sun. I could hear the crunch of his fingers toying with the grass in between us, and without realizing it, my hand landed over his.

"Oh, sorry," I said, starting to pull away.

But his fingers closed over mine, and he threaded our hands together.

"Keep it," he murmured. "You're not bothering me."

He was holding onto my hand so tight that it felt intimate. A little *too* intimate.

My pulse spiked so hard I felt it in my throat. I prayed my cheeks didn't betray me, even as his thumb traced lazy, unhurried circles over my skin like he wasn't thinking about it all. But knowing Max, he absolutely was.

When I glanced at him, the lake light caught in his eyes, and I felt it again. That low, slow ache that had been building between us for seven summers.

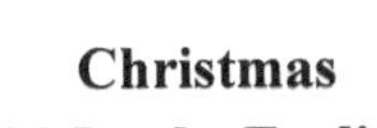

Christmas
7 Months Earlier

I was curled under three blankets in my room, fairy lights dripping gold across the ceiling, when my mom's voice floated up the stairs.

"Mackenzie! Max is on the phone!"

I was out of bed before she finished the sentence, bare feet hitting cold hardwood. I snatched the landline off my desk.

"Hey."

"Hey, Trouble." His voice was so warm. He sounded like a late-night drive during summer. I could hear the curve of his smile through the line. "You sound tired."

"I am. Ag—uh, my uncle's been trying to make me eat gluten-free stuffing all day." I almost slipped and said Agent West, but caught myself. Fear gripped my throat, and an unsettling paranoia crashed through my body.

"Need me to kill him?" His laugh was low.

I didn't say anything back, but a weird, crippling feeling tugged at my heart. He sensed my hesitancy and said, "I'm kidding. It feels like forever since we talked. I don't know how to joke with you anymore."

It had been three days. For us, that was an eternity.

"Did you flip the table?" he asked. "When he told you to eat it? We all know you have anger issues."

"Almost." I grinned into the receiver. "And I don't have anger issues. I'm just persuasive. What about you? How's Christmas?"

He was in Oklahoma with his sister and her four kids.

"It's good. They're wearing me out, though. I don't know how she manages to survive this every day. They keep asking if I'm married yet. When I tell them I'm eighteen, they look at me like I'm defective and ask, 'So? You ugly?'"

I laughed, but my stomach twisted. Did he have a girlfriend? We never went there.

There was a pause, then, almost like he'd read my mind, he said, "I don't have one, by the way."

My heart did a stupid, slow flip.

"Well… maybe you should get one. So that they'll stop asking."

I wanted to bite the words back immediately.

"I don't know, too much work. Promise." His tone was half-sarcastic, half-hopeful. "You and me, always? You're easy."

I wanted to say, 'Yes, forever.' But I was with Jackson, and Max didn't know.

"I'm down," I said, lightly. "Bonnie and Clyde style."

He was quiet for a few beats, and then—

"What is that thing that people do where they say if they're not married by 40, they'll marry their best friend?"

"I don't know. But is that what you want? A friendship pact?"

A hesitation came across the line, and then he said, "I'll take it."

On his end, I heard the quiet creak of a mattress, the shift of his weight. Then silence, long enough for me to listen to his breathing.

"I think about it sometimes." His voice was so soft I almost thought I'd imagined it.

My throat went tight. "Think about what?"

"You. Me. What it'd be like if..." He trailed off, with a faint laugh like he was shaking his head. "Never mind. Dumb."

"Max."

He didn't answer.

"Tell me," I pressed. "You can tell me anything."

If he told me he wanted me, I'd probably dump Jackson. But the feeling of Jackson's hands around my throat from days earlier snapped me back to reality.

"You're such a fucking whore, Mackenzie," he had hissed after secretly listening to mine and Max's conversation. "Such a fucking whore for him. Can you be a whore for me?"

There was a darkness inside Jackson, one I couldn't escape. Even if Max knew, he wouldn't be able to save me. No one could.

A long breath came over the line, like he was surrendering

something. "I just… wonder what it would be like if we weren't always saying goodbye."

And there it was. The unnamed thing between us. That ache. That gravity.

"Me too," I whispered. "All the time."

His exhale was almost a groan. Then, because he was Max, because we couldn't stay in it too long, he said, "So… did the gluten-free stuffing taste more like paper or dirt?"

THE MEMORY FADED LIKE THE SUN SLIPPING BEHIND THE horizon, but the ache it left deepened in my chest. Max's hand was still wrapped around mine like it was meant to be there, like *I* was meant to be there, next to him. We never talked about that night, about that phone call, but it lived between us anyway.

A soft breeze danced across the lake, pulling strands of my hair across my face. Max reached over and tucked them behind my ear, fingers lingering, brushing against my skin just a little too long.

"You, okay?" His voice was gentle, as if we were still miles apart, talking on the phone instead of sitting right beside each other.

"Yeah," I murmured, looking away. "I missed this place."

"Me too."

"You know what would make it better?"

He smiled knowingly.

The iPod Nano had been our thing. Same scratched silver case, same twenty tracks we'd worn out every summer. We had played mostly Incubus, shared between one set of headphones.

"Tell me you brought it," I said, watching the spark in his eyes.

"Safe in our room. Not sure it has much life left," he nudged me with his shoulder. "You have a phone now. Could have a million songs. We should create a Spotify playlist together."

"Yeah, but it's not the same. Just us and the little Nano that could…"

"And Brandon Boyd," he added.

I laughed. "Always, Brandon. You can't compete."

"I've been trying for years," he muttered. "Told you I could fix the Nano, though. It will be a pretty easy fix."

I knew he could do it. He was so skilled with technology, it wasn't even funny. Kind of creepy. He was way too smart.

But before I could answer, I looked up into the dark eyes of Jackson. He dropped his towel beside mine and sat, gaze fixed on Max's hand still holding mine. His expression was unreadable, but his jaw was tight.

I slid my hand away. Max sat up beside me, but his knee brushed mine and stayed there. We always seemed to find each other, even subconsciously.

I turned from Jackson's stare, then felt something crawl up my back. A jolt of pure panic ripped through me.

A spider.

"Oh my God!" I shrieked. "There's something on me!"

Max was on his feet instantly. "Stop moving."

I felt the tickle on my spine.

"It's in my clothes! It's *in there!*"

He caught my shoulders, trying to still me. "Hold still, I'll…"

But I was already clawing at the back of my swimsuit cover-up.

"Take this off," he ordered, voice sharp.

I froze. His hands brushed my hair aside, his body close enough that I felt the heat of him at my back. "Off, Trouble."

"I can't! What if it falls and crawls into my ear?!"

He laughed once, trying not to, then yanked the cover-up over my head in one quick motion. His hands were immediately on my bare back, warm and sure, sliding under the strap of my bikini top.

"Found it. It's tiny. But fast as hell."

My skin buzzed under his palms. Jackson's stare burned into me, but Max didn't notice. He chased the spider with his fingers, and suddenly his hand froze. We both looked down at the same time. I heard him inhale.

His hand was underneath the cup of my bikini top. He hadn't realized where his hands had been going, but here they were.

Our eyes met. His throat bobbed. His jaw flexed.

"Yup," he said, voice just a shade too high. "Saving your life. Totally normal. Nothing weird is happening here."

But he wasn't breathing, and he definitely wasn't moving his hands away. I let out a raspy exhale, and he flicked the spider to the ground, scooped up my cover-up, and handed it over without meeting my gaze.

"I'm not looking," he muttered quickly, shielding his eyes with his hand. But when he cracked two fingers open just enough to peek and flash me a crooked grin, my stomach somersaulted.

He was actively checking me out. And despite the heat of embarrassment on my cheeks, I really liked him looking at me that way.

"Thanks," I said softly, embarrassed. So *fucking* embarrassed.

"No prob." His voice was heavy with restraint.

The ghost of Max's hands was still on me, warm, trembling, lingering beneath my skin.

His pulse had been racing under his fingers, erratic and uneven, matching the stutter of my own heartbeat.

He wasn't looking at me now, but I could read his thoughts by the way he was sitting. He was stiff, quiet. There was a muscle ticking at his temple. His fists curled in his towel, as if he had no idea what else to do with them.

Max never unraveled. He was steady in storms, composed

when everyone else lost their heads. But this? Me, half-naked and pressed against him, his hands between my breasts while Jackson stood there ready to explode? Yeah, that had rattled him.

His chest rose and fell too fast, color creeping up the side of his neck. I'd never seen him look so unsure of what to do next. But I knew one thing. He'd touched me with a hunger that I'd never seen from him. He'd crossed a line. And he'd wanted to.

Hell. I think he wanted to do it again.

"Alright, counselors. Welcome to the first day of camp," Graham's voice cut through the air. "We're going to play a few icebreaker games. Everyone, pick a partner."

Max's hand was on mine instantly, lifting my arm. "She's mine," he said, too fast.

"You need to pick someone new, Max," Graham replied lightly.

"I don't want to." Max's voice dropped. It was actually kind of scary. I had never heard his voice that deep before.

I was seeing a new side of him—territorial and a little possessive.

It was a little off-putting. I wasn't sure what to think of this new Max.

Graham hesitated, then let it go. "Alright. Jackson, partner with Heather since you're new."

I looked over at the girl sitting next to Jackson. Her red top clung to her curves, her beach-blonde hair catching the light. Jackson's gaze slid from me to her and back, but she wasn't looking at him. Her eyes were locked on Max.

"Shouldn't we be with an experienced counselor?" Heather said, voice playful, chin tilted toward Max.

"Yeah," Jackson said, "dibs on Mackenzie."

Max's grip on my hand tightened, his irritation pulsing through his fingers.

"You have a point," Graham said, "Sorry, but Mackenzie. Max. Pair off."

Heather and Jackson closed in like it was a game.

Max didn't look away from me, his grip grounding me. "You're going to be okay," he said under his breath. "I'm right here."

Heather stepped closer to him, pushing her hair over her shoulder. Max gave her the crooked smile he'd given me minutes ago, and I hated that it wasn't reserved for just me. She leaned in, chest forward. His eyes dropped, briefly, but long enough for my jealousy to flare hot and sharp.

I forced my gaze to Jackson. The sunlight caught in his dark eyes, his gold chain flashing against his olive skin. He looked exactly the way he had the first day we collided in the hallway of our senior year: beautiful, but impossible to trust.

Jackson sat down beside me, reaching for my hand.

I pulled away. "Don't touch me."

"Come on, Kenz. Don't act like that." He said in that broad southern drawl.

"Oh? Such as?" My voice was razor-sharp. "You know what you did, you psycho. I don't owe you anything."

"Psycho, is it? The last I checked, that's what you liked…"

The smile on his face was unnerving. It was cocky, arrogant, and borderline unhinged.

Behind me, I could feel Max go still again, every muscle wired tight. He was listening, and if Jackson pushed me, Max wasn't going to stay quiet.

Max didn't know what had happened between Jackson and me, but I could see the unease beginning to take hold in his chest. Everything now felt dangerous. I could sense the slow, peaceful story of summer slipping into a dark abyss. One where only one of us would come out alive.

Graham's voice carried over the lake, all cheer and obliviousness. "Alright, it looks like everyone's paired off. Time to put you into groups of four!"

He pointed to Max and me, and then Jackson and Heather.

"You four, together."

Graham handed me a bowl of folded slips. I drew one, fingers brushing scrap paper, and unfolded it.

"Two Truths and a Lie," I read aloud, my lips curling into something I hoped passed for a smile. The words caught in my throat halfway through the rules.

Heather gave a nervous laugh. "Oh wow. This is going to be hard."

Max leaned back on his hands, voice carrying. "How are we supposed to win if we don't know each other?"

"That's the point," Graham called back. "It's like speed dating. But you're getting to know your other counselors."

Heather grinned at Max. "Aw, cute. Max, I'm ready for our first date. We should do this romance-themed!"

Max gave her a polite half-smile, but his shoulders were tight. "Fine," he said, low. He was definitely *not* into that idea.

I could do romance. Safer than digging too close to my history.

Jackson shifted beside me, his fingers skirting down my spine. He was too close. "We've got this, Kenz," he said, smiling like he owned the air between us.

I hated his nickname for me. Kenz. It made my blood boil.

I rolled my eyes and glanced across at Max. He was watching us. Arms crossed. Jaw tight. His expression wasn't just dislike. It was something darker.

I had never seen that expression on Max's face before.

Jackson's hand found my arm. His fingers gripped like a warning. His smile was casual, but the press of his thumb on my skin marked me as *his*.

I remembered his hands on my throat, the bruising pressure, the way my vision spotted at the edges. He liked to choke me, whenever anything didn't go his way.

"You're such a fucking slut, Kenz. You liked it? When you saw me fucking her? You like to watch. Don't worry, baby. She

doesn't mean anything to me. It's always going to be you and me. Til death do us part."

The memory wasn't just in my head; it pulsed through my skin, stuttering through my body.

Max saw it, the way I reacted. His body coiled, jaw ticking like something dangerous had just been switched on inside him. He looked like a predator about to go on a hunt, and the prey was Jackson.

Jackson noticed, too. His smirk dared Max to step over a line so that he could cut deeper. His hand slid to my waist, his fingertips skating over my hips.

"Don't touch me," I snapped.

Max stood. His fists clenched. He looked at me, silently asking permission to intervene. I shook my head. He sat again, but the heat in his eyes didn't dim.

Jackson's gaze cut between us. Cold calculation was there now, like a man cataloging weapons.

Graham's voice broke the tension. "Alright, time to start. Go."

I felt unease rip through me, and I nervously started the game, stumbling over my words.

"Once I kissed someone so well, they fainted." My gaze slid between both men, letting the moment hang. Jackson wore his usual smugness. Max's jaw was stone.

"Two: I've faked an orgasm." The words landed heavily. I watched Jackson, waiting for his reaction, but it was Max who flinched.

"Three: I've been head over heels in love." The last statement came out softer and more unguarded.

"The second's the lie," Jackson said immediately. "I'd know."

Max's eyes narrowed. "It's the third. You've never been in love. I'd know."

It wasn't a question. It was a declaration, and the way he said it… like the thought of me loving someone else was a blade he wasn't ready to take.

He was glaring at Jackson. Max had always been so competitive, and I was beginning to realize that the prize in this game was something I wasn't ready to give up: myself.

"You're wrong," I said softly, looking at them. "The lie was the first."

Jackson muttered something under his breath, clearly pissed. Max didn't move, but I could feel his thoughts closing in on me.

"You're serious?" He asked, his voice quiet. He had said it more for me, but everyone else could hear him.

I nodded once, not breaking eye contact. "I wouldn't lie twice during two truths and a lie. That's cheating."

His gaze searched mine, eyes flicking from my mouth to my eyes and back again. I could practically feel the shift happening inside him.

"Like *really* in love?" He asked slowly.

"It's obvious it's me. Let's move on," Jackson said, sitting up straighter. "I dated her for a year."

Max looked at Jackson with a fierce glare, full of anger. But as usual, Jackson was oblivious to the threat.

"I have to point out that, for the record, I have a huge dick, and Mackenzie would've never faked an orgasm with me. So not sure why she even made that an option," Jackson added like an asshole.

Max's jaw tightened the second Jackson mentioned us having sex.

"How would you even know if I faked it or not?" The words came out like a splinter.

Jackson's eyes darkened, and he licked his lips as he looked at me.

"You came all over me, babe. I can still smell you, taste you."

Max's face twisted. He was about to blow up.

"Okay, Jesus. Max, you go next. I'm ready for my turn," Heather said. "This is getting so boring."

Max finally looked away from me, just enough to acknowledge Heather again. But his body was still angled toward me, as if I were a magnet he hadn't decided to stop following.

He cleared his throat and ran a hand through his hair. "Alright." His voice was steady, but it carried the weight of a war he was battling. He was holding himself together, thinking about every word before speaking it. It was as if he was choosing the right sentence to keep the character of the golden boy he played so well. But underneath, I felt it, his desire to burn the mask away and be reckless, and uncharacteristically bad.

"First," he said slowly. "I once broke my arm falling out of a tree trying to impress a girl."

That got a laugh out of us. Even Jackson cracked a grin.

"Second," Max continued, glancing at the ground now. "I've had the same best friend since I was twelve, and I've never once gotten tired of her."

Max's gaze slid to mine for half a second before moving on as if nothing had happened.

"Third," he said, his voice barely above a murmur. "I think I'm in love with someone who makes me want to do insane things. Things I didn't even know I'd like."

No one laughed this time. A heavy silence settled over the group. I couldn't sit still. My skin was buzzing, and my heart was hammering in my chest. Max's words replayed in my head on a loop. *I think I'm in love with someone who makes me want to do insane things. Things I didn't even know I'd like.*

"Which one is the lie?" he asked.

"It's not the first one," I said suddenly, cutting through the noise of the group's guesses. My voice was steady, but inside I was a storm. "You did fall out of a tree during summer five, right after lunch."

Max's eyes locked on mine. His eyes held a look of soft surprise. He didn't think I remembered.

"And the second truth?" I added a smile, tugging at the edge of my mouth. "You've never shut up about how much you love your best friend."

His throat bobbed as he swallowed. I saw the corner of his mouth twitch, like he was trying not to smile.

"So," I said, voice a little lower, more vulnerable now, "the third one is the lie. Right?"

I sensed the implosion before it happened. At first, it was a silent detonation, gradually spreading among the four of us like a bomb. And then, he took us all out one by one.

"You're fucking kidding me," Jackson barked, sitting up so fast. "Are you serious, Mackenzie?"

"What?" I asked.

"He's fucking talking about *you*. Are you seriously going to stand there and pretend you don't get it?"

Jackson let out a bitter laugh, running a hand through his hair, eyes wild.

"God, *of course*. You always had this little thing, this... *attachment* to him. Always ditching me to call him on your fucking landline phone, laughing at his dumb jokes. And I was cool with it. I was chill."

"Jackson..." I started, but he cut me off with a sharp, humorless grin.

"No, no, no. I get it now," he said, his voice tipping from anger into something unstable. "You never even looked at me the way you look at *him*. I can finally see it now. And don't try to deny it because everyone fucking sees it. I'm not stupid."

I didn't say anything. Max remained still beside me, eyes fixed straight ahead, jaw locked.

Jackson's voice dropped, venomous and chilling now. "So, what is this? Some big reveal? After all these years, Max finally drops his pathetic little crush, and now we all have to clap for him?"

"Stop," I said quietly, but he was spiraling further, fueled by bitterness and jealousy.

"He's been in love with you since that first summer. Everyone knows it. I knew it. I just thought you were smart enough not to fall for it."

"That's uncalled for," Max said. "We haven't even finished the game, and you don't know anything about me."

"I'm fucking done with the game, bro," Jackson snapped. He leaned forward, his smile twisting into something darker. "But don't you hate it?"

"What?" Max said, fists clenched, tension thickening.

"That I fucked her first. That I was fucking her while you were talking every night."

Max's face soured, as if his soul was being torn apart.

"Ohhh… You're so in love. It hurts, doesn't it?" Jackson jeered, unhinged.

"Jackson, shut the fuck up," I snapped, my voice trembling with rage. Jackson's glare bore into me, his fists clenched tightly, as if he were about to wrap them around my neck.

I instinctively flinched, retreating from him. Max refused to look away from Jackson, but I caught the flicker of fear in his jaw and the raging fire in his eyes. He had seen me flinch.

"That mouth of yours ever stop running?" Max said, voice low and deadly as he scooted closer to me.

"Nope, Mackenzie keeps it busy," Jackson smirked. "Or I guess not anymore. Just letting you know she sucks at giving head."

"Funny. She had me moaning her name earlier while that sweet mouth was wrapped around my dick."

6

MACKENZIE

The sound I made was soft, involuntary. The entire group went silent.

"You seriously think I'd believe that?" Jackson sneered, rising with deliberate menace. Max was on his feet in an instant, matching his cold energy like a beast.

"I know you haven't even fucked her," Jackson spat, eyes gleaming with cruel confidence. "All that talk from you, but you're just noise, Max. All bark, no bite."

Max's glare sliced through the air. "And how exactly would you know that?"

"Because I had her pressed into the back of my truck two months ago. She told me she was a virgin." His voice dropped to a sickening whisper. "She was tight. Tight enough to bleed all over me."

My heart lurched with a sickening thud as the terrifying memory of that night crashed over us.

Two Months Earlier
Marigold, Georgia

THE LIGHTS FROM THE SOCCER FIELD WERE STILL GLOWING faintly in the distance, casting long shadows across the empty parking lot. The game had ended over an hour ago, but Jackson didn't seem in a rush to leave. He sat on the tailgate of his truck —shirt off, hair damp with sweat, cleats still on—legs dangling like he had nowhere else to be.

I sat between his knees, facing him, the cool night air brushing my skin.

"You were amazing out there," I said, voice soft. My fingers traced the faint curve of muscle on his arm.

He smirked. Not cocky this time, but proud. "I'm glad you stayed for the whole game."

"Every second," I smiled, stretching up to kiss him lightly on the lips. I hesitated, then pressed another to his cheek, then his neck. I felt his pulse thrum beneath his skin. I heard his breath hitch, felt his fingers twitch on my waist.

"You always make me feel like the only guy in the world. I don't know how you could love somebody like me," he whispered in my ear.

I blushed. My heart fluttered. When he was like this, it was easy to forget the hours he went silent. How he could flip cold without warning, and warm again when it suited him.

Right now, he was golden. The Jackson I was falling for. Because I was an idiot.

"I want this to be special," I murmured, brushing my hand through his damp hair. "You're all I think about."

He swallowed hard, nerves tangled with something warmer, darker.

"Are you… sure?" he asked, his breath catching. His thumb grazed my cheek. "I promise I won't hurt you."

I believed him.

We crawled into the back of the truck. The blanket he pulled out scratched against my legs. He kissed me like he had all the time in the world, whispering things that made me feel wanted, seen. But his hands were rough when he took my clothes off, and when I lay down, he didn't wait for me to tell him I was ready.

When he slid the condom on, my thoughts immediately went to Max. I wanted to tell Jackson to stop—that I'd changed my mind, that I wasn't ready—but within minutes he broke through my barrier and was inside me. The pain sliced through my body, stretching, burning. I wanted to cry. He stayed completely silent.

Jackson… I—" I pushed at his chest, but he grabbed my hands instead, pinning them above my head against the seat, holding me in place. His eyes were black, dark, and devilish.

He didn't ask if I was okay. He didn't say a single word. He just rocked into me, mechanical, and in a few minutes, he was done. When he pulled out, I winced.

"Oh. You bled all over me," he muttered, looking down.

His words hit me, and a feeling of dread surged through my veins. Every sound from outside the truck suddenly became loud. The distant hum of stadium lights cooling. A lone cicada screeching from the treeline. The metallic tick of the engine settling. I curled inward, pulling my knees to my chest, trying to make myself small.

His fingers hovered near me. My stomach churned. When he finally drew his hand back into the light, there was blood smeared across his skin.

"So beautiful," he murmured, his voice carrying a feverish quality, as he lifted his fingers and placed them inside his mouth.

I gasped, breath catching like a knife lodged in my throat. For the first time all night, my heartbeat wasn't fluttering—it was racing.

It was almost like I was staring into the dead eyes of my father.

Every instinct in me screamed to run.

PARANOIA SNATCHED ME BY THE THROAT AS I SURFACED FROM the memory. I scanned for Max and found him staring at Jackson, face stone cold. But there was a terrifying calm in his eyes —like the quiet before a bomb goes off.

The part of him he'd been holding back was about to surface.

"Say that again."

His voice was barely above a growl. It was low, lethal, promising destruction.

Jackson's grin spread, triumphant, as if he'd just dealt the final blow.

"She was dripping, begging for it. Swore she'd never done it before. I thought she was faking it… but then she bled. I probably shouldn't have worn a condom, would've been so much fucking better than it was."

Without warning, Max lunged.

He didn't scream. Didn't swing. He grabbed Jackson by the collar so violently that Jackson's smug expression shattered like glass. Max's eyes were wildfires, burning with rage and a savage, desperate possessiveness. His jaw clenched until the muscles strained, every fiber in his body taut and trembling.

"You don't talk about her like that," Max growled, voice raw and deadly. "Not to me. Not to anyone. It's disrespectful."

Jackson shoved him off.

"What? You mad she gave it to me before you?"

Max laughed so loudly I thought his body might splinter in two. He stepped in front of Jackson, their noses almost touching, and his laughter abruptly stopped.

"Don't worry. I've fucked the memory of you out of her."

I know I shouldn't have reacted the way I did, but hearing those words come out of his mouth ignited a heat that surged through my entire body. It was dizzying, raw, and so wrong. So, so wrong.

Jackson's grin dropped, and he stepped towards Max with pure anger in his eyes.

That's when I stepped between them. My hand pressed firmly against Max's chest, just enough to make him hesitate, though I could feel the tremors of his fury under my palm.

"Max," I whispered, steady and soft. "It's not worth it."

He looked down at me, chest heaving. His breath was ragged, like he was trying to cage some volcanic rage. In his eyes, I saw everything: heartbreak, desperate desire, and this fierce, aching tenderness that was mine alone. It disarmed me a bit.

Around us, the counselors had stopped, frozen like statues, watching the storm happen.

"Boys, enough!" Graham's voice cut through the tension.

Max ran a hand over his face, shoving the rage down with a shaky exhale. Slowly, reluctantly, he raised his hands in surrender, and the golden boy was back with his aloof crooked grin.

Jackson's smirk twisted into something colder, more sinister.

"Good luck with her," he hissed as he turned away. "You have no idea where she came from, *who* she comes from."

His words hung like a dark curse as he disappeared into the crowd.

I stood frozen. Jackson's words were crawling under my skin. What did he mean?

You have no idea where she came from, who she comes from.

The repetition echoed, warped, sinking its teeth in. Panic started to rise in my chest. My thoughts scattered. Did Jackson know about me? Did he know about my dad?

"Max…" I whispered, desperate, the panic overtaking my entire being.

He didn't look at me. His jaw was tight, his gaze fixed somewhere far past the tree line.

"Max. Please. Look at me."

His head snapped up. Eyes sharp.

"I fucking hate him."

I grabbed his elbow, not even glancing at Heather who watched us like a vulture. I pulled Max into the woods until the shadows swallowed us. He immediately grabbed my hand as we walked further into the dark.

Once the trees hid us, I turned, facing him head-on.

"I know. He's a bastard," I breathed. "But I'm not fragile. I don't need you fighting my battles."

I didn't want him to get hurt. But I also didn't know what to do if he found out the truth.

"You shouldn't have to do this alone, Trouble. He acts like you're his. I don't like it." The raw intensity in his voice made me hesitate. He ran a hand through his hair; that part of him that was slowly clawing out was trapped again.

"Max, I—"

"You matter," he cut me off, rushing his words. "You've always mattered. And I swear, every time he touches you, talks about you, I want to rip his hands off." He sighed in frustration but kept going, stammering, fidgeting as if he was about to burst out of his skin. "These are new feelings for me, and I don't know how to control myself. I want him to see there's not a single part of you he can claim anymore."

His honesty hit me hard.

Jackson's words lingered. His reminders of where I came from, who I was, seeped into my mind like a shadow of dread. That doubt slithered beneath my skin, gnawing at my nerves, as an icy dread took hold. In my head, I almost heard Agent West's voice echoing, 'Get rid of him.'

An unsettling chill ran through me as I scanned the dark, twisting edges of the woods. I could feel my father's eyes burning into my back, watching, waiting. Was I being watched now?

My gaze flicked to Max. A reckless, impossible thought coiled within me: we had to play Jackson's game. In his twisted game, he believed he was king. I needed to crush him with a true opponent, and that opponent's gaze was locked on me—fists clenched tight, eyes burning with a darkness I'd never seen before, as if something evil had awakened within him.

I was noticing cracks in his armor. The strong, dangerous Max—the one struggling to break free—was about to emerge. There was a shadow within him I hadn't met, yet he was still the only person who made me feel truly safe. I trusted him with my life.

"So, how do we win?" I asked, nerves buzzing.

Max blinked. "Win?"

I nodded, stepping closer. I could feel his tension spike the closer I got to him.

"Jackson thinks he owns me. Like he's figured out a code, like he's won a game he's been playing for years. But what if..."

Max arched a brow, sharp and impatient.

"What if what?"

"We prove him wrong?" I said, swallowing the lump in my throat.

He studied me. A war waged in those fierce eyes.

"I need you to be my boyfriend," I said softly. His eyes nearly popped out of his skull.

"What?" His voice was sharper, more aggressive than I expected.

"I mean, fake boyfriend. Just for the summer. To get Jackson off my back. Then we go back to... whatever we had."

I shrugged, trying to look casual, but my fingers clenched my arm.

He mulled it over. I could almost see the gears in his brain grinding.

"You think that'll work? Us faking it? You think Jackson will back off because I say you're mine?"

"I think," I said carefully, "he just wants control. And right now, I'm giving him too much."

Max's gaze remained steady, his expression now impossible to read. Until he moved closer, and his face stilled with quiet determination.

"And what about me?" he asked.

My heart stumbled. "What about you?"

"I don't fake shit well," he warned. "Not with you." He hesitated, then asked, "What do I get out of this?"

The air thickened. My voice shook. "What do you want?"

He held my gaze, steady, deadly serious.

"I want full boyfriend privileges. When we're pretending, I want the real thing."

That wasn't what I expected.

"But don't you…" I stammered, unsure how to say it without sounding like I was chaining him. "You can sow your oats. Or whatever. When I'm not around, I don't want to hold you back."

He laughed.

"Sow my oats? Are you in the 1800s, Trouble? You mean fuck?"

Damn, Max. This dangerous side of him was confusing as hell because I liked it a lot.

"I mean… yeah, if that's your thing," I said, barely meeting his eyes. Sweat dampened my hair at the nape of my neck.

"Yeah, definitely. But Jackson doesn't think we're fucking. How are we going to make him believe it? Me just saying we're dating isn't going to affect him."

He stepped closer, the scent of him crashing into me. My heart slammed into my chest.

"Uh… I don't know." His finger traced down my arm as he caught my nervous gaze.

"I want to touch you. Where I want. How I want. When I want," he whispered. "I'll be a good boy and follow your rules. But when it's showtime, I'm not holding back."

Holy shit. Maybe I wasn't ready for this. Max was in the big leagues, and I was not.

"We have to keep it believable. Just enough to…"

"Believable?" His laugh was low. "I told you, I'm not holding back."

I stayed toe-to-toe with him. Our eyes locked, letting the silence stretch, letting him wonder what I'd do next. He was so confident.

Could he hear my heart racing? Could he sense the way my breath trembled? Could he smell me? Because in that moment, I was a complete mess, undeniably drenched. I pressed my thighs together to ease the pressure that was forming right *there.*

"I know you're not ready for that," he murmured. "Show me the line, Trouble. Show me what's okay."

I slid my fingers into his hand, pressing them to his chest. "This."

He tilted his head. "That's nothing. We do that all the time."

I stepped closer, my shoulder brushing his chest. "This?"

His eyes were locked on mine. "Cute, but still nothing. I had my hands on your tits earlier, Trouble. If we were fucking, I wouldn't be able to keep my hands off you, so I think we need to include that. Come on, we're both adults here. Don't be shy. It's just me."

That was the problem, it was *him.* He was my best friend, and he knew me better than anyone else. I wasn't sure if I was ready to dive into that layer of intimacy with him.

He took my hand and dragged it up to his jaw, his stubble rough under my fingertips. His eyes closed for a beat, memorizing the touch. "Too much?"

"No," I said too fast. I was surely going to pass out.

He slid his hand to my waist, drawing me even closer. His fingers tightened on my ass, and his hands were so large they seemed to envelop me completely. A groan escaped me, making his eyes flutter shut. When he opened them, his pupils were so dark they almost consumed the blue of his irises. I could see him battling his inner demons.

"This too much?" he whispered.

"I… it's a little bold, but I'll accept it."

He smiled, sliding his hand to the back of my neck.

"You're mine. Whether it's fake or not, I don't share. You okay with that?"

Our hips and knees were touching. We were so close that our breaths were mingling. Fireflies flickered like tiny stars around us, like the sparks we both pretended to ignore.

I tried to pull away, and he grabbed me by the waist again, pulling me into him. I hitched a gasp. He smirked.

Max pressed a finger beneath my chin, tilting my face up so I could see every flicker of blue in his eyes. His lips were so close to mine. His breath was hot on my cheek.

"Are you okay with this?" he whispered.

Dusk held its breath with me.

"It's… I'm okay."

He held my gaze, then slowly pulled back. He looked like he wanted to devour me whole.

I'd never seen him like this.

"Okay," he breathed out.

"Okay," I repeated.

He snarled, low and fierce, "I want that motherfucker frothing at the mouth every time he sees us. I'm going to bury him alive."

I liked this version of Max. The thought twisted my stomach. What was wrong with me? More than that, I *wanted* him like this. I wanted the danger. But I felt like I was stepping into a place I wasn't supposed to go.

I trusted Max. And I felt like if we entered the fire together, we could burn the whole world down.

I imagined us, side by side, unstoppable. We could do it. We had the chemistry. We had the history. We knew each other so well, and that was both a weapon and a liability. A flicker of worry started in my chest. What if my secret slipped? What if Max said or did something that unraveled everything I'd worked so hard to hide?

I shouldn't want this. A part of me knew I was doing this because I wanted to be closer to him. More than friends. The pull of him was too sharp to ignore. I knew he could protect me, but what if he burned me alive in the process?

I turned back toward camp. But his footsteps pounded behind me.

"You don't get to walk away from me that fast," he said, catching up to me with a sly smile. "I deserve to hold your hand for agreeing to this bullshit."

He took my hand, lacing his fingers with mine, and we walked back together, past every line we'd ever drawn. Neither of us noticed how fast our hearts were pounding.

7

MAX

I fucking loved holding her hand. Loved it too much. Because this wasn't just best friends holding hands anymore. We were more, at least in my mind.

The second her fingers laced with mine, and she looked up at me like I was the only safe thing in her universe, I found myself grinning down at her with the silliest smile I'd ever had.

Fuck.

Was I falling in love with her?

Like *really* in love?

I couldn't be.

Could I?

I wasn't some sap who instantly fell in love with people. I know I had said it during the game, but really, it was to get under Jackson's skin more than anything. But my pulse was too loud in my ears as I thought about all the years Mackenzie and I had shared together.

Maybe I was losing my mind, then. This was definitely not love.

She looked back at me, smiling with her tongue in between her teeth. Her hair fell into her face, and I watched her wrap it up on top of her head with a ponytail holder. She reached out her pointer finger and lightly gripped my pinky.

My God. My heart sprinted yards ahead as I gripped her finger. I was falling for her. *Hard.*

The lines blurred, and I was finally letting out a part of me that had been caged for years.

I stared at her, and this feeling of absolute terror and bliss crashed inside my chest. I could feel my love for her clawing up my throat. My brain was short-circuiting just looking at her.

Oh, shit. I was in trouble.

This was fast, way too fast. But I had known her for seven years. We talked every day, sometimes multiple times a day. Sometimes for hours. She was the first call in the morning and the last one before bed.

Maybe it wasn't fast at all. Or maybe I was just trying to rationalize that this was okay, that I was normal. A normal guy falling in love with his best friend. A normal guy who would do absolutely psychotic and insane things for his best friend. Thoughts that were totally fucking scaring me. A normal guy who wanted to pin his best friend to the bed and fuck her unconscious. I was normal.

Totally normal.

But I wanted Jackson to know she was *mine.* I wanted him to feel the loss in his chest every time he looked at her and saw her with me. I wanted to erase every memory she had of him, and I would be the first everything for her. I hated him for touching her. For having parts of her I couldn't get back. The thought of it was enough to make my hands itch to break something.

"You want to get the kayaks?" she asked, smiling playfully.

"Yeah," I said, too eager.

She walked to the docks to talk to Graham. The sun bled orange across the lake. She stood there with her arms wrapped around herself. Her hair was in a messy bun now, strands curling in the breeze, and she looked so goddamn unattainable it made my teeth ache. She wasn't just my best friend anymore. She wasn't just the girl who knew my coffee order or hummed off-key when she was nervous. She wasn't just the one who stayed up talking to me over the phone when I was sick.

She was *mine*.

I almost felt guilty thinking of her that way. But the nerves didn't stop me from wanting it. I wanted it so badly.

She didn't know it yet. My claim on her. I'd decided somewhere between the woods and right now. There was no coming back from it. I wasn't planning on pretending.

I wanted her. *All of her.* I wanted to possess her soul. I didn't know what that made me, only that I couldn't stop wanting her. Every part of her. Even the parts she hid from me.

My chest ached, not a shallow burn of lust, but a slow, consuming kind you can't shake. It kind of fluttered, like a moth trying to escape a jar. Every time I looked at her, it swelled.

It was the kind of feeling that makes you protective in ways that aren't entirely healthy. The kind that says you'd do whatever it takes to keep her.

Was I wrong to feel this way? To feel so protective and territorial and downright psychotic around her?

We knew each other so well. She had to feel it too, right?

If she tried to run, I'd follow. Always.

She turned then, like she could feel my eyes on her, and I didn't look away. Her silhouette was gold in the dying light, and for one dangerous second, I thought about kissing her.

But I was nervous. Nervous about the way I was feeling. Nervous because this was Mackenzie. I didn't want to fuck this up.

"You okay over there? You're staring pretty hard," she laughed as she walked back towards me.

God, she had no idea.

"Can't help it," I said, voice low. "You look... unreal right now."

Her smirk faltered. "It's the sweat and bug spray combo, right?"

I stepped in, shaking my head. "No. It's you. Just you."

She studied me like she wasn't sure if I was teasing, and for a moment, I thought she might say something that would tip us over the edge. But then she smiled and bumped her shoulder into mine.

"You're getting sappy. I think the fake boyfriend thing's going to your head."

Oh, honey. I'm not your fake boyfriend. I am your boyfriend. You'll see.

She turned toward the kayak, and I let my eyes linger on the curve of her neck, the swing of her hips, cataloguing every detail because I was going to need it later. I was already too far gone to play this off like a game.

She was the real thing. For me, at least.

Nothing had ever felt better than this.

Nothing ever would.

"You ready?" I asked, my voice low.

"Yep! Let's go!" she said, smiling. "It's going to be dark soon; I thought we could go swim at the Blue Baths."

I didn't care where we went. She could've said we were heading straight into a storm, and I'd have followed without hesitation. But the Baths did spark something. It had been years since we'd been there. Back when we were sixteen and too young to name the things we were feeling.

"Did Graham give the green light?"

"Yeah, he said today and tomorrow are perfect. The water's clear."

I could feel Jackson's stare before we even pushed off. He stood motionless on the bank, arms crossed and jaw clenched so tightly I feared he might shatter his teeth. His piercing expression sent a wicked thrill through me. He could watch all he wanted—she was mine, and he was powerless.

She was laughing, fixing her hair again, joking that we'd sink because I was 'too big now.' Yet, I saw the flicker of tension in her shoulders, the way she furtively glanced back toward shore, as if nervously expecting something to go wrong.

"It's showtime," I murmured. "He's watching."

Her eyes cut toward me and narrowed. "Who?"

She knew.

She'd already clocked him. Still, I tilted my chin toward Jackson.

"Tall, brooding, looks like he wants to stab me."

She huffed, small and sharp. God, she was beautiful when she was irritated.

I dug my paddle in and steered us further out, the dock shrinking behind us.

"I can kiss you if you want," I said, casual on the surface but inside every nerve was on high alert.

Her head whipped around so fast the kayak swayed.

"What?" she squealed.

"To make him jealous," I shrugged nonchalantly.

"You're unbelievable. I thought we'd set boundaries." She was trying to be serious, but I could see the small smile on her lips.

"I'm just committed to the gig," I said with a slow smile. Her eyes softened, and I knew she'd considered it.

"You're forgetting the ground rules," she said.

I smirked. "You said we could improvise."

I leaned forward, resting my hand on her hip. She froze for a heartbeat but didn't move away. My thumb brushed over the thin fabric of her shorts.

"I think we need to go slow. Do you want to kiss me that badly, *boyfriend?*" she asked.

I flicked my gaze toward the shore. Jackson looked like he was chewing through the inside of his cheek.

Good. Let him choke on it.

"Yeah… I want to fucking kiss you, *girlfriend.*"

I wasn't pretending, so I might as well lay my cards out now.

She inhaled a breath. She didn't hesitate the way a timid girl might. Instead, she leaned a hair closer and rested her palm against my thigh. She was showing me that she was in control, that she owned me.

"Then show me how far you'll go," she murmured. "Make him watch."

"Do you trust me?" I asked, a faint hum of excitement coursing through my veins.

"Yes," she whispered. That single syllable lit something in my chest that was far more dangerous than desire.

I didn't rush. I let the silence swell, thick and heavy. My thumb stroked lazy circles against her skin. She was breathing faster, and I could feel her struggling to control herself.

"You don't have to kiss me if you're not ready," I said, voice dipped low enough to make it intimate. But in my head, I was already thinking about how easily I could take what I wanted.

She was practically begging me.

Her eyes locked on mine, searching. "I said I trust you," she repeated.

I leaned in, not enough to touch her, just enough to trap her in my gravity. "Then tell me how far you want this to go."

Her lips parted, but she looked away toward the shoreline. "I want him jealous."

I grinned, letting my fingers press a little more firmly into her hip and raising them just a bit higher underneath her shirt.

"That's a dangerous offer."

"You afraid of danger?" she teased.

I laughed under my breath, leaning closer until my thigh pressed against her back.

"Danger should be afraid of me."

I slid my hand up, tugged her cover-up just enough to bare her shoulder, and bent down, brushing my lips over her warm skin. It was a claiming kiss. I trailed kisses up her shoulder and neck, stopping right beneath her ear. I didn't need to push further. The way she was looking at me told me I already had her. That pull started in my chest again.

"You think he's jealous?" she said breathlessly, her voice one octave higher than normal, as she dropped her paddle into the water, and we started gliding toward the Baths.

I didn't look back at Jackson. I didn't need to. I already knew he'd keep seeing it in his head. My hand on her, my mouth on her skin. And if I had it my way, that image was going to haunt him.

"Oh, yeah."

About ten minutes later, the sun was gone, swallowed by the night. We drifted into the clearing where the water changed, and at first, I thought we'd gone too far out. Until the black surface beneath us began to glow.

A muted, electric blue clung to our paddles, trailing us in shimmering ribbons.

"It's like we're floating on stardust," Mackenzie squealed.

She reached into the water and gasped when her fingertips sparked to life under the surface. The glow danced along her skin, clinging like it wanted her. Her laugh was quiet.

"God… I forgot how beautiful it is."

I didn't answer. I wasn't looking at the water. I was looking at her. That fluttering feeling was back in my chest, and suddenly I felt like I might hyperventilate. I didn't know how to control myself around her.

The blue painted her from below, making her seem untouchable. Celestial. Her hair had fallen loose, curling over her shoulders in messy strands. The way her curls fell reminded me of that one night last summer when we stayed up late to watch the stars over the lake. She had held my hand that night. I had felt something for her even then, but I hadn't wanted to admit it.

She twisted slightly, catching me staring, and when her eyes met mine, something in my chest wrenched tight.

"You're staring again," she said lightly, but her tone had softened. She was curious about my behavior.

"Yeah," I admitted.

"Why?"

I set my paddle across my lap, letting us drift into the glow. "Do you want the boyfriend's answer or Max's answer?"

Her brows lifted. "Max."

I exhaled slowly, watching the light swirl around her hand. "Because I like seeing you like this. Happy. It makes me... I don't know. Feel things."

She was still, her eyes locking on mine as if she was weighing something heavy. The air became charged like the moment before a lightning strike.

She shifted to face me fully, knees drawn up, just close enough that I could reach out and tuck the curl from her cheek. I imagined leaning in and closing the space between us until her breath mingled with mine.

For a second, I thought she'd let me. Her lips parted slightly, her gaze flickering to my mouth.

And then she pulled back.

The glow on her face dimmed as she retreated, her shoulders curling inward. She didn't meet my eyes.

"We... we should head back," she said quickly. Her voice was tight.

"You don't want to swim?" My disappointment was sharper than I wanted to show.

She shook her head. "It's late. I'm tired."

Her voice was composed but not innocent. She was making a choice, playing a character.

I recognized the move. When things got real, she folded away. But this time she wasn't fleeing so much as controlling the endpoint. She'd started this game with me; she could stop it whenever she wanted. She knew exactly what pulling back would do to me, and she was going to do it.

"Alright," I said, picking up my paddle.

I caught the flicker in her eyes. It was a quick flash of satisfaction, like she'd *wanted* me to want more than she'd ever planned to give.

"Keep playing, and I'll have you begging for me by the week's end," I snapped, and the satisfactory grin on her face told me everything I needed to know.

She was fucking teasing me on purpose.

The trip back to the cabins was quiet. We both stole glances at each other, pretending not to notice. When we reached the cabin, the place was silent, and most counselors were already asleep. We tiptoed to our shared room.

As soon as we were alone, the door closed, she busied herself with pajamas and washing her face. I just sat there, watching. Every slight movement was another reminder that she was so close, and yet I still didn't have her. Not the way I wanted. Not yet.

She talked about how the water grew colder after the sun went down, about the glowing algae—probably with some Latin name she remembered from eighth grade—about the mosquito bite on her ankle.

She was talking about everything except for one thing that mattered. *Us.*

It was making me crazy.

I changed into sweats, towel-dried my hair, and let my gaze drift to her. She had asked to sleep in one of my shirts tonight.

My eyes skirted up her entire body.

My shirt's hem barely brushed the tops of her thighs. Bare legs. Bare feet. Leaning against the bathroom door with a toothbrush in her mouth, her hair damp and messy. She probably thought she looked casual. That this was a normal conversation between best friends.

But damn, did she look fuckable. My dick was twitching in my pants, and I had to hold the towel in front of me so she didn't notice.

I considered telling her to put on shorts. But why the hell would I give her the chance to cover herself up? She felt comfortable with me, and I didn't want that to change.

"You, okay?" I asked, my voice low enough to make her look up.

She nodded quickly. "Yeah, just tired."

She was such a liar.

I stepped closer.

"Mackenzie."

Her eyes snapped to mine, startled. I hardly ever used her real name.

"You don't have to talk about it," I said, "but you don't get to pretend I don't notice what's happening between us."

Her throat worked. "What's happening between us?"

"It's fine," I said, even though it wasn't. "You panicked. I got too close. I get it."

"I didn't panic," she shot back. Then, quieter, "Okay… yeah, I did."

"I'm not mad," I told her, because I wasn't. Frustrated? Sure. Did I want to pin her against the wall until she said what she really wanted? Absolutely.

"I'm not here to pressure you," I said, which was half-true. "I told you I'd let you lead, and I didn't. That's on me. I went too far."

Her head shook immediately. "No. You didn't go too far."

My jaw flexed. "Then stop acting like I did."

She didn't answer. She just crossed her arms, eyes fixed somewhere past my shoulder, like she was bracing herself against something invisible.

"I told you I can't fake," I said.

"Yeah, well… you're good enough at it that I can't tell

what's real right now," she said quietly. "I shouldn't have asked you to play along. We're too close."

She stopped and bit her lip. For a fraction of a second, I saw something like contentment flicker across her face. She wanted me to work for it, for her.

She was such a fucking tease.

She started to walk away, and I grabbed her hand. She stopped, not turning her head completely, but she didn't move her hand out of my grip. I started inching my grip up her arm, little by little, catching her elbow and gently pulling her into me. When her shoulder touched my chest, I turned her body so that we were looking straight into each other's eyes.

Everything else faded. Our hearts beat in sync as we stared at each other. Then I bent my head down so that my lips brushed against her ear.

"You like teasing me?"

Her breath stalled, and I could feel her pulse skyrocketing against my lips as I brushed them down her neck.

"You're blurring the lines again," she whispered back. But she wasn't pushing me away.

"I think you want me to blur them a little," I said, pulling my shirt down a bit off her shoulder and kissing the bare skin there.

Her breath was erratic now, her fingers gripping the front of my shirt like a vice. I pulled my lips off of her and looked back into her eyes.

She was hungry. The green irises were now molten lava. I wanted to touch her, taste her, sink into her. But she was my best friend, and I needed to take it slow. But my desire for her was so strong. It was overwhelming.

I bent down, my lips hovering right over hers.

So close. She closed her eyes, angling her face up to mine.

She wanted me to kiss her.

Her breath brushed my lips, and I swear I could taste her.

But I wanted her to work for it a little bit, too. I stepped back, biting my lower lip and holding in the tiny smirk I wanted to give her. She opened her eyes slowly, and when she saw that I wasn't going to give in to her, a flash of pure anger rolled over her face.

She turned her back on me, hair spilling across the pillow like a halo as she lay down in her bunk. I stood there, pulse still pounding. I'd agreed to this fake-dating shit for her. And yet, here I was, falling for it. For her.

She could at least give me the benefit of the doubt.

But because I was such a fucking gentleman, I plugged in the nightlight I'd brought her, setting it close enough for the glow to spill over her. She didn't turn around. But then she reached out and caught my hand. It was a quick brush of fingers before she pulled back like a petulant queen.

I shook my head with a soft smile because I was a fucking idiot and thrived off this shit.

I turned off the main light, took off my clothes, and climbed into the top bunk, the frame creaking under my weight.

"Goodnight, Trouble," I said into the dark.

There was a long pause before I heard it.

"Goodnight, Max."

My phone pinged at the same moment hers did. The screen's glow illuminated her face in the dark. I didn't need to lean over to know what it said.

I had already read it.

JACKSON KENSWICK

That little kayak date was cute.

Too bad, you'll never escape me.

The message was childish, but it made my jaw tighten. He was still circling her.

I let out a breath and looked up at the ceiling.

I had fucked up.

As soon as I saw her, a part of me I had locked up became obsessed. To be honest, I had been lowkey obsessed with her for years. I had stolen pieces of her journal, smelled her shirts when she wasn't looking, and even thought about stalking her during the school year. But I had never acted on it, because I was a standup guy. She would kill me when she found out how fucking obsessed I was with her.

I don't know why, but every time I was around her, I became a completely different person. And for some reason, this summer was when I decided to let everything implode.

I rubbed my hand across my face, blowing out another breath.

I had let my brain rationalize the most insane parts of myself, and I had crossed a line she didn't even know I could cross. A line I told myself to *never* cross.

I wanted to protect her because I loved her. I was just finally coming to terms with it. I knew Mackenzie had secrets. I had guessed a while ago that she was running from someone, and that all these 'aunts' and 'uncles' weren't family members.

Her drawings gave her away. I just didn't know the extent of her trauma. *Yet.*

I couldn't fault her for hiding it from me, because I had secrets of my own.

She thought I was just smart, the golden boy who got into MIT and two Ivy League schools. She thought I didn't have depth, that I just played ball.

She didn't know the truth, that my dad had taught me to hack before I could drive, that I'd been breaking firewalls and building bots since I was twelve. That I lived in an online world she didn't even know existed.

I had done it before I even realized what I was doing. I had a clean, easy doorway into a life I was dying to be part of. *Hers.*

When I helped her set up her phone, I accidentally hacked in. Okay, not *accidentally,* I knew what I was doing.

I was discreet about it.

I wasn't supposed to use my skills for stuff like this. Dad had told me this was just for fun, and one day I would use my skills for something useful. Was that day today? Probably not. But I was going to tell myself it was.

I couldn't stop. Not with her. I needed to know what was happening. Every threat, every secret, every shadow she didn't want to say out loud, I was going to know about.

I was always going to be one step ahead in whatever game Jackson was playing with her.

It was a little harder to hack his phone than hers. He was good at covering his tracks, but while he had been busy stewing about Mackenzie earlier, I had grabbed his phone and jailbroke it. I had made sure the little backdoor left no obvious footprints. Now, I could watch Jackson's accounts, trace his IP hops, catalogue his messages, log his times, and view his browser history.

I was browsing through his files when I discovered it. In his documents, a file labeled **"Game_2_MK."**

MK. Mackenzie? Or Max McKinnon?

The file was encrypted, even with the backdoors I had built. That meant he wanted it hidden. I couldn't open it, but I didn't need to. The name alone told me what I already knew: Jackson was planning something, and we were being watched.

I think part of her suspected something was off with him, but I don't think she realized the full extent of his psychosis.

In his files, there had been pictures I'd managed to retrieve. They were so grotesque I almost threw up when I saw them. There was a weird crest on all of them, though—thirteen-pronged. It kind of looked like a star.

I didn't know what that meant, but I wasn't going to think about it much.

Jackson was a fucking psychopath. And my job now was to keep her away from him. The only thing that would keep me from ripping his throat out was her.

Every second she spent near him, every smile she forced in his direction, I wanted to tear him apart. He thought he had her, but I had the chess piece.

She was the only thing he and I had in common. The difference was that I actually knew how to protect her. Psychopaths are predictable. They follow patterns. Jackson was no exception. Jackson wasn't a threat. He was a variable. And variables can be eliminated.

I wasn't just some golden retriever trailing after her. I was a Doberman. Her Doberman. *Hers.*

I was starting to scare myself with the lengths I'd go for her. I mean, fuck, we had only been back at camp for less than 24 hours, and I was already turning into a raging, reckless lunatic thinking about killing her psychopath ex-boyfriend. Something was changing in me. I didn't want to fight it because she needed me. I was her personal vigilante.

She didn't need to know how far I'd go. Not yet. But one day, she'd see that every insane, fucked-up thing I was about to do was because I was in love with her.

She was my entire purpose now.

My soulmate.

She had always been.

And I die before letting her go.

8

MACKENZIE

The cabin was quiet, safe from the cicadas' lazy symphony outside. Fifteen minutes after Max had climbed into his bunk, I noticed his breathing had evened out. My eyes drifted to the small light he'd left on for me.

I felt like such a fool.

He was the kindest, most patient person I'd ever known. He didn't understand why I feared the dark; he'd only asked once, casually. Yet here he was, making sure I felt safe.

And I was being a bitch. I was using him. I *was* teasing him.

I turned onto my back, staring at the underside of his mattress.

I couldn't stop replaying the way he looked at me tonight, the weight behind his voice when he said he was starting to feel things. Every syllable had carried the truth.

He liked me. Like, *really* liked me.

I rolled onto my side, hugging the thin blanket tighter around my waist. My skin still tingled where his hand rested, his thumb tracing slow patterns over my hip, leaving goosebumps. It hadn't been casual. It hadn't been playful.

And I felt it. Deep down, painfully. The *want*.

But that was the problem.

This wasn't supposed to be real. Max had already ruined the illusion in just a few hours. I was stupid to think we could play at something this intimate without consequences. As soon as I proposed the fake dating scenario, it was as if a doorway had opened, and suddenly, we both realized we liked each other. That we had liked each other for years.

He had looked so good on the lake tonight. And the invisible string between us was tightening, suffocating, drawing me in until it felt like falling for him wasn't just possible. It was inevitable.

Max saw me for me. Every jagged, broken edge. He read my silences, my moods, and didn't flinch. He didn't try to fix me. He just saw *me*.

I didn't want to admit to myself how attracted I was to him. It scared me how badly I wanted him.

I paused, making sure his breathing was still slow, and then my hand slid beneath the sheets, down between my thighs. I was desperate and aching. I bit my lip as I imagined my hand was his —his mouth, his weight pressing me down and making me forget everything but him.

I thought about the way his gaze lingered too long, heavy, and hungry, like he wanted to devour me. My hips lifted into my own hand, chasing the release.

We'd been friends forever, two halves of the same messed-up whole. Being with him made sense, perfect sense. And when I finally shattered against my palm, muffling a moan into the pillow, the only name in my head was his.

He meant everything to me. And maybe that was why I couldn't bear the thought of losing him.

As friends, I was able to keep him at a distance. It was easy to keep things from him when we were talking on the phone miles apart. But if we dated, that shred of privacy was gone. He would find out because I wouldn't be able to hide it from him.

And then, what would that even mean—for Mom and me?

We'd been federally protected assets for seven years, but I still wasn't sure what we were being protected from. My dad? Or something else?

Whenever I asked, Mom said it was "complicated," and Agent West said it was "classified," that normal witness protection rules didn't pertain to us.

Other protected families didn't have agents; they just resumed their lives in the normal world, but with new names and new identities. I didn't understand why we were always monitored. Why had everything stayed the same, but different?

But the rules were simple. Don't talk about Dad. Don't talk about the *past*. Don't get too close.

I knew my Dad was a bad person. I heard my mom call him "the Butcher" once, her voice low like she didn't want the walls to hear.

When I asked too many questions, like about the bodies, or why my Dad did what he did, West got quiet in that way that made me feel like I'd broken something, and Mom would change the subject.

But where did dating fit into this world I lived in?

Jackson had been vetted, West said. He was clear. I had been okay to date him. But where did Max fit in? Dating him meant questions. Questions meant details. And Max always had questions.

My phone pinged, jolting me out of my thoughts.

JACKSON KENSWICK

If you fuck him, you die.

A deep feeling of dread rippled through me. A memory of last winter broke through, dragging me back to my bedroom in

Marigold. A memory that reminded me that some things aren't meant to be so simple.

7 MONTHS EARLIER

I WAS PACKING IN MY BEDROOM, LAUGHING AT SOMETHING MAX had said on the phone that morning. I felt the lightness of excitement. Mom was taking me to Colorado for the first time. We had finally gotten FBI clearance, and this was my first real vacation. Agent West was coming with us.

I jumped as Jackson's voice cut through the air behind me.

"What's so funny?" he asked, his voice dark with jealousy.

I froze. "Nothing… just something Max said this morning."

The click of my bedroom door closing jarred my senses. He stopped, turning towards me.

"You think I don't see it?"

"See what?" I asked, trying to keep my tone steady as irritation rose.

"What he wants."

"He's my friend, Jackson," I said, folding clothes into my duffel bag.

"You think I'm blind?" His voice dropped to a low, dangerous rumble. "You talk to him every single day. Twice a day, sometimes. I see how much you like him."

My throat went dry as dread seeped in. I spun around too late. He slammed me against the wall with brutal force. His hand clenched my head, pressing so hard it felt like my skin would tear. My neck cracked painfully. I struggled to move, but he held my head down.

A ragged gasp escaped my throat, unnoticed by him. His eyes

were hollow, vacant—completely devoid of humanity. He was a stranger. A monster who could crush me without a second thought.

"Do you want to fuck him?" His breath was hot against my ear.

I didn't answer.

"Tell me, Kenz. Do. You. Want. To. Fuck. Him?"

His hand slid down my leg, fingers digging into my thighs, slipping beneath my skirt. I froze, my heart pounding. The air around us seemed to pulse with menace, the room narrowing until I barely had room to breathe.

"I know you get fucking ideas in your head. When he calls you, don't you forget who owns you." His teeth grazed my earlobe, tugging hard. I grimaced, a surge of dread tightening in my chest.

I didn't fight. I couldn't. Fear had shadowed my life, but now it was different. This was terror, guilt, and self-loathing.

"You smell so good," he whispered, his voice icy and dripping with malice. It sent shards of terror racing down my spine. "Like yellow flowers in a field," he hissed, a sinister edge sharpening his words.

I blinked, paralyzed by horror. My childhood memories flashed before me: daffodils in our backyard, my secret hiding place.

How could he know?

"So pretty, Kenz. Just like you." My dad's voice echoed cruelly in my mind, a twisted reminder of what I was supposed to be—a girl who reveled in this pain, a girl who deserved a monster like Jackson. The daughter of "the Butcher."

"Do you think I'm pretty?" my voice cracked, trembling under the weight of pain.

Jackson leaned in closer, oblivious to my tears and trembling. His obsession was pure, deranged, and all-consuming.

"Yea... yeah," he stammered, eyes blazing with an insatiable hunger that sent chills down my spine. "You know they picked you specifically for me."

My breath hitched, heart pounding. I clenched my teeth as a sharp pain shot through my jaw. What did he mean? Who had chosen him for me? What the hell was he talking about?

But then he pushed in deeper. I wanted to scream, to run, but I was paralyzed. The darkness within him seethed with a terrifying reality, Satanic and all-consuming, and I was ensnared inside it.

He was my nightmare incarnate.

I BLINKED INTO THE DARK, MY HEART RACING FROM THE memory. Since Jackson had registered for camp late, he ended up in a different cabin. Still, his presence made me uneasy. In the middle of the night, it was worse, like the shadows thickened with him.

If I dared to look out the window, I was certain I'd see two eyes waiting for me. I could almost feel his fingers dragging over my skin, phantom touches that made me want to claw myself out of my own body.

I stared up at the underside of Max's mattress, gripping my blankets tight. I listened to his even breathing. Heavy. Deep. Max would never hurt me. I knew that. He was the only one who made me feel safe.

Jackson's snapping was inevitable. If I gave myself to Max, if I let this happen, I knew I'd never escape it alive. Jackson would probably kill me. I didn't deserve someone like Max—not after everything that had happened. He was too good, and I was already too broken. I had watched my Dad murder people. That alone had shattered my soul.

I closed my eyes briefly, and the darkness closed in around

me. Suddenly, I wasn't in the cabin anymore. I was back inside my burning house in New York. Smoke clawed down my throat. Sirens wailed in the distance, but they were far, faint things.

"God, I dropped her," Agent West's voice echoed.

Then the growl of a motorcycle engine, growing louder, closer, until a voice cut through the flames.

"Mackenzie."

I turned, and there was Max, standing inside the fire like he belonged to it. But he wasn't the Max of today. It was him at twelve. His sunburnt cheeks, his baseball cap. His voice cracked, boyish and sure all at once.

"Wake up. Wake up, please."

I shot up in my bunk, lungs clawing for air. My sheets had twisted to the floor, sweat drenching my skin. Big, steady, grounding hands were on my shoulders.

"Trouble. Jesus, are you okay?" Max's voice was hoarse with panic. His face was pale, drained, his boxer briefs clinging to his hips. His eyes scanned me like he could find the source of my fear and rip it out.

"Yeah, I'm fine," I lied, rubbing my eyes. "Just a nightmare." My smile felt brittle, but he didn't call me out.

He bent, scooping the sheets from the floor, and tucking them back around me with a tenderness that made my chest ache. He hesitated, chewing on his lower lip, before climbing into the narrow bunk with me. The mattress dipped under his weight, and I nearly fell off.

"What are you doing?" I whispered, my voice shaking with relief.

He slid closer, his body radiating warmth and comfort as he cocooned me next to him.

"That was one hell of a nightmare," he murmured. "I'm sleeping with you."

His heartbeat drummed steadily against my back, soothing the terror still rattling in my bones.

"It's okay, Max. I think I'm fine now."

But he didn't move.

"Well, I'm comfy," he said after a beat. "So, you're shit out of luck if you think I'm going back up to my bunk."

I huffed. "What about everyone else?" I nodded towards the front of the cabin. I couldn't see anything out there. The darkness closed in through the open doorway, and the panic crawled up my throat.

"I don't give a fuck," he said simply. "No one can see us back here."

He shifted, finally letting his hand rest on my waist. His other arm wrapped fully around me. The contact was grounding. I inhaled his scent, a mix of lake water, smoke, and that sweetness that was just *him.*

It instantly comforted me. It was as if it had been made just for me. I was discreetly trying to catch a whiff of him when his voice broke through the silence.

"You were screaming my name," he whispered. I stilled, and he felt it. His hand tightened on my hip.

"I was?"

"Yeah," he said, his voice breaking a little. "You said my name a lot. You sounded… terrified."

"I don't know why I did that," I lied, forcing a laugh. "But thanks for waking me up."

He stayed quiet, holding me, his front to my back.

"You know you can tell me anything," he said softly.

I knew that. But he didn't need the weight of this. I was terrified that if I opened up my mouth, I would spill my secret.

His voice was so raw, deep, and full of longing for the truth. It tore me apart that I couldn't confide in him.

"Max?" I whispered.

"Yeah?"

"Thank you."

"For what?"

"For always knowing when I need you."

A whisper of warmth touched the back of my neck as his lips grazed my scar. My entire body stiffened.

"I didn't mean to…" he started, pulling back, but I caught his hand and held it tight, turning towards him.

He looked embarrassed. His blue eyes were shadowed by his anxiety, worried that I might pull away from him.

"It's okay."

I could hear his heartbeat pulsing inside his chest with nerves, and I slowly turned so we were face-to-face. I was careful not to knock us off the narrow mattress. I put my hand on his cheek, my thumb tracing his jaw.

"Truly. It's okay."

Something shifted in his eyes as my fingers dragged down his face. I leaned forward, intending to brush the corner of his mouth, but he angled just enough to claim my lips instead. The shock that rolled through me made him gasp, and I tried to give him a soft, sweet kiss back.

But he conquered me. His right hand went up to the back of my head, while his left hand pulled me in closer to him. His tongue slid against mine as his teeth tugged my bottom lip.

It was dominant, the way he kissed me. He wanted to be in control.

A needy sound escaped me before I could stop it, and the answering groan in his throat nearly unraveled me.

"We shouldn't be doing this," I whispered against his mouth. "We're supposed to be pretending."

"Yeah… " he moaned, sucking on my bottom lip like his life depended on it. "You want me to stop?"

"No." My voice was breathy, uncontrolled.

Heat surged between us, my body aching with the memory of what I'd done while he slept. I so badly wanted this, and if he tried, I don't think I would say no.

I unconsciously began rocking my hips against his, and his hands became wilder as they moved over my body.

"Fuck, Mackenzie," he groaned, kissing me harder. "Don't do that."

I was about to wrap my leg around his waist and climb on top of him. But he pulled back, his eyes big, his mouth open, his lips glistening from my tongue.

"I… want to keep going, but I know if I do, I won't be able to stop." He smirked faintly. He was so proud of himself.

"Okay…" I whispered, trying to distance myself from him because if I felt his body on mine any longer, I might actually explode. But Max had other plans. He hauled me against him, chest to chest, holding me like I was his lifeline.

Our eyes locked.

I was wet, wanting, and disappointed. He was hard, wanting, and disappointed.

We could hear each other's thoughts. We both wanted it, but we were going to hold back. It didn't feel wrong, what we had just done, but he *was* right. I don't think either one of us would stop if we let it continue. This was all pretend.

Right?

We stayed like that, breaths mingling, our mouths swollen and close enough to tempt another kiss, locked in a stare that left everything in silence.

I'm yours, I wanted to say.

And I heard him say back in his head, *I'm yours, too.*

And somehow, impossibly, despite the intense yearning, we drifted to sleep tangled together. For the first time in ages, I found myself without dreams.

9

MACKENZIE

The sunlight slipped through the cracks in the blinds, gold slashing across the thin cabin walls, painting Max in sharp, holy light.

I peered up at him. The sun carved shadows down his chest, tattooing his body in needle-like lines.

God. He was warm against me. We were still face-to-face, our lips so close to each other. His arm looped low around my waist, fingers twitching in his sleep, and I felt them under the hem of my shirt. His palm pressed to my stomach, fingers splayed over my ribs. He held me like I was his.

I hadn't slept next to someone since I was five years old. But now that I had, I never wanted him to go back up to his bunk.

I lifted my head slowly, memorizing him. His mouth was slightly parted, his hair rumpled, his lashes dark against his cheeks. He looked so painfully beautiful and peaceful. Pain had never found him. Not like it had for me. Pain had scarred me.

I pressed my fingers to the scar on the back of my neck, tracing the raised knot of skin where the staples had been. It didn't feel like a badge of survival. It felt like a weight I would never shake.

Jackson's voice slammed into my thoughts.

"If you scream, I'll kill you," he had said as he pressed the lit end of his cigarette into my skin.

That had always been my punishment for doing something he disliked.

He always looked at me like I was an annoyance, a nuisance he didn't want to deal with. But at the same time, I was something he wanted to conquer.

Max looked at me differently. He kissed my scar last night. No one else had ever done that.

When he kissed me, it felt as if he was trying to transfer his soul into my body. I wanted to do it again. I felt the butterflies when he kissed me, and I wanted that feeling back.

It made me forget everything—even the darkness. I wonder what he'd do if he knew how badly the darkness torments me.

His eyes fluttered open. He blinked, dazed, and then gave me a slow, lazy smile that knocked the air out of my lungs.

"Hey," he rasped, his voice rough with sleep.

"Hey," I whispered back, my head propped on my hand.

We were still tangled, his leg draped over mine, his hands on me as if he had no intention of letting go.

His gaze lingered on my face, dropped down, and came back up again. Hunger bled through the cracks in his composure. It wasn't just his fingers tightening on my waist, or the way his breath hitched when I licked my lips. It was in his eyes, heated glances, a barely contained growl in his voice when I adjusted my bare leg against his.

I could feel him hardening against me. His desire wasn't quiet or polite. But he was holding back, waiting for permission.

Jackson never waited. Jackson *took.* Max would be wild too, but not in the same way. He'd rage like a storm, yes, but he'd let me *choose* to step into it. He'd want me to feel every second of it. He'd like me to take control.

"What?" I teased, feigning coyness.

His smile was small. "First time I've seen you in the morning like this."

"You've seen me all the time," I rolled my eyes.

"Not like this. Not the first thing. Lying next to me." He bent close to me and whispered, "In *my* clothes. You're beautiful."

He shook his head slightly, as if he couldn't believe he had said that. He reached out, brushing a strand of hair from my face. I was really starting to like that gesture. He did it often. I smiled at him, and he paused, studying me so intently I almost flinched. Those aquamarine eyes were open, unguarded. He wasn't just looking at me; he was truly seeing me.

He looked at my lips, and I knew he wanted to kiss me again. Suddenly, nervousness took over my chest. It rippled through my core in tight waves. My breathing quickened.

I liked him too much. I was falling. Too fast. We were supposed to be pretending.

He must have sensed my anxiety because his hand gently moved up to my arm and stayed there, steady, warm, comforting. My breathing slowed, and I suddenly blurted out, "I want to get a tattoo."

His brows rose. "Oh, yeah?"

I nodded, chewing the inside of my cheek. "Over my scar. I'm tired of knowing it's there."

"You sure?"

I nodded again. He watched me, his eyes hooded, and then he said, "Alright. Let's go."

It was so decisive, it startled me.

"Wait, what?"

He didn't ask why. He didn't try to fix me. He just stood, pulling a dark shirt over his head, jeans half-buttoned, hair a mess from sleep, morning light kissing the curve of his back.

"Yeah, let's go."

He meant it. No hesitation, no judgment, just support. The ache in my chest cracked open.

He hadn't asked me once about the nightmares. He didn't need to. He was my anchor when I drifted, steady when I spun. And here he was—anchoring me back to my course. But still, the fear coiled. He didn't know why I had the scar. He was going to actually see it. What if he looked at me differently then, like I was broken? Like I was a monster? Was I a monster?

I swallowed, tearing my gaze away. But when I glanced back at him, he was already watching me; his gaze warm, his smile gentle, and my paranoia subsided.

"Come on," he grinned. "We've got a tattoo to get."

I dressed quickly, and I followed him to his truck. Our campers didn't arrive until tomorrow, which meant, for once, it was just us.

The drive into town felt like a dream. Max had the windows rolled down, one hand loose on the wheel, the other resting on the console between us. I moved my hand close enough that our pinkies brushed.

His sunglasses were crooked, his hair wild from the wind, and still he looked maddeningly relaxed. Happy. Free. And the strange part was, I felt the same. I wasn't looking over my shoulder for once.

"How far is this place?" I asked, propping my feet up on the dashboard, my anklet shining in the sun.

He smirked without even looking at me. "Twenty minutes. Less, if you stop distracting me."

"Distracting you?" I tilted my head, feigning innocence as I fiddled with his phone. I couldn't download any apps to mine, so he had set up a playlist on his Spotify for us.

"I'm just sitting here. Being an excellent DJ."

"11 a.m." by Incubus broke through the speakers.

"You're sitting there looking like that," he muttered, eyes flicking down my legs, before darting back to the road.

I laughed. "Hmm. You like what you see?"

He gave me a look that said he wanted to say something

filthy back, but he bit his tongue. His fingers were gripping the steering wheel so tight his knuckles were white.

"I'm not going to respond to that, Trouble."

I was a bit disappointed. This wasn't like Max. He usually told me whatever was on his mind. But now, he was holding back the part of himself I loved the most. I wanted him to be bad. I wanted his restraint to falter a bit.

I didn't know why he was hiding from me.

"Why? You acted like you liked it last night."

I wanted to see what made him tick, and apparently, it was me. His jaw twitched, and a soft look of challenge flickered across his face.

"You're staring too," he said after a moment, a smirk tugging at his mouth.

"I'm not."

"You are," he countered easily. "I think you like what you see."

I rolled my eyes, heat creeping to my cheeks. But I was relieved his brief absence of Max-isms was over. "You're so cocky."

"All 8 and a half inches would agree."

His grin stretched smugly across his face when he saw my mouth drop open. He cranked up the music.

We pulled off into town, and instead of heading straight to the tattoo shop, Max parked in front of a tiny corner diner.

"I'm starving," he said. "And you need food, otherwise you get... moody."

"Moody?" I arched a brow, getting out of the truck and meeting him on the sidewalk.

He mimicked me, sticking his bottom lip out in a dramatic pout. *"Max..."* he whined in a high-pitched voice. *"I'm so hungry, I'm shaking."*

I shoved his shoulder, laughing, but he caught my wrist and spun me into him.

For a second, we were too close. Chest to chest. His gaze dropped to my mouth, lingered, and for one second, I swore he might actually—

He cleared his throat and stepped back, releasing me. "Come on, baby. Pancakes."

He mimed an eating motion, and I stared hungrily at the way his arms flexed with the movement.

Baby. He had called me, *baby*.

Get a grip, Mackenzie.

His hand squeezed my waist on the way inside, just enough to make me squeak. I needed to start calling him *dangerous*, because he was making me feel things I had never felt before.

The diner was washed in sunlight, and the booth was too small for someone his size. He grunted as he tried to get comfortable. We sat side by side, despite the tight squeeze, practically on top of each other. His thigh brushed mine every time he shifted, and though my mind pretended not to notice, my body did.

We were too entuned to each other. It was hard not to react. I could feel his restraint rippling through his movements, too. We were both trying to behave, but we didn't want to.

"Want a milkshake?" I asked, clearing my throat and flipping open the laminated menu.

"It's 10 a.m.," he said, looking down at his menu.

"So? Afraid it'll ruin that perfect body of yours?" I teased.

His head tipped back slowly, a mischievous smile tugging at his lips as he draped one arm across the back of my chair, his thumb resting provocatively close to my shoulder.

"That's the third time you've mentioned my body, Trouble," he said. "I'm starting to think you've got an obsession."

His tone was cocky, but his eyes softened, like he liked the idea of me wanting him. Like it made him weak in ways he'd never admit.

The soft click of the jukebox cut through the chatter in the diner. "Dreams" by Fleetwood Mac began to play, and I let my gaze drift over to Max. His knee bounced under the table, jittery, fingers toying with the napkin holder. He was nervous.

A slow, wicked sort of confidence unfurled inside me, settling in like I'd just been handed the next move in the chess match.

"Maybe, I do." I bit my bottom lip between my teeth, my eyes dragging over his shoulders and the veins in his forearm. "Or maybe, I just haven't decided what I want to do with you yet."

The words tumbled out before I could stop them. I didn't even realize how breathless I sounded until the words came out. The thrill hit me low in my stomach. I'd never flirted like this with anyone.

And *definitely* not with Max.

He blinked. His mouth opened, then shut. No sound. Nothing. Not one damn word. Just a low, soft grunt that told me everything I needed to know.

I could see the red blush forming under his skin as the color crept up his neck. His fingers curled against the table like he needed something to hold onto. His jaw flexed, and his knee bounced hard under the table, like his whole body was wound too tight, and the only thing that would cure the ache was me.

"Christ," he muttered, almost a growl. His voice was thick with heat. "You're gonna make it real hard to finish breakfast."

10

MAX

I was going to combust. Right there in that stupid vinyl booth, in the middle of a half-dead diner with peeling wallpaper and sticky syrup bottles. The universe had planned the worst possible stage for my downfall.

One second, she was talking about milkshakes, and the next, my brain was busy undressing her, flipping through a highlight reel of every way I wanted her. I had already thought about it all night and all goddamn morning.

Maybe I just haven't decided what I want to do with you yet.

What the fuck was I supposed to do with that? How did I fucking respond to that?

My jaw locked. My fingers flexed against the table like I could crush the wood if I just squeezed hard enough. I needed a stress ball because she was giving me high blood pressure. Tension coiled low in my stomach, hot and mean, like a fuse waiting for a spark. My knee bounced like I was sixteen again, not a guy two months shy of nineteen who was supposed to have a handle on himself.

The problem was, I didn't want to control myself. I didn't want to play the good guy. Ever since that kiss, I was losing it. I wanted her. Every look. Every touch. Every laugh that ended with her shoulder brushing mine made me feel like I was drowning. And she had no fucking clue.

"Something wrong?" she asked sweetly, batting her lashes like she wasn't about to dismantle me, piece by piece.

I gripped the table's edge like it could ground me. Holding onto something was good for me. It kept me from flying straight out of my body.

"You're dangerous," I said, because it was either that or groan her name across the damn diner.

She smiled. "You know, I was thinking of giving you that nickname."

Yep, I was about to groan.

She licked her lips. "You kind of like it, right?"

Like? Like?!

No, no, I was addicted. I was trying to be a good boy. But she was fucking flirting with me, and I wanted to bend her over this table and make her feel how addicted I was.

"I love danger," I quipped back, smirking.

"Good, because I'm just getting started."

"Careful," I warned, "I don't like being messed with."

I'd let her mess with me, though, only her.

She tilted her head, smiled, and then decided to go full nuclear.

"Yeah? Then what are you going to do about it, sweet boy?"

My elbow slid off the table, and I nearly cracked my skull like an idiot. She couldn't be serious.

She twirled a loose piece of hair around her finger. She was serious. Drop dead, crazy in the head, serious. I mean, damn, she could pick up the knife off the table right now and carve my heart out, and I'd let her feed it to me on a platter.

I let out a low laugh and leaned closer to her.

"Oh, baby..." The word slipped out before I could stop it. "Keep teasing me, and we won't make it to the tattoo shop."

Her grin sharpened. "You'd like that? Making me yours?"

I mean, she already was. But I'd let her keep thinking I was playing the game until the time was right.

I swallowed, dragging my eyes from her lips. "I don't think you're ready for that yet."

She had no idea what I would do to her.

"You underestimate me," she said, twirling her hair again. "I'm not a little girl anymore. Maybe you're not ready for me."

I wanted to tell her everything, all the filthy things building in my head. But I bit my tongue.

"I'm trying to be good, Trouble," I admitted, staring at the menu. "But if you keep talking like this, this *fake* relationship of ours? It's going to have problems."

"What kind of problem are we talking about?" she teased. "Principal's office? Detention?"

I grinned then. "Oh no. Worse."

Her eyes sparkled. "Oh, worse? Wow. What, then? Do I need to beg for some extra credit? Bend me over a desk and—"

I nearly choked on my water. I froze mid-sip, as if someone had unplugged me from reality. My brain short-circuited, as visions of her bent over a desk with her skirt hiked up around her waist flashed through my mind. She had been reading my mind again.

I didn't know what to say to her. If this were anyone else, I would've quipped back with something snarky. But it was Mackenzie. When I was around her, I reverted to that twelve-year-old nerd she had befriended. My body was hot, my palms sweating. She said it so casually, like she hadn't just pulled the pin on my grenade.

She was a freak. And I loved it.

"Fuck," I whispered, because it was either that or confess every fantasy right there between the salt and pepper shakers.

The waitress popped next to us, saving me from complete combustion. Mackenzie jumped a little, breaking our bubble. I ordered a milkshake with two straws like some smug idiot in a rom-com movie, and she gave me a look.

"What?" I said. "You're gonna drink half of mine anyway."

The waitress came back with our drink, and the second her lips closed around that straw, I felt it. That hum, that pull, like we were standing on the edge of something we couldn't come back from.

She licked the chocolate from her mouth, and my eyes dropped without permission. My thoughts weren't even subtle anymore. They were full-blown confessions.

"Stop looking at me like that," she warned.

Like that.

I knew exactly what she meant. I was going to tear her apart. Watch her beg. I wanted her so wrecked she couldn't walk straight for days.

"If you're going to flirt with me like that, then fuck, baby, buy me breakfast first."

I gave her a killer smile, waiting for her to fold. But in true Mackenzie fashion, she just matched me.

She didn't laugh. She didn't tease. She just looked at me. And that look? That was the moment I realized that she didn't want to fake. But she hadn't admitted it to herself yet.

MACKENZIE

MY HEART SLAMMED AGAINST MY RIBS. I HADN'T MEANT TO BE so forthcoming, but I was turned on just by sitting next to him, and I wanted him to know it.

I was going to tell him to make me beg for it, that I wanted to, but before I could respond, the waitress slid by, and Max started ordering like he hadn't just promised to ruin me.

When she left, I finally found my voice again.

"You think this is a done deal," I said, looking away.

"What?" he asked.

"Us. You and me."

"It is a done deal." His voice was so deep I could feel it vibrate through me. "I told you that if you keep teasing me, we'll have a problem."

"And the problem is?" My eyes flicked back to his.

"I'll give it to you right now." His smile was sharp, wicked. "And you're going to fucking like it."

My pulse stuttered. Was he joking? Teasing? Or serious?

"Oh, Dangerous." His eyes lit up when I said his new nickname. "You think we can do that without feelings?"

He hesitated, then looked down, fiddling with his fork. He knew exactly what I meant. We'd been undressing each other with words seconds ago, but this wasn't just flirting anymore. We were moving into a new territory. The air changed between us. It wasn't just tension anymore. This was something real.

"I don't know," he admitted finally. "I told you, I'll do whatever you want. I just… need to know the limits."

"I told you the limits," I whispered.

"Those have changed now, don't you think?" he said, his eyes dark and hungry.

I inhaled slowly, forcing myself to meet his gaze. "That's because you keep blurring the lines."

He leaned forward, his fork spinning lazily between his fingers. "I'm not blurring them. You are."

"*I* didn't do anything." The protest felt weak, even to me.

He hummed low, then pounced.

"What about when you told me you wanted me to bend you over a desk? Was that nothing?"

Heat rushed to my face. He had me, and he knew it.

"Maybe we quit," I whispered.

His head snapped up. "No."

The word came out so fast, too firm. "I'm not quitting," he added. "I said I'd help you, and I will."

I raised an eyebrow. "No sex. Okay?"

I didn't mean it. I wanted to… so badly. My mouth said no, but my body said yes.

He looked at me, and in his gaze, there was his easy confidence, but underneath, something gentler, steadier. He wasn't pushing me. He was letting me steer. But God, the way he looked at me made me want to drive off the cliff myself.

"We'll be careful," he said softly.

He wasn't agreeing with me on the no sex.

His hand brushed mine on the table so faintly I could've imagined it. He gave me a smile then, not his crooked one. But a small, mischievous one that told me everything. He didn't want to quit because he wanted me.

The waitress returned with our food, shattering the moment as if it were nothing. She placed our plates on the table.

Max leaned back in the booth, grinning like we were friends grabbing breakfast. This was so like him. One second, we were word fucking each other, and then the next, we were back to being besties.

I stole a strawberry from his plate and popped it into my mouth with a slow exaggeration.

He froze mid-bite. "Really?"

"Girlfriend perks," I teased.

His grin deepened, but his eyes lingered. It made me squirm in my seat. He was loving this.

"So," he said lightly, "what's the plan for the rest of our fake, totally-not-complicated day?"

I rolled my eyes. "Tattoo. Public appearances. Make Jackson sweat."

"Love that for us." He clinked his fork against mine like a toast. "Alright, what's step one?"

"Step one: act unbothered. Like you being all over me is just… normal."

"Am I allowed to be all over you?" His grin was infuriating.

"Don't be a dick," I said dryly, ignoring the flip in my stomach.

"Too late. Okay, so hand on your back, whispers in your ear, grabbing your thighs, got it."

I arched a brow. "You've thought this through."

"I've had some ideas." His gaze didn't waver.

"And step two?" I asked.

"Don't know yet. I say we see how fast Jackson cracks before we get there."

I dragged a fingertip along my glass, leaning in. "And when he does?"

Max met my gaze head-on. "We blow it up."

The silence that followed stretched taut between us, buzzing.

"You're a convincing fake boyfriend," I said finally, leaning back, trying to breathe again.

"Convincing?" His grin turned sharp. "I'm the best boyfriend you'll ever have."

I noted how he didn't say "fake."

MY LONGING FOR HIM WAS OVERWHELMING AS WE STEPPED OUT of the diner.

His truck rumbled to life, the radio a low hum beneath the tension.

"So," Max said, clearing his throat. "What are you getting for your tattoo? A heart with my name in it?"

I snorted. "Please. I was thinking something meaningful.

Subtle. Oh, I know. A middle finger. For you." I lifted mine in demonstration.

He grinned. "Bold of you to think I wouldn't find that fucking hot as hell."

I rolled my eyes. "Right. Forgot, you've got a tattoo fetish."

"Just on you," he said too quickly, then backpedaled, eyes flicking between me and the road. "I mean, any girl with ink is hot in my book."

I caught myself staring at his hand resting casually on the console. I wanted to hold it.

"Sabotage," by Beastie Boys, filled the silence a moment too long before he asked, "Okay, seriously. What are you getting? And am I allowed to see it?"

"I'm still deciding."

"Will I get to see it though?"

I paused. "You'll have to undress me first, but yeah."

I was joking, but now even my jokes were coming out flirtatiously.

His head turned, just enough for me to see his expression. Not playful. Not mocking. Just that steady, scorching look that said, *stop fucking with me unless you mean it.*

I met his gaze, and for a second, it felt like we were teetering on the edge of something we couldn't undo. I'd told him no sex because I was terrified of what it would do to us, of what it would do to me. But the string between us was burning with our barely controlled longing for each other, and I was about to be scorched.

What would he do if I climbed over the console into his lap? Would he fight me off, or let me take control?

What would we do if we passed the line, more than we already had? Would we survive it? He was my best friend in the whole world. If I lost him, I wouldn't ever be the same.

Max shook his head in disbelief, pulling us back from the brink.

"I can't believe you're doing this. I can't wait to see what you pick."

"I can't believe it either," I whispered, though my chest buzzed with something dangerously close to joy. For once, I felt like I wasn't chained to my past. I was reaching for something new.

His eyes softened when they slid over me, lingering at the scar on the back of my neck.

"It's going to look so pretty on you."

He had to stop saying things like that, things that made me fall harder for him. The rush of air through the open windows wasn't enough to cool the heat crawling over my skin.

His fingers immediately laced with mine. I wanted to fight it, this feeling, but I couldn't. Because it felt exactly like it was meant to.

Maybe I didn't need to keep running. As long as I was with him.

MAX

We rode in silence. Not the easy kind we'd fallen into a hundred times before, but something wound tight. It was tense. She was holding something in. It hurt to watch. She looked like she was figuring something out, and it was scaring the shit out of her.

I risked a glance at her. Her jaw was set, her eyes locked on the window, but her hand was gripping mine so tight I could barely feel my fingers.

"What's wrong?" I asked softly, keeping my eyes on the road.

I eased my hand from hers only to place it on her knee. She didn't realize it, but she always clung to my touch when she was anxious. And I always gave it to her, as if I could transfer my strength to her and take her fear away.

She didn't answer. My chest tightened. The longer she didn't respond to me, the more I began to fidget. But then she turned, and fuck, her eyes.

Not just green. They were wild, storm-after-the-rain green, cutting through me, pulling me under. The kind of green that made you forget what you were about to say. They weren't soft and delicate. Sharp, always watching, always calculating, like she could see the parts of you that you kept hidden.

I loved her eyes because they were so expressive. When she was mad at me? They burned like glass, catching sunlight. But when she laughed or smiled? They turned into moss and clover and everything about summer that felt like home.

I could get lost in her eyes and never want to crawl back out.

"I'm good." Her voice was too calm, the kind of calm that hides something sharp beneath it. Her gaze dragged down my body, stopping at my waist before flicking back to my face. But it was the flush in her cheeks that damn near undid me.

I had to look away. I was so wound up from our conversation at the diner, I wanted to pull the truck over and tell her to get in the backseat.

I forced myself to breathe, to keep it together, despite my hardening cock in my jeans. I seriously could not control myself around her. I tried so hard not to look at her again, but my eyes betrayed me, drifting back to her.

I was always drifting back to her.

She was beautiful in that messy, infuriating way; cutoff shorts, a braid falling loose, looking like trouble and freedom and home all at once. Every time I looked at her, my body reached for hers before my brain could stop it. We were tuned to the same frequency. Always riding the same wavelength.

Mackenzie wasn't just perfect. She was everything. I craved intimacy with her because I just craved her. I wanted the connection. She was my fucking soul.

She laughed, breaking the silence. "Remember when we were fifteen, and you dared me to jump off the cliff into the lake? You thought you were *so* brave going first to catch me, only to nearly drown."

I laughed, the sound pulling us back into familiar territory. "I *was* brave. You were the one screaming the whole way down."

She rolled her eyes. "I was not screaming."

"Please. You sounded like a banshee auditioning for a horror flick." I howled like a wolf, and she jabbed me in the ribs.

"Shut up," she said, but her grin told me otherwise.

I grinned wider. "You were the one who wanted to go up there. You've always chased the high. Maybe that's why I keep getting dragged into your chaos."

She tugged her hand free, though her smile stayed. "Or maybe it's because you like the chaos as much as I do. You like to think you're protecting me."

I shot her a look, squinting.

"Maybe. But some chaos is worth it."

Her expression flickered, serious for just a second. "We've always been a mess together, huh?"

Without hesitation, I reached for her hand again, threading our fingers.

"Yeah. But I wouldn't want it any other way."

"Me neither," she whispered, smiling.

Then, like she needed to shatter the electric energy between us, she asked, "So... did you ever find that girlfriend back home?"

My smile dropped. Her words punched me square in the gut. That's what she'd been thinking? That I was taken? Why the fuck would I be doing what I'm doing with her if I had a girlfriend?

"Uh... no. I... dated a few girls, but none stuck," I said, exasperated. "I told you this."

She nudged me, teasing, but I caught the careful curiosity beneath it. "Come on, spill. Who was the most memorable mess?"

I gave her a sideways glance. "Memorable? None."

Because none of them was her. None of them ever stood a chance against Mackenzie.

I thought about shutting down this conversation for a second, but then I caught the look in her eyes, the one that said I could trust her. That she really wanted to know.

"There was one girl," I admitted finally. "Kind of wild. A little reckless."

Her brows lifted. She gave me a look to continue, but I saw it. Jealousy. There was a dark cloud hiding behind her eyes, and her breathing accelerated.

"What happened?" she asked.

I raked a hand through my hair, buying time. "We just… went our separate ways. She wanted to be serious, and I didn't."

What I didn't say was that I had been caught staring at a photo of Mackenzie. I was given an ultimatum, and I chose Mackenzie. And that was that.

"Sounds rough," she murmured, sympathy softening her features.

Our eyes caught, something raw sparking between us.

"Yeah," I said, shutting it down before I spilled too much.

She smiled. "You deserve someone special, Max. Someone who loves you completely."

My throat burned with the thing I wanted to say. *You. It's always been you.*

But I kept quiet. Because if I opened my mouth, I wasn't sure I could stop.

We stepped into Wildwood Ink, a hole-in-the-wall, but there wasn't much to choose from out here.

The air inside the tattoo parlor smelled like ink and antiseptic. She glanced around curiously, a nervous energy buzzing off her, and I was forced to focus on anything other than her body when her shirt rose on her back as she leaned over to look at the fresh designs on the wall.

Her jean shorts fit snugly at her hips, while her oversized tee was tied at the waist. She glanced back at me, tossing a small smile over her shoulder, which was almost worse. It was so sweet, and my thoughts were so filthy.

She started talking to someone at the front desk, and I mumbled something to John, the artist who would be doing her tattoo. Before I knew it, he had already led us to the back of the room.

There was something about the way he appeared—too suddenly, too quietly—that made the hair on the back of my neck stand up. But a giggle from Mackenzie pulled my gaze away.

She sat on the cushioned table, her fingers tapping restlessly against her knee to hide her anxiety. But I could see past her act. Her leg bounced nervously, and she started to overanalyze the situation, biting the inside of her cheek.

"You sure about this?" I asked quietly, keeping my voice low even though the buzz of the tattoo gun and the music from the front drowned us out. "We can leave. Just let me know."

She was humming to the music; it sounded like something she would listen to. Heavy guitars, deep screaming. It was calming to her.

She looked up at me and nodded, "I want this."

I believed her. But I also knew that there was another reason why she was doing this. It was the same reason she was having these nightmares. Mackenzie had many secrets. There was always more beneath the surface with her. I didn't fault her for keeping them from me. I wanted to tell her she didn't have to carry it alone, even if she hated me for knowing.

That journal of hers, I didn't read it. Not really. But she left it on her bunk a lot over the years, and I'd seen enough of her sketches to know they weren't just doodles. They were confessions, stories. Scratched out figures, frayed lines, harsh shading.

There was one page I couldn't forget. A man's silhouette, towering over a petite figure. She hadn't drawn his face. She'd just darkened it in, pitch black, like even remembering him was something she couldn't let herself do.

It didn't take much to connect the dots.

I knew something had happened, something with her dad.

She never said it outright, but she didn't have to. I remembered the way her voice flatlined when his name came up once.

And then it all clicked when Jackson said I didn't know who she was or where she came from. The boundaries, the fear, the way she sometimes looked at me like she wanted to be close. Something was always holding her back.

It pissed me off that Jackson knew, and I didn't. I wanted to tell her that she could trust me, but that wasn't what she needed.

Because even if she couldn't say it, I already knew. I had seen it in her eyes in the truck. She wasn't afraid of me. She wasn't even afraid of me finding out about her past. She was scared I would *leave* her.

I hope she knew that I wasn't going anywhere.

She turned in her chair, her back to me, revealing the pale, knotted scar on her neck. I had glimpsed it before, while swimming, changing, or running together at camp, but I really saw it for the first time today. She always hid it from me, but today, she wasn't.

There was trauma linked to that scar, a pain she was trying to escape. When I kissed it last night, I wanted her to know how I felt about her. I didn't know how to say it out loud.

"Is this what you want?" John whispered, his voice low and chilling, making me jump. He was a towering figure, covered in tattoos that twisted like dark veins across his arms, a septum piercing glinting ominously in the dim light.

I moved to stand in front of her, trying to shield her from him, while remaining within his line of sight in case something went wrong. Leaning against the cold wall with my arms crossed, I forced myself to appear casual, though my entire body felt lit up. The moment the needle pierced her skin, she didn't flinch. She didn't even wince. I was trembling more than she was, my nerves fraying at the edges.

She just gazed at me. Her piercing eyes locked onto mine for an agonizing hour. She didn't break eye contact until the tattoo was finally finished. Then, slowly, she sat up, brushing a strand of hair from her face as if emerging from darkness.

God, she was *fucking* beautiful.

"Well?" She asked, spinning around, holding the mirror up. "What do you think?"

I stepped forward, reaching out instinctively. My fingers hovered just above the freshly inked stars. I wanted to touch her. So fucking bad. But I knew I couldn't because of a possible infection. She flinched slightly as my fingers lingered over her skin, tracing the stars in the air.

"It's perfect."

I glanced at her. Her eyes were full of tears, and I felt an overwhelming connection to her. Her feelings, her scar, and just *her*.

"My turn," I murmured, gently removing my shirt.

"Wait, what?" She asked, her voice trembling with surprise.

"Yeah, while you were busy looking at designs earlier, I told John here that I wanted whatever you picked out, too," I said, a slow smirk playing on my lips.

"But what... what if I had picked out something like a butterfly or a heart or a moth?"

I chuckled darkly.

"A moth? Seriously? I'd probably skip that one, but a butterfly?" I shrugged. "I'd look pretty sexy, right?"

Her eyes flickered with a mixture of desire and suspicion before she burst into laughter.

"I love you," she whispered, and my chest tightened with a dark, aching need.

John shook his head.

"You two are super cute," he said with a sugar-coated layer of cynicism.

I ignored him, but I thought to myself, *Yeah, we are pretty cute.*

"I want it right here, a little bit bigger," I stated, pointing to my left shoulder. "The same as hers."

She watched me like I was made of glass. Like she didn't want to miss a single second.

Fuck, getting the tattoo hurt. She had made it seem so painless, but I was dying.

Don't let her see how badly it hurts. Don't let her see how weak you are, I told myself.

But I was a pussy. I was about to cry.

Her hand drifted to my knee halfway through, like she needed to touch me, and honestly, it made me feel better.

"It hurts, right?" she asked, voice gentle.

"Fuck yeah, it does," I said with a shaky laugh, exhaling slowly.

"You've got this."

The needle's whine drilled into my skull. I clamped my hand over Mackenzie's, her pulse fluttering beneath my fingers.

"Big guys are always the worst," John observed, wiping blood away with a sterile pad. "Relax."

"Fuck off," I said, sweat beading at my hairline.

The needle buzzed again, tearing hot lines down my shoulder. Mackenzie flinched when I flinched.

John glanced up, eyes flicking between us without moving his head. "You two together?"

She swallowed. "What makes you think that?"

John leaned back, stretching his gloves with a snap. "Most couples who come through here either break up or get married. If you two survive each other, come back for more. I'll discount it."

My heartbeat tripped. Marriage. The word shouldn't have hit as hard as it did. The picture formed too fast in my head—her with my name, my ring, my future carved into her skin and her life.

I imagined her wearing my name under her skin, inked where only I would ever see.

The shop's overhead LEDs buzzed faintly, catching on the stainless steel tray and the neatly laid-out needles. The delusion of marriage in my mind snapped.

What the fuck was I thinking?

I forced a breath out. "Then don't fuck it up. We might be back."

John snorted without looking up from his setup. "I never fuck up."

She looked away first, and I felt the loss like cold air rushing in.

Afterward, with both of us wrapped tight in fresh Saniderm, I reached for her—then hissed, pulling back with a half-laugh. "Shit, it burns."

She laughed, reaching for me.

"Can't even touch it," she said, fingers tapping lightly on the unwrapped part near my elbow instead.

"You can touch me everywhere else," I offered, maybe too fast.

Her eyes suggested she understood all the implications, yet there was also a subtle snapping hinting at her restraint.

"I wanted it to be mine," she whispered, eyes locked on my arm. "But it's even better now that it's ours."

Ours.

"Thanks for doing this with me. For me," she added.

Her voice shook, and I swear my soul climbed into her palm when she cupped my face. Her thumb dragged just below my eyes, and I went still, because if I moved, if I breathed, I'd say it. I'd say everything. I was a fucking sap.

But I'd have done it a thousand times over if it meant being the person she reached for when the world got too heavy.

"Always," I said.

Could she feel it? That I'd already given her every piece of me without asking for anything back? That I'd burn down the world for her with a grin if she asked?

It had happened so fast. Maybe it had been happening for years. Maybe I just needed someone else to point it out so it would feel real. I knew it at the lake, but I had kept fighting myself. But now I really knew it, and I couldn't ignore it.

Fuck.

Loving her wasn't going to kill me.

Not loving her would.

12

MACKENZIE

We listened to the cleaning instructions and left the parlor. My nerves burned under my skin like a fever. Things were unraveling, slipping through my fingers before I could even decide if I wanted to hold on. Not even twenty-four hours into this fake relationship, and Max was already ruining it with his stupid soft smiles, matching tattoos, and the way he looked at me.

He felt *safe*. And that was the most terrifying part. He felt like home, like belonging, and I had no idea what to do with something that dangerous. I didn't deserve someone like Max— and the worst part was I still wanted him anyway.

He would hate me when he found out about the things I carried. The rot I kept buried inside me. Memories I'd never said out loud.

Like the chilling echoes of screams that had haunted my basement. Or the guttural grunts of my father as he dragged yet another unwelcome load through the back door.

Or the dull sound of the saw on bone while my mother hummed a lullaby to lull me to sleep. Things I should never have been forced to witness as a child.

But with Max, all the darkness that haunted my life dissolved. One look at him, and a desperate desire to kiss him seized me—body trembling, craving something I knew I shouldn't want. Love, affection. Those words felt hollow here. This was supposed to be controlled, a fleeting distraction, a performance staged in shadows. Instead, it twisted into something darker, more visceral. Perhaps I was just waiting for a new horror to consume me.

The truth was, we'd been more than friends long before either of us admitted it. At sixteen, it was the kind of restless awareness that made me avoid his gaze. At seventeen, we knew exactly what we were doing when our hands brushed a little too long. By last summer, it was already a slow implosion.

He was intense, always had been. But that intensity was becoming something more. An unspoken devotion that was scary as shit. We were always on the edge with each other, waiting for years for it to finally happen. But we were both in denial.

I let my gaze linger on his a second longer than I should have, and then I ripped myself away. But the ache stayed, lodged in my chest. I was possessive over him. Jealous that he could move through life happy and unscathed. Part of me wanted to touch the light, flutter towards it like a moth to a flame. Another part wanted to diminish the light just to see if he'd stay. I wanted him so badly I almost wanted to crawl into his skin and make myself a home.

I shook my head. When I dared glance back, his eyes were still on mine, steady and sure, as if he was waiting for me to catch up to what he already knew.

Perhaps he wasn't in denial, after all. I was the only one who hadn't caught up to the plotline. Was this the part of the story where the unobservant girl was murdered?

I talked a mile a minute in the truck, words spilling out to fill the silence. Max listened patiently, as if he were trying to understand every word. But the way he looked at me, as if I were an entirely different person, made me restless and uneasy.

I was absolutely terrified of him now. The ink burned on my skin, a permanent reminder of our bond. Our tattoos weren't just marks; they were chains, tying me to him in a way I couldn't explain, and couldn't escape. I didn't know if he felt it too, that pull, that inevitability, but to me, it was almost like a vow I had secretly agreed to.

Like he was my soulmate.

I didn't know what to do with all these conflicting feelings in my chest. All I knew was that I was his. And that might destroy us both.

We walked from the camp parking lot side by side, the grass brittle beneath our shoes, the air thick with heat. My arm brushed against his, and my chest immediately clenched tight.

I could still feel the heat of his cheek under my palm from earlier, still feel the echo of his gaze tearing me open. I didn't know how to exist beside him without drowning. Because I wanted to dive into him.

As we rounded the bend to the cabin, that's when we saw him.

Jackson.

He was by the fire pit, hauling a crate of kindling, his shirt sticking to his back. He looked up immediately, as if he'd been waiting for me, and his stare slid over Max before landing on me. His gaze was cold and possessive—unsettling in the daylight.

A cold whisper of dread climbed up my spine. I didn't think. My hand reached for Max's on instinct, like my body knew what I needed before my brain caught up. His fingers closed around mine without hesitation, grip solid, his thumb brushing over my knuckles with muscle memory.

Jackson's smirk faltered. Satisfaction sparked hot and sharp in my gut.

I stopped walking. Max turned to me, brows drawing together.

"You ready?" he whispered.

I rose onto my toes, wrapping my hands around his neck so he had to bend down. I pulled him closer—not for a kiss, not yet, but close enough that my forehead pressed against his. Our lips hovered, breath mixing and tangling. His hands found my waist, gripping me firmly as if he'd been waiting for this moment. His dark, intense gaze locked onto mine. I stared into his eyes, sinking into the blue depths that unveiled his secrets and opened the door to his heart.

Max consumed every thought I had. He leaned in suddenly, closing the gap between us. The desire was all over his face. His eyes fluttered shut as he attempted to kiss me, but I jerked away instinctively, my heart pounding as Jackson's gaze burned into us. I turned aside, desperate to escape his control, clawing at the oppressive feeling of him taking over my mind, as fear surged through me.

I started to panic. I could see Jackson watching us, and I was scared. Scared of what he would do to me after this. Scared of what he might do to Max for kissing me.

Max's thumb on my chin snapped me out of my thoughts. He pulled my face up to him, forcing me to look directly into his eyes.

"Look at me," he whispered, bringing me back to him. "Don't think about him, look at me."

Relief washed over me as we looked into each other's eyes. He smiled, his eyes brimming with warmth, hope, and love.

"Thanks for today," I murmured, my voice trembling.

"Anything for you," he answered, and his voice was trembling back.

He was nervous. It was cute. I heard Jackson let out a low, angry growl, his heels digging into the dirt on the path near us as he began turning away in a huff.

"I think he bought it," I whispered. I could feel Jackson's eyes burning into the back of my neck, fixed on the strip of Saniderm over my new tattoo.

I pulled away from Max, prepared to return to the cabin and face my fate at Jackson's hands, but Max clutched my shirt, gripping the fabric tightly, and hauled me back into his arms, crashing his lips hungrily against mine.

I gasped, utterly overwhelmed. Then I kissed him back, fierce and insatiable. His taste was heat, salt, and everything I had been refusing to admit, and when his hands seared around my waist, I knew I was as lost as he was. We fused together in an intense, fiery embrace—melting into each other.

His hands came up, cupping both sides of my face, holding me in place like I might run, but I couldn't. There was nothing soft in his kiss. It was a silent vow between teeth and tongue. Max kissed me like he was trying to bury himself in my bones, like he needed to mark me.

His hands dropped to my ass, and he yanked me even closer to him. I moaned against his mouth, and he swallowed it. He wanted everything. Every breath. Every sound. Every fucking part of me.

His grip bruised; his kiss bruised deeper. He kissed me like he was starving. Like I was the first real thing he'd ever tasted.

And I let him. Knowing full well we were digging our graves.

I fisted the front of his shirt harder, needing something to hold onto as heat tore through my veins, settling deep between my thighs. I was shocked at how quickly it happened—the wetness. It pooled in my underwear so quickly. I burned for him.

We moved together like magnets, pulled by something unshakable.

The kiss didn't softly hint at our love; it roared it. So fiercely that even the woods seemed to tremble. A flock of birds exploded from behind the treeline, swirling around our heads as we inhaled each other's souls.

It was the best damn kiss of my entire life. The kind of kiss that didn't ask for permission. It was messy and hungry, just like us.

When he finally pulled away, our chests were heaving, breaths ragged, eyes locked as if we were the only two people in the world. His eyes burned like molten lava, flooded with his love for me.

I wanted to stay in this moment forever. But I tore myself away just enough to look at Jackson. His eyes gleamed with madness. His cheeks were flushed, his grin stretched too wide, fists clenched so hard his knuckles turned white. He wasn't just angry. He was unraveling, consumed by a dark, careful kind of hatred.

The way he stared at Max made my stomach turn. Like he was already imagining where to put the body.

"Little one. Hold the shovel, please."

My father's voice slid to the forefront of my mind. The memory of him dragging the remains of his latest victim toward an open hole in the backyard.

I had stared at a single yellow daffodil growing beside the grave. My anchor to a life I didn't want to be part of. I shut my eyes, pretending I couldn't hear the shovel hit dirt. Or bone.

I was always surrounded by monsters. Even in my memories.

Maybe I was one of them.

Max tightened his grip on my hips, fingers digging like he knew I was disappearing.

"I'm here," he whispered. "I'm always here. Come back to me."

I looked up at him, our eyes connecting. I fell into him as he continued to watch me like I was everything in the world that mattered to him. Like I was the moon, the stars, and everything in between.

Max was my yellow daffodil.

He didn't want chapters written on him. He wanted the whole damn story.

He wanted *me*. I wanted him.

But only one of us would survive Camp Blackshear.

13

—

MAX

I could still taste her when I pulled away. Sweet like watermelon.

She had melted into me. No resistance. No hesitation. Just heat and want and something deeper I hadn't dared hope for. That hadn't been a kiss. I had fucking imprinted my entire soul into her body.

Her hands were still tangled in my shirt, like she wasn't ready to let go either. Her lips were swollen from my kiss. Her cheeks flushed pink. Her eyes were wide, stunned, glassy with need, looking up at me like something wild had been unleashed.

My hands were still tightly around her waist, holding her as if I needed the reminder that she was real—that this had just happened. She needed me to keep her grounded. I could see a faint veil behind her eyes as she drifted into her thoughts.

I was never going back now.

She was fucking mine. And I was hers.

She pulled away, forcing my hands to drop like I was laying down a weapon I didn't want to part with. My fingers ached from the restraint. My body shivered with adrenaline. I pushed my hands into my pockets before I snapped and roughly dragged her into the woods, tearing all her clothes off in a heated frenzy.

I caught Jackson's face, and holy hell, that motherfucker was seething. His jaw locked, eyes burning holes through us. The sight lit me up.

Good. I wanted him to choke on jealousy.

I slung my arm around Mackenzie's shoulders, pulling her in close, making damn sure he saw exactly who she belonged to. My grin stretched slowly and sharply, the kind that begged for a fight.

Fuck off, Kenswick, I thought.

I didn't want him angry. I wanted him gutted and hollowed out. If I could tear his guts out with my bare hands, I would. I wanted him to know she'd never be his again, and that the sight of us together was the closest he'd ever get to her.

If he wanted to take a swing at me, I'd welcome it. Hell. I hoped he would. Because I'd swing back, and I wouldn't stop until he was on the ground, choking on his own blood. Maybe I'd kill him. Perhaps I'd like it.

I took a breath. Honestly, I was a little shocked at my own thoughts. A feral monster had been unleashed from me with that kiss. The monster was ugly. But I didn't give a damn. I was a fucking lunatic for Mackenzie now. Possessive. Territorial. Obsessive. Call it what you want. She was the oxygen I needed to breathe. And anyone who tried to take that from me… I'd bury them.

I didn't speak as we walked back toward the cabins. I couldn't. My head was a warzone, and my pulse hadn't slowed since her mouth touched mine. I still had her hand in mine, and the thought of letting go made me feel like I wouldn't last long without touching her again once we got inside our room.

By the time we reached the porch after climbing the two steps, I had already decided that her shirt and shorts were the first to go, but I'd take my time with her underwear.

She'd object at first, saying we were moving too fast. But I was done pretending. Honestly, I didn't even want anything in return; I just wanted to touch her, pleasure her, and obsess over her. I was picturing the whole thing in my mind when a syrupy voice hammered into my skull.

"Hey, Max."

I stopped and turned to see Heather leaning against the porch railing like she'd been waiting for us. Her tits were straining for attention in a red bikini top, her shorts half-buttoned, her ponytail high and glossy, makeup heavy.

I blinked, thrown off guard, and Mackenzie slipped her hand out of mine.

"Uh… Hey," I managed, my voice flat, my brain still wired on Mackenzie and her beautiful freckles sprinkled across her nose.

Heather sauntered closer, eyes dragging down my shirt. "That shirt looks really good on you."

My chest tightened when I saw Mackenzie stiffen next to me. My autopilot took over because I had no idea what the hell to say. My whole system was crashing under this much attention, and I honestly didn't know how to respond. There was only room in my mind for one girl, and that was Mackenzie.

"Uh… Thanks, you look good, too, I guess."

The second the words left my mouth, I knew I'd fucked up. Mackenzie's body froze, like ice in the air.

Shit.

Heather smirked.

"We're heading down to the waterfront later. A couple of us are swimming if you want to come."

I opened my mouth to answer, but Mackenzie cut in, casual on the surface, sharp underneath.

"He's busy," she said, stepping a little closer. Not clingy— just there. Her voice didn't need volume; the possessiveness in it did the work. "Right, baby?"

I nodded once. "Yeah. Plans."

Heather lifted her brows like she wasn't buying it. Her hand skimmed my forearm, fingertips brushing the edge of the Saniderm under my sleeve. I flinched before I could stop myself.

"Oh—damn, did you get a tattoo?" she asked, pulling her hand back.

"Yeah," I said, adjusting my sleeve so she'd stop touching the wrap. "Still healing. I can't get in the water, yet."

"Looks good," she said, letting her eyes linger for a second too long. "I've got a thing for tattoos."

She didn't touch me again. But her gaze slid to Mackenzie, waiting for a reaction.

She got one. Mackenzie's jaw tightened, eyes dark with something territorial. It was subtle enough that Heather wouldn't name it, but I felt it like a hand around my throat.

Mackenzie smiled, but it didn't reach her eyes. "Good for you."

Jealousy looked good on Mackenzie. Too good.

"Well, if your plans get boring," Heather said with a shrug, "you know where we'll be."

Heather walked off, and I didn't even have a second to think before Mackenzie turned on her heel and walked towards our room without waiting for me. My stomach dropped.

"Trouble, wait—"

"You flirted back with her." Her voice was sharp, clipped.

"I did not!" I hated how pathetic I sounded.

"You just stood there and let her touch you like she wasn't two seconds from sucking your dick?"

Her cheeks were flushed, her eyes burning. She looked furious, but underneath it, hurt. That gutted me more than her anger ever could.

We had finally broken through to each other, and I had fucked it up.

I stepped forward. She stepped back. My chest hurt. Like, really fucking hurt when she did that.

"Trouble, listen, I wasn't trying to hurt you. I didn't even realize she was flirting."

Her jaw set, hard. Resolve was written all over her.

"You know what? I have no reason to feel this way. I told you. You can screw whoever you want outside of our appearances." She tugged her braid loose, her brown hair spilling over her shoulders in waves. It was cruel, how beautiful she looked while she cut me open. "Go ahead. Don't let me stop you. Thank you for the kiss. You did your job for today."

Rage ripped through me.

"Are you *fucking* serious right now?" My voice snapped sharply, angrier than I meant. But I couldn't reel it back.

She wouldn't look at me. She just stood there with her arms crossed, acting like she hadn't gutted me.

She was a fucking butcher. Ripping me open vertebrae by vertebrae with every single word.

"Fuck, Trouble." I dragged a hand through my hair, pacing the room before whipping back to face her. "You really think I want Heather? You think I care about anyone else after that kiss?"

Her jaw tightened. That silence was enough.

"You want me to fuck whoever I want?" I stepped in close, my voice low. "Repeat it. Say it like you mean it."

Her eyes snapped to mine then, wide. But she stayed silent.

"I'm not touching Heather. Or anyone else. Not because I'm some good guy or because I give a fuck about your stupid rules. I won't because I *can't*. I'm locked in. To you. Only you. You're fucking *mine*. I'm yours."

I let the words cut between us.

Her arms crossed tighter across her chest, like she was holding herself together, but her voice cracked. "She wants you.

She had her hands all over you. She can probably give you what you want. She's more… experienced."

My jaw dropped open. This girl was delusional as fuck if she thought I wanted anyone else but her. I was obsessed with her. I was fucking hacking into her cell phone and becoming a raging lunatic just to be *near* her.

She turned, moving into our bedroom, and I closed the door as soon as we both walked through the threshold.

Within seconds, I had her pinned against the wall, grabbing her waist to keep her from falling over.

My heart was beating a mile a minute.

"I'm going to say this one more time, and I'm never repeating it after this, okay? I don't want Heather. The only person I want is you. Stop being so fucking stubborn."

She looked at me like she wanted to claw my skin off or climb inside it. I could see the battle in her eyes. She wanted to tell me to fuck off, to go screw myself, but her body was telling me something else.

"I can smell how wet you are," I whispered in her ear. "You know you want me, too."

She licked her lips and shook her head. That fire I loved returned to her eyes.

Her body pressed against mine, and I could feel the weight of her presence, the heat radiating off her like it was daring me to lose myself. She tilted her head, green eyes flashing, lips just close enough to mine to make my teeth ache with want.

"I'm sorry. I think I have a little bit of a possessive crush on you," she whispered, a soft, teasing smile on her lips.

The groan I let out was loud enough for her to hear.

She smiled. "You know. You're cute when you try not to lose it around me."

"Cute? I'm not cute. I'm tough like Batman, I'm—"

What the fuck was I saying?

Her fingers brushed along my chest, up my arm, tracing the

edge of the wrap where my tattoo was. I shivered, trapped in her pull.

She leaned in, brushing her nose against mine. She was just a breath away, and I could feel the slick tension of anticipation coiling through me. My hands tightened on her wrist. Every muscle was straining, every thought consumed with her. *Her.* Not anyone else.

Only her.

Her lips brushed my ear, soft and teasing. "Tell me, Batman...," she giggled, and that sound sent an electric shock straight to the tip of my dick. "How far would you let me go if I wanted to push you over the edge?"

"Oh, *fuck.* Use me, Trouble. You know you want to."

This was it.

Her eyes lit up, and I almost lost it right then. Almost. My fingers twitched, gripping her thigh, lifting it up around my waist. I forced myself to hold back, though the ache in my chest was raw.

Something primal ripped through me.

"I'm going insane for you," I breathed, voice ragged. I swallowed hard.

"Maybe I want you insane," she murmured. "I want you thinking about me when you're alone. I want you to need me... want me more than you can handle. You're not in control, Max. I am."

She laughed softly, letting her hand slide down my side, cupping my ass and pulling me even closer. My chest pressed against hers with a thud. She was tormenting me.

Fuck me.

Was this really my best friend in front of me? Because I had to do a double-take. I didn't recognize this mysterious girl in front of me.

I closed my eyes, heart hammering, chest tight. She already had me. Every glance, every brush of skin, every whispered word, the entire world had shrunk to her. This Mackenzie. She was slowly becoming my favorite version of the woman I loved. I liked this possessive, fiery, untouchable Mackenzie.

I wanted to worship her.

"I… can't…" I rasped, shaking my head, trying to regain control I didn't even have.

Her lips twitched in a smirk, and I knew she *loved* the effect she had on me. I was high on this fantasy we were sharing. And I loved that she knew exactly how to destroy me and still made me crave more.

"Do you even realize what you're doing to me?" I rasped, voice rough.

"I think I do," she whispered, dragging her nails along my chest, teasing. "And I like it. How long have you wanted me, Max?"

I wanted her more than I'd ever wanted anyone. I wanted to lose myself in her control. To let her consume me. To let her take what she wanted. And I wouldn't fight it.

"A long fucking time," I whispered, moving even closer to her face.

Every thought, every heartbeat, every inch of me was hers. I wasn't supposed to like it. I wasn't supposed to enjoy being at her mercy. But I did.

I pushed my hips into hers, and she gasped when she felt how hard I was for her. I rolled my hips, and she closed her eyes. My cock was about two seconds away from blowing through my jeans, and her shorts were so thin I might as well have ripped them apart.

I bent forward, closing my eyes, getting ready to kiss her. I could smell her arousal, so sweet. I wanted to feel how drenched she was. My fingers tapped restlessly on her hip, moving closer and closer to their destination. I rolled my hips against hers again, this time allowing my hard cock to rub against her clit through her shorts. I couldn't feel much through my jeans, but she could feel me. She bit her bottom lip, trying to control herself, but I could see it in her eyes.

I kissed her gently, allowing her to deepen the kiss on her own accord. She did, and I swallowed her alive until I came up for a breath and said, "If I took your shirt off, would you let me?"

"Y… yes," she stammered.

I grabbed the hem of her shirt and pulled it gently over her head. She was wearing a black push-up bra, and my eyes almost fell out of my head when I saw her tits. They were full, perfect, and round. My hands itched to touch them, but I froze like an idiot, just staring at her.

Jesus Christ.

The straps framed her golden shoulders, the curve of her cleavage spilling over just enough to make me want to bite, to mark, to worship. I wanted to bury my face there, lick the sweat from her skin, hear the way her breath moved when she finally gave in.

The way her chest rose and fell, faster now, told me she was giving up her control. She wanted me to make the first move.

I swallowed hard, my cock pressing painfully against my jeans. I needed some relief.

She reached down, gripping me through my jeans, almost as if she was reading my thoughts.

"Fuck, Trouble…" The words stumbled out of me.

Her lips curved, just slightly. But I knew a dare whenever I saw one.

I reached out, tracing the line of her bra strap with one finger, down across the swell of her breast until she sighed. I reached around her back and unsnapped her bra in one quick motion. And when it fell to the ground, I honestly forgot how to breathe.

"Holy fuck," I breathed, my voice hoarse.

Her tits were perfect—my absolute dream. Her nipples, tight pink pebbles, drew me in. Her breasts were full and round, more than I could handle. Her eyes flicked up at me through her lashes, revealing she wanted to be embarrassed, yet she knew exactly what she was doing to me. She tried to cross her arms over her chest, but I caught her wrists, gently pinning them above her head on the wall.

"Don't you ever hide from me," I growled, my voice low and possessive.

Her lips parted, a sharp inhale catching in her throat as I leaned in, brushing my mouth along the edge of her jaw and down her neck, breathing her in eagerly. She arched against me, her pulse pounding under my lips.

I trailed kisses down her throat and across her collarbone, my tongue flicking out to taste the skin above her ribs, eliciting a soft moan. Her body jerked as if shocked.

"Maxxx…," she whined, voice trembling.

"I know," I said against her skin, my words muffled as my lips grazed down the curve of her breasts.

I released her wrists, my hands sliding down to her waist, gripping her hard enough to leave marks. She didn't push me away. Instead, her fingers tangled in my hair, tugging, guiding me lower.

I bit softly across her right breast, right where her nipple pebbled. She moaned as I took it in my mouth, and that was it. My control snapped.

"You like that, baby?" I rasped against her chest, my tongue circling. She didn't say anything, but I could feel her nodding.

Her back arched, pressing her tits harder into my face.

"Fuck, Trouble." I groaned against her skin. "You're gonna kill me."

I continued my gentle assault before switching to the other breast. Her nails scraped down my back, making me hiss through my teeth.

Could you die from an erection? Because I was so hard, my dick might actually fall off.

She was trembling beneath me, but she didn't tell me to stop. Her thighs squeezed together, hips shifting, grinding against me while I worshipped her chest.

I slid one hand down, over her stomach, catching the waistband of her shorts. I pressed my palm flat, right over the heat between her legs. Even through the shorts, I could feel how wet she was for me.

Fuck, I wanted her.

She gasped, her whole body jerking from my touch on her pussy through her shorts.

"Tell me to stop," I muttered, my lips brushing her collarbone.

She lifted her hips into my hand. "I don't want you to fucking stop," she whispered.

That was all the permission I needed. I popped the button on her shorts and pulled the zipper down, grabbing the sides and sliding them to her ankles in one quick motion.

Her body shook against me, anticipation written all over her flushed face. I kissed her again, this time rough and hungry, my tongue forcing her lips apart.

The thin barrier of her panties was damp, and the second I brushed my fingers over the material, her whole body went taut like a bowstring.

"Christ, Trouble," I groaned against her mouth. "You're soaked."

She whimpered, shoving her hips into my hand, her nails digging into my skin.

I pressed harder, circling the tips of my fingers against her clit through the fabric of her underwear, swallowing her moans as they vibrated through my mouth.

"Max, please touch me, pleasssseee," she begged.

I grasped the sides of her underwear, preparing to slide them aside, when the speaker suddenly shrieked from the front of the cabin, jolting us out of our trance. We quickly separated.

God damnit. I was crushed.

I watched her. Her beautiful chest heaving with rapid, shallow breaths. Her eyes were blown out, wide and hungry for me. Her cheeks flushed. I was captivated, completely ensnared in her web.

I'd do anything she wanted me to do. She wanted to put a collar around my neck and drag me around like a dog? I'd bark for her, and I'd take it like a fucking champ.

She giggled like she was reading my thoughts, and then said, "Come on," as she bent down and put her bra and shirt back on.

I watched her walk through the door. My fingers were soaked from her arousal. I put my fingers in my mouth, tasting her. Damn. She tasted as good as she smelled. I had never wanted to eat out a girl so badly before, but with Mackenzie, I was starving, and I wanted to ruin her.

Fuck that speaker.

14

MACKENZIE

He looked wrecked, sad, and disappointed, as if he was trying to hold himself together. That only made me smile. His body had felt too good pressed against mine—immense, overwhelming, like he could crush me if he wanted. And maybe that's why I couldn't stop thinking about it. About him. About how he'd spent seven years just being my best friend, and how, in one kiss, he'd become something entirely different. Someone I wanted to devour whole. I wanted him to consume me.

I wanted to tear him apart. The Mackenzie I became around him was new to me. She was *powerful.* Maybe it was born out of every shadow that had followed me, every secret I carried. Perhaps it was because Max wasn't afraid of the parts of me that were dark. He fucking craved every single part I hid. He could handle me.

I hadn't sketched a single thing since arriving at camp. My sketchbook used to be my only escape, the only way to breathe free from the ghosts of my father and the violence woven into my blood. But Max had devoured every part of me, body and soul. He forced me to stop fleeing and ignited a desire to play with the fire rather than hide from it.

The dining hall was buzzing with its usual chaos when we entered: trays clattered, campers shouted, and a small speaker blared summer tunes. But all I could feel was him. Max sat close, so close our legs brushed under the table, and every nerve ending in my body ignited.

I was still raw from the cabin. I was wet. Wound up. Hungry.

Jackson sat rigidly across the room, glaring at us with a feral intensity, as if swallowing shards of glass. His tray remained untouched, his jaw clenched in silent rage. Max leaned in closer, his voice a tense whisper.

"You hanging in there?"

"I'm fine," I said roughly.

Max's hand slid onto my knee under the table. Electricity shot up my thigh, hot and fast, pooling low in my stomach. I licked my lips without thinking.

How could my body react so quickly to his touch?

Max froze, like he felt it too. His jaw clenched, and his hand flexed just slightly on my knee.

"Are we still faking?" he murmured, voice strained. "'Cause this doesn't feel like pretend anymore."

I bit back a laugh, biting the inside of my cheek until it hurt.

"Behave," I whispered, leaning in until my lips almost brushed his ear.

"I can still feel your pussy on my fingers," he breathed. "I won't be behaving for a long time."

I swallowed, my eyes blurring as I nearly went cross-eyed, hearing him say that. He offered a small grin, never taking his eyes off mine.

Across from us, Jackson was watching Max's hand as if he were mentally calculating how to break every bone in his body. I smiled sweetly, tilting my chin toward Max, and casually plucked a piece of bread right off his tray.

Max's brow arched. "What's with you stealing my food today?"

"We're dating," I said casually, loud enough for Jackson to hear every word. "What's yours is mine."

"You want the rest?" His voice lowered, smooth as velvet, but with a hint of edge underneath. "I'll feed you."

I grimaced. "Ew. No."

"Too much?" He murmured, but his gaze had already dropped to my lips.

"Way too much," I whispered back, leaning so close my mouth barely brushed his. The heat between us crackled. That ghost of a touch set him off. His hands clamped down on my waist, possessively, and I gasped before I could stop myself.

"Don't blow up on me," I teased. "Just kiss me."

Max's eyes darkened. His pupils swallowed the color. His thumb brushed my bottom lip as if claiming it. He tilted his chin down and kissed me. It was brief, rough, with his tongue flicking against mine for only a heartbeat before he pulled away.

It was too quick.

He was trying to regain control, but I could feel the storm beneath his kiss.

He kept me pinned in place, chest rising hard, eyes locked on mine. His stare was dangerous, starving. I told myself it was just lust, but the way he looked at me made me wonder.

Jackson's chair screeched sharply across the floor as he shot a venomous glare, muttering something about air before storming out with a wild, unhinged look.

Max didn't flinch. He didn't even glance at Jackson. His eyes never left mine.

I tore my gaze away, my skin burning. "You think he bought it?"

Max's brow furrowed, as if confused, then he looked toward where Jackson had been sitting, a resigned expression crossing his face.

He leaned back, shaking his head, a nervous smile spreading across his face as I saw his nerves beating in his throat.

His pulse hammered so loudly I almost felt it beneath my skin.

"Yeah," he said roughly, his voice trembling. "He bought it."

I watched him carefully. This was supposed to be pretend, but every time we looked at each other, I forgot which side of the lie we were on.

I cleared my throat.

"You should eat," I murmured, my eyes flicking to his trembling hands. "You're shaking."

MAX

HOLY MOTHER OF GOD. SHE WAS GOING TO BE THE ABSOLUTE death of me. I'd never been this nervous over a girl, let alone Mackenzie. Her kisses—*God*. Every kiss was straight out of my fantasies.

When we returned to the cabin, she passed out almost immediately, like she hadn't just detonated my entire world with a single touch. I lay awake, stiff on the top bunk, staring at the ceiling. My chest ached with the weight of what we were becoming. I couldn't stop replaying what had happened earlier. I wanted to finish it.

The cabin was silent except for the creak of wood and the occasional rustle of bodies asleep. Her nightlight cast her sleeping shadow on the wall, a halo I couldn't ignore.

I ran a hand down my face. I couldn't sleep. I couldn't think, not with the scent of her shampoo and the ghost of her lips still burning a mark into my psyche.

Every inch of me was tight. When I looked down at her curled beneath the blanket, dozing in my t-shirt, one bare shoulder exposed to the air... a restlessness rippled through me. I couldn't stay up here anymore thinking about it.

I needed her. Her phone hadn't stopped vibrating since I left the dining hall, a constant shrill echo in the quiet of the night. I unlocked my own, the blue glow illuminating my face, revealing the encrypted files I couldn't afford to ignore.

JACKSON KENSWICK

More staged kisses for me?

Don't worry. No one is buying it. Just remember—if I can't have you, no one can.

I shoved my phone beneath my pillow, clutching it tightly. I was going to erase her messages, erase everything she might see. She shouldn't read those. I had to find a way to get rid of Jackson. He was starting to really piss me off.

I should've walked outside or taken a cold shower. Anything but what I was about to do.

Instead, I climbed down. I snatched her phone off the floor, opened it, deleted all her messages, and then looked down at her.

"Trouble," I whispered.

She stirred immediately, blinking those sleepy eyes up at me.

"I can't sleep," I said. "Can I..."

She lifted the blanket without hesitation.

Fuck. Okay.

I slid in beside her, and the world narrowed to her warmth. There wasn't room for me. In this tiny ass bunk, we could only have full-body contact. Her body pressed against mine, her chest rising with every breath, our legs tangling. My arm found her waist instinctively. I was so tall that my feet were hanging off the bed.

She rubbed her feet against my legs, and I shivered at how cold they were. I squeezed my legs around hers to warm her up.

"Is this okay?" I whispered.

She nodded, eyes fluttering shut for a moment. "Yeah."

Her sigh rattled through me like a drug. She sounded like she'd been holding her breath all day, and only now she could exhale. She curled tighter against me. Her hand slid over my waist, clutching me like she could fuse us if she pressed hard enough.

Our hips brushed, our mouths hovered, her breath spilling across my lips. I pressed my forehead to hers, breathing her in like oxygen. Like I'd die without her.

Because honestly? I felt like I might.

She didn't say anything for a long time. The silence stretched, thick with all the things we weren't brave enough to speak.

I couldn't stop the thoughts spiraling in my head. I wanted her so badly it hurt. My body screamed for her. I tried to convince myself I was not attracted to her, but the darker part of me, the one that had already decided she was mine, didn't give a fuck about stopping these feelings.

"You make me feel safe, Max," she whispered into the dark. She pressed her mouth to the corner of my lips, just a brush, teasing me. It wasn't enough.

I fucking whimpered. I could feel her laugh against my mouth.

"You want me so bad, don't you?" She whispered, her breath skimming my skin. She pressed her hips into mine.

My dick got even harder from the movement. If I touched her now, I wouldn't stop. I couldn't. I pulled her even closer to me, grinding my hips down on her, rubbing my dick against her leg.

I couldn't control myself. I felt the liquid heat in my dick from the base of my shaft to the tip, and every touch she gave me made me want to devour her, eat her alive, and consume her.

I had wanted to fuck girls, sure. But not like this. I wanted her so badly that it physically overpowered me. And it wasn't just the sex. I wanted to be close to her, to know her, to *really* know her.

Her hand dragged down my chest, stopping just above my boxers. My stomach tightened like she'd reached inside me and pulled something raw.

"I could let you have me. Right here. Right now."

A sound escaped me as I heard those words fall from her lips. I didn't recognize it as mine. She was destroying me, unraveling every bit of control I'd tried to hang onto since the second I saw her again.

"This feels anything but friendly," I whispered. "Are we still just friends, Trouble?"

I leaned into her, body begging, every muscle screaming to take. To claim. To taste her again.

And then, she pulled back. Smiling. Fucking smirking.

"Just friends."

My chest caved. Air punched out of me like I'd been hit.

"Trouble—" My voice cracked.

She was saying no, but her actions said yes. Her lips brushed down my jaw, and I groaned because it wasn't where I needed her.

"Think about me tonight." She whispered, but she was looking right at me, taunting me. I wasn't going to let her be in control, not tonight.

I rolled on top of her, spreading her legs with my knee, and pressed my hips against hers. My balls tightened at the sound of her shocked gasp.

"I told you I don't like being messed with," I whispered. I lifted her shirt, exposing her stomach. My hands moved up her inch by inch until they hovered just under the swell of her breasts. She looked up at me, her eyes wide, her skin pale from the moonlight coming through the blinds.

"What do you want from me?" she whispered; her breath raspy.

"I want to take this off," I said, pointing to her shirt. She lifted her arms. I gently pulled the shirt over her head, making sure not to snag her arms. I threw it on the ground next to her, quickly glanced at her amazing breasts, and immediately started edging the waistband of her pajama shorts with my fingers.

"You like this, teasing me?" I whispered again. She licked her lips as I ran my hand up her bare leg.

"Yes," she gloated. "Call it foreplay."

I nodded my head in acknowledgement.

I leaned down so my lips hovered against her lips. "I've had seven years of foreplay with you. I'm pent up. So stop fucking teasing me."

She put her hand on my bare chest, never taking her eyes off me. Earlier, we had been caught up in the moment, but now? This felt different. There was a heat, a real heat, that had been skimming the surface for so long. It was boiling over now. We were deliberately passing a line, daring each other to go farther than the other.

This was intentional. A choice. One that we were making together.

She looked up at me with a distinct hunger in her eyes, and I matched it. Her fingers grazed my ribs and stopped, hovering like she wasn't sure if this was happening.

I slid my hand down, pulling her shorts off. She let me, lifting her hips so I could slide them off easily. I ran my hand down her abdomen, palm skimming the soft skin of her waist, waiting for her to stop me.

She didn't. Instead, her lips parted, and she moaned. That sound sent me into fucking space.

I cupped her breast, thumbing over her nipple until she whimpered. Her back bowed. My hips rutted forward on instinct.

"I'm going to lose my mind," I murmured, my forehead pressing to hers, our mouths brushing. "Being able to touch you like this, it's…"

I was actually kind of lost for words. I didn't know how to tell her how much I fucking loved her, how much this meant to me, how much she meant to me.

She grabbed my hand and tugged it lower, sliding it under the waistband of her panties. Not going to lie, I was going to fucking explode if she continued to take the lead like this. We were two matches to a flame.

"Still want to fake it?" I whispered. I really wanted her to say no.

She didn't answer. Instead, she guided my hand between her legs, and *fuck*—she was soaked.

My control snapped. I dragged my fingers over her slick clit —slow and deliberate, circling her in tight circles. I had thought about touching her like this for years. Now that it was happening, I honestly was losing my shit over it.

She let out a strangled moan, tipping her head back and exposing the soft line of her throat in a wordless invitation. I claimed it, my mouth finding her skin, sucking at her pulse just firmly enough to leave a mark.

Her hips moved with my touch.

"Max…" she breathed out. Her voice was cracked and needy. "I need… more."

I hesitated for a second and then inserted one finger into her. I was gentle.

"This, okay?" I whispered, watching her eyes flutter closed. I needed her to say yes.

"Jesus…" she whispered, clutching my shoulder like she had to hold onto something to keep her on this earth.

"Is this okay?" I asked her again, and she nodded. I pushed in deeper, all the way to my knuckle, and she cried out.

"Fuckkkk, Max."

"You're killing me." I dragged my lips up her neck.

Her hand slid down my stomach, skimming the waistband of my boxers, and I groaned. Suddenly, she froze. I sensed her hesitation, fear weaving beneath the desire. I stopped immediately, my hand still gently cradling her, but not pressing any further. The air shifted. Every nerve in my body screamed to keep going, but her silence said stop louder than any word could.

I wanted her. God, I wanted her. But this was Mackenzie. The last thing I wanted was to hurt her.

"Hey," I murmured, brushing her hair off her face. "We can stop. We don't have to go any further."

"I want to," she whispered. "I just—I'm... I'm nervous... about touching you. I've... I'm not as experienced as you."

Oh my God, she was such a fucking turn on.

"I've got you," I said. "Just relax. This is about you. You don't have to touch me back if you aren't ready."

She relaxed, her body humming, as she opened her legs up wide for me. I wanted nothing more than to pleasure her, not caring whether I received anything in return. All my attention was on her. I kept my touch gentle, drawing slow circles until she was trembling, whispering my name as if it were the only thing anchoring her.

"Faster, Max, please..." She moaned.

I growled, speeding up.

"You like me finger fucking your sweet little cunt?" I pushed another finger inside her, moving my pointer and middle finger in and out of her quickly, still circling her clit with my thumb. "You're such a fucking bad girl teasing me all day."

"Oh my God, Max..."

I felt the crescendo rising inside her, my mouth opening automatically as I watched her close her eyes, arch her back, and let out a silent cry.

"Cum on my fingers, Trouble," I rasped out.

Her pussy tightened around my fingers, pulsing and throbbing. It was amazing. Even better than my dreams.

I kept going, holding her through it, pressing kisses to her temple, her shoulder, anywhere I could reach. She buried her face in my neck to muffle her cries, and she held onto me tighter as her body shook, coating my fingers with her thick cum.

I looked down, watching my fingers move in and out of her, wanting so badly to replace them with my cock. But I'd wait.

I'd wait until she was ready.

I bent down, gently biting her bottom lip, and she moaned so loudly that I was sure the other counselors heard her.

I let her dig her fingernails into my skin. I could feel the blood beginning to prickle, but I didn't pull away or flinch. I wanted her to feel at home with me.

Because she was my home. And I wanted her to know it, even if I was too nervous to say it out loud.

15

MACKENZIE

A soft light filtered through the blinds, waking me up. I stretched slowly, rolling onto my back and raising my arms overhead. I reached for Max, but he was gone. I sat up, staring at his empty spot, with memories of last night playing over and over in my head, like some kind of mental loop torture. I wanted more. After he touched me, he smiled, kissed me, and cuddled up next to me like I was his lifeline, like I was his anchor, and we drifted into sleep together, tangled in each other.

It had been… romantic.

The bed felt cold and empty without him. Where was he?

I silently slipped out of my bunk, glancing into the shadowed main part of the cabin. The other counselors lay sprawled across mattresses, limbs tangled in restless sleep. I hurriedly pulled on my yellow camp shirt and black shorts, pretending I was a normal eighteen-year-old girl with a normal brain. Not someone consumed by the memory of her best friend's grasping hands all over her.

I went through my morning routine on autopilot, my movements almost mechanical. I brushed my teeth, tied my hair into two braids, and slathered SPF onto my face, each act a desperate distraction from him. His toothbrush and aftershave sat next to my hairbrush and makeup on the bathroom counter, a haunting reminder of how close we were. A *real* couple, by all standards.

But here we were, trapped in a twisted game of cat and mouse with no qualms about the consequences. How long could this chaos last before we shattered everything?

A small red mark on my neck made me freeze. I leaned closer to the mirror, examining the splotches beneath my ear. Had he given me a hickey? My fingers brushed the red print.

Yes, he had. That jerk had marked me!

I scanned the room, searching for him like he was going to appear out of thin air. I wanted to punch him, to make him pay. The silence was deafening, and I felt a strange sensation of being watched.

I didn't like being without him.

As I stepped outside, the morning sun was already thick and heavy. The deafening screech of cicadas echoed eerily through the trees. I flicked a mosquito off my arm, a small prick of blood erupting on my skin. I immediately regretted skipping the bug spray. I hurried toward the nurses' station to get mosquito repellent, when suddenly I froze, my senses sharpening as a silence crept in.

It was almost as if the air had thinned down to this single moment—warning me that he was here.

There he was. Running shirtless down the trail, sweat slicking across his chest, gray shorts hanging dangerously low. His muscles flexed with each stride; every step calculated. He yanked off his baseball cap, dragged a towel across his brow, and then shoved his cap back on. My eyes, traitorous and thirsty, followed the sharp cut of his V-line like it was a treasure map I wanted to trace with my tongue.

I shut my eyes, but the image branded itself there anyway.

When I opened them again, it was too late. His gaze was locked on mine, and he gave me a shit-eating grin.

Crap.

I nearly ducked behind a bush, but he was already walking toward me, peeling out his AirPods.

"Hey," he said, his voice rough from the run.

"Hey." My cheeks burned. He knew. That smirk wasn't random. Max McKinnon never did anything without intent.

"You're up early," he drawled, his breath heavy from his run. I tried not to watch the way his chest rose and fell with each breath.

"I could say the same for you."

"I couldn't sleep." His eyes dragged over me. "I couldn't stop thinking about you."

My pulse thrashed. He stepped closer, close enough that I could smell him. He was temptation wrapped in a package made just for me.

"Are you thinking about it?" he asked, not even waiting.

When did Max McKinnon become such a tease?

"No," I lied, turning my face away.

"I think you are." His smirk widened.

The air between us snapped tight, electric, the same pull that had been strangling us for years.

"You working hard?" I asked, acknowledging his sweaty body, pretending I wasn't seconds from ripping his shorts off. "You know—after you gave me a fucking hickey last night."

I pointed to my neck.

He stretched, laughing, and my gaze betrayed me, tracking every flex.

"Gotta keep up with this body," he said, cocky. "Can't let the girls at college think I've gone soft."

The words landed sharply. His tone was joking, but his eyes cut to me. He was waiting for a reaction, for jealousy, or possession.

Unfortunately, he got it. The flare of it burned in my stomach before I could school my expression.

He, apparently, liked it because he ran his tongue along his bottom lip and checked me out so hard, I thought his eyes might fall out of his head.

"Besides, I gave you more than a hickey last night," he smirked, rolling onto the balls of his feet.

My eyes dropped down his body, and when they snapped back up to his face, he was smiling like he had won a game.

"You checking me out again?" he teased, like he hadn't just baited me on purpose. "You make this too easy."

"Make what easy?"

"Keeping up your facade," he said, and before I could move, his hand hooked my waistband and yanked me against him. His mouth brushed mine in a kiss that was quick, taunting, and just enough to make me crave more.

When he pulled back, that devil's grin was plastered across his face, smug and infuriating.

"Don't let it go to your head," I muttered, shoving him back.

"Too late," he laughed. "You looked so beautiful underneath me last night."

I exhaled sharply, my body betraying me. I turned towards the first aid cabin. "I'll see you at our station at nine."

But before I could step away, his hand slid down my arm and closed around my elbow. It was incredibly possessive, the way he grabbed me.

"Trouble, wait—" His voice dropped, quieter now, softer. "I didn't mean to be a dick. I'm just teasing you."

I looked at him for a beat. "It's okay, Max." My fingers brushed his hand before I could stop them, a squeeze meant to soothe. "I don't think you're a dick."

But I sure as hell was thinking about his dick.

His jaw clenched tightly, and his eyes fixed on a burn scar on my arm with a piercing suspicion, as if he desperately wanted to say more. I instinctively raised my hand, covering the mark. It was little, right above my left elbow.

"If I ever find out that you hooked up with him, I'll do far worse than this to you," Jackson had hissed, as he held me down in the back of his car, extinguishing his cigarette into my skin. The smell of seared flesh filled the air as I let out a shrill cry.

"Trouble, I…" Max's voice broke me out of the memory, but he abruptly cut himself off, leaving a heavy silence hanging between us.

"What?"

"Never mind." He shifted, letting out a resigned sigh. "What are you doing?"

"Looking for bug spray," I said, turning away. "Unless you want to watch me get eaten alive."

His lips curved, eyes darkening, and I knew exactly what he was thinking. Something indecent.

I could have him eating out of the palm of my hand if I wanted. I smiled as I walked towards the nurse's cabin.

The air was cool inside, and the cabinets were lined up. I started rifling through them.

"Band-Aids, gauze, Dramamine… seriously, where does she hide the bug spray?"

Max lingered at the door, leaning against the frame, his large body filling it entirely.

"Trouble…" he said suddenly, voice lower now. "Can I ask you something?"

"About what?" I asked distractedly, then dragged a small ladder from the corner and climbed it. I balanced it as I opened the highest cabinet.

"Last night, you said you hadn't done that with anyone. Was that true?"

I froze. The question hit me so hard I nearly toppled off the step ladder.

"I didn't say I hadn't done that with anyone. I said I wasn't as experienced as you."

A veil of jealousy crossed his face.

"So. It's true then. Did you really fuck Jackson?" he spat.

"*What?*"

"He said you did. During two truths and a lie. I want to know from you."

His voice dripped with hatred, his cheeks flushed in anger.

"Max!" I snapped, heat rushing to my cheeks. "That's none of your business."

He huffed, his jaw flexing hard in frustration. He stepped closer to me.

"Mackenzie. Stop this."

I snapped my head down toward him when he said 'Mackenzie.' His eyes were pleading with me.

"Stop what?" I asked, feigning indifference. I knew exactly what he was implying, but I was too nervous to have this talk with him.

"Acting like this is pretend."

I inhaled.

"It is pretend," I whispered.

He ran a hand over his face, took off his cap, and smoothed the dark locks around his ears.

"Oh my God, Trouble. *Fine*, fuck," he rasped out. "If I'm gonna play your boyfriend, I need to know what I'm up against. Where you've been."

I eyed him.

"It's none of your business," I bit out. "All you need to know is what happens between you and me."

That made him go still. His eyes locked on mine, darker than I'd ever seen them.

"What's happening then?" His voice was gravelly, every word dragging. "Between you and me? You said this is pretend.

You said no sex, but I think we passed that barrier last night. So, where do we stand?"

I groaned, trying to mask the pulse pounding between my thighs.

"Don't take everything I say so literally, Max. I don't fucking know what this is." I motioned between us.

"Funny," he murmured. "Because all I want is to take you literally, horizontally, vertically, however you want."

My pulse soared, and I quickly turned away to avoid his gaze. I felt as if I might melt right into the floor.

"Shut up, asshole," I scolded. "Are you jealous?"

A darkness crept over his face, and I saw it in his eyes. Possession.

"Do you want me to be?" His tone was playful, but he was holding back from revealing how much he truly felt. I could see on his face that I was pissing him off.

I know I should've felt bad, but a thrill ran through me. I liked that he was jealous. It meant that I owned him, in all the ways I wanted to.

I did feel kind of bad, though. I was playing with him.

I rifled through the shelves, ignoring him because if I spoke, he'd pick up on how badly I wanted him. Finally, I spotted the bug spray, shoved high on the top shelf. Rising on my toes, I stretched too far.

"Need help?" His voice was a taunt.

"I'm fine."

"You say that every time you're about to do something stupid," he muttered.

A moment later, his body was behind mine, heat pressing in. He reached up, taller, stronger, his arm brushing mine as he grabbed the bottle with infuriating ease. Except when he did, his hand grazed my chest.

"Sorry," he smiled, though his eyes burned with anything but friendliness.

"Sure, you are." I laughed lightly, stepping down. My foot slipped then, but his arms were already there, catching me, dragging me hard against him. His hand landed high, on the inside of my thigh. I could feel his fingers right *there*.

His fingers twitched slightly, as if he hadn't quite decided what to do with them, but then I saw the emotions on his face as he leaned in and said, "I want a repeat of last night."

I swallowed hard. "You're the one with your hand between my legs. Do something about it. It's familiar territory for you now."

His gaze dropped to my mouth. He pressed his fingers just a fraction higher, tracing the seam of my shorts with maddening patience. Heat surged through me. Every inch of me was humming. He looked at me like he wanted to rip my clothes off. And then, he grabbed my hips and gently walked me back to the wall, never taking his gaze off of me.

My back hit the wall as he held me in place. I squeaked.

"Shhh, be quiet." He gave me an aloof smirk before dropping to his knees. His hands remained tight on my hips as he looked up at me, the playfulness vanishing from his face.

"I've been thinking about your pussy all morning," he said, licking his lips. "Did you like it when I touched your clit with my fingers last night?"

My eyes went wide, my knees shaking as I simply nodded my head.

He grinned.

"What if I licked your clit? Would you like that? I haven't had breakfast yet, and I'm fucking starving."

He leaned forward, pressing a kiss to the top of my inner thigh, and I let out a raspy sigh. My breathing quickened, nearing hyperventilation at the thought of his mouth on me. When he kissed the inside of my other thigh, my knees started to shake.

"God, Mackenzie. I can smell you through your shorts. You smell so damn good," he whined.

I fidgeted, my knees clamping around his head in anticipation.

"Be still," he demanded, opening his hands on my hips and slowly pulling my shorts down.

A deafening crash of the cabin door slamming into the wall startled us apart.

"Good morning, Mackenzie and Max!" Nurse Campbell's cheery voice sliced through the room.

Max got up so quickly I thought he might fall over, his eyes locked on me for one scorching second before he bolted for the door.

"Yeah," he muttered. "Morning."

Nurse Campbell looked at me with wide, attentive eyes, her face calm yet alert. She gave me a knowing glance before moving around the cabin with practiced efficiency, restocking gauze and making notes on her clipboard. Her presence was calm and clinical, radiating a composed professionalism.

"Mackenzie..." She stopped me right as I was about to walk out. My face was flaming in embarrassment.

"Yes?" I asked, my voice high-pitched.

There was a pause. Then, completely unfazed, she said, "Can you come here, please?"

I sucked in a breath. Was I in trouble?

She glanced nervously around me, eyes flickering upward into the darkened air and into shadowed corners, as if searching for something unseen. Suddenly, she grabbed my arm with a trembling grip and whispered hoarsely, "I have exactly one minute, but I need to tell you something. *You're not safe here.*"

The floor fell from beneath my feet.

"What?" I whispered.

She pulled me in closer to her, wrapping her arms around my neck as if we were hugging.

"I need you to be quiet and listen to me. Do not say anything back."

My heart hammered in my throat, and a ringing hummed in my ears.

She leaned in closer, pretending to fix my hair.

"Your game is about to start. If you don't play it, they will come for you."

"Wha—what? Who's coming for me?" I asked, my voice trembling with fear.

"Don't say a word!" she whispered urgently, glancing nervously around her.

"They change the game frequently. The players are constantly changing. Don't trust anyone. Not even Max."

By the time I blinked, her expression had recomposed into sterile professionalism. The only tell was the faint tremor in her hands as she went back to arranging paperwork on her desk.

My stomach was in knots. What the fuck was she talking about? What *game?*

She opened her desk drawer, rifling through her supplies until she found a small pink packet. When she closed the drawer, she glanced at the clinic hallway before passing the package into my palm.

"Take this, please," she murmured. "Start it tonight. Do not skip."

I stared at her, throat dry. "What is it?"

She nodded her head as if to say, 'I will not answer that.'

I looked down at the package. Birth control pills.

"I don't... need these," I said quietly, trying to hand them back. "I'm not—"

She recoiled before I could finish, snatching her hand away like I'd tried to burn her. "Start it tonight," she repeated, voice trembling under the surface. "And don't ask questions. Not here."

Her eyes flicked back over to the clinic door again. Someone walked past outside. She held her breath as we both heard footsteps, then silence. Nurse Campbell pressed her lips together so tightly they blanched white.

"I'm not sexually active," I whispered, instantly hating how weak I sounded.

She blinked once. "Don't assume anything, Mackenzie. Everything you've known up until this point is a lie."

My pulse thundered in my ears. "What? Why?"

She ignored me, turning away. She sanitized her hands, straightened a stack of folders, and smoothed her shirt, as if she could tidy her panic back into place.

By the time she faced me again, she wore a polite smile. It was eerie. She looked at me as if we hadn't just crossed a line into a different fucking reality.

"Drink plenty of water in this heat," she said brightly. "I recommend at least one gallon a day. Max needs double that with how big he's gotten."

Then she sat down at her desk.

"Have a great day, sweetheart."

I STEPPED OUTSIDE INTO THE OPPRESSIVE, BLINDING SUNLIGHT, the air clinging to my skin like a suffocating shroud.

The screen door groaned loudly as it shut behind me. I had barely taken two steps before Jackson appeared, blocking my path.

"Whoa," he said softly, his hands pressing firmly on my shoulders. His grin stretched too wide, like a wolf showing teeth.

"What do you want, Jackson?" I asked, hurriedly sidestepping him. "Being a creep?" I watched him closely, searching for any hint of his intentions. Was he a player in my part of this game? He remained an impenetrable wall, emotionless and cold.

His head tilted unnaturally. "What were you doing in there?"

"Bug bites," I said quickly.

His eyes slowly trailed up my body until they landed on the hickey on my neck.

"What's that on your neck?"

"Nothing," I said, denying it too fast.

Before I could react, his fingers brushed my neck, sending a shiver down my spine. The touch was intrusive, unsettling, and made my skin crawl. I flinched.

"Jackson. Stop."

"Seriously?" His voice was flat now, emptied of humor. "Did he do that to you?"

I stepped back, pushing him away from me. But he grabbed my wrist, his grip tight. His knuckles whitened as he clung to me. I struggled to break free, but he tightened his hold until I felt like the bones in my wrist were about to snap under the pressure.

"It's none of your business," I snapped.

"Bullshit." He let go of my arm and stepped closer, shadows in his eyes. "I know you. And I know the two of you aren't fucking. So I want to know how the fuck you got a hickey on your neck!"

"Leave me the fuck alone, Jackson." I took a hesitant step back, my heartbeat pounding erratically.

He chuckled then, a shrill, menacing sound that sent chills down my spine.

"That kiss he gave you yesterday? That was a friendly kiss. Want me to tell you the difference?" He leaned in, hot breath scalding my cheek. "I've fucked you. And trust me, I didn't kiss you like that after."

I froze, rage and nausea tangling in my throat. He had never kissed me. Not once. Not after the first time, not after the last. He'd treated me like a body, not a person.

I was nothing more than a piece of flesh for him to torment and use. I was overlooked, insignificant. The kiss with Max had meant everything to me. But now a flicker of doubt, fueled by Nurse Campbell's words, spiraled through my mind.

Don't trust anyone. Not even Max.

I was starting to second-guess everything.

What game was I in?

Who was coming for me?

The feeling of paranoia was gripping my throat, and the longer I talked to Jackson, the more I felt like I was going to pass out.

"He doesn't kiss you like a man who's been inside you," Jackson sneered, eyes narrowing, venom in his voice. "Max—someone like him, he wouldn't be gentle. He'd destroy you. He'd own you. He's not as nice as you think."

I froze, absorbing his words. What was he implying?

"Well, too bad for you," I forced out, my voice trembling, "he's fucking me, and he's... nice." Panic surged as my breathing quickened, the ache of hyperventilation pressing beneath my skin.

A beat of silence passed between us before his grin faded entirely. His face hardened into an icy mask.

"You're lying," he murmured softly, a cold edge to his voice. "And you're a terrible liar, Kenz." His eyes darted toward the cabin. "But if I find out he touched you, I'll cut out his fucking tongue for tasting you and make you keep it. A reminder of my love for you. And when I'm finished with him...," His voice dropped lower. "I'll fuck you over what's left."

What the fuck.

My stomach twisted, bile clawing up my throat.

"Fuck off, Jackson," I spat, shoving past him. My hands were shaking. I was absolutely terrified of him.

I felt his smile follow me like a knife pressed to my spine. Jackson wasn't just cruel; I was starting to see that he might actually be a psychopath.

As soon as I reached a clearing between the cabins, I immediately launched myself towards the building. I placed both hands on the wood, resting my forehead against its surface.

My breaths came in hot, short bursts. I counted silently in my head.

10... 9...

I was trying to calm myself, but it wasn't working.

I squeezed my eyes shut, searching for anything remotely calming. Of course, the first thing I heard was Max's voice in my head.

"You're okay," he would have said if he were here. *"Nothing will hurt you. I'm here."*

Gradually, my breathing slowed, and calmness rippled through my body. Even as everyone else made me doubt him, he remained my anchor, the beacon of light leading me out of the storm.

But could I trust him? I wanted to believe I could, but now, uncertainty clouded my mind.

Shit. How do you protect yourself from the feeling of being hunted when everyone around you is a predator?

16

MAX

I had to head straight to the showers. I couldn't see straight. I was so pissed off that I couldn't keep myself together around her. I had almost gone down on her in the nurse's cabin for fuck's sake.

I couldn't shake the heat of her thighs under my hands, the way her breath stuttered, the way she looked at me like she'd let me take her right then and there. She had trusted me naturally, instinctively, like her body was already mine to take.

And that was why I was so fucking attracted to her.

She was eating me alive. She had her hand wrapped around my heart, and would probably take a bite out of it if she could.

This wasn't just a crush anymore. I had moved beyond attraction. I needed her like air. She was my oxygen. Every single rational thought I had went out the window as soon as I was around her.

Under the water, I tried to wash her off of me and ended up with my fist wrapped around my dick. I thought of her, only her, and I didn't care what line I was crossing. I came so hard I nearly fell to my knees.

Once I got to our station, I watched her walk towards me,

almost in slow motion, as if she wasn't detonating me. Her yellow camp shirt was knotted above her waist, black shorts that should've been criminal, braids bouncing as if they were designed to murder me one swing at a time.

She smirked, and my chest tightened. She knew. She fucking knew I couldn't keep my shit together.

"You feeling okay?" I asked, though my voice came out strangled.

"Never better," she said sweetly, but her eyes were different. She was holding back from me. Something was up.

She leaned close, brushing her fingers over my chest as she adjusted her name tag. She smelled like coconut sunscreen.

Fucking delicious.

"You're staring." She glanced at me through her lashes, then averted her eyes.

"Just waiting for the campers." My jaw clenched. If I admitted the truth, that I was imagining dragging her into the trees and pressing her against the bark until she begged me to stop, I'd never come back from it.

I was losing my damn mind thinking about her. But why was she acting so weird?

Her chest grazed my arm when she reached past me for the clipboard, her fingers skimming the bare skin at my waist as they briefly crept under the hem of my shirt. She'd done it on purpose. She was testing me.

I caught her wrist.

"Seriously?"

"What?" She was innocently mocking me.

"I told you I don't like being messed with."

Her smile curved slowly. "I'm just playing the role, Danger-ous. Isn't that what we agreed on? The game, right?"

The game? What the fuck was she talking about?

"This is not what we agreed on. But I'm *game* if you're

ready to take this up a notch. I think the rules are null and void now."

"Maybe, I mean, I've had your tongue in my mouth, your fingers inside me," she whispered, lip caught between her teeth. "What's a little PDA?"

"Don't tempt me."

She didn't even flinch. She matched my energy.

"I bet the other counselors have bets on when we hook up."

"Bets?"

She shrugged, casual. "Maybe next Saturday. Maybe tomorrow."

Fuck Saturday. Fuck tomorrow. If she kept looking at me like that, I wasn't making it through the night.

"We already hooked up, baby." But my voice came out shaky, trembling, just thinking about her.

She leaned in; her breath warm against my ear. "You okay, Max? You look... flustered."

I took a half step back, every muscle straining. She was fucking with me, and I was over it. The caged animal I had been holding in was about to claw himself out.

"I'm just thinking about all the ways I'm going to fuck you when you finally give me the green light. I'm not just your bestie anymore, sweetheart."

She smiled, no longer shy, and followed me. She dragged her hand down my back.

"Yeah? You'd like that, wouldn't you? Wanna do it right now?"

She wanted me rabid for her. When the chorus of campers' voices carried across the hill, it was the only thing that saved her from me snapping right then and there.

"Trouble," I muttered under my breath. "Keep this up, and I swear to God—"

"You'll what?" she asked, smiling like the devil. "Turn me into the game masters?"

I looked at her, confused as hell, but grinned back. "I'm not going to be fucking gentle with you."

Her lips curved, soft and lethal.

"Maybe I don't want you to. I mean, what are the game rules?"

"Rules?" What was she talking about? Our rules?

"Yeah, I mean, you said they were null and void now, so tell me the line."

The rules had shifted. No, the rules had been obliterated. And I was fucking here for it. But what game was she talking about?

"No rules. No boundaries," I said, tugging her over to me by the hem of her shirt. She looked up at me as I moved her hair back from her forehead, and then leaned down so my lips were hovering right next to hers. "You think you can handle that?"

"Try me," she whispered.

Oh, I definitely fucking would. Max the bestie was officially gone.

MACKENZIE

It was 3 p.m. The last of the kids were gone, and the campgrounds were quiet. Nurse Campbell's voice was still ringing in my ears, but Max hadn't done anything to make me feel like I couldn't trust him. I had been dropping hints all day to see if he flinched at me referencing the game.

But he was just Max. I'll admit, we had been flirting with each other all day, and honestly, it just felt right.

The sexual tension between us was so high, but neither one of us was brave enough to pull the trigger. Honestly, maybe

Nurse Campbell was just an old bat, and I was thinking too much into it.

Max leaned against the fence, the sun in his hair, his shirt clinging to his chest, and radiating an illicit level of charm.

"You missed a spot," I said, pointing at the smear of red popsicle on his arm.

He raised an eyebrow. "Wanna lick it off?"

"Please, I have standards."

"Sure, you do." He pushed off the fence, closing the gap between us. "That's why you're dating me."

"Exactly. Low risk, high reward. Cute face, good ass, built-in snack provider." I flicked a blade of grass off his shirt.

"Wow. You've been checking out my ass?"

"I love how that was the only part you picked up on." I rolled my eyes.

I hadn't told him about Jackson cornering me outside of the nurses' station. I'd been toying with it, wrestling with it all day because I wasn't sure if Max could be trusted. However, I chose to ignore what Nurse Campbell said. I trusted Max. He would never do anything to hurt me; he was my best friend.

Max didn't know that Jackson had been texting me. Every day. All day. They were short, hungry lines at first, then rants, then promises.

The messages had shifted from possessive to pure threat. But they were getting worse. My phone had been blowing up with texts from him all day.

JACKSON KENSWICK

I miss you

Then an hour later,

I'm going to fucking kill you both.

He had even sent me a picture from the archery range with one word:

Mine.

But that wasn't all. This morning, I had seen footprints in the muddy path behind the cabin, prints that ended beneath my window. A latched screen that had been nudged open an inch.

I thought I had escaped the terror in my life, but with Jackson, it still lived under my skin. And now, I was unsure about everyone around me. Terrified that I was living inside a fishbowl, in a game where I was being targeted.

West was stuck in real FBI work, so I couldn't call him. The thought of waiting for a grown-up rescue made bile rise sharply in my throat. Max was the only person who made me feel safe. He was reckless, sure, dangerous, and maybe a little too territorial, but he was the protector I needed. I needed someone who would stand between me and the thing that kept showing up in my life.

Fear.

I needed to be honest. And maybe if I did, Max would give me some hint if he couldn't be trusted.

I dropped my voice. "Listen. I need to tell you something."

The smile faded from his mouth as soon as he heard my tone. His body went still.

"What?"

"After you left the nurse's station this morning, Jackson cornered me."

Max dropped the cones he was carrying. His whole frame tensed.

"Why would that fucker corner you?"

"He's obsessed with whether or not… we've done anything."

Max's voice sharpened. "Why does it matter? I think we made it clear you're mine."

I exhaled.

"He saw me with something. It set him off."

"What was it?"

"The hickey on my neck."

The silence that followed was louder than shouting.

"So?"

"Max. You marked me. He's pissed. He said some things that were not normal."

He stepped close to me, grabbing my chin and lifting my face so my eyes were looking directly into his.

"I don't care what he said. You're mine, and I'm glad he finally knows it."

My mouth parted, stunned into silence.

This was an entirely different side of Max. I had never seen him like this before. He had been joking about being more than friends, but this? There was a darkness inside him that was about to come out.

"I'm not really yours, though." My voice was quiet because I knew it was a lie, and by his reaction, he certainly knew it was a lie.

His hands clenched at his side, as if he was barely holding himself back. "Don't say that. I told you I don't share. You're mine, I'm yours. End of story."

I let out a small squeak, and he smiled so broadly it almost blinded me. The heat in my chest tangled with nerves. He was *serious.*

His smile dropped, and he tensed again, seeing my facial expression.

"What is it?"

I opened my mouth, but suddenly froze. He looked at me, like he already knew.

"Say it," Max demanded.

Every word spilled out of me. The threats, the way Jackson looked at me. Max didn't interrupt. He didn't blink. He just absorbed. His fists curled so hard his veins stood out, but his face was a mask. I watched it hit him like a wave, but he refused to be swept away by it.

"I'm fine," I lied, trying to defuse the bomb that was about to detonate in front of me. "I'm just worried… about you. Jackson is extremely jealous."

I'd seen Max angry before. I'd seen him jealous, stubborn, possessive even, but this was something else.

"You're not fine." His voice was steady. Then a silent resolve hit him. "I'll handle it."

"Max—"

"If he comes near you again, I'll kill him."

He didn't mean it. Right? At least, I told myself he didn't, but the look in his eyes said otherwise. There was no bluff in his voice. The air left my lungs.

"Your daddy is not a good guy, Mackenzie. But we just ignore the things he does. When the time comes, we'll escape," my Mom's voice echoed in my head.

"Max… come on, I'm serious," I laughed nervously. "You just can't go around killing people. That's insane. Jackson is… something is wrong with him."

His eyes snapped to mine. He was hurt and furious.

"It's not insane. When it comes to you? I'll do whatever it takes. I…" He shook his head, closing his eyes and looking up at the sky. I didn't say anything back. I mean, what would I say?

He picked up my hesitation and said, "You think I won't end someone for putting their hands on you? For looking at you wrong? I'd fucking rip out my spine before I let anyone hurt you."

I was seeing the man he was becoming. He was no longer the nerdy boy who liked archery bows and video games. He wasn't the boy who tripped over his shoelaces and blushed when I caught him staring. That boy had grown up. He was turning into a full-fledged protector before my eyes, territorial and possessive. And he definitely was not part of any *game*.

A part of me craved it, this side of Max. I liked knowing that I could drag him into the dark with me, and instead of shrinking back, he'd bare his teeth and follow.

I wanted to tell him the truth. I knew now that he could handle it.

But I just *couldn't*. I hated having to keep it from him. I looked around us. We were standing in the middle of the field, no one around. Not even the trees. Were we being watched right now?

Maybe I could whisper it to him. I opened my mouth to tell him, but held it back.

"You don't have to destroy yourself for me," I whispered, stepping closer to him. "I like your spine."

A small smile crept on his lips, and he said, "I'd do anything for you. You know that, right?"

I felt everything inside me start to unravel. The grief. The fear. The need. The truth I didn't want to say out loud. But it lived in every look between us.

"You shouldn't have to deal with this bullshit alone," he added. "I'm here for you. With you. Whatever you need. I'm here."

"I didn't say I wanted to deal with it alone," I said quietly. "I want to deal with it with you. I like doing this with you."

His eyes searched mine, and he grabbed me by the waist.

"Oh yeah?"

"Yeah." I smiled.

"What else do you like doing with me?"

"Oh, I don't know. We haven't done it yet. But I think when we do, it will be my new favorite thing."

He hesitated and then said, "I want you. Like, I really want you. For real."

My father's voice suddenly echoed in my head, *"They're*

always fucking watching, Emily! Always! You and Mackenzie will never be safe."

I started to pull away. I couldn't do this. I wanted it so badly, but now that he had said it, I was panicking. I was putting a target on his back. Nurse Campbell's voice was in my head, Jackson's words were in my head, and I was terrified of who was watching us.

My brain wasn't in sync with my heart. I couldn't get my stupid mouth to stop, and God damnit, I hated the look on his face right now as I pulled away.

"I can't... Max, I'm sorry."

He let go of me and took a few steps back. His reaction was not what I had expected.

"I'm tired of you playing with me, Trouble."

"Max—I'm not. What's wrong?"

He huffed out a breath in frustration and stepped away from me.

"Do you even hear yourself? You kiss me, you tease me, you sleep with me, you tell me you want to fuck me, and that's a big fucking deal to me. I finger you. We make out. And then you turn right around and tell me you want to use me to fuck with Jackson, that this isn't real, that you can't be with me."

I lifted my chin, matching his fire. "You were aware of the terms when we agreed to this fake relationship."

"Fuck the terms."

His voice was stern, high-pitched, not at all like him. He was screaming... *at me.* I don't think he had ever raised his voice at me before. We had gotten in fights, sure, but not like this.

Fury shook through me. "Don't scream at me."

"I'm sorry, Trouble. I'm sorry. I'm just... I'm so fucking obsessed with you, I feel like I can't get a grip. FUCK!" He ripped at his hair, pacing.

I stepped closer, letting my finger trace a deliberate line down his chest. "We agreed to this *game*... we agreed..."

"I already told you I'm not fucking playing a game. Jackson is threatening to kill you. He's threatening to kill me. We're past whatever the fuck this is, Mackenzie. We're past all of that. This is fucking real now. We're real now."

"I know it's real…" I hesitated. He was pacing now, his breath heavy and rapid.

"You know, you have been my best friend since I was twelve years old. I know everything about you. But you hide things from me. I want to break down the walls. But you won't let me, and I've accepted it. However, what I can't accept is being treated this way. I lied when I told you I could do this because I can't. I don't know what you are talking about with a game, or whatever. But I want you, Trouble. You set my goddamn soul alive."

I wanted to sink into his words. I wanted to kiss him, hold him, let him absorb me. But I couldn't. And I had to push him away. He was going to get hurt by whatever was chasing me.

"I'm not some easy thing you can control, Max. There are things you can't know about me. I'm not a normal girl. I could never be a normal girlfriend to you. I can't give you what you want. This is all I can give you."

He gave me a look, which was both questionable and unreadable. It was as if he was figuring me out, but he didn't want to tell me that he knew.

"I get it, I do. I just… I don't know if I can keep fucking doing this for the rest of the summer. I know it's only been a few days, and this might seem fast, but for me, it's been years. *Years,* Trouble. You're not just some girl. You're everything to me."

It had been years for me, too. I wanted to stop him, tell him I loved him, that we could live happily ever after, but this was real life, not some fairytale. Something was happening to me, and he was going to get hurt. It was better that he remained in the dark.

"Max—I don't know." The tears welled in my eyes before I knew it, and they started to spill over my bottom lashes.

His hands cupped my face immediately, wiping the tears away with his fingers.

"Fuck. I'm sorry. I'm not sure this is coming out right. I didn't mean to start a fight with you. I'm just trying to tell you that I belong to you. Even when you're impossible, even when you scare me to death. I belong with you, and you're tearing me apart."

I pressed my forehead against his.

"You're terrifying," I whispered. My hand slid around his waist. "Do you know that?"

He gave me a condescending look and then growled against my lips, close enough that I could feel the heat radiating from him. "I'm losing control. This means… too much to me."

I could feel the storm inside him, the heat behind his eyes, the raw edge of obsession. I hated that I was causing him this pain. He captured my bottom lip with his thumb, and I could see that he wanted to walk away. But he couldn't.

I didn't pull back. I pushed against him, lips pressing, teeth grazing, hands tangling in his hair. I knew I needed to pull back. I knew I needed to end this, but I couldn't control myself, either. He sighed, hands roaming my back, pulling me impossibly close, trying to dominate me, but I fought him. I arched into him, teasing, testing, refusing to yield.

We were equals in fire, obsession, and dark desire. Soulmates who could spar and burn and bite and push each other to the edge, and still, somehow, come together in that perfect, dangerous, electric collision.

"Mmm… you're impossible to ignore, Trouble," he hissed against my mouth, one hand gripping my waist, the other tangled in my hair. "I could…"

"Could what?" I taunted, breaking the kiss just long enough to flash him a wicked smile. We always came back together with a sense of humor. Maybe we could now.

He snarled, dropping his forehead against mine, lips brushing mine in quick, sharp bites. "Stop fighting this."

He was being too serious.

"I'm not," I whispered, hands sliding under his shirt, feeling the brutal heat of him.

His teeth grazed my jaw, his hands all over me.

"God…" he groaned, pressing against me. "I hate that I want you this much. I've never felt this way before."

"Me too."

He kissed me back, and it was so deep, so intimate, I almost passed out. And then, he whispered in between kisses, "I love you."

He said it like it hurt. Like he couldn't stop the words from tumbling out, even if he tried. My heart nearly stopped. We had passed the line. I wanted to say it back so badly it burned my throat.

But if I gave him that piece of me, he'd own me. I was so scared about what this meant.

I kissed him harder, trying to pour it all into that moment. I wanted him to hear in that kiss how much I loved him. Could he hear my thoughts? Because they were repeating it over and over:

I love you. I love you, too. I love you, Max.

My tongue twisted with his as I kissed him deeper, and he moaned into my mouth, but the longer I didn't say it back, the slower his kissing got until he quickly pulled away, his hand on his chest as if his heart might fall out.

"I need a minute."

I looked up at him, surprised by the hurt in his voice. It was so deep, it felt like my heart was breaking into a million pieces. I almost fell when I saw his eyes. They were wet with tears. He was crying. Because of me.

He walked off, leaving me wondering what the hell just happened. And the worst part?

I had become a villain in my own story. A *monster.* An exact replica of the one I was running from.

17

———

MAX

Was this what a broken heart felt like?

Because I felt like I might throw up.

I didn't go far after I left her. Just enough that I could breathe. I needed to think before responding to her.

Every time I was around her, I lost my mind. I went from flirty to devastated to angry to fucking obliterated in under five minutes.

I hadn't meant to tell her I loved her. It just fell out of my mouth.

I was so fucking in love with her, I couldn't stop thinking about her. She was the goddamn love of my life. Every time I closed my eyes, it was her. Her hair, her laugh, the curve of her mouth when she smiled, the fire in her eyes that made me want to break every rule I'd ever known. And she was killing me. She was playing a game with me.

Because she was hiding things. I could see it in her eyes, in the little hesitations, the way she measured her words. Every secret she kept, it hurt. And I couldn't do a damn thing about it.

Even though I knew.

I had always known there was more. I just didn't know how deep it went.

The puzzle pieces were starting to fall into place quickly. I felt bad because I was watching her struggle with her internal conflict. I knew she couldn't tell me, but I was hoping that the fiery Mackenzie, the one who didn't follow the rules, would break through, and she would ignore her orders.

But she didn't. And I think that hurt the most, because she had always told me everything, except this.

It always started the same.

Around 2 or 3 a.m., I'd feel her shift restlessly beside me. A tremor would pulse through her legs. Her breath would catch, ragged and uneven. Sometimes she'd mumble incoherent fragments, other times she'd whisper desperately, "Don't go, please don't go."

I'd glean pieces of her story she'd never spoken aloud, glimpses from her nightmares. Now, those fragments haunted my mind, drifting endlessly through my thoughts.

"Dad... running... hiding... can't see him."

"You promised not to go."

"I dropped her."

"I'm so fucking tired of always pretending."

"Don't go in the basement."

"Max, I see you."

"He's gone. He's gone."

"They're watching us. They're always watching us."

Each line replayed in my head. She'd been drifting from memory and fear, and I held her all night as she moved from scene to scene in her dreams.

I wanted to tear down every wall she built around herself. I wanted to see every dark corner, every hidden piece, and claim it. I didn't know who to reach out to. I didn't know who could help her. Did I call her mom? Did I call her uncle? I figured that it wasn't her uncle.

She doesn't know I stay awake most nights, and I lie there listening, counting the spaces between her breaths, memorizing the shape of her fear. I Google the names she mutters in her sleep. I've started keeping notes on my phone—times, details, and fragments of phrases.

I wanted to save her, to shield her from the darkness threatening to consume us. My love for her was a fire that haunted my restless nights. The image of her lying vulnerable, dreaming in secrecy, shattered my resolve. I couldn't afford to lose her. Every fragment of my soul was entangled with hers. Desperation drove me to the edge, seeking answers in the shadows.

Last night, I infiltrated the system that holds sealed juvenile records. Specifically, the confidential database used by federal protection agencies. The one I shouldn't have even known about.

It wasn't my proudest moment, but I was already reading all of Jackson's sickening messages to her. As soon as I cracked the code, her secrets spilled out like they had been lying in wait for me. Her old address, her original birth records, and FBI relocation logs. Disturbing, twisted details about her father: a man who wore a deer skull and mutilated 21 women. A true psychopath.

A newspaper clipping from the Ashbourne Gazette piqued my interest.

It was clipped from the October 17, 2012, edition. Mackenzie would've been almost twelve years old, a few months before she met me.

POLICE HUNT FOR 'THE BUTCHER' AFTER 21ST VICTIM FOUND NEAR ASHBOURNE

ASHBOURNE, N.Y. - STATE AND FEDERAL AUTHORITIES ARE intensifying their search for a suspected serial killer dubbed 'The Butcher' after the dismembered remains of a woman were discovered late Thursday in a wooded ravine outside Ashbourne.

*Investigators say the victim, an unidentified female believed to be in her late twenties, is the **21st woman** linked to the killer over a span of five years across three states. Law enforcement officials describe a "signature" at each scene. Victims are found with ritualistic injuries, and several crime scenes have contained animal bones and antlers arranged near the bodies.*

"We are dealing with an extremely organized and sadistic offender," said Special Agent Tony West of the FBI's Behavioral Analysis Unit during a Friday press briefing. "He is mobile. He is meticulous and escalating. We are asking the public to remain vigilant and to report any suspicious activity immediately."

Neighbors in the rural outskirts of Ashbourne reported hearing sirens and seeing emergency vehicles converge on the ravine just after midnight.

"We've seen the missing posters on TV, but you never think it's going to be here," said local resident Marlene Cooper. "Now everyone's looking over their shoulder."

*Authorities have released very few details, citing the ongoing investigation. However, authorities have confirmed that the murders appear to be connected by a combination of forensic evidence and a pattern of interstate travel. Sources close to the case say at least one potential witness and her family have been placed under **federal protection,** though officials declined to comment on the claim.*

Anyone with information about 'The Butcher' is urged to contact the Ashbourne Police Department tip line or the FBI field office in Albany.

IT ALL CLICKED INTO PLACE. HER DRAWINGS. HER PUSHING ME away. She had been living in a state of terror her entire life. It sickened me to know she had endured such horror, that her father was still out there, on the run, hunting her. She never knew when he might return, and that thought haunted me as well.

I should've felt guilty for hacking into her life like this. But I didn't. Because I needed to know. I needed to know her completely. I should've stopped there, but the urge to push forward gnawed at me.

I wrestled through layers of encryption, frustrated at first, but ultimately breaking through. A sick pride surged within me.

Strangely, I'd started to see patterns in her files—unusual names recurring, the same obscure organizations lurking in the background. Contacts that made no sense, hidden connections between people she trusted. She was involved in something far larger than she realized… and so was I.

My brain didn't register it when I first saw it.

THOMAS MCKINNON, CIA, 07-18-82.
LEGACY PRIORITY HANDLER.
DO NOT DISTRIBUTE.

For a second, it was just text.

Then my stomach dropped. The name sharpened on the screen, everything else smearing into a peripheral blur. Thomas McKinnon. My dad.

Why the fuck was my dad's name on these files?

The room seemed to tilt, like the headboard had slipped a few inches back. I blinked, read the line again, slower this time, making myself pick through each word. Then I scrolled down into the metadata.

Dates. Classification tags. Internal routing codes I didn't recognize. I traced phone numbers back to satellites and followed chains of command that didn't belong to any sheriff or county patrol. This wasn't just high-level. This was untouchable, vault-level, oath-sealed, dangerous, CIA-real shit.

And I had fucking found it.

That was the part that scared me the most—how straightforward it had been. No encrypted drive, no air-gapped server, no impossible backdoor. Just... there. Too easy.

The ease of it felt wrong, like a door left wide open in a bad neighborhood. Either someone wanted this to be found, or they were confident no one like me would ever come looking.

Why the fuck was my dad involved in this? I'd grown up thinking he ran a car dealership. Boring invoices, late nights at the office, a normal life. I had never—not once—considered CIA.

But as I stared at his name, old scenes started slotting into place in my brain. The whispered arguments in the kitchen I'd written off as work stress. The "old friends" who showed up late and never gave their last names. My dad's half-smiles and deflections whenever I asked what he actually did.

It added up now, and it made me feel stupid for not seeing it.

What really fucking pissed me off, though, was that he wasn't just in some random document. He was threaded directly through Mackenzie's case file.

He had known who she was all along.

Her file flagged her under something called the Legacy Program.

What the fuck did that even mean?

If he'd known who she was all along, then what did that make us? Had our meeting been an accident, or something scheduled years before I'd ever walked into Camp Blackshear? Had we both been dropped onto the board, nudged along by invisible hands?

For the first time, it occurred to me that maybe none of this had started with me at all.

Jackson kept referencing a game in his texts to Mackenzie, and now Mackenzie was questioning me about a game. We're we in a game now? Did she know?

Anger flared inside me. I felt the root of betrayal settle. The man who taught me right from wrong, who kissed my forehead when I was sick, was part of something monstrous. Something that was terrorizing the woman I was deeply in love with.

I closed the laptop, hands trembling. Someone would notice eventually. That I had hacked in. I didn't do a great job of covering my tracks on this one. But for now, I had a plan. I needed to protect her from Jackson, from her father's world, from everything that was hunting her.

Including the CIA and the FBI. I didn't trust those fuckers.

I had no idea what the fuck I was up against, but I loved her enough that I would enter the game with her. I was quickly realizing that everyone here at Blackshear was a predator.

Even in her sleep, Jackson was there. Inside her brain, haunting her. He'd already shown me he didn't play by any rules. Every ping, every shadow, every move was unhinged. He was a predator who wouldn't stop until he'd taken everything. I needed to figure out a way to ensure she was completely safe from him.

I had watched her as she slept. The rise and fall of her chest, the soft curve of her lips, the fragile way she clutched my hand. Obsession clicked into place. Possession. Protection. Love. Something primal that didn't care about right or wrong.

I couldn't stop thinking about her, memorizing her. The twitch of her lip when she lied, the twist of her bracelet when she was anxious, the way her pupils dilated when I whispered things that made her body react without her knowing.

I'd follow her into hell. I'd walk through fire, bleed, burn for *her*.

Her cries, her nightmares, her secrets, even the darkness she carried—all of it belonged to me now. I would guard her, whatever it took.

Because I loved her. Completely. The closer I got to her, the more it burned. If this obsession were to destroy me, I'd wear it like a crown. She was mine, in ways she didn't even know, and I'd be her king if she let me.

I closed my eyes and shoved my hands into my pockets. I let

the dark settle around me, thinking about everything I had discovered. The stars now reflected off the water, bright and sharp, reminding me of our tattoos, of the light she brought into my life. She was the only light that made this chaos bearable.

I was going to fucking marry her. Not for show. Not for romance. Okay, a little bit for romance. But mainly for protection. The only way I could guarantee she'd be safe from Jackson, from the shadows circling her, from the world she didn't even understand she was part of, was by having her take my name. My dad was CIA, so he had to earn us some protection, right?

He'd protect his daughter-in-law. I just needed to figure out how to make her say yes. And the first way to get her attention was to ignore her, because Mackenzie loved the chase.

18

MACKENZIE

The darkness seeped in quickly, consuming the cabin entirely. The sound of Max's footsteps reached me before I saw him. He entered the bedroom, his eyes briefly meeting mine with an unsettling stare, then silently he grabbed his swimsuit from the dresser.

"Max…" I whispered. He didn't look at me. He didn't say a single word to me. Not one.

We might as well have been strangers.

Deep down, I knew I'd hurt him. But I had no idea how to make things right. I was terrified that if I got too close, the truth would come out. Max was too bright, too perceptive. He was constantly fiddling with his computer, typing out code, and doing things I didn't understand. He knew me too well. He wasn't going to let me get away with it forever.

And when he finally figured it out, he'd leave. He'd just run away. The thought of losing him, even if it was his decision, was unbearable. It was a pain that sank deep inside me.

He didn't wait for me. He just walked off toward the lake, with Heather asking to join him. He nodded his head yes, and she lapped next to him like a dog. That one small choice ripped

185

me apart in ways I couldn't even describe. Jealousy consumed me.

My heart actually felt like it was shattering, like tiny pieces of glass exploding inside my chest. When I tried to swallow, I could feel the shards pressing into my vocal cords, silencing the scream that threatened to come out at any moment.

By the time I reached the water, the air hung thick with the sickly scents of sunscreen, sweat, and pine, blending into an unsettling aroma. Our counselor group was mingling with some of Jackson's. I didn't recognize most of them. Only Rhett Callahan stood out—he was the one who'd helped me earlier when one of the kids got sick, but now his eyes seemed darker, hungrier. He dragged his eyes up and down my body. I felt like a specimen, like a moth trapped inside a clear glass, fluttering awkwardly to escape.

Was I in my game now? Was he a player?

Rhett and the others shouted and splashed, already knee-deep in the shallows, while Heather and Megan lounged on the dock. Max wasn't with Heather, which gave me some solace. I stood at the lake's edge; my towel slung casually over one shoulder. I was trying not to watch Max, who I also noticed was trying not to watch me.

He looked agitated yet stoic. His shoulders were tense. I could see his muscles straining against his shirt as he tried not to look at me.

His backwards cap barely kept the messy waves out of his face, and then, as if he knew I was watching, he reached for the hem of his shirt.

My stomach clenched as I watched Heather's head turn.

His cotton shirt peeled up his torso, revealing every inch of that golden, lean muscle underneath. His broad shoulders, his abs sharp, the tattoo on his arm flexing. I'd seen him like this every single night, every single morning, with only a thin layer of clothing. I'd felt that body pressed against mine, but it wasn't the same as seeing him now. He had an audience, and he was aware of it.

And he wasn't mine to claim, because I had told him so. Because I was an idiot.

From across the dock, Heather's mouth was nearly hanging open. She nudged Megan, whispering and giggling as if she stood a chance with him.

I mean, did she stand a chance? He had walked with her to the lake. Maybe he had moved on from me already.

That realization hurt. I knew I deserved it. I had been pushing him away. But it didn't make it easier to deal with.

I looked away before my face gave me away. My jealousy was stirring up anger. If Max wanted to play, so would I.

The second I dropped the swim cover-up, I felt his gaze hit me. He froze mid-step.

The yellow bikini I was wearing was daring, much more risqué than I would typically wear, but I wanted Max to look at me.

His eyes dragged over my body discreetly at first, and then hungrily. He kept going back for another look. His jaw went slack, lips parted. His tongue darted out as if he hadn't even realized he was doing it.

And then his expression changed.

His gaze sharpened and darkened. It was as if he was fighting every instinct to cross the space between us and claim me. His hands clenched at his sides like he wanted to grab, touch, hold, and pull me in so close that no one else would dare look.

His eyes dipped to my chest, lingering far too long, and then lower, over the stretch of bare skin on my stomach, the dip of my waist, the high-cut curve of my hips. His throat worked as he swallowed hard. He was remembering everything—the feeling of his hands, his lips, his tongue on my body. I could see it in the way his hands twitched at his sides, the way his body gravitated toward me.

His mouth opened like he wanted to speak, but nothing came out. He was furious with want. He looked like he wanted to drag me into the lake, rip the bikini off with his teeth, and remind me exactly who I belonged to.

Jackson's whistle broke through the noise from the water. His eyes were glued to me, and one brow arched in that familiar way, cocky and *interested*.

"Damn," someone muttered behind me.

Rhett stood a few feet away, gaze dragging down the length of my body like he had no shame. "Didn't realize the lake came with a view."

Max's head whipped around. I could feel a chilling crackle in the humid air, like static ready to burst. Max's eyes locked onto me—dark, stormy—his entire posture stiff. He took a step forward, then abruptly halted.

Why was he hesitating?

I fought a smile as I walked past him, brushing my shoulder against his.

"Problem?" I asked, my voice low, innocent. His eyes flicked down to the curve of my hips and back up again, jaw tight.

"You tell me." His voice was deep. He was *pissed*.

The water was cooler than I had expected, sending a shiver down my spine as I waded up to my thighs. Goosebumps prickled across my skin, but I tilted my face up, eyes closed for a second.

Then I heard splashes behind me. I peeked over my shoulder.

Rhett, all cocky confidence, was making his way toward me, and Max was stalking right behind him. The tension followed them like storm clouds.

"Didn't peg you for a thong bikini kind of girl," Rhett said, eyes unapologetically dragging across my body. "But I've never been happier to be wrong."

I raised a brow, forcing a casual smirk. "What kind of girl did you peg me for?"

"Trouble," he said, grinning. "The fun kind."

I opened my mouth to respond. It was weird that he called me Trouble, Max's nickname for me. But Max was suddenly beside us, the water lapping at his hips, chest rising and falling like he was trying to stay calm. But the way his eyes looked, as if he were going to punish me, told me everything I needed to know about how he was really feeling.

Rhett didn't seem to notice or didn't care. He kept talking.

"You know, I've got a late-night dock shift next week. I could use someone to keep me company," he winked. "You interested?"

Max's jaw clenched so hard it looked painful.

"She's busy."

I turned toward him, startled by the edge in his voice. His eyes weren't on me. They were locked on Rhett like he was trying to figure out how many seconds it would take to drown him. Rhett didn't flinch. He just grinned, as if he were too stupid to recognize danger.

"Relax, man. We're just talking." His gaze dragged over my body again. "Where's Heather, anyway?"

Max didn't blink. "Why would I give a damn about Heather?"

"She said you two were hooking up," Rhett said it casually, glancing to shore where Heather was shimmying out of her shorts. Her eyes were on Max.

Everything around me stopped. Max went still in that way he only did when he was lying. His jaw was tight, his eyes a little too blank. His gaze never even flicked to Heather; it locked on Rhett like he was the problem.

"What?" Max snapped; his voice so tight it barely made it past his teeth.

"Yeah, she said you guys hooked up tonight at the lake. She's been talking about it for hours. I thought that meant Mackenzie was now fair game, since you're done chasing her."

No, no, no. I knew Max. I *knew* him. Didn't I?

Max's eyes went wide, his mouth parting, but he didn't say anything. He looked shocked, unable to come to terms with what was being said. But he didn't deny it. He just looked at me. It was the kind of silence that cut deeper than any lie.

I could see every part of his mind shutting down, the light fading as if he couldn't think anymore.

Heat surged through my chest. I could hear Heather's smug little laugh in my head, see her body pressed against him. Maybe she *had* been with him tonight. He had been gone for a while. And they had walked to the lake together. Perhaps I was just some stupid girl he liked to play with. His childhood best friend. He made me think he loved me, while he snuck around with the big dogs.

She knew what she was doing. I didn't.

I had told him he could do this, fuck around. But I didn't think he'd actually do it. I thought he'd be loyal to me. But I had pushed him away, and apparently, I had pushed him straight into Heather's welcoming arms.

I felt myself sway, losing my balance.

Max saw it and immediately reached for me.

"Trouble," he breathed out, stepping toward me, panic flashing in his eyes. "It's not what you think—"

"Isn't it?" I whispered, my voice barely holding together. The ache in my throat burned like betrayal. "Then say it."

He looked like he wanted to say something, but couldn't. He was slow, too slow. Max was a smart guy and usually quick to defend himself. But right now, he looked defeated, scared even.

Rhett shifted uncomfortably.

"Didn't mean to start anything. Just trying to figure out who's off limits here."

Max turned on him with the slow precision of a lethal killer.

"She's not *fucking* available," he growled.

Rhett raised an eyebrow. "Could've fooled me."

That was it.

For a moment, I thought Max was going to lunge, drag Rhett under until he stopped breathing. But instead, Max turned sharply, water splashing as he stormed out, muscles tight, shoulders bristling with fury he couldn't unload.

I didn't follow because he hadn't denied it. And I was *heartbroken.* I wanted to grieve, run away, hide, but as always, fear was watching me. It was always watching me, waiting to torment every single small piece of happiness I had left.

Like a nightmare rising from the deep, Jackson stepped into view. His presence sucked the warmth from the air. The air emitted a loud, screeching cry around him.

He didn't speak right away. He just watched me with a smile too sharp to be human, his eyes glinting like he'd been waiting for this exact moment. To get me alone.

"Lover's spat?" he asked, his voice velvet and venom combined. "Looks like you touched a nerve."

He then turned to Rhett. "Get lost."

I barely registered his words. My mind was stuck in a loop.

She said you guys hooked up tonight.

Max was a damn good actor. He had fooled me. He had made me think we were something more; that we were meant to be together. Why would he tell me he loved me?

"You new here?" Jackson asked, voice low and threatening.

Rhett blinked, disarmed by Jackson. "Yeah, Rhett. I'm—"

Jackson cut him off. "Right. Rhett. Just so we're clear—" He got close. Close enough for the threat to be unmistakable. "Mackenzie is my property. I own her. There are some other boys here claiming she is theirs, but don't be mistaken; a man actually takes her. Me. Don't ever fucking look at her again if you want to keep breathing."

"Dude, chill."

"I am chill." The danger in Jackson's eyes was cold and terrifying.

Rhett held his hands up and took a step back. "Alright. Got it. Jesus, Mackenzie. You sure get around. Everyone has a claim on you tonight."

Jackson didn't say anything, but I could see the darkness in his eyes. He finally turned to me, his eyes dragging down my body with possessive heat.

"Nice bikini," he murmured. "You always did like being the center of attention."

I swallowed hard. I took a step back into deeper water. "It's just a bikini, Jackson."

He followed.

"I've never seen it before."

Before I could respond, his hand was suddenly on my waist, sliding down my back. His touch was too familiar, but compared to Max's, foreign. I tried to shrug him off, but he pulled me closer.

"Don't," I snapped, but he wasn't listening. His mouth was in my ear, whispering.

"You think they're all staring because you look hot?" he said. "You think Max is jealous because he wants you? Or because you're making yourself look easy?"

My lungs clenched tightly. He pulled me even closer, a predatory grin on his face. Suddenly, his hand slammed against the back of my head, smashing me under the dark, suffocating water.

The water was freezing as it forced its way into my lungs, a numbing sensation that made me scream in agony while he held me down mercilessly. In an instant, darkness consumed my vision. At first, it felt unreal—a cruel joke, a twisted display of power. I flailed desperately, expecting him to loosen his grip, but he didn't. Instead, his hold grew tighter. Water shattered my eardrums, muffling the screams. I thrashed around, panic ripping through my chest like a beast unleashed.

The seconds dragged into eternity. I opened my eyes underwater, darkness pressing in around me. My lungs screamed for air. I clawed at his arm, desperate to scream, but only bubbles escaped my mouth. A suffocating weight enveloped me. I was drowning.

Memories of my father's motorcycle outside our burning home flashed violently in my mind. I could almost hear his screams, *"I've had enough!"* He often shouted that from his basement.

I broke the surface of the lake with a harsh cough, but the terror still gripped me. Then I was pulled under again, drowning in darkness. I could hear Jackson's mocking laughter through the water. Was this a cruel joke to him? A wave of panic and adrenaline surged through my veins as I blindly kicked out, desperate to break free. I managed to hit something, and then he yanked me out of the water.

"Oh, shit. You, okay?"

I opened my eyes, rubbing the water out of them.

"What the hell is wrong with you?" I choked out, wiping water from my face, my voice shaking. Everyone around us seemed too far to hear. No one was paying attention. "You trying to fucking drown me?"

Jackson's smile was calm.

"You needed to cool off."

My entire body trembled.

"You're an asshole."

His eyes were dead—flat, empty, terrifying. For a moment, they stayed that way before suddenly snapping back to their normal honey brown, the horrifying emptiness still lingering behind.

And then the tears began. They flowed down his face, hiding his evil.

"I didn't mean it! Promise," he sobbed. "Please don't be mad at me, Kenz."

My entire body shook. My chest felt like it was on fire.

Tears, mingling with the lake water, poured down my face in torrents. I was consumed by an overwhelming terror—much greater than anything I'd ever known. You always expect to escape terror by running. But in moments of pure panic, your mind turns against you. You struggle to accept what's really happening because it's impossible, right?

You're not going to die.

It's impossible.

You feel sluggish, unable to process any emotion except the fear pulsing through your body.

That's exactly where I was. I was facing the impossible. My breath came in frantic, searing bursts as I fought to keep myself together. My mind was an empty void, churned by terror and devoid of any rational thought.

He put his hands on my waist, and I quickly slapped them off.

"Don't touch me, you fucking psycho," I threatened him.

He put his hands up, the sobs continuing.

"Okay, okay! Look, I'm sorry for what happened back home. I was an idiot, and I've been trying to call you for weeks. It's unfair that you ghosted me when we broke up."

Was he… *serious*? He had to be bipolar. His dueling personalities were giving me whiplash.

"So, you're trying to kill me now? Way to get back at me," I scoffed, nearly sprinting out of the lake. The water clawed at my legs like tiny hands, dragging me backward as I fought to move forward.

I grabbed my towel, wiped my face, and looked around for Max. I needed him. I didn't care what had happened with Heather. I *needed* him. I was terrified, shaking with fear. And I just fucking needed the one person I knew who would make me feel safe.

But he was gone.

Where the fuck was he?

Probably fucking Heather, my subconscious thought.

A fury like I had never experienced consumed me. I turned away from Jackson, who was now glaring at me with such coldness that the hairs on my arms stood straight up.

"You're mine. You know that? You'll always be mine. Wherever you go. We're blood-oathed."

His words catapulted me back to a memory of myself when I was five.

Mackenzie—Age 5

THE HALLWAY WAS REALLY DARK. MY TOES FELT COLD WHEN I walked, and the floor was slippery. I wanted my Mommy because I had a scary dream. I walked to the bathroom. I saw Daddy's room. The door was open just a little bit, so I peeked inside.

Daddy was in his chair, looking at the wall. He had a big shiny knife on his lap. He talked to it in a whisper. I froze, but Daddy saw me anyway.

"Come here, sweetheart," he said, smiling at me.

I wanted to run to Mommy, but my feet just kept going, so I went to Daddy. If I didn't, I'd get in trouble.

He touched my hair, and it felt weird.

"You're mine, you know that?" he whispered. His breath smelled bad. "No matter where you go. You'll always be mine."

I didn't cry. I knew I wasn't allowed to cry with Daddy. Because that was bad. Really bad. So, so bad. I was bad.

I turned back to Jackson.

"What did you just say to me?" I stilled.

Jackson smiled, the black centers of his eyes widening beyond the honey brown. "Kenz, don't be like that, come on. You know you'll always be mine."

"I'm not yours, and I never was." My entire body was frozen with fear.

"Yeah, alright. So, all those times we fucked, you weren't mine then?" He tsked his tongue, wringing his hands in a move I recognized as anxiety. "Why did you stop talking to me?"

I couldn't believe him.

"That's what happens when you break up with someone. You generally don't speak again."

I was trying hard not to hyperventilate. The lake water was still inside my chest, and I felt like I was about to puke.

"We were together for eight months, Mackenzie," he said, upset. "I can't believe you'd let all that go away."

I stared at him. Jackson was the kind of attractive that made people look twice. He was tall, with rich, tan skin that glowed golden in the sun, and a chiseled jawline that looked as if it belonged on a magazine cover. His eyes were deep brown, almost black, intense, and unreadable. But when he was sweet, the Jackson I had loved, his eyes were honey.

His hair was cropped close, neat, and always styled just enough to look effortless. He smiled easily, the kind of smile that could charm a room while hiding something sinister. I had fallen for it, too. Jackson was so precarious because he could make you believe he was a good person with good intentions, then turn everything on its head with a single look or action.

I should've known back then that he was evil. The problem was that I never knew what he was thinking. He had always been so closed off.

He gave me whiplash, and I didn't know what was real with him. He lived in a different world from mine—a fractured reality where he was two beings. And I spent most of our relationship wondering which version of him I would end up with.

The human version, or the demonic entity that had consumed his soul.

I should have picked up on the signs back then, but I didn't. He was a fuse, always seconds from being lit. People noticed him because of his looks and charm, but I saw him for what he truly was: completely unhinged.

A monster.

Memories of that night during spring break flashed through my head.

Three Months Earlier

"Jackson. Oh my god!" The girl screamed as he forcefully thrust into her. All I could see were his lean arms, his muscular back, muscles tensing with each movement. I shrieked, covering my mouth with my hand, frozen in the doorway of that stupid party. I had just received my acceptance letter to GCU and made the soccer team.

I couldn't wait to tell him.

He whipped his head around suddenly, his eyes locking onto mine, still pounding into her with brutal intensity. He paused, then stared directly at me with a cold, deadly stare that sent chills down my spine.

"Oops," he muttered. "You weren't supposed to see this."

Anger boiled underneath my skin. I was done playing the victim.

"Let's think about this a bit. You slept with another girl. Not only were you still inside her when I caught you, but you said 'Oops', and continued to fuck her in front of my face," I screamed. "You think that's appropriate? Do you think I'd want to talk to you after you fucking did that to me?!"

"Oh yeah, like you're some saint? *Oh, Max is my best friend, Max needs to talk to me. I need to call Max.*"

"You need to get over this obsession you have with Max!"

"I see the way he looks at you. He's fucking in love with you." He ran his hands through his hair, pulling at the edges.

He wasn't in love with me, I thought. Because he went with *her*.

I stared into Jackson's dark eyes that had killed me repeatedly. I wanted him to hurt. I wanted him to die like I died when I heard him fuck her, when I saw him fuck her, when he held me down and fucked me repeatedly afterwards.

I had told Max that Jackson and I had only had sex twice. It was a lie. Jackson had forced himself on me so many times.

I had been so delusional in thinking I didn't deserve love that I allowed it.

"Fine, you want the truth?" I asked. He looked at me expectantly. "I'm in love with him. He's in love with me. We've been fucking for years. All those things I wouldn't do with you, I do with him all the time. Happy?"

He was consumed with rage when I said that, and I smiled.

The change in him was immediate. Jackson vanished in an instant. I could see it in his eyes—jet black, unrecognizable. The true monster lurking within had been revealed. Rage overtook him when I described it, and I couldn't help but smile.

Because if he was the devil, I was the devil incarnate.

"You lied to me," he said, his voice cold.

"Yeah, I lied," I said, staring directly into his devilish eyes. "Oops."

Anger twisted his features, shadows twisting darkness in his eyes as he struggled to suppress his rage.

"It doesn't matter because you and I are bound by blood," he hissed with a sinister edge. "It's unavoidable. As soon as you graduate, we're getting married. You have no say in it."

He clenched his fists tightly at his sides and stepped dangerously close to me.

"I'm going to kill him, anyway," he hissed, leaning in. "He's in my way. And if I find out he's touched you, I won't go easy on him."

"It's too late, Jackson. He's always touching me," I said coldly.

"How many times?" His voice cracked with panic and rage.

"Want numbers? Or just highlights? First time? Camp. Two years ago. In his bunk bed. Then the shower. The floor. Twice in his car. Three times at the lake. Once right here on the dock." I was getting creative with my lie, and Jackson finally looked at me with a haunting expression, making me feel like I was in control of him.

I tilted my head, my eyes daring him to explode.

"How many times does that make it, Jackson? Oh, right. More than you ever managed to get without lying or forcing."

"Shut your fucking mouth," he snarled, grabbing my arm violently and pressing two fingers viciously against my forehead. I gasped as his grip tightened around my throat, cutting off my air. His twisted smile grew as I struggled for breath, then he made a chilling gunshot sound, aiming an imaginary barrel at my head.

"Bang," he whispered cruelly.

Before I felt the blackness overtake me, Max's hand shot out from behind me, gripping Jackson by the throat with terrifying force. A guttural voice, unrecognizable as Max's, snarled, "Fucking walk away. Now."

19

MAX

I shouldn't have walked away. The second Rhett opened his damn mouth about Heather, I knew I had lost control of myself, the situation, and Mackenzie.

I didn't know what fucking game Rhett and Heather were playing, but I wasn't in the mood for it.

Earlier, I was too busy trying to play hard to get with Mackenzie when Heather stepped in like she'd been waiting for us to implode all along.

"Hey," she said, stepping in line with me before I could even open my mouth. "You heading to the lake?"

"Yeah."

"You, okay?" Her voice was honey-sweet and fake.

"Fine."

"You don't look fine." She tilted her head, all doe-eyed and manipulative sympathy. "Can I help you take your mind off her?"

That made me stop.

"Excuse me?"

Heather smiled, slow and knowing.

"I'm just saying… she's not the only girl here. You've got

options. I'm an option." She reached out, her hand grazing my forearm. "If you want to forget about her, I can help with that."

I yanked my arm away.

"I'm not interested."

She blinked, taken aback. "What? I was just—"

"I'm not interested. I've never been interested."

Her expression hardened instantly, like she'd been slapped. "Wow. Okay. You don't have to be an asshole about it."

"Listen, I wouldn't have to be an asshole if you'd stop trying. I'm with Mackenzie, so drop it."

Heather's face twisted with anger and humiliation. "You think she's gonna choose you? She's fucked up, Max. Jackson has been telling me all about her and her life. And you're going to end up just like every other idiot who tried to save her."

I stepped in closer, furious.

"Say one more thing about her," I said. "I fucking dare you."

She flinched, but she didn't back down.

"She's going to break your heart."

I didn't answer. As soon as we got to the lake, I walked away from her. The worst part? Heather was right. Mackenzie was going to break my heart. But I was still all in.

But then Rhett ruined everything, and I completely fucked up. My anger took control, and things spiraled into chaos.

I went back to the cabin and picked up her journal. She hadn't sketched anything in a while, and some selfish, fucked-up part of me hoped I was the reason.

But most of it wasn't drawings, anyway. It was mainly tangled, messy thoughts. Some of it was her dreams, scattered nonsense I couldn't make sense of. But then there were the parts about me—pages of them. What she wanted to do to me. What she hated about wanting me.

I lingered there too long, letting the words sink into my head. I shouldn't have. I was invading her privacy, *again,* but I needed it. I needed to know if I was in her head the way she was in mine. And for a second, I convinced myself she was because there was an excerpt that she had written about me. It was finally the truth.

Max, I love you.

I've loved you since the first summer when you stumbled over a canoe, trying to act like the bleeding didn't happen. You were stubborn, hilarious, and too good at Capture the Flag.

You drove me crazy, even back then. But now? This isn't just a crush. It's waking up with you as my first thought. It's watching you laugh at something completely unfunny, and wishing I could bottle that sound because I don't know how many laughs I'll have.

I want every single one of them.

Every moment I'm with you, I can finally breathe; every moment apart, I feel like I'm drowning. I love you in that terrifying way where I can't breathe or look at anyone else. I want you. Even the dark parts. I love you so much. But I can't tell you, and I hate that.

The words blurred, and suddenly, I felt weightless. I reread it.

Max, I love you.

Every part of me wanted to run through the woods and

demand why the fuck she'd kept this from me, why she made me think I was the only one drowning in this. But I knew why. She thought that by not being honest with me, she was protecting her secret. But she was mine; she had always been.

A twisted relief flooded me. I began to laugh maniacally and unsettlingly, because I wasn't insane. All the obsession, the way I couldn't stop wanting her, it wasn't one-sided. She wanted me the same way. I grinned, reveling in the sick truth I finally knew.

Because now? I wasn't letting go. This was it, the moment. She was mine. Not because I owned her, but because if I didn't have her, I wouldn't survive. I wanted forever with her. And today? I wasn't holding back anymore. She wanted a knight in shining armor? Fine. I'd be the only thing she craved. Maybe with a little dark edge, but I'd do it. I'd fucking do whatever she wanted.

As I made my way back, I was prepared. I was going to tell her that I knew everything. I was going to come clean, and we would live happily ever after. I almost skipped back to her.

But then I heard it. Her voice. Sharp, unsteady, trembling with a horrifying edge. When I reached the lake, every fiber of my being screamed to run to her. Mackenzie was soaked, water cascading from her hair onto the ground as she shrieked at Jackson. I moved faster toward them, but stalling when her words sliced through the air with terrifying clarity.

I don't think I'd ever been this angry in my life. Not when I'd lost a game. Not when I'd gotten screwed over by coaches or teammates. Nothing compared to this. Hearing the way Jackson had disrespected her and made her feel small, it was like someone had wrapped barbed wire around my chest and started pulling tighter.

She deserved better than that. She deserved someone who would worship every inch of her body, who would fuck her like she was sacred, and love her with every breath. And knowing he had tainted her with anything less than that? It made me want to break every bone in his body.

He lunged at her abruptly, his grip tightening around her upper arm. Mackenzie braced herself against his chest, struggling to push him back. Her face was contorted with fury, and something darker I recognized immediately. Fear.

When he made a pretend gun motion, that was it; everything turned red.

I stepped in front of her, my hand closing around his throat in a cold, brutal grip.

His neck was tiny, and I almost snapped it in half.

"Fucking walk away. Now."

I ripped his hand from her, my grip bruising.

"Touch her again, and I'll snap your neck and shatter your fucking jaw."

I let go of his neck and shoved him hard, hard enough to make him stumble. The crack of the impact echoed between us as he fell to the ground.

He jerked upright with a cruel, vacant stare that made my skin crawl. My vision blurred into a tunnel, fixated on his face, and for the first time in my life, I truly understood what it meant to want to destroy someone.

I must've looked unhinged because even Mackenzie flinched.

"This is a private conversation between my girlfriend and me. Fuck off," Jackson said, scrambling back onto his feet.

I don't know what gave him the right to think he could even call her that.

"*Ex-girlfriend,*" I bit out, stepping forward until we were nose-to-nose. My voice dropped, the kind of sound that came from a place buried deep in my bones. "Don't come near her again. Don't *fucking* test me, Jackson."

Jackson smirked, tilting his head slightly like he was amused. Like I was a game he was looking forward to playing.

"That's not your decision… *bro,"* he said. "She's mine. She always was. Why don't you back the fuck off before I kill you?"

Jackson might have the devil's smile, but the beast inside me? The one that had been locked away for years? He was ready to play ball.

I sneered.

Game on, you twisted bastard.

"I'd like to see you try. The only body they'll be dragging out of the lake is yours," I said flatly. "Your death will be endless, brutal, and horrifying. The last thing you'll remember as the water fills your lungs is my hands holding you down, and the cruel certainty that Mackenzie was always mine. I will marry her. I will give her *my* babies. Not yours. Mine."

It was settled. I was staking my claim on her, whether he liked it or not. I didn't care if the entire camp heard.

"You're finished. You don't talk to her; you don't even look at her. You so much as *breathe* in her direction, and I'll make sure you regret it every single day you're still able to open your eyes. You think you're scary? Try me. I'll rip the smirk off your face and make you choke on your teeth. One wrong move, Max, and I'll remind you exactly why you should have never touched her in the first place," Jackson spat in my face.

I balled my fist and pressed it in the center of his chest, pushing him backward again.

Rage flickered in his eyes. I hope he swung first. I *prayed* for it.

"Okay, testosterone overload, *cool it,"* Mackenzie said, putting a hand on my chest. "No one's killing anyone tonight without my say in it."

"Careful, baby. If you want to be the ringmaster, people might wonder if Daddy passed on more than his eyes," Jackson taunted.

Mackenzie's face went pale.

"You threatening her now?" I asked, my voice deceptively calm.

Jackson's lips curved. "Not a threat. Just a reminder of who she is. Deep down, you know it. You've always known. It didn't take you long to figure it out, did it?"

Mackenzie was frozen next to me, and I could feel her eyes on the back of my head. Jackson had just royally fucked up everything. I moved closer to him, toe-to-toe, my rage barely simmering under my skin.

"Touch her again," I said. "And you won't have to worry about reminders. You'll be lucky to fucking walk."

Jackson's jaw ticked, but he didn't move.

"Hey, guys? Why don't we play a game before you two kill each other?" Megan called from over near the water.

A campfire had started, and the group had now dispersed to a small number of us.

I grabbed Mackenzie's hand, pulling her into my side. I wrapped my arm around her and strolled to the campfire, shielding her with my body.

We sat near the fire, and I rested my arms on my knees. Her voice broke through then, soft and barely above a whisper. She wanted only me to hear her. "Max… how much do you know?"

I could feel her hesitation, the quick hitch of her breath, the way her fingers pressed against mine. She looked incredibly vulnerable, and seeing her in this state stirred something dark and protective within me.

I didn't answer immediately. Instead, I squeezed her hand, my voice low.

"All of it. Okay? Don't be mad. Just know that it doesn't change anything. You got that?"

Her eyes widened with terror, pupils darkening, a shiver running down her spine. I sensed the tremor in her, the shock that I could care this much, that I could see this. A flicker of relief passed over her face, and I watched her finally take a deep, steady breath.

I wanted to tell her that she didn't need to be scared. That I had a plan, a fucked up one. But a *real* plan to protect her.

I let my grip linger, the heat between us palpable. We could finally bury all this bullshit behind us and move on. She didn't need to know how far I'd gone—about my hacking history. She just needed to know that I was hers and that nothing and no one would take her from me.

Heather crept over and settled beside me, her presence suffocatingly close. Mackenzie froze entirely, her eyes dark with growing jealousy that threatened to consume her again.

Fuck, babe, please don't do this right now, I thought. *I'm fucking yours.*

But I was too pissed to say it out loud. I watched Jackson sitting across the fire, looking at Mackenzie with a grimace. He looked like a predator. Good thing I was worse.

Megan pulled out a cooler filled with drinks and handed me a beer. I cracked mine open and knocked it back so quickly I heard Mackenzie groan in disapproval beside me.

"Max… can we go somewhere in private?" Mackenzie whispered next to me.

I was about to say, "fuck yeah," when Megan interjected.

"Okay, so here are the rules," Megan called out. "You pick the never have I ever prompt. If you've done it, you drink. But here's the thing, I play this game dirty. If things get a little raunchy, I'll start calling out some dares."

"That's so stupid," I snapped, a heat of irritation rising within me. A part of me was itching to leave with Mackenzie. I wasn't interested in wasting time with this pointless game.

Mackenzie coughed, her eyes narrowing as Heather's hand rested on my knee. A flicker of envy crossed Mackenzie's face, and her expression darkened with rage. I immediately shifted, and Heather's hand dropped.

"I think it's fun," Heather said, dragging a finger down my arm. I flinched, scooting closer to Mackenzie. I didn't know why Heather was still fucking trying.

"Okay, never have I ever... had sex in a public place," Megan said.

Jackson drank, Heather drank, and I took a sip. Mackenzie's eyes snapped to mine. The moss on clover that I loved so much was shadowed, darker. She was trying to hide just how jealous she was, but she was failing.

"Seriously?" she said, her voice tight.

"It didn't matter, Trouble," I said, shrugging.

Fuck.

This was going to be bad. I might as well jump into my grave now.

"That's the thing about Max," Jackson grinned. "You probably have no idea how many girls he has run through."

"Shut up, Jackson," Mackenzie snapped. But she eyed me like she didn't know me.

My jaw clenched. I was fantasizing about how I would kill him. Baseball bat to the head? Yeah, that was it.

"Oh, c'mon, it's a game, Kenz," he sneered. "Let's be honest here. Never have I ever had a threesome."

Heather and Jackson both took a sip. I held onto my beer and noticed Mackenzie hadn't taken a single sip of hers yet.

"No? Not yet, huh?" he taunted her.

"Fuck you, Jackson. I should've known you were doing all that shit when we were together," she said icily.

Heather leaned into me, brushing her hand down my arm again, and I wanted to puke. Mackenzie was so pissed that I could feel the heat radiating off her body.

"Never have I ever had sex more than five times with the same person," Heather purred, her eyes locking onto mine with a chilling intensity.

Heather and Jackson exchanged a look, and something

inside me went cold. It wasn't just a glance—it was an understanding. A secret. They were working together. Something was going on, and I knew, whatever it was, it wasn't going to end well for me.

Both Jackson and I took a sip. I kept my eyes on him the entire time.

"More than five times? Who?" Mackenzie interjected, her eyes wild with untamed jealousy. She was losing her shit now.

"It's nothing, Trouble. I promise. It didn't mean anything," I said uneasily.

It hadn't.

"How many girls, Max?" she snapped.

I didn't answer right away. The silence said it enough.

I should've lied. I was fucking this all up now. I looked over at Jackson and watched as he greedily devoured it. This had been his plan all along.

"Yeah, *Trouble,* you thought you were 'The One'?" he said mockingly.

"You have no business talking to her," I snapped. "You cheated on her. Then you stalked her as if she were something you could hunt. Don't think I don't know about the messages—those paragraphs you send at three in the morning. I've seen how you stand across the trail and watch for us. You don't get to act like you know anything about this. You're a fucking parasite. A psychopath who doesn't understand 'no' unless it's carved into you."

"Oh, I stalked her, yeah? Why don't you tell her about all your online activity?" he grinned.

Fuck.

"Okay… guys, stop it. Seriously. You're ruining the game," Megan said. "Here, everyone, Jell-O shot break."

She handed out some Jell-O shots from the cooler, and we all started taking them. I managed about five before Mackenzie took two. I cracked open another beer, gulping it down so quickly the aftertaste felt unsettled on my tongue. I had to pause, my hands trembling slightly from the adrenaline.

Mackenzie finished her beer, her eyes flickering with something unspoken, as if she sensed the shift between us.

Before I knew it, I'd lost count of how much I'd drunk. My vision blurred, and disjointed voices echoed around the campfire. Everything around me seemed louder. I felt a sudden heat blaze through my body, the alcohol scorching my throat. We had been stuck in this ridiculous game for over an hour, and I was intoxicated, feeling reckless and numb, but also deeply unstable. My limbs felt heavy, my thoughts spiraling into chaos, my senses fraying at the edges as I lost my grip on reality.

And Mackenzie?

She was drunk. Not sloppy, but loose. Jackson was sitting next to her now, leaning into her like they were together. I was fucking spiraling watching the two of them because all I could think about was slitting his throat.

I grabbed her waist and pulled her in closer to me. Her head snapped up, and I could see it, the pure anger in her eyes. She pulled away from me.

She laughed loudly at something Megan said and avoided looking at me again. The alcohol only complicated things further.

"Alright—my turn!" Heather called. "Never have I ever given or gotten head at a party."

I took a sip and looked away from Mackenzie.

"Wow," she scoffed quietly. I noticed she hadn't taken a sip of her beer, which thrilled me. I was a dick. But the thought of her doing anything with anyone pissed me off beyond belief.

"Mackenzie. It's your turn," Megan said.

Mackenzie stared at me, a subtle smirk on her lips. The expression in her eyes was crushing. She wanted to end me. I just wanted to stand up, take Mackenzie back to the cabin, and be the two of us again.

Every single time I felt a resolve with us, like things were going to go our way, it all went to shit within minutes.

Mackenzie lifted her beer with a glint in her eye.

"Never have I ever… cum on someone's face."

The fire cracked as Mackenzie downed her entire beer, holding eye contact with me the whole time. She dropped the empty bottle to the ground, wiping her mouth with the back of her hand.

"Oh shit! Damn, Mackenzie!" Heather shrieked. "That's the fucking energy we need!"

My vision went black.

I wasn't angry. I wasn't jealous. I was fucking feral; crazed; wrecked. My fingers clenched into fists in my lap, my nails carving crescents into my skin.

And before I could stop myself, the words came out.

"It wasn't him, was it?"

The group fell quiet. My voice didn't even sound human. It was pure gravel, the sound of someone about to *snap*.

Mackenzie seemed utterly unfazed by the tantrum I was about to throw. She shrugged. "Doesn't matter, McKinnon."

Ah. *McKinnon.*

She only used my last name when she was mad at me. I twisted the beer bottle in my hand, messing with the paper wrapper on the side.

"Cute. Practicing your last name?"

She smiled, but it was malicious.

"Don't hurt yourself thinking too hard about it. That's a pipe dream."

"Mmm… okay. Well, here's something for you to think hard about," I leaned forward slightly, my entire body tight, my stare locked on hers like a sniper. "You can hate me. You can lie to yourself. You can even fuck somebody else. But you'll never belong to anyone but me. Not really. Not ever. This fake relationship is now officially real, so don't fuck with me."

She scoffed, but I saw it, the flicker of hesitation in her eyes. That split-second where the air lingered heavy between us shifted from playful to dangerous. And then Jackson, the fucking ghost of every bad decision, opened his mouth.

"Still dreaming about her, huh, Max? Shame you'll never know what it's like to have her screaming with her thighs locked around your face." He leaned back on his palms. "It gets me hard just thinking about it."

And there it was.

Fuck this. *Fuck. This.*

My entire body screamed to move, to do something—throw him into the fire, drag her into the darkness, mark her so no one would dare come near her. But I held back. She could feel it— my rage. I was doing a shit job hiding it.

I watched the way her spine straightened; her breath stuttered just once. But she knew what she had just done. She was watching me unravel right in front of her. She could see the storm in my eyes. The fury. The hunger. The absolute fucking *possession.*

The Max I kept caged was officially unleashed, and I wasn't playing fair anymore.

"So uhhh... let's keep this going then, yeah? Max. Your turn," Megan said, her voice a little too upbeat to cover the tension building.

I didn't move.

"Come on, Max, don't freeze up now," Heather teased. "Unless you've got something better to do with that mouth."

I didn't even look at her. But Mackenzie did. Her head snapped toward Heather, eyes narrowed to slits, her whole body radiating anger so sharp it could've killed all of us.

Oh, now she wants to pretend that she's jealous?

Fine.

Let's play, baby.

"Never have I ever," I said, voice flat, void of anything, "had someone beg to suck my dick before I even touched them."

Gasps echoed around the circle. Nervous laughter broke out. People shifted uncomfortably. But not Mackenzie. She didn't laugh. She didn't flinch. Her eyes locked onto mine, burning with jealousy and hurt. All of it swirled in those green eyes I was in love with.

Good. I wanted her to feel it. I wanted her to hurt like she hurt me.

But did I?

I didn't like the way she was looking right now. It left a hole in my heart. She began to swirl in front of me, and I swayed a little to keep myself upright.

Fuck. I was drunker than I thought. The angry shadows I kept inside me were coming out, and the love I had for her was being pushed down. I needed to fight harder to make sure that the light wasn't extinguished.

Heather giggled, twirling her hair around her fingers. "Okay, now I'm interested in seeing your dick because it must be pretty awesome if you have girls begging you for it."

I took a slow sip of my drink, never breaking eye contact with Mackenzie. She was glaring at me like she wanted to throw her bottle at my face.

I wanted her to. I wanted her to fight for me.

Throw it at me, punch me, bite me. I just want you to do something to make me feel like you like me. I fucking crave it.

"Classy," she snapped.

"You started it," I said, my voice rough.

She knew what I meant. Everyone else might've thought this was about the game. But her and I? We were playing Russian Roulette. Except we were shooting words, and every hit drew blood.

Megan let out a frustrated breath.

"Okay, wow. Things are getting intense. Let's switch it up, Truth or Dare?"

There were cheers from the others, but I didn't even register them. I leaned back, eyes never leaving Mackenzie. Her fingers dug into her knees. Her body wound so tight; I knew she was seconds from breaking.

"Alright, Heather, you start us off. Truth or dare?" Megan grinned.

Heather smirked.

"Dare."

"I dare you to kiss Max," Megan announced.

Mackenzie's body tensed like someone had just struck her. And fuck, I felt it like a slap straight to the face. My gut twisted. The fire, the flirting, the games, I didn't want any of it. I was hurting her. And I didn't like that. I took it back. I took it all back.

"Nah, I'm not..." I lifted a hand to object. I wasn't playing this game. But it was too late.

Heather was on me before I could finish the sentence, grabbing the front of my shirt like she owned me, legs wrapping tight around my waist, her mouth crashing into mine.

The kiss was sloppy, desperate. I couldn't even push her off. She was holding onto me so tight that I couldn't breathe.

She tasted like a mix of beer and watermelon Jell-O shots, with a sour undertone. Her tongue forced past my lips without invitation, and I let out an exasperated groan. I was absolutely disgusted. I wanted to vomit. I tried to push her off, but she grabbed me even tighter. When she finally pulled back, she looked victorious, like she had just won a prize.

"Mmm," she purred, glancing sideways at Mackenzie. "You taste good."

My blood went cold. I wiped my mouth with the back of my hand, trying to wipe her kiss off me. And then my eyes snapped to Mackenzie.

Fuck, fuck, fuck.

She was staring straight ahead, face flushed like she'd been slapped. Her mouth trembled slightly, and she was blinking too fast. Then I saw it. The single tear forming in her right eye, hovering. And it felt like a goddamn knife to the chest.

"Mackenzie…" I choked out. She didn't even look at me. Not once. She didn't speak. She just stared at the fire like it might swallow her whole.

I would've set myself on fire if it meant undoing the last thirty seconds.

And then Heather, smiling in her delight, leaned back on her hands and said in that sweet, venom-laced voice, "Truth or dare, Mackenzie?"

The group froze. The flames cracked.

"Dare," she said, her voice cold, small. She didn't sound angry. She sounded tired. And that was much worse. Because I knew that tone, I knew that edge. It was the voice of a girl who had nothing left to lose. The kind of voice that made people *bleed.*

That made me bleed. And she was going to make me suffer over it.

I let myself look away from Mackenzie, just for a second. I found Jackson staring at her across the fire.

My hands curled into fists.

"Enjoy the show?" I asked quietly.

His eyes flicked to mine, slow, almost bored.

"Careful," I went on, my voice dropping so only he could hear. "You keep watching her like that, one night you're going to feel someone watching you back." I leaned in a fraction, letting the fire throw my shadow over his shoes. "And I promise you, Jackson—it won't be her."

A log shifted in the pit with a loud crack.

He flinched.

20

MACKENZIE

I couldn't breathe.

I felt that kiss between Heather and Max like it had happened to me. Heather's lip gloss was on his mouth. He didn't stop her. How long did it take him before he pushed her away?

So, they *were* fucking. It was apparent they knew each other well.

Heather sat back like a cat with blood in her mouth. Max looked sick. Guilty. But the damage was done.

My throat was tight. My heart thundered in my chest like it wanted to escape.

I didn't want to cry in front of him, but when I felt the tears in my eyes, I looked away quickly. I loved him, and this hurt. So much more than I could've imagined.

"Truth or dare, Mackenzie?" Heather asked, a smug smile on her lips. I wanted to punch her.

"Dare," I said, my voice dry, wobbly.

Heather paused and said, "I dare you to kiss Jackson."

Silence dropped over the group. Max tensed next to me. I felt it in my bones. But I wouldn't give him the satisfaction of looking his way. This was his chance to say something. To do something. To prove that I was *his*.

My pulse pounded painfully in my ears. I should've said no. I should've laughed it off, rolled my eyes, or told him to get lost. But the image of Heather on Max's lap haunted my mind, more vivid than ever. I was drunk, hurt, blinded by a pain that cut deeper than jealousy. Everything was so blurred, so uncertain—I didn't know what to do, only that the ache was so overwhelming I couldn't imagine us ever going back to being friends after this.

I stood up and walked over to Jackson, who had moved next to the cooler.

Every step felt like a betrayal of the distance I had built with Jackson and the relationship I was starting with Max. But I kept moving.

Jackson was already smirking, a sinister gleam in his eyes. When I reached him, he leaned back on his hands, his cocky demeanor masking something unsettling.

"Are you sure, baby?" he whispered, his tone now edged with menace. I hated it when he called me baby. "Wouldn't want to upset your little boyfriend."

I hesitated. I didn't want to do this. But the burning jealousy inside me drove me forward.

"He's not my boyfriend," I spat out.

I grabbed the front of Jackson's shirt like I had done so many times and was about to put my lips on his when a pair of strong hands grabbed my waist.

"This isn't fucking happening." The voice was deep, full of rage.

Before I could react, my feet were off the ground. Air rushed past as the world flipped, my stomach slamming into a stiff shoulder. The impact punched the breath from my lungs, a startled gasp tearing from my throat.

The ground swayed below me, distant and tilting, as I realized where I was. I was draped over Max's shoulder, his arm secured around my legs.

I clawed at his back, staring down at the forest floor as he hauled me away like I weighed nothing.

"Put me down!" My voice cracked, more desperate than defiant.

"No," his grip tightened, his breath rough against my side. "I'm not watching you self-destruct like this. Not with him."

My chest constricted.

The woods devoured us entirely as he dragged me deeper into the darkness, the night oppressive and silent except for the ragged sound of our breathing, growing frantic and uneven. We pressed on until we reached the old trail marker, a shadowy relic in the gloom. I looked at the tattered sign stapled to the tree, "Don't go off the trailhead," it read.

He released me abruptly, but held tight to my hand, his grip trembling. His eyes flashed wild and unhinged, quivering as if he thought I was mad at him.

"I didn't mean for that kiss to be—, I mean, I wasn't okay with Heather kissing me," he said, his voice small, almost regretful. He was stuttering, consumed by rage and jealousy, more drunk than I thought he was.

That was what he was apologizing for? I tried to think through the drunken fog in my brain, but I was pissed that he had kissed her, but not as pissed as I was about him intruding into my life and finding out my secret.

"Look, I'm sorry. I'm so fucking sorry," he spat out in broken words, his speech slurred. He sounded like he was on the verge of tears.

"Are you serious right now, Max?"

MAX

She waved her hands around, flustered, shrinking into herself again like she constantly did when things got real. There was no way I was allowing that fucker near her again, no fucking way. Not after everything I just heard them talk about.

I was done with him.

She wrapped her arms around her chest, closing me out.

"Don't fucking shut down on me," I spat out.

She wasn't doing this to me. Not this time. I needed her to tell me everything: how she felt, what she was thinking. *Everything.*

"Max, I can't believe you know. How the fuck do you know?" She was shaking with nerves, drunker than I realized. Her eyes were glassy, red-rimmed, brimming with tears.

My mind was going a mile a minute. I was on the edge of losing it, feeling like I was about to burst out of my own skin, trying to find a way to say, *"I've hacked into your life. It's because I love you. I do. I know your dad is a serial killer, and you're in the Witness Protection Program. And hey, my dad is CIA and has known who you are my whole life, and we're probably being watched right now, and we're in some weird game that I don't understand. And oh, our meeting seven years ago was probably part of an FBI plan."*

It sounded insane. Fucking insane. I was going insane... for her.

"It doesn't matter, okay?" I said. " I want you to know that it doesn't matter. I don't care what has happened to you. I mean, I care—Fuck, this isn't coming out right. I'm drunk."

My brain felt like it was sloshing inside my skull. Mackenzie was swaying like she was on a boat. She was just as drunk as I was, if not more.

"I... I... I just can't do this with you. I can't do this! I can't fucking do this!"

She ran her hands down her face, clawing at her neck like she wanted to tear her throat out. She started to back away from me, but I caught her by the wrist and held her in place.

"Don't leave," I hissed. She rolled her eyes and then gave me an exasperated look.

"I've spent my whole life living in secret, and I've been told that if anyone finds out about me, it puts my mom and me at risk. Shit. Max. How the hell did you find out? I need you to tell me the fucking truth!"

"I... uh... I..." I was stumbling for words. I didn't know how to break it to her. I didn't know that what I had done would jeopardize her safety. I was a fucking idiot. I had let my obsession with her take over everything.

"Forget it," she said flippantly, watching me struggle to figure out what to say. "I don't know how Jackson even knows. I've told him nothing. I'll probably end up getting sent away again, with a name change..."

She was crashing out in front of me.

"No, no, no, no. I can't lose you." I grabbed her by the shoulders, bending my head down a bit so I could look straight into her eyes. "We'll figure this out, okay?"

She looked at me then, incredulous. "I'm not figuring out anything with you. You really hurt me tonight. How could you do something like that to me, especially after knowing everything I've been through?"

"Don't play that game with me," I snapped, letting her go. "Heather kissed me! I didn't kiss her back."

"Why would you even allow it, after everything we've been doing together?"

"I'd never fucking cheat on you. I wouldn't. I'm faithful to you. Heather basically raped my face."

She looked away, unable to keep her eyes on mine.

"We're not together," her voice was small. "It wasn't cheating... at least I don't think. It just... hurt to watch."

That was a slap in the face. I didn't know what she wanted. One minute she was all over me, and the next I was just a friend.

"You're so unclear on what you want," I snapped.

"My thoughts have been pretty clear, Max," she deadpanned, looking me straight in the eye with a cold, callous glare.

We had always been able to read each other's thoughts. But not this time. She was so hot and cold. I had no idea what she was thinking these days. I mean, I had to basically read her damn journal to see how she really felt about me.

The heat in my face grew as my anger started to boil over. I'll admit, I was a hot head. I struggled with my anger issues. When I was drunk? All bets were off.

I snapped.

"I'm not a mind reader. Tell me you fucking want me. Use your words like a big girl."

She blinked as if I'd crossed a line, and maybe I had. But I didn't care. I saw the fire ignite in her eyes. Trouble was stubborn, fiercely independent, and hated being bossed around. Whenever she felt challenged, her fire emerged.

I saw it now: a quiet determination set her features, her jaw tightening, her eyes blazing as she took one step towards me.

"If you talk to me like that again, I'm going to grab your balls and squeeze them so hard you're going to squeal like a pig," she said with the bitchiest tone of voice I had heard from her this summer.

And I was fucking into it. This was the Trouble I wanted.

"Mmm. I'll probably like that because I've been imagining your hands on my balls every goddamn minute of the day."

Her mouth twisted. "Not happening. Whatever this was? Over."

"You think so?" I let out a short laugh. "Good. I can finally be put out of my misery then."

My voice was loud, really loud, and I was matching her drunken sway with my own. I looked around us. It was dark, the moonlight beaming down on us. I instinctively took one step towards her, trying to shield her.

She was quiet, not saying anything, but I could see her bottom lip trembling. I started to pace. I wanted to be more romantic in my words to her, but I was fucking pissed, actually.

"I know it's not fair. But I can't help it," I looked over at her, watching her body tremble, shake, as she held back the tears. "I look at you and wonder what he got from you that you won't give me. Why won't you give it to me? I've loved you since I was twelve years old. What the fuck else do you want from me?"

"You love me? You love me so much; you hacked into my life and have been fucking Heather behind my back?" she snapped. "Because I still can't get it out of my head. Her mouth on yours. Or the way you sat there and let the whole fucking circle think you got head at some party like you were proud of it. How many times has Heather sucked your dick?"

I gritted my teeth. First off, I couldn't believe these words were coming out of her mouth. Secondly? I was so fucking done with her thinking I was interested in anyone else. And lastly? Her fighting with me was turning me the fuck on.

"What the fuck is wrong with you?" I growled, stepping so close our bodies nearly collided. "You think you're some inno-cent angel? You bragged about cumming on someone's face. You think I didn't picture him when you said it? You think that didn't gut me?"

Her jaw dropped. Her eyes flashed, wounded and furious.

"It wasn't supposed to hurt you."

"Well, it did. It *really* fucking hurt. Why did you say it?"

"Because you hurt me first! You let Heather kiss YOU!"

"I didn't want that! She ambushed me. I told her to fuck off earlier."

"Could've fooled me," she shot back. "You looked like you wanted to."

I ran my hand through my hair.

"I cannot believe you are still fucking doing this! I sleep next to you every single night. I protect you. I fight for you. I would burn this whole fucking world to the ground if anyone touched you, hurt you. I got a tattoo with you. I let the entire camp believe we're together because you asked me to. I've kept your secret safe. I've been killing myself, telling you that I'm in love with you, that you are the love of my life, and you stand here and act as if none of it matters."

Her voice broke as she shouted, "You think I'm not hurting? You think this didn't gut me, too? You're my best friend, Max! The only person I trusted."

"I'm so far past friendship, Trouble. I can't even see the fucking line anymore. I don't care how messy you are, how many walls you've built. I'll tear down every single one. You're my home, Trouble. The only one I've ever had."

She stared at me, and I stared at her. I saw it all over her face: her guilt, rage, heartbreak. We were destroying each other.

"You're going to leave," she said quietly. "It's going to be too much for you when you really find out who I am."

"Oh, for fuck's sake, Trouble!" My voice cracked with anger. "I'm never walking away. Get that through your head. You're it for me. The love of my fucking life. Do you hear me? Nothing you've done, nothing you've lived through, changes that."

I stepped closer to her.

"Is your brain turned on tonight? Because I have a message for it." I cupped my hands around my mouth and aimed towards her. "*I can handle you.* You want to kill someone? Fine. I'll help you dispose of the body. You want to light your house on fire? I'll bring the gasoline. You want to go on a secret federal mission? Cool. I'll dress up in an FBI outfit. I think I'd look pretty hot in it."

She cracked a small smile.

"You want to slap me, punch me, bite me, throw me into a river, I'll let you do it, and then I'll drag my ass back to you. You want to run away and get married? I'll be there at the altar waiting for you. Fuck, I want to marry you now. I want it so badly. You. Are. The. One. I want YOU. I want all of you, even the pieces you hide from me. For the love of God, please, *please,* stop pushing me away."

We instinctively moved closer to each other. We were so close, our noses touching, and the fire between us was burning so hot that we were about to be engulfed in flames.

Her breathing stalled, and I could tell her anger was subsiding, replaced by a desire for me. Her eyes said it all; she loved me, too. My body was about to implode. I wanted to show her how much I loved her, craved her, and obsessed over her.

"Max… this is too real." She whined, but it was more of a whisper.

"Just tell me you love me. Tell me, please." I was begging now, but I had no shame in it.

I looked at her eyes, her mouth, her tits, and back up to her eyes. She licked her lips and pushed her hips into mine. I saw her take a few moments to decide if she wanted to say it, and then she looked right into my eyes, and I melted.

"I love you," she whispered.

I hesitated, laser-focused on those words coming out of her mouth. They cut through my drunken haze and buried themselves in my chest. The rational part of me was telling me to slow down. I needed to take things slow. She was suffering from trauma, and I needed to support her journey.

But the irrational part of my brain woke up as soon as her lips parted, and her eyes drank in my body, and then she whispered again against my lips, "Yes, I love you. I love you so much."

I blinked, listening to her voice crack when she said it, and then I snapped.

"Fuck it."

21

MACKENZIE

He pressed his mouth firmly against mine, his arms gripping me tightly. His strength was overwhelming. I didn't resist; within seconds, we were perfectly in sync. Our kiss deepened, passionate and hungry, as if we couldn't get enough of each other. Every sensation heightened, and everything else faded into the background. It was just us, lost in the intensity. We stumbled backward, my back hitting a tree as our desire ignited.

I wrapped my left leg around his waist, and we melted into each other. He pulled my swimsuit cover off and ran his hands over my body.

"So *fucking* perfect," he whispered into my mouth.

I moaned. My entire body lit up.

"You're mine," he growled against my skin. "Not his. Not anyone's. Say it."

"Yeah… yours," I moaned against his lips.

"No, that isn't good enough. Say my fucking name," he demanded, biting my bottom lip and sucking on it hard. I tasted copper on my tongue.

I swallowed, consumed by him.

"Max McKinnon... I'm yours."

He sighed into my mouth, his kisses growing more aggressive.

"Did he touch you like this?" He said, running his hand from my knee to my inner thigh. I ran my hands all over his chest, dragging the tip of my tongue up his neck. He tasted like lake water and pine. That subtle, sweet taste of him lingered on my tongue. He let out the most resounding groan, his eyes blown out wide.

"Did he kiss you like this?" He toyed with my hair, bringing my body closer to his, thrusting his tongue into my mouth. I matched him. Thrust to thrust, suck to suck. I grabbed the waistband of his swim shorts, fiddling with the string, trying to lower them.

"Fuck, Trouble. Touch me. Fucking touch me."

I was a complete mess when I heard him say that. I untied his swim trunks, slipping my hand inside, and grasped his length. He was thick, veined, and the size of him made my chest tighten with a mix of nerves and longing.

He moaned as I wiped my thumb on the head of his cock, feeling the warm pre-cum on my fingers. I gasped a little. His cock was throbbing, aching with his need for me.

"I can't fucking think straight with your hands on my dick," he whispered. "I'm dying to be inside you."

He pulled his shorts down and lifted me. I wrapped both legs around his waist, and he quickly pulled my bikini bottom to the side, swiping a finger down my slick center. I closed my eyes, letting out the deepest moan I think I had ever heard come out of my mouth. Every nerve ending was alive from his touch.

"So fucking wet. All for me," he grunted. I could feel him at my entrance, the tip of his cock hovering just there, right where I needed him. Desire pooled in his eyes, dark and deep as his gaze met mine.

"I love you," he whispered. "I can stop if you want me to, but I fucking want this. Please tell me you want this too."

I hesitated for just one second. We didn't have a condom. This was stupid. *So stupid.* But instead of stopping him, I nodded my head, and in one swift motion, he started pushing the head of his dick inside me.

I licked my lips and looked away then. I was nervous. I was scared I wouldn't be enough for him.

"Look at me," he groaned. "I want to see you. I want to see how good I make you feel. I want it all over your face."

I looked at him as he pushed even more into me, my body resisting him. He closed his eyes for a second before offering, "I can… go slow?"

I didn't want him to go slow. I shook my head, matching his thoughts. "I want it hard and fast. But I'm scared."

His throat worked, and he nodded, the weight of my words sinking into him. For a moment, something dark flickered in his gaze, but it softened almost instantly. His hand brushed along my jaw, trembling but steadying me all at once.

He kissed me softly, and then stilled in front of me, pushing the rest of his cock inside me to the hilt.

"You can fucking take it, baby," he groaned as I adjusted to him. "All of it."

I gasped out, feeling him stretch me open. I was so full, I could feel every inch of him.

"That's it, baby," he whispered. "You're mine. Every inch. Just let me in."

He filled me so completely I thought I might break apart, but underneath the pain was heat. My chest rose and fell against his, my pulse racing as I tried to catch my breath.

"I… oh God, Max." My voice trembled, but he remained still inside me, waiting for me. I held him tighter, craving the firm weight of his body. My body instinctively pressed against him, aching for movement, for the friction of his touch.

I started moving naturally on my own against him. His forehead pressed against mine.

"Are you on birth control?" His voice was so needy.

"No," I stammered. "We probably shouldn't do this." It was weak, even he knew we weren't stopping.

He nodded his head.

"It doesn't matter. I'm making you my wife after this." He said it so seriously, and I almost choked on my spit.

"Wh—what?"

"I want to protect you. Fucking forever. No one else is going to get you after this."

This was crazy. Was he... proposing to me while he was balls-deep inside my pussy? He sounded like a man half-crazy with fear and love and desire. I looked into his eyes.

He was dead serious.

I dropped my head onto his shoulder as he started thrusting into me. I should've stopped him. But I lifted my hips, meeting his thrusts. I was his, and I had been ever since that very first day we had met when we were twelve years old.

MAX

FUUUUUUCKKKKKKKKKK.

I had never been with a girl without a condom before.

Holy fuck. I could see why people did it. Her pussy was gripping my dick so tight, and I was ten seconds away from cumming inside her. I had to stop myself; otherwise, I would.

"Fuck, you're so tight. I can barely get in. You feel that?" I pushed more, completely sheathing myself inside her. "Holy shit. Your pussy takes me so well. No one else could ever fit like this," I groaned, my eyes closed. "You good, baby?"

She gasped loudly, nodding her head, and she clawed at my back as if she were trying to crawl inside me. I held her up against the tree with one hand while my other hand gripped her thigh. I grounded myself as I thrust hard and deep inside her.

I sank into her, inch by inch, until I couldn't tell where she ended, and I began. She was so tight it felt like her body was trying to push me out, but I forced myself deeper. I was being incredibly greedy with her, but I wanted to claim every bit of space.

We were drunk on each other. She sloppily kissed me, biting my bottom lip, and I moaned, literally moaned, into her mouth. I had never done that with anyone before. I had completely lost control.

"You feel fucking amazing, Max," she breathed out.

It was more of a scream than anything. But I wouldn't make it if she talked to me like that, screamed like that.

"Trouble, Jesus. Please fucking say yes. I want you forever."

I was so flustered and consumed by her that I could barely think, and I couldn't stop the words from tumbling out of my mouth. I was a lunatic for proposing to her this way, but I fucking wanted it. Mackenzie was moaning so loudly in my ear that I thought she had burst my eardrum. I must've been loud too because she kept whispering, "Sshhhh."

And then a soft, "Yes," came out from her mouth. I grinned as I bent down to kiss her.

She was mine.

I was fucking her so hard I was starting to see stars. The sound of our skin slapping against each other echoed through the trees. I was pretty sure I was hitting her cervix because her moans were damn near shrieks at this point. Every scream made me even harder.

I wasn't paying attention to anything around us. I was

completely consumed with the sounds of Mackenzie moaning, our bodies melting into each other, and the insane groans I was emitting. Suddenly, the wind picked up sharply, and a disturbing sound echoed behind us, startling me and sending a chill down my spine.

"Holy shit! Oh, my fucking, God!" Megan screamed.

I froze, snapping my head around. Megan's mouth was wide open as she took in the sight of us fucking each other against the tree. Mackenzie whispered in my ear, "Oh my God, I can't… Max. I can't stop it."

Her body convulsed around me, pulling me deeper. The sound she made, half sob, half moan, was enough to shred the last of my control as I felt the beginning of her orgasm shatter against me.

I turned back towards her. I drove into her, chasing it, needing it, whispering in her ear, "Cum for me, baby." My release slammed through me at the same time hers did, both of us shuddering. I damn near passed out.

"Fuck," I whispered, dropping my forehead against hers.

Mackenzie buried her face in my neck, trembling, both of us humiliated. I held her tighter, breath ragged. It would be just our luck that the first time we fucked, we would have an audience.

We were always being watched.

Mackenzie gave me a quick look, and I'd fucking die in those eyes. I didn't think it was possible, but I loved her even more now.

Megan stumbled back, her eyes darting as if she wasn't sure whether to run or applaud.

"What the—what the fuck, guys. That's—Jesus. I knew… I knew you were fucking!"

Mackenzie shoved me off her, unwrapping her legs from my waist, and I whimpered like a wounded dog when my dick fell out of her. I wanted to live inside her.

My heart was in my throat. My shorts were halfway hanging

off my ass, my dick throbbing from the loss of contact. Mackenzie's bikini top was crooked, one of her tits hanging out. She so intoxicated me that I couldn't focus on what was happening.

Megan turned, covering her eyes.

"Oh shit, okay. I didn't see anything. Damn, damn, damn… Max. Fuck." She covered her eyes, then looked again at my dick, shock across her face. She ran back towards camp, stumbling a bit.

Mackenzie immediately grabbed her swimsuit cover, pulled it over her body, and fixed her bikini bottoms.

She whispered something to me.

"Huh?" I had no idea what she had just said because I was a madman from her touch, her kiss, her moans.

We both stared at each other, the weight of what we had just done settling in over us.

We had unprotected sex. I had cum inside her. Fuck. What had we done?

She looked away first, and my chest cracked wide open as she walked away from me. I watched her go, the night swallowing her. I was hurting because she had taken a piece of me with her tonight—the piece that would never be able to let her go.

I should've been more upset about possibly getting her pregnant, more nervous. But the sick part?

I wasn't. Because I was now a part of her. She couldn't shed her skin without shedding a part of me.

22

MACKENZIE

The walk back to camp was quiet. Max jogged beside me, his fingers brushing mine once, as if he wanted to retake my hand but didn't. He was breathing heavily.

My lips tingled, and my body still ached for him. I was so wet, his cum was dripping out of me, and I could barely walk. He had felt so good. I couldn't stop thinking about it. His hands were all over me, his strength supporting me against the tree. His kisses. His moans. His everything.

I had never felt such a deep connection to another person as I had with him. It was undeniable, our chemistry with each other.

And I guess we were engaged? Oh my God. We were nuts. We were both so drunk, not thinking clearly at all. But it felt… right? He had fucked the sense out of me, and I wasn't even sure if I wanted it back.

God, we were idiots.

The campfire flickered in the distance, shadows dancing between trees. Laughter floated in the air. Megan was telling everyone how she had caught us. That we had fucked like rabbits, that she hoped I was on birth control because Max probably got me pregnant with the way we were carrying on.

"I swear to God. I've never seen anything like that in my life. They were all over each other. It was straight-up porno level. Like, Max is a fucking freak. I'm jealous. I've never had sex like that."

The laughter died as soon as we emerged from the trees.

Max's hair was disheveled, his lips swollen. I probably looked the same. It wasn't a secret what we had just done. You could see it all over us. Max gravitated towards me even closer now than he did before.

The first person I noticed was Heather. Her face instantly fell as soon as she saw Max. I glanced at Max to see if he was looking at her, but he was only watching me. The love shining from him was both disarming and endearing, and by the way he was looking at me, I could tell I shared the same expression.

We were undeniably in love with each other. My love for him surged through my entire body. His love was bursting from his skin. But a sharp laugh from the left pierced my soul, pulling me out of my love-filled daze.

"So what? You two fucking now?" Jackson's gaze fixed on Max, and it no longer flickered with jealousy or hate. It was dark —something twisted, cold, and simmering beneath the surface.

Max remained silent. I moved to step in between them, trying to diffuse the tension, but Jackson was already approaching.

"Must've been something with the way you two were carrying on. You forgot you had an audience? Sounds echo through these woods. We all fucking heard you."

Max's jaw clenched. "Back off."

Jackson's lips curled into a snarl.

"Why? You think you have her now? You think that because you fucked her that she's yours now?" He leaned into Max's face, licking his lips. "That's not how this works."

My stomach dropped, and a cold wave of dread rippled through me.. "How does *what* work?"

Jackson took another step towards me, reaching out to grab my arm, and Max lost it.

He moved faster than I'd ever seen him, a blur of aggression. One second he was beside me, and the next, he was slamming Jackson back with both hands on his chest.

"Don't touch her," Max snapped, his voice a low, guttural growl, territorial and savage.

Jackson blinked in surprise, then smirked defiance like someone dared him to do worse.

"Oh. Is she yours now? We'll see about that."

He lunged forward and swung wildly.

Max reacted instinctively, ducking the punch and answering with a brutal uppercut that cracked against Jackson's jaw, sending him staggering back. Jackson howled in pain, clutching his face as blood trickled down his fingers.

Campers screamed and scattered in all directions, chaos erupting around us. The noise was deafening, overwhelming. When I looked up, only Megan, Max, Jackson, and I remained, caught in the nightmare.

"She's going to scream your name while I take her apart, and you'll be rotting in the ground, helpless to stop it," Jackson hissed, his voice cracked with madness. Max didn't hesitate. He charged forward like a linebacker, wrapping both arms around Jackson and throwing him down onto the grass, forcing him into the earth with a brutal force that trembled beneath them.

They collapsed in a hissing tangle of limbs and dirt. I stumbled backward, my foot catching on a hidden root. The world spun wildly as I fell. The jagged edge of a rock at the path's rim slammed into the back of my head with a sickening crunch. Bright pain exploded behind my eyes. I tasted metal.

I tried to rise, but my head swam. Megan was suddenly there, grabbing my arm with frantic strength. "Mackenzie! Mackenzie, look at me!" she yelped, yanking me upright.

Adrenaline surged through my veins, giving me a fleeting sense of safety. Then, Megan's tone shifted. "You're bleeding!"

I stared down, my vision dimming as blood darkened the hand that had touched the back of my head. Blinking painfully, stars burst behind my closed eyes. The world tilted violently, and in that moment, I saw it—something glinting sharply in Jackson's hand.

"No!" I screamed, voice cracked with fear.

I lunged toward them, desperate to block whatever was happening, but a brutal, unfamiliar sting suddenly numbed the pain in my head. A scorching, hot pressure seized my side.

"Oh." My breath hitched as I crumpled, clutching my side and collapsing to my knees.

Max's scream shattered the tense air. He sounded pained, frantic, warped with terror. I tried to turn, but everything narrowed, sound tunneling into a deafening roar.

Max broke free with a burst of strength, sliding toward me like a runner heading for home, leaving Jackson writhing on the grass behind him, clutching his arm in agony. Was his arm broken? It appeared shattered.

Max reached me in an instant, his hands burning with heat and desperation, frantic as he worked at my side.

"Mackenzie… Hey, baby, look at me. It's Max. Breathe, baby. Breathe."

His voice was everything. It was full of terror and frantic command, cutting through the chaos. It yanked me back, holding me there with him. He pressed his palms hard against my shirt, where warmth was spreading, fingers clenched as if trying to stop the world with sheer force.

"Call for help!" someone screamed. Megan's face hovered close, ghostly pale. I smelled smoke, grass, and the sickly metallic tang of blood. Max's voice grew more frantic. He kept talking to me, pressing down, holding on.

Was he crying? I heard heavy sobs, echoing as black shadows threatened to swallow my vision.

I tried to speak, but only a hollow, rasping sound escaped. My legs folded beneath me, and the last thing I saw was Max's face looming over mine. Blood stained his forehead, his lips parted in silent panic, eyes wide with terror. He kept talking, voice cracking, telling me about tattoos, light, and stupid little things he loved—things that felt miles away now.

He told me how much he loved me. He told me about the first time he knew he was in love with me, and about all the babies we were going to have together. I let the rhythm of his words hold me as the world went soft and distant.

Then it all faded.

Except for his voice.

23

———

MAX

Her voice faded away. The silence echoed softly among the trees in a quiet moan.

All I could hear was my staccato breathing, Megan's gasps, and Jackson's uncontrolled hissing. My whole fucking world cracked in half as I looked down at Mackenzie.

Blood blurred my vision, sticky and thick in my mouth, damp on my hands. Around me, the world narrowed to a tunnel of terror, trees looming like a silent, malevolent army.

"I… Oh my God… baby, wake up." I continued to press my hands onto Mackenzie's wound. The blood was pouring out of her. It was all over me. "Hold… hold her, please."

Megan got down onto her knees and cradled Mackenzie, while I took off my shirt and bunched it up. I pressed it down hard against Mackenzie's wound and then pulled her back into my arms.

"She's going to be okay, right?" Megan's voice cut through the chaos.

I turned to Jackson, who was cradling his arm, drenched in blood. The bloody knife was on the ground.

"You fucking stabbed her, you sick fuck!" I screamed. A

panic unlike anything I'd experienced before ripped through my chest. I thought I knew fear, but this? Seeing her slip away right in front of my eyes was agony.

This was hell.

I pressed my hand against her cheek, desperate to wake her. But her eyes rolled into the back of her head, and she lay perfectly still in my arms.

"She's… she's not okay. She's not opening her eyes! She's not fucking opening her eyes! Mackenzie. Mackenzie, look at me, baby. Look at me, please."

"Max!" Megan sobbed violently. "We have to call 911. I'm calling an ambulance." She yanked her phone out.

I shook Mackenzie lightly, terrified to shake harder. My chest was caving in, my ribs splintering under the pressure of losing her.

I would never survive it.

"Oooh, is she dead? Too bad. I was looking forward to peeling her skin off on our wedding night."

I looked up at Jackson, watching him smile through the dark blood dripping down his face.

I was going to kill him. I was going to bash his brains out with my baseball bat and then feed his brain to a dog. I had never wanted to commit murder before, but the act of it was something I welcomed. The thought of it brought me joy. Because my hatred for Jackson was the strongest it had ever been in that moment.

"I'm going to fucking kill you," I snarled. "And everyone you've ever known." My voice was venomous, filled with rage that he clearly sensed. His smile faded instantly, replaced by a flicker of terror.

He thought he was bad? I was worse. I was always going to be worse. All bets were off when it came to Mackenzie.

Megan shifted nervously, eyes darting between us. "Jackson,

you've got about ten minutes before the cops arrive. You'd better run."

"Fuck that," I snapped, rising to my feet. I handed Mackenzie back to Megan and pressed my blood-stained hands against my face, smudging the gore into a grim mask. The caged Max was finally unleashed. "I'll give you a head start before I rip your limbs off, one by one."

A small hand pressed against my chest, stopping me in my tracks. I looked down to see Megan's cold, distant eyes.

"Max. Mackenzie needs you. Your chase is over," she said quietly, with an unsettling calm.

I glanced back at Mackenzie's distorted, lifeless body, and then turned to Jackson, who was frozen, staring at her.

"Don't you dare look at her like that, or I swear I'll gouge your eyes out. Promise me, Jackson—next time I see you, I won't hold back. Run, motherfucker."

He didn't hesitate. He took off into the darkness. I was about to pursue him, but a soft, agonized sob slipped from Mackenzie's pale lips, drawing me back down to her, clutching her trembling form.

"Baby, look at me. Please. You're mine, do you hear me? You're not leaving me," I rasped, my words harsh and trembling as sobs choked my throat. I pressed my forehead against hers, my mind consumed by an overwhelming fear. I was thinking of how deeply I loved her, how I had always loved her, and the terror that gripped me at the thought of losing her forever.

"Open your eyes, Mackenzie Anne Hamill! Please, just open them!" I begged, desperation thick in my voice.

"Max… the ambulance will be here in fifteen minutes," Megan's voice was distant, almost drowned out by the pounding in my ears. Only the frantic, ragged sound of Mackenzie struggling to breathe against me remained clear.

I lifted my gaze and met Megan's wide, panicked eyes. Something inside me shattered.

"I'm taking her to the hospital now. I won't wait for her to die," I said, my voice haunted and urgent.

My decision was final. There was no universe where anyone could argue with me. I stood, cradling Mackenzie in my arms, her head lolling into my chest. The sight of her blood soaking into my shirt nearly brought me to my knees, a scream trapped in my throat.

Megan started to say something, but I cut her off with a murderous glare so sharp she silenced instantly. No one was stopping me.

"I've got you, baby," I whispered into Mackenzie's hair, my lips brushing her damp forehead as my hands trembled violently. "I've got you."

Rage and terror flooded through every step I took toward the camp gates, my breath ragged and shallow. I ran to the cabin with her in my arms, grabbing my wallet and truck keys in a frantic blur. Bloody fingerprints smeared across the nightstand as I seized them, mind racing.

"I'm not losing you," I muttered like a vow, clutching her tighter as if to hold her from slipping away. By the time I shoved open the camp's front gates, my chest heaved wildly, my mind a chaotic storm. Rational thought had vanished. Only raw, primal instinct remained: get her safe, get her healed, keep her alive at all costs.

If anyone tried to stop me, I would destroy them.

As I forcefully charged through the ER doors 15 minutes later, chaos erupted around us. People were shouting and screaming at the sight of us. I was half-dressed, drenched in a sickening mixture of my blood and Mackenzie's, the scent almost suffocating. The squeal of gurney wheels echoed like nails on a chalkboard. Someone desperately tried to yank her from my grasp, but I clung on, brutally unwilling to let her go.

"She... she hit her head. She was stabbed... D-don't you dare waste time..." My voice cracked into a guttural cry, losing all composure. I could feel my mind slipping, unable to hold back the terror and despair.

"Sir, please, step back," a nurse commanded, grabbing my arm roughly.

"Don't fucking touch me!" I spat, my grip tightening on Mackenzie. "She isn't leaving my arms until you swear she'll be okay."

Two orderlies moved in quickly, their faces cold and intimidating. Realizing I was blocking the way, I reluctantly lowered her onto the stretcher, my hands shaking as I gently brushed her blood-matted hair from her face.

"Get vitals," a nurse said quickly. The cuff inflated around her arm with a hiss.

"BP eighty over fifty, pulse one-forty, tachycardic. Respiration's shallow," another nurse rattled off, already clipping a pulse ox to her finger. "SpO_2 ninety-two percent."

The ER doctor appeared in the same instant, eyes sharp and voice calm. "Airway's intact for now. She's talking?"

"No, unresponsive," the nurse answered.

"Okay—two large-bore IVs, fluids wide open. Oxygen, non-rebreather, fifteen liters. Apply direct pressure to that stab wound, left flank. Get a type and cross, send blood, and page trauma surgery now."

Gloved hands pressed gauze to the wound, red blooming through the white. Someone slipped an oxygen mask over her face. Machines began to beep.

"FAST exam at bedside, CT head and abdomen once she's stable."

"Step back, sir," the charge nurse barked without even looking at me. Her tone was flat, practiced. My legs obeyed before my brain could argue.

"I'm not leaving her." My voice cracked.

"You can follow in the hallway," she shot back, already pushing the stretcher. "But she goes to trauma now."

And then she was gone, swallowed whole by an overwhelming tide of scrubs and clipped voices, while I stumbled after, powerless. My heart pounded so loudly it drowned out the monitors. Inside the trauma bay, chaos erupted.

Gloves snapped onto hands, monitors screeched, voices shouting over each other in frantic, disjointed commands. Orders yelled amid the chaotic, synchronized movement of the team: gauze pressed desperately into the bleeding wound, IV bags spiked and hung, machines blared ominous numbers into the suffocating air.

"Stay with us," a nurse's strained voice whispered as they shoved meds into her line. I stood paralyzed at the edge of the turmoil, helpless, watching strangers fight desperately to keep her alive. I clutched Mackenzie's hand tighter, feeling the cold grip of terror and helplessness.

"Sir, I'm sorry, but next of kin only." The nurse put her hands on my chest and tried to push me out of the room.

"I am her next of kin," I said curtly. The lie was instinct, primal. It just happened.

"And you are?" The nurse eyed me inquisitively.

"Her husband."

The nurse paused, sizing me up. I was eighteen, but my size made me look older. She relented, grabbing a clipboard and a pen.

"Okay, husband, I need details on our Jane Doe. Patient ID, age, allergies, medications, blood type."

"Mackenzie McKinnon…"

My voice was shaking, but I rattled off all the information as if it was second nature because it was. I knew Mackenzie. I knew her so well.

"Any past medical conditions or surgeries?"

"Concussion from soccer last year. Her appendix was removed three years ago." The sobs were taking over my entire body.

"Okay, Mr. McKinnon," the nurse said briskly, already moving me back towards Mackenzie. I stood frozen, my chest caving in with every clipped order. She wasn't responding. Her hand didn't squeeze mine back. Her pulse—God, I could feel how weak it was.

"Mackenzie… please," I whispered. My throat burned. "Don't leave me."

They lifted her to a transport gurney, voices around us sharp.

"Sir, you can't follow into CT," the nurse cut me off firmly at the door. "You'll wait in her room. We'll bring her back as soon as imaging is done."

I nodded weakly, watching the doors slam shut behind them. I clutched the railing tightly, my hands trembling uncontrollably, a sinking dread pooling in my chest as I fought to breathe. Just as darkness threatened to overwhelm me, cold, unyielding hands settled heavily on my shoulders.

"Are you Max?" A calm, almost too-perfect voice pierced the chaos.

His tailored charcoal suit was crisp, his white shirt casually undone at the collar, a heavy, gleaming watch strapped to his wrist. His polished black shoes echoed sharply on the silent tile floor.

He carried himself with an unsettling confidence, like someone who owned the place, or believed he could destroy it if he didn't get what he wanted. Broad-shouldered, clean-shaven, hair slicked back with precision. His eyes held a coldness that stared right through me, as if I were nothing more than an obstacle.

For a second, I thought mafia. He looked like the kind of guy you'd see slipping into the back room of a dimly lit club, making men twice his size sweat bullets with a cold, blank stare. He stepped back a few feet as I sized him up, and the corner of his mouth tilted in a slow, sinister grin.

"Yeah? Whose asking?" I said in my deepest, hoarse growl.

I didn't care that tears blurred my eyes, pooling and spilling over.

Then he cracked a smile, but it didn't reach his eyes. "You must be… the… boyfriend."

There was a faint hesitation, like he was calling us out on our bluff, or testing how much we could take.

"Who are you?" I shot back, my voice sharper, standing straighter without realizing I had.

He didn't flinch, just looked at me with an unsettling calm.

"I come in peace," he said, raising his hands slowly, fingers twitching. "Names West. Tony West."

"You watching us?" I asked, voice trembling slightly, a chilling sense of dread creeping in.

He smiled again, but his expression was sad. "Does it matter?"

"I'm not interested in whatever fucked-up game this is."

He let out a breath and looked towards the trauma bay. A look of concern flickered across his face, then vanished.

"She's going to be okay," West said quietly, more to himself than to me. "But you need to calm down, or you'll make this worse."

I snarled, shaking my head. "I don't fuckin' know you."

West's jaw tightened. He leaned in until his voice was almost a whisper. "When someone you care about gets hurt on your watch, it cuts deeper than you can imagine. You become fiercely protective. But you also get practical. Step aside for those who know how to fix this without risking everything. If you want to help her, stop making it about you."

My fists clenched. "Nah. Fuck off."

West didn't answer. He simply shoved his hands deeper into his pockets and tilted his head, studying me with a half-smirk, half-grimace. His gaze was heavy, measuring, weighing his words with calculated precision. I hated the way it made me feel, like a fragile specimen on display.

"I think you're capable of a lot when it comes to her," he finally said, his voice flat and cold, almost clinical. "But she's also your weakness. When she breaks, you break. And when you break, you get dangerous."

Those words clawed at me because they weren't wrong. But what the hell gave this guy the right to question who I was?

My eyes narrowed. "You got here pretty quick," I spat, voice thick with suspicion. "How many cameras are set up at the camp, huh?"

I threw it at him to see if it landed, and it did, as a flicker of irritation flashed across his face.

"Didn't take you long to figure it out, did it?" His voice was steady, then he let out a short, cold laugh. "We flagged the breach the second you touched the firewall. You were clever, but reckless. Your dad told us you'd figure it out."

He was baiting me. It irritated me more.

"I don't want to talk about him now," I shot back. "I'll deal with him later."

West's voice turned flat, almost mocking. "He's the one who laid the trail for you, the breadcrumbs you followed. Did you really think it'd be that easy to hack into FBI files?"

My stomach dropped. My dad had wanted me to find Mackenzie's history. Why would he do that?

"If you'd watched Mackenzie half as closely as you watched me, she wouldn't be in this hospital fighting for her life. I blame you both." I stepped closer, close enough that he had to look up at me. "And I know for a fact the FBI doesn't tell the CIA shit."

West's face tightened, something private crossing it. He looked away for a beat. Mackenzie was his weakness, too. He didn't want to admit it.

"What is she to you anyway?" I asked, my voice catching as I looked him straight in the eye. He bit his bottom lip, hesitating just a moment before saying, "She's family. I... see her as a daughter."

The words hit me harder than I expected, a stabbing blow of reality. He was actually being honest. I took a step closer, my voice trembling. "So, if she's your family, you'd do anything to protect her, right?" I pressed, vulnerability flickering. "She's my family, too. I love her. I'd do anything for her."

My eyes darted down the hall, longing to see her walk toward me, to end this nightmare. "Look, I get it, she's got a past. That stays between us. But I don't like being messed with. And I certainly don't like getting watched. I don't know what game you're playing, but I'm sick of it. So, hear me now—fuck off."

West's face remained calm, but his eyes pierced through me, icy and sharp. "Fast reactions save lives, Max. But anger doesn't. Keep that in mind." His tone was flat, but I sensed the threat underneath. My chest still hammered with panic and adrenaline, yet beneath it all, my mind spun. He hadn't intended to reveal everything, but unfortunately for him, I was smarter than he realized.

They're tracking everything: every step, every second. And I didn't even notice until now.

West studied me, that faint smirk pulling at the corner of his mouth.

His eyes lingered on me, intensity burning behind them. "You've got focus, instinct—a talent for reading people under pressure. If you could just channel that..." His gaze dragged over my body. "You'd be a problem. The kind you don't want to face. In the best way."

I froze, shivering despite myself. A problem? The word echoed in my mind. I already was a fucking problem. He just didn't know it yet. Before I could speak, the nurse reappeared, wheeling Mackenzie's gurney into view. She was still unmoving, eyes closed. West and I stepped forward instinctively.

"She's stable," the nurse said hurriedly, her voice tinged with urgency, noticing the panic flickering in my eyes. "We've stopped the bleeding from the stab wound. No major vessels hit.

The wound's sutured and packed. She's not actively hemorrhaging anymore. Her blood pressure remains stable with fluids, and her oxygen saturation is good. The CT scan came back clear. No skull fracture, no intracranial bleed. She's still unresponsive, but her pupils are reactive. She's breathing on her own."

A strangled sob escaped me as relief flooded over me.

She was breathing.

"Thank you," I choked out.

"She's not out of danger yet," the nurse said softly, her voice cold with necessity. "But she's alive. She's stable. That's good news."

I nodded fiercely; my throat felt constricted, my words caught in my throat.

"Can I sit beside her? Please."

She studied me long and hard, then finally nodded. "Alright. Just stay out of the way of the team."

I didn't wait for her to change her mind. I was already moving when West stepped into my path.

"Let me."

The nurse blinked at him, her expression cautious. "And you are?"

"I'm her step-dad," West said smoothly, a hint of coldness lacing his tone.

Well, that was news to me. I fought to hide the shock that flashed across my face, but failed.

"Sorry," the nurse said, her voice clipped and firm. "Immediate family only."

West tilted his head slightly, playing it cool, then nodded toward the waiting room. "Come on, Max."

"Mr. McKinnon can come in. He's her next of kin."

West froze, his eyes narrowing into slits. A flicker of calculation behind them. In an instant, I saw him piece it together. He was noticing the way I moved, the way I claimed her, the way she belonged to me. This wasn't some teenage fantasy. We were deeper.

For the first time, West's posture shifted. He wasn't confident anymore; he was guarded, wary. He was sizing me up, weighing his words.

"Next of kin?" he asked, voice tight and tense.

"Yeah," I said, glaring at him. "Husband. Thought you knew." The nurse glanced between us, rolled her eyes, and hurried back into the room.

A tense silence settled, broken only by a faint, knowing smile spreading across his face. "We'd have been alerted if you two got married. Don't try to lie to me."

"I proposed, she said yes. Same difference."

"I underestimated you," he exhaled, voice edged with disdain.

I stepped closer, voice cold. "We're meant to be together; it was a long time coming. When I finally make her mine legally, I'm taking her away from all this fucked-up bullshit."

He nodded slowly, but his eyes stayed fixed on mine. "Sure. Call me when you have news. Mackenzie knows how to reach me." He turned to leave, shoulders stiff, but his voice cut through the air as he faced me again. "You may call yourself her fiancé, Max, but this is bigger than you. Lying about next of kin gets you in the door, but it complicates evidence, custody, and all sorts of legal messes you don't understand. You just made yourself a target."

"I don't give a fuck," I spat.

He tsked once, thinking, then something in his face shifted, his expression cold and determined. "If you want her protected, I can assure you she's being protected." He spoke with a chilling calm. "We started with the obvious. I already filed a formal assault report, notified law enforcement, and pushed for an immediate arrest warrant for Jackson. I'm working to have the hospital security secure the area and place her under constant guard. We'll secure an emergency protective order, and I'll personally demand priority for the investigation."

"That's not nearly enough," I said flatly, my voice tense. "Don't forget—you've been watching her, and you couldn't even protect her. I can do a far better job than you and your team ever could."

He paused, fixing me with that same, unblinking stare. "I know what you're thinking. But marriage doesn't buy safety."

"With me, it does."

He scrutinized me from head to toe, a grim smile creeping onto his face. "She won't have the same level of protection from you that she has from us."

"Make me one of you then," I snapped, my voice sharp and fierce.

"You're not ready," he responded calmly, looking at his nails as if he had already been thinking about it. I stepped closer to him, so close that he had to look up at me. His pupils dilated. He wasn't scared, but a smirk on his lips revealed he respected me.

"I'm ready."

He tilted his head, studying me with that flat, unreadable stare.

"You think this is a badge and a gun, and suddenly you're untouchable? It's not. This is training, surveillance, rules you don't even know exist. It's years of losing pieces of yourself."

"I don't care. If it keeps her safe, I'll do it."

His mouth curved into a faint smile.

"I get that. But the Bureau doesn't just hand out shields because someone's desperate. We recruit, we evaluate, we test." His gaze flicked to me again. "And you don't even know what we'd ask of you."

"I don't care," I said louder, my voice echoing with a hint of desperation.

West's eyes softened just a fraction, but beneath that, an icy chill lingered. "Careful, Max. You're opening a door you can't close. You're not ready yet. But… maybe someday." He tapped his finger against the wall like a silent gavel.

"I can't believe I'm saying this. Mackenzie's mom is going to kill me, but if you two want to make this real and legal, I can speed things up: contact a magistrate, push the paperwork, and find someone to witness it here. I'll also facilitate channels if she needs to be relocated or placed under protective custody again."

"Great," I said, turning away. "Do that."

"You know what's more useful than vows right now, Max? A prosecutor ready to file charges, a judge prepared to sign a protective order, and a security detail that doesn't sleep."

"That's not enough," I snarled bitterly. "There's something— someone—watching her constantly. Do you really think all that will protect her? We're up against some crazy, sick conspiracy group, if everything in her file is accurate. Am I wrong? Is she part of that legacy program? They want to breed her, right? Don't feed me bullshit."

He paused.

"You dug farther than I thought," he laughed softly, a hint of menace behind it. He hesitated briefly before adding, "Your dad will be proud."

His eyes lingered on me, measuring, assessing. I could feel the weight of his stare. I rolled my eyes.

"Again, I'll deal with my father later."

He smirked darkly, nodding slowly.

"Listen, kid. You're smart, real smart."

His gaze dragged down my frame as if he was trying to see something deeper. I towered over him, six-four, broad-shoul- dered, more like a linebacker than a college ballplayer. West was barely five-ten, wiry, compact, bearing the mark of someone who'd seen too much. Age, training, the weight of the badge— all of it showed. But standing this close, the difference was impossible to ignore. I could crush him in an instant.

"I know you could handle yourself… handle Mackenzie. But

you need to understand the stakes. This is adult-level shit that you're not ready for. I can help you. I'll cover the legal and security sides, but don't think lying will protect you. It's a liability." The room seemed to close in around me with his next words, as if the shadows grew darker.

"They're going to come for you, you know that, right? The *Alliance*."

I knew what he was talking about. I had read it in her file. The group that was watching us. But it was the first time someone had said it out loud. I should've been nervous, scared even, but I wasn't. Because I'd do whatever I needed to do to save her.

"I'll be ready," I said, because I *was* ready. I'd take on anything that came her way. "By the way, isn't your job to protect her from them? Or have you fucked that up too?"

West's jaw dropped the barest degree, then he nodded once.

"Fuck you, Max," he said, his voice edged with a tense, almost threatening tone. "Just stay out of the way."

I clenched my jaw so tightly my teeth ached. "You don't get it. I already vowed. She's mine. She said yes when I asked her. And if being her husband on paper makes one more person think twice about touching her, that's what I'm doing."

He studied me, eyes narrow, waiting for me to back down. I didn't. My pulse pounded loudly in my ears, my chest aching at the thought of her slipping away.

Finally, West exhaled slowly, reluctantly. "Marriage is a big fucking deal, kid. You really want to chain yourself to that decision right now? You're not even nineteen."

"Yes." My voice was sharp, unwavering, resolute. "I'll call your boss if I have to. I'll go to the media and tell them everything. An FBI agent marrying his protective order? An FBI agent shadowing two high school kids at a summer camp? An FBI agent letting a secret society surveil them? I know there's some illegal shit happening here. Tell me that doesn't reek of corruption."

His brows drew tight, a faint tic in his jaw. He was already imagining the calls he'd have to make.

"Jesus Christ," he muttered, running a hand over his mouth. "You don't let go, do you?"

"Not with her." My voice broke, but I stayed firm. "Never with her."

Resignation flickered in his eyes. He shook his head once.

"Fine. I'll see what strings I can pull. I'll get a protective order secured for both of you. I'll reduce the number of people watching you two, but I'll keep one or two protective assets in the shadows. But when this blows up, it's on you." He stepped closer, voice cold and final. "And when Mackenzie wakes up and finds out what you've done, I hope she beats the shit out of you."

I laughed deeply and heavily. The sound of my laughter echoed off the walls, settling between us.

"Sounds like a plan… *dad.*"

I didn't mean to say it, but the way his face changed told me I wasn't wrong.

24

MACKENZIE

A rhythmic, shrill beeping echoed through my head.

Beep, beep, beep.

The sound echoed harshly off the cold, barren walls. I slowly forced my eyes open, feeling the gritty grip of a heavy hand clutching mine. Where was I? I turned my head and saw Max. He looked... unsettling, somehow. Older, with an unnatural energy flickering beneath his skin, his blue eyes glinting dangerously. They softened just slightly as he watched me struggle to stay conscious.

My heartbeat pounded deafeningly in my ears as he crouched beside the bed, his hand tightening around mine. "You're awake. Finally," he whispered, his hands suddenly cupping my face, fingers tracing through my damp hair.

Dried blood streaked his clothes, darkening his hair, sharpening his features into something menacing. He peppered frantic, lingering kisses over my face, neck, and hair, as if trying to drown me in his madness.

"What… what happened?" My voice came out high and fragile, nothing like my usual tone.

"You were stabbed." His voice cracked, eyes wide, knuckles

white as he gripped my hand. "Right side, near your ribs. I... I thought I'd lost you. They said you were bleeding fast, your blood pressure dropped, and your pulse skyrocketed. You went into shock."

"What?" I screeched out in a hoarse voice.

He sucked in a shaky breath. "They stabilized you... lost a lot of blood. You scared the hell out of me."

I tried to move my legs. Hospital sheets scraped harshly against my bare skin. The gown hung awkwardly on my body.

"How... how did I get here?" My voice was trembling.

He glanced nervously at the door, then back at me, a hint of urgency in his eyes. "I brought you here."

A sudden dread clutched my stomach. We were in a public place. No sign of authority, no FBI, no nothing. What if someone recognized me? What if they knew who I was?

"I can't be here. I don't have ID, anything—no birth certificate, no wallet..." My voice cracked.

He shook his head slowly, voice low but steady, almost too calm. "Don't worry. It's all been handled."

"Handled?" I repeated, my heart pounding. "What do you mean by 'handled?'"

He fidgeted, his hands twisted nervously in his lap. "I lied a little. West showed up with a stack of forms and this whole 'federal protection' script. He got you flagged as a protected witness and rushed some emergency licenses. We signed everything at your bedside and pushed it through. Everything's done, filed, and sealed."

My pulse hammered against my ribs.

"Paperwork? You met Agent West? What the hell are you talking about?" I tried to sit up, but the monitors and IV lines restrained me. My head was throbbing, and I barely registered the pain.

"Don't," he snapped sharply, a cold edge sharpening his

words that made me shiver. "We're being watched. You need to stay calm."

His voice dropped to a trembling whisper, almost a gasp. "I thought I was going to lose you. I had to make sure you were safe. Everything I did, every lie, was to protect you. I'm not sorry for that."

"Max… tell me," I croaked, my throat dry and burning.

He swallowed hard, eyes flickering away from mine for a tense moment. "You're… married. Surprise."

A wave of nausea churned in my stomach, forcing me to lie back to avoid vomiting all over my sheets. I was married? Tears blurred my vision as disbelief consumed my thoughts.

I blinked rapidly, my heart pounding erratically. "I… what?"

A crooked, guilty smirk curled his lips. "You don't have to be scared anymore, Trouble," he whispered, lowering his head slightly. "You can live a normal life."

Shock ravaged me.

"Are you fucking kidding me?"

He winced, ducking his head as if expecting to take a punch. "Don't hate me. We had no choice."

"No choice?" My laugh was sharp, hysterical. "You married me off while I was unconscious? Do you even hear yourself?" The monitor beside me screamed as my pulse spiked wildly.

"Calm down," he snapped, glancing toward the nurse's station. "It's been about 36 hours. You were out for a day and a half after the surgery. But everything's fucked right now, and we saw no other way to keep you alive. And no, I didn't marry you off to just anyone." His eyes bore into mine with an unsettling intensity. "I married you. We were engaged anyway."

My chest hollowed out. For a moment, I couldn't breathe. He was serious. He had actually done it. I stared at him, horror twisting my face as I wondered who the fuck this Max really was.

"What the fuck," I muttered. "What the *actual* fuck, Max?

You can't do that without my proxy. My mom would've never agreed. You need witnesses…"

His hesitation was quick, measured.

"You're an adult. But your mom's listed as your medical proxy and emergency contact. West had her on the phone while you were under. He sent her the emergency consent forms, you know, power-of-attorney type shit, and she signed. She said she'd rather know you were legally tied to me than left vulnerable. Honestly, she didn't take much convincing. She said she wants you taken care of, and that I can do that."

"You bastard."

He ran both hands through his hair, words tumbling out like a practiced goddamn liar. "West pulled the strings. He got the emergency license issued, dragged a judge to your hospital room, pushed the certificate through the clerk's office. He signed as the federal witness on the whole thing."

"There are laws," I rattled out. "You can't just marry someone who's unconscious. I was incapacitated, eh, that voids consent."

"Trouble, you don't need to worry about all the legal crap. West made it all sound airtight."

Red swirled at the edges of my vision, my chest tightening with a stifled gasp. "You forged my name. You made a decision for me while I was unconscious. Do you have any idea how fucked up that is?"

"I—" Max's voice cracked, desperation flooding through his tone. "I was trying to protect you."

"Protect me?" I scoffed, my laugh brittle, trembling with rage and fear. "From who? Jackson?"

"Yes. He tried to kill you. He would have if he could."

"You don't get to control me, Max," I hissed, my voice trembling with rage and fear as I shook my head. "My life's been stolen from me too many times—by my father, Jackson, and now you. Congrats. You just joined the fucked-up club. I don't even know you."

A thick silence descended between us, heavy with unspoken threats. His chest heaved rapidly, while I fought to keep my breath steady, my anger simmering just beneath the surface, ready to boil over.

"You know what, Max?" I whispered. "Since you decided to play God with my life while I was gone, we're doing this my way from now on."

A rough, humorless laugh escaped him, and I saw a flicker of relief in his eyes.

"You'll survive, Trouble. You're mine. Just... let me help you heal first. Then—"

I cut him off abruptly, leaning forward with a tight grip on the edge of the bed as if holding on to life itself. "Did I give you permission to speak?"

For the first time, he hesitated. The corner of his mouth twitched—an unsettling blend of amusement and resignation. He seemed smaller, the fire in his eyes dimmed by a hint of submission.

"We're doing this my way," I insisted, voice sharp. "And don't think this means you can just stroll in and claim me. You earned nothing while I was unconscious."

His jaw clenched, blue eyes narrowing as they locked onto mine. I noticed the same mixture of fire and restraint that I both feared and relished.

"You chose for me," I said coldly. "Now I'm taking back everything else. We're having a real ceremony—my ceremony—on my terms. You'll earn it, Max. Every part of this is mine to control."

He swallowed hard, tension radiating from his shoulders, barely concealed. "And if I say no?"

"Then you're out," I snapped sharply. "I'm not going to do

this half-assed. And I won't let anyone, especially you, turn my life into some FBI case while I'm trying to recover."

A flicker of a grin played on his lips. He was accepting the challenge, a masochist to the core. "You're insane," he murmured, rough and unrefined, but the spark—full of defiance and hunger—still burned in his eyes.

"Looks like we're made for each other," I shot back, smirking. "But I'm your wife now. I set the rules. And I plan to make you pay for every second you decided for me while I was unconscious."

He groaned, dragging his hands down his face in frustration. He knew it. I had him cornered. "You're going to kill me," he muttered.

"You're mine, McKinnon," I said, with a cold threat. "And if you cross me again, I'll cut your throat with a hatchet."

His eyes flicked to mine, mouth twitching despite himself.

"Better practice that name, sweetheart. You're Mrs. McKinnon now."

I leaned back on the bed, looking up at the stale white ceiling, ignoring his cocky smirk.

I was so pissed at him. Furious. A dark, simmering rage bubbled beneath my skin, and all I could think about was tearing him apart. I wanted to wrap my hands around his throat, to squeeze the life out of him, feeling his struggles weaken under my grip.

"We had sex once," I said, teasing coldly, "and you married me immediately after."

He shrugged, a crooked, reluctant grin twitching at his lips. "What can I say? It was the best I've ever had."

"The only thing you're getting for the rest of your pathetic life," I whispered, "and if you even think about stepping out of line..." I leaned in, voice sharp as a blade, "You'll wish you hadn't."

He swallowed hard, throat working, eyes darkening with fear and something darker.

"Do you understand me?"

"Yes... Yes, ma'am," he breathed, voice trembling, obedience replacing the earlier bravado.

"Good," I said, a slow, menacing smile curling at my lips. "Because you belong to me now. Entirely. And don't even think about arguing."

He groaned, dragging a hand through his hair, but there was no doubt in his eyes. He knew I meant every word.

ABOUT 12 DAYS LATER, ONCE I COULD WALK ON MY OWN AND had been discharged from the hospital, we made it official. The chapel smelled musty, with the harsh scent of old wood polish mixing with the faint, lingering incense. A single stained-glass window let fractured, sickly morning light spill across the pews, casting jagged, distorted shadows that danced unevenly across the cold stone floor.

We were in the hospital chapel. It was just us and a justice of the peace. Despite already being married, it didn't take much to convince Agent West to do this for me. He looked troubled, guilt gnawing at him for his impulsive decision.

Fucker.

Fuck them both.

He made sure we had clothes, but they offered little comfort. My dress was cheap. I could feel the thin lining and the itchy seams biting into my ribs. A dull ivory that caught the faint, unnatural light each time I moved. The skirt fluttered just enough to mimic innocence, yet it offered no warmth or solace. Lace sleeves brushed my wrists, fragile and delicate, hiding the bruises from the IV.

My hair was pulled back with a simple clip, hiding my tattoo and the fresh scar beside it. No veil, no bouquet—just me, exposed, honest, trembling.

The pain was relentless; I moved carefully, painfully slow. Max had been surprisingly dedicated. He never left my side, sleeping on a pullout in the room, only rising for the restroom or cafeteria. He walked me through the halls daily until I was gasping for breath. He monitored everything I ate and drank with an obsessive precision. He read to me, watched movies, did everything a husband should. But nothing could erase the sickening truth. He had married me while I lay unconscious, as if I were some prize to claim in the darkness.

Max was already waiting at the foot of the altar when I stepped inside. He was clean now, scrubbed raw from the hospital shower. He complained about the water pressure but refused to return to camp.

Despite my anger toward him, I froze in place when I saw him. He was wearing a cream-colored suit, the jacket slightly too broad at the shoulders. His towering height made it difficult for Agent West to find a suit on short notice that fit his frame. His bruises, though fading, were still visible. Grim reminders of the fight. His damp hair curled at the edges from the shower. No blood stained him now, only sharp lines, unblemished skin, and eyes that seemed to fixate where I stood.

The moment his eyes locked onto mine, he froze, too. His jaw clenched tightly. His chest heaved and stuttered as if he had forgotten how to breathe. He stared at me as if I were a ghost, a specter that might vanish if he blinked.

The way he looked at me, as if I were his salvation, burned through the frigid silence of this cold, empty chapel.

As soon as I made it halfway down the aisle, he surged forward, grabbing my hand and yanking me toward the altar with frantic urgency.

The officiant began, asking us to recite our vows, and Max opened his mouth first.

"I, Max—"

I raised a hand, palm flat like a command. "Stop."

Max stopped mid-sentence, brows clenched in confusion. "Mackenzie…"

"No." My voice sliced through the tense silence. I took two deliberate steps forward, the silk hem of the dress dragging along the chapel floor with a sinister whisper.

"You don't get to start this. You tricked me into a contract while I was unconscious. You stole my agency. My freedom, my choice. If you want me, Max—," I cocked my head, savoring the way his jaw twitched, lips parted in helpless anticipation, "—you're going to fucking earn it."

His throat worked furiously, Adam's apple bobbing as if he were choking on his own panic and shame. I pointed down at the ground at my feet. "On your knees."

The justice of the peace sputtered, voice trembling. "Miss, this isn't exactly—"

"Do it," I ordered. My eyes remained fixed on Max, burning with intensity.

Max hesitated only briefly before collapsing onto one knee, then both, his palms flat on his thighs like a man awaiting judgment from the gallows. His gaze never wavered; it was fierce, defiant, desperate. Those beautiful blue eyes pleaded for salvation as he looked up at me with a grimace.

"Good boy," I said softly, menace lacing my voice. I stepped closer, forcing him to tilt his chin up to keep me in sight. "Now say what you mean. Not vows, not promises—say what you really feel. And if you screw up, Max—" I leaned in, whispering into his ear, "—this marriage ends here, and I'll tear you apart."

He inhaled sharply. Then, slowly, his words escaped in a hoarse, raw whisper.

"I promise," he rasped, "I'll never trap you in chains you

didn't choose… ever again. I'll bleed first. I'll kneel before you and worship the ground you walk on until you're sick of me, and even then, I'll follow you into hell. I'll protect you, fight for you, burn the world down for you. You're mine, Mackenzie. Always mine. But I'm yours first."

The chapel was silent except for the crack in his voice at the last word.

I exhaled slowly, feeling the power shift, the control sliding into my hands where it belonged. Then I extended my hand, palm up.

"Get the fuck up."

He rose suddenly, towering over me with an imposing presence. But I wasn't afraid of him because I had him. I had the entire dark, sinister essence of him. The justice of the peace cleared his throat nervously, breaking the tense silence. "Uh… shall we continue?"

My lips curled into a victorious smile. "Yes. Now we can."

I didn't realize we had rings, but when the officiant said we could exchange them, Max produced two black boxes. He must've worked with West overnight to prepare this. When Max slipped the ring onto my finger, I drew in a sharp breath. It was actually perfect. A slender band of tarnished white gold, a single diamond set in delicate filigree that shimmered, as if it had been made just for me.

Even amidst the chaos, Max somehow managed to pick something that truly represented me. He knew me too well.

I turned my hand in the dim light, marveling at how it caught the flickering sunlight streaming through the stained-glass window. He slipped the matching band onto my finger and looked down at me, a strange glint in his eyes.

"He sent me a couple of texts last night with options. I knew it was this one the moment I saw it. Your mom… your mom agreed this was the one."

My mom.

I hated that she couldn't be part of this. Max knew what I was thinking because I could see it all on his face.

"I'd die before letting you wear something that doesn't feel like you," he said, his voice low and steady. "Also, I paid for it, not the FBI. I just wanted to clarify that. I used my money from baseball lessons during the year." His finger brushed over my rings, and I felt branded, like a scar repeatedly reopened. But for some reason, it felt good, right, like it was the way it was supposed to be.

His ring was nothing fancy — a plain, sturdy band — but it suited him, rugged and understated, just like him. Together, the two rings were chaos and elegance, fire and grounding, just like us.

The officiant cleared his throat and pronounced us husband and wife. Max didn't wait. His hand slid to the back of my neck, careful not to press too hard on my wound, his mouth crashing against mine with something halfway between hunger and relief, echoing with a raw desperation.

When we finally pulled apart, we walked out together, hand in hand, hearts pounding. The chapel doors swung open to the empty hallway beyond, the air thick with the scent of stale coffee, replacing the faint, lingering traces of incense and wood polish.

Yet, there was an eerie silence hanging in the air.

I could almost feel it.

25

———

MAX

I pulled into the hotel parking lot, and she shot me a look like I'd lost my mind.

"Where are we even going?" she snapped.

I turned off the ignition, my jaw clenched.

"You were out cold for the first thirty-six hours of our marriage," I muttered, teeth grinding. "Then I spent two weeks going crazy because I couldn't touch you. We need to consummate this marriage now, or I swear I'll lose it."

"You're basically kidnapping me," she scoffed with a forced smile, though I caught the faint curve of her lips.

She was calling me out, technically, but since she was legally bound to me, it wasn't kidnapping.

I looked at her. God, she looked beautiful. My chest tightened seeing her in that dress, soft and flowing yet sharp, just like her. Two weeks ago, I prayed for her in the woods. Now she's mine. Forever.

I must've been making a face, because she smiled.

"What?"

"Nothing," I muttered.

Just trying not to drool all over my legally kidnapped wife, I thought.

"I just can't believe you're mine, Mrs. McKinnon. I can't wait to make you mine repeatedly tonight."

Every inch of me burned, imagining taking her upstairs, tearing that dress off. I knew she was still recovering, and I needed to go slow. But my blood was molten. My control? Hanging by a thread.

"We'll see about that," she said dryly, sliding out of the truck.

West had packed us an overnight bag—pajamas, camp clothes, some semblance of normalcy. However, I fully planned on her being naked the entire night. She wouldn't need pajamas. But I had made him get them monogrammed with her new initials. He told me he hated me for making that request.

What can I say? I was sentimental and just a teeny bit psychotic. But just for her.

Walking to the hotel room, the tension between us was electric. Every step made my dick harder. She was pissed at me, but she wanted me. I could smell her wetness. It was fucking addicting. There was something about the way she smelled that just naturally turned me on.

Once we got to the hotel room door, I slid an arm behind her knees and the other around her back, careful to avoid her injured side, and lifted her. She let out a sharp gasp, fingers clutching my shoulder.

"Max," she warned.

"I've got you," I said, slowing my steps so I didn't jostle her. "If you think I won't carry my wife over the threshold just because she's pissed, you're mistaken."

I bent down and kissed her on the forehead. "I'm going to be so gentle, Mrs. McKinnon."

The second the door clicked shut, and I put her down, she shoved me. My back hit the wall with a loud thud. It was harder than I expected from her, given everything she had just gone through. She winced, one hand flying to her side briefly before she straightened.

There was fire in her eyes. Her lips were swollen, parted. She looked fucking *dangerous*.

"Strip," she demanded.

My cock twitched in my pants. My blood spiked.

Oh, hell yes.

She was taking control. I loved every second of it, but I needed to make sure she was okay.

"I like you being the boss," I muttered, searching her face for any sign that this was going too far. "But we can take our time. Why don't we order dinner?"

"No. I'm not hungry for food. It's time for you to be punished," she shot back.

I moved fast, shedding my shirt. I was slow on removing my pants, but I kept eye contact. I wanted her to watch me.

She had zero patience, though. She bent down, ripped my pants off, freeing my cock. I was hard as a rock seeing her on her knees in front of me. She let out a small gasp when she saw my size. This was the first time she had actually seen me. We had fucked in the woods, but she hadn't really taken the time to look at me. It had been so fast, so dark.

I watched as she dragged her gaze from the base of my shaft to the tip, and she licked her lips as she looked up at me with those fucking beautiful green eyes.

I had imagined this moment for years.

My groan barely made it past my teeth as she leaned forward, lips tracing my shaft, and I inhaled.

Fuck. If she blew me right now, I wouldn't make it through the night.

Instead, she kissed the head of my dick, standing up abruptly.

"You're not a good boy. Good boys don't get rewarded," she whispered.

Good boy? GODDDDDD.

I was a fucking lunatic for her. I wanted that praise. Fucking *lived* for it.

I slumped against the wall, immobilized by her intensity.

She stepped back, hands on my chest.

"Take my dress off."

I obeyed, savoring the curve of her back as I unzipped her, careful not to drag the zipper too close to her bandage.

She had been my obsession, my everything for years. And now she was my wife. I was going to worship every inch of her.

The dress fell. She slid off her bra and stood in front of me— bare, trembling, fucking mine. My gaze dragged over her curves, every slope, until my eyes caught on the bandage stretched tight across her ribs. The stark white reminder of what he did. A reminder of how close I came to losing her.

She shifted slightly, one hand brushing the edge of the gauze, like she was still getting used to it being there.

The sight of it should've made me pull back, but instead it ignited something sick and primal in me. That mark wasn't a weakness; it was proof she'd survived. I wanted to tear the bandage off with my teeth and kiss the scar beneath.

She was alive because of me. And I'd kill anyone who dared look at her and see anything but perfection because she was perfection to me.

She dragged her eyes down my naked body.

"Mmmm… Silver lining, I've got a husband who looks good in clothes, and out of them," she teased.

My hands were itching to touch her. But she hadn't permitted me yet. I was trying so *fucking hard* to follow her rules.

She slid her underwear down and bent to remove her heels. I muttered, "Keep them on."

I wanted to look at her more. I had seen her naked, but this was the first time we were both standing in front of each other like this.

I wanted more time to reconnect with her, but she wasn't interested. She nodded, took my chin in her hand, and her nails dug into me.

"I didn't tell you to talk. Get on the bed."

I practically sprinted to the king-sized bed, jumping like a dog in a pile of leaves, and lying back. I was entirely at her mercy, and I loved it.

"You want me in control, don't you?" she whispered.

"Yes," I whispered back.

I felt her close to me as she started to settle her body on top of mine. Her hand closed around my throat, surprisingly tight for someone who'd been stabbed two weeks ago.

"I'm going to punish you. Make you hurt. You like being punished, right, baby?"

"Oh… fuck yeah," I swallowed. "Hit me, bite me, choke me."

She loosened her grip on my throat, settling her hips down on mine. She started moving herself up and down my cock. She was fucking soaked. I could slip in any moment, but I was letting her call the shots. I groaned, tilting my head up to the ceiling, when she started rolling her hips.

"You gonna be loud for me? You want everyone to hear us?"

"I can be loud." My voice was rough. "I want everyone to know my wife is fucking me."

She gasped sharply. She could fight, resist, tease, but I knew she craved this as much as I did.

"Tell me you don't love it," I smirked.

She grabbed my chin again.

"Kiss me."

I sat up, grabbed her hips, and kissed her. She pushed my head back onto the pillow, leaning over me as she grabbed a tuft of my hair and yanked so I had to look directly into her eyes.

"Not there."

My hands were on her instantly. I slid back until my head

was right next to the headboard, then gently began guiding her movements above me.

"Wh—what are you doing?" she asked.

Her innocence was such a fucking turn-on. She was trying to control me, but I knew she was hurting, so I was going to guide her, even if she didn't realize it.

"Hands on the headboard, open your legs, and sit on my face," I commanded.

She laughed.

"What??"

"Sit on my fucking face. Now. I want to watch my good girl cum."

She obeyed, spreading her legs. Every inch of her was tense and waiting. I watched her. I watched the way her hips tilted. I watched her chest rise and fall. Then I looked directly into her— open, wide, wet, for me.

"Can you breathe?" she asked. I appreciated her checking in on me, but I couldn't breathe, and that was the point.

"No." I inhaled her. God, it was fucking psychotic how good she smelled.

"Good," she whispered.

"Fucking suffocate me, Trouble." She relaxed, putting all her weight on my face.

I dragged my tongue over her clit, slow at first, learning her, listening to every broken sound she moaned. Her moans were soft at first. She was nervous. I could feel her shaking on me.

But when her hips started moving against my face, I lost whatever control I had left. I pushed in deeper, tasting her, devouring her, chasing every reaction like I couldn't get enough.

Her moans turned rough, desperate. Her fingers twisted in my hair, thighs locking tight around my head, and I let it happen. I let her hold me there, let her use me, while I kept going, starving for it, for her.

"Max, holy shit—" she cried out.

Was it too much for her? She was shaking so badly. I wrapped my hands around her thighs and squeezed.

"Ahhh, fuck," she screamed.

"Mine," I growled, my voice lost against her skin.

"All yours," she gasped. "No one else. Just you."

That did it. I pushed a finger inside her, mouth working harder, deeper, chasing every sound out of her until her hands slammed into the headboard and she screamed my name.

I held her there, gripping her thighs as she arched, shaking, coming apart over my mouth.

"Fuck—yeah," I breathed. "That's it. Give it to me."

Her orgasm exploded against my mouth, the tiny pulses pounding against my tongue. She tasted fucking amazing. The best thing I had ever savored.

I grabbed her hips, flipping her down onto the bed. My hands never left her skin.

"You okay?"

Her eyes were glassy, hair a mess. She looked perfectly ruined. And I smirked, because yeah, I had done that.

"Yeah, I'm okay," she said breathlessly, looking up at me.

I stared at her for what felt like five whole minutes because I had no idea how to rationalize that this was happening. That Mackenzie was my wife, and I was her husband. This meant more to me than she would ever know.

"You have no fucking idea how long I've wanted this," I said, my voice rough. "I can't stop thinking about how good you felt in the woods."

I leaned down, biting her bottom lip.

"Well, I've wanted to fuck you since the first day of camp," she whispered.

I growled, leaning back just enough to see her face. She was open now, looking at me like she wasn't holding anything back. And I couldn't look away.

"Oh yeah?" I ran my hand down her inner thigh. "What were you thinking about?"

She wasn't embarrassed; she just looked at me and said, "When I first saw you come out of your truck, I could barely talk. I thought all types of things when we discovered we'd be back in that room together."

I leaned in, voice low and coaxing. "What were we doing in your thoughts?"

She bit her lip.

"Um, this. I thought about you kissing me, touching me. I thought about you naked, I thought about the way you would feel."

My jaw flexed, and I said, "I want specifics."

She hesitated just a minute and then said, "I touched myself in the shower three times after I saw you shirtless for the first time, and I touched myself in my bunk while you were asleep."

Fuck.

That was not what I had been expecting.

I was going to destroy her.

"You touched yourself while I was asleep?" My fingers were high on her inner thighs, my dick hovering right there, *so close.*

She nodded her head yes.

"What did you think about when you were touching yourself?"

"I thought about how you'd look if you lost control, if we stopped holding back." She leaned forward so that her mouth was hovering against mine. "I thought about what you would sound like."

She looked away, and I grabbed her face so I could look into her eyes. I groaned, hips grinding down against her, the head of my cock sliding up and down her wet center. I was shaking now. Desperate. Barely holding on. Our mouths collided again, all tongue and need.

"Repeat it," I breathed against her mouth.

She shivered. "I touched myself thinking about you."

My hands gripped her thighs, spreading them wide, and I slid my fingers up her again.

"So wet," I said. "Is this how wet you were when you touched yourself?"

She arched her hips into my hand, her fingers clutching the sheets.

"Yes. God—yes."

26

MACKENZIE

I moaned as he slipped one finger inside me, then two, curling deep while his thumb traced slow circles over my clit. My breath hitched, eyes fluttering closed.

"Or did you do it like this?" He whispered, his voice rough and low against my ear.

I melted into the sheets, embarrassed by how he unraveled me, by how wet I already was. But the way he watched me told me he loved every second of it.

He moved at exactly the pace I needed, like he knew my body by heart. When my moans grew louder, he leaned down and covered my lips with his, swallowing them, breathing hard as his fingers kept working inside me.

"Baby, I fucking love those noises," he murmured against my mouth.

My stomach flipped at the word baby, warmth blooming in my chest.

"Yeah?" I breathed back, barely able to form the word.

His gaze lingered on me. He was trying so hard to stay in control, but I was tired of men controlling my life.

The moment I reached down and wrapped my hand around

his cock, I knew he was relenting. The sharp intake of his breath confirmed it. I matched his rhythm, slow and needy, like we were learning each other in real time.

"Oh my God, Trouble," he groaned, as I rolled my hand up and down his length. "Fuck."

He pushed his fingers deeper in response to my touch, and if I hadn't been lying flat on the mattress, I swear I would've tipped right over the edge.

"You're such a dirty girl," he murmured, voice thick. "You like that… when I finger fuck you?"

I nodded, maybe a little too eagerly. No one had ever spoken to me like that before. And, selfishly, I reveled in it, in the way his focus narrowed until it felt like I was the only thing in his world.

"Yeah," I whined. "Max—oh my God—stop, I need, I need you inside me."

He slid his fingers free and shoved them into his mouth, groaning low as he tasted me, like it was the most natural thing in the world. The sight was filthy and intimate all at once, sending a shiver through my entire body.

I watched as he shifted over me, all hard lines and flexing muscle, his cock flushed and heavy, desire written plainly across his face.

And then I really looked at him.

This was my childhood best friend. The same boy who cried when Han Solo died. The one who used to ramble endlessly about insect anatomy and black holes. The kid with mismatched socks, jars of beetles, and sunburned shoulders from summers spent fishing, playing baseball, and wasting whole days at the lake. The boy who made me laugh harder than anyone else ever could.

And now…

Now he knelt over me, broad-shouldered and grown, hair messy, eyes dark, wearing that slow, knowing smirk that still made my knees weak.

My husband.

God help me. What he'd done was unforgivable, and part of me clung to that anger. But another part of me kept softening, pulled under by him like always. Nothing about us had ever been simple. Our marriage least of all. With Max, everything ran on instinct and emotion, messy and intense and impossible to ignore.

It pissed me off that I was letting myself soften toward him again.

But this time… I didn't want him in control.

I wanted him to work for me.

I wanted him to beg.

He wrapped a hand around himself and dragged the tip slowly down my center, almost like he was trying to punish *me*. His head tilted slightly, as if he was watching art unfold, like he was about to destroy his favorite masterpiece.

Something shifted in his eyes then. Feral. Unsteady. Like he was holding himself together by a thread.

His gaze trailed down my chest, lingering. I was completely exposed, trembling beneath him, and all he did was look. He'd touched me, been between my thighs, had watched me come undone, but this was the first time he had seen me like this— spread-eagled on the bed with a drenched pussy entirely at his mercy.

His face went slack, and then he pushed inside.

One slow, overwhelming thrust that stole the air from my lungs. My nails dug into his back on instinct, a broken cry slipping from my throat.

"Oh my God," I gasped, arching into him.

His head dropped to my shoulder, lips parting against my skin as a deep groan tore out of him. It came from somewhere deep in his chest.

"Oh, fuck," he breathed, voice rough and reverent all at once.

He didn't move right away. He stayed there, buried deep, letting the moment stretch until I could barely breathe, grinding slowly like he was settling into something familiar… like home.

"I'm going to try to be gentle, Trouble," he whispered against my ear. "But you've gotta tell me if I hurt you, okay? Because I love you… But fuck, I want you to feel like I don't."

His hips rolled, slow and heavy.

"You feel fucking perfect. You." Thrust. "Are." *Thrust.* "Mine." **Thrust.**

Each movement carried more force, the headboard knocking against the wall in a steady rhythm.

He kissed my mouth, my breasts, my shoulders—anywhere he could reach, he pressed his lips there, like he couldn't help himself. My legs locked tight around his waist, pulling him closer, deeper.

We tried to stay quiet, swallowing each other's sounds, breathing each other in. But a rough groan tore out of him, loud enough that I clapped a hand over his mouth without thinking.

His tongue slid against my palm, teasing, and I grimaced.

He laughed—actually laughed—low and wicked against my skin.

His hips snapped into mine harder, faster, our bodies slick with sweat, rhythm turning urgent.

"Fuck, baby," he breathed, already losing control.

I cried out as he picked up the pace, grunting into my mouth, one hand sliding to my throat while the other pressed between us, thumb moving in tight circles against my clit that made my whole body shake.

He watched me the entire time. His eyes locked on mine, drinking in every reaction, like he was witnessing something sacred. And then it hit me. I tightened around him, the release crashing through me without warning.

His eyes widened, a flash of surprise breaking through the hunger.

"Fuck... I can feel it," he breathed, voice rough.

My legs locked tighter around his waist as I went over the edge. It was so strong I felt it everywhere. The release rolled down my spine, behind my eyes, sparking through every nerve in my body.

Then, I felt the exact second he started to lose control. His rhythm was stuttering, his breath uneven, his pupils blown wide. He was close. Too close.

Not happening.

Not today.

He wasn't going to get his release until I said so.

I flipped us with a strained breath, wincing at his weight for half a second before he shifted with me, letting it happen, letting me take over.

Max barely had time to react before I was straddling him, palms planted on his chest as I drove my hips down.

The sound he made—half groan, half broken moan—punched the air from his lungs like I'd just wrecked him completely as I slid down, taking his entire size inside of me.

His hands shot to my thighs, trying to take back control, but I slapped them away.

"No," I panted, grinding down against him, watching his eyes roll back. "You said you're mine. Then let me show you what that means. You don't get to cum until I say you can."

I needed this. I needed to take back my agency, and he knew it.

"Fuck, Mackenzie..." he rasped, voice shaking. His jaw clenched as I started to move. I was slow at first, deliberate, dragging him in and out of me with a rhythm meant to undo him. Every time I felt him getting close, I stopped.

His head fell back, chin tilting toward the ceiling, breath ragged.

"You're gonna fucking kill me."

"Good," I whispered, leaning down until my lips brushed his. "Then die knowing I'm the only one who gets you like this."

I rocked harder, faster, and he lost whatever control he had left. His hands flew back to my hips, but I caught his wrists and pressed them into the mattress, pinning him there.

He was trembling beneath me, chest heaving, muscles drawn tight like a bowstring. The cocky brat who used to tease me was gone.

Now he was completely at my mercy.

He stared up at me like he couldn't believe what he was seeing.

"Jesus, fuck," he groaned, completely helpless now, hips bucking up into me with every desperate thrust. His eyes were pleading, blown wide with need. "I'm—fuck, baby, I'm… am I allowed to cum? I… can't… last…"

"No." The word came out firm, final, and it made him shiver. I stilled my hips, feeling him pulse inside me.

"Please… please, Mackenzie… please," he begged, voice breaking.

"Are you going to be a good boy?"

"Yes—fuck—yes. I'll do anything you want. Anything you tell me."

"Are you my bitch?"

His throat worked, a strangled sound leaving him. It wasn't amusement, but disbelief, pride fighting desperation. "No—"

I reached behind my ass and dug my nails into his balls just enough to make him choke on the word. His eyes opened wide.

"Say it," I ordered. He shook his head, wanting to say no again, and I squeezed.

"I'm your bitch," he whimpered, the last of his resistance collapsing.

"Cum for me," I whispered, grinding down in slow, tight circles as another wave built inside me.

My hands slid to his throat, holding him there, grounding

him, and with a broken sound, Max surged up into me one last time, fingers fisting the sheets as his body jerked.

After, he just looked up at me.

All the feral heat was gone from his eyes, replaced by something softer. His eyes were open, unguarded, achingly familiar. The way he watched me then made my chest tighten. It wasn't about control, or punishment, or who had won.

It was love.

He didn't care that I'd pushed him, or made him break, or taken control. None of that mattered.

He still loved me.

He leaned his forehead against mine, both of us still catching our breath.

"Holy shit," we said at the exact same time.

I laughed softly and rolled off him, but he immediately followed, his hand settling warm and possessive against my left breast, like he needed the contact.

"I… I didn't know it was going to be like that," he murmured, voice husky. His arms tightened around my waist, holding me close, caging me against him like he wasn't ready to let go. "We really fucking consummated the hell out of our marriage."

Every inch of me throbbed, pleasantly sore. His lips brushed over my temple, my jaw, the corner of my mouth. He gave me soft, lingering touches, like he couldn't stop himself. Like he needed to keep reminding himself I was real.

And then I saw it.

A faint flush spreading across his cheeks.

My brows lifted, a teasing grin tugging at my lips. "Max McKinnon… are you blushing?"

His smile went crooked—half sheepish, half dangerous.

"Shut up," he muttered.

I laughed, breath still uneven. "Oh, come on. Don't get shy

now. Not after everything you just said to me. Not after what you did."

His hand slid down my back and squeezed my ass hard enough to make me gasp.

"Careful, baby," he whispered against my neck. "I'll flip you over and remind you exactly what I did."

My pulse jumped. I bit my lip, heat flaring all over again.

"I'm serious," he continued, voice dropping, that cocky edge creeping back in. "You keep mouthing off, I'm gonna make you beg for it. Is that what you want?"

I gave him too long a hesitation.

In one smooth motion, he rolled me onto my back and hovered over me, smirking like he already knew the answer. He carefully touched my bandage, reassuring himself that I wasn't hurt, and then said, "That's what I thought."

27

MAX

She lifted her head, ready to tease, that smartass grin already forming. But then, she saw my face and froze. She thought I was playing. She thought this was over. But I wasn't fucking done. Not even close. I had waited seven fucking years for this.

My hands slid back over her skin, rough and greedy, no hesitation now as I pulled her back over me, dragging her into place like I owned her.

"Wait, already?" she laughed, breathless. "You don't need time to recover?"

I stared up at her like she was insane. "Nope," I growled. "Didn't get nearly enough of you."

She was so fucked, and I think she knew it.

I rolled us again, caging her beneath me. I wanted to take my time, trail kisses across her body like vows, make her feel every single promise I'd told her tonight. But then my eyes landed on her tits, and everything soft inside me burned to ash.

They were perfect. Full. They were bouncing just slightly, given how hard she was breathing.

All fucking *mine*.

I kissed her again, this time slowly. And then I was trailing my mouth down her throat, between those perfect tits, across her stomach. She sighed, a broken, needy sound, and I fucking groaned. That sound would haunt me.

When I reached between her legs, she hissed and jerked her hips. She was still sensitive. I'd been too rough.

"Max… fuck. I can't," she said, voice trembling.

"Yes, you can," I said, low, right into her skin. "You can take it; I know you can."

She whimpered. I kissed down her inner thighs, teasing, licking, letting her feel how much I wanted her, how fucking desperate I was for another taste.

Her moan cracked through the room. I licked her once, twice, slow and deep, before devouring her like I was starving. My tongue circled her, sucked, and flicked. She bucked, keening underneath me. When I slid two fingers inside her, I felt her stretch, her walls already fluttering. Still soaked. Still tight. Still so fucking perfect.

She reached down to touch me, and I growled, catching her wrists and pinning them beside her hips.

"You gonna behave?"

"No," she whispered. "Not unless you make me."

Christ.

I pulled her off and flipped back, dragging her with me, careful not to hurt her. She was breathless.

"I want you on top again," I said, voice ragged.

She let out a noticeable inward gasp. I saw doubt flicker in her eyes. She wasn't sure if she could manage it.

Her hesitation was hot, *so hot.*

"I'll help you, baby," I whispered.

I held her hips, lined her up, and started guiding her down, slow and ruthless.

"One… two… three," I counted, just to fuck with her. She was so wet, I slid in too easily. I could feel every inch.

"Four… five… six, *fuck*," I groaned, eyes rolling back. I was never going to get enough of her.

She braced herself on my chest, panting as I filled her, and she continued counting… seven… eight…

"Score," she gasped, and holy shit, the way she said it, breathless, not even trying to hide how good it felt, I fucking lost my mind.

"Yeah, that's it," I growled, fucking up into her. "Ride me. Just like that."

It was our wedding night. I wasn't going to hold back.

We were soaked in sweat, panting, bodies colliding again and again. She was so fucking good at this. So good at being mine.

"You were made for me," I hissed, spanking her ass hard. She clenched around me and cried out. "So, fucking tight. Look at you, my perfect girl."

"Max… I'm gonna …"

I sat upright so that we were face-to-face. She looked away, and I grabbed her hair again, yanking her head forward so she had no choice but to look me in the eyes.

"Cum for me," I commanded. "I want to feel that pussy clench around my dick."

And holy fuck, did she. Her body locked around me, tightening like a fucking vice, and she came screaming. That raw, shaking, earth-shattering kind of orgasm that tore through her entire body.

I grabbed her hips and slammed into her so deep I could feel her heartbeat against mine, and I came with a savage groan.

I didn't pull out right away. I stayed inside her, clenching her hips, breathing hard as she collapsed into my chest, completely done.

Eventually, I lifted her gently and eased out, laying her beside me.

"You, okay?" I asked, brushing her hair off her sweaty face.

She smiled.

"Yeah."

I watched her stretch out beside me, her skin flushed and dewy. My cum was dripping out of her, sliding down the inside of her thigh.

I ran a hand through my hair and let out a slow breath, trying not to panic at how hard that image hit me. How primal it made me feel.

I should've pulled out. I knew I should've. But I didn't. Because somewhere deep in my sick, obsessed, possessive little soul, I liked it. I liked seeing her like this, marked, used, filled.

I wanted to brand her. Bury myself in her until there was nothing left of her but me. I wanted every inch of her—mind, body, soul, name, future—all of it.

And the worst part? The part I could barely admit, even to myself?

I didn't hate the idea of her getting pregnant. Not even a little.

My eyes dropped to her stomach, and something twisted low in my gut.

I could already see it. She'd hate me for it, and I'd give her everything. She smiled, still dazed, still drunk on me, and when her legs shifted, I watched more of my cum slip out of her.

Jesus.

I was getting hard again.

"Max?" she murmured, eyes fluttering open. "You, okay?"

I gave her a slow grin. "Oh, baby, I'm better than okay."

"You're staring," she said sleepily. "You're thinking hard about something."

Yeah. I was.

Nothing weird here, just me, the guy who married her while she was unconscious, casually imagining pushing my cum back up inside her.

Totally normal thoughts from a totally normal person.

But I wasn't normal, and neither was she.

"What are you thinking about?" She asked me, getting up on one elbow to look at me.

"Just how hot it is knowing I might have just gotten you pregnant tonight."

She froze, blinking at me. "What?"

"Nothing," I smirked, cocky as hell now. "Just thinking about filling you up again."

She rolled her eyes, but I didn't miss the flush on her cheeks. Or the way her hips subtly tilted into mine.

Yeah, she liked it too. She was a little freak.

"I love you," she said in my ear.

I looked over at her, and I knew I was never going to be the same.

"I love you, too."

She sat up, looked down at me, and then gave me a hard slap across the face. The sharp crack stunned me. The sting of her hand burned on my cheek. I raised my hand to the spot where she had hit me.

"Oh, baby. You're in fucking trouble."

"Shut up and kiss me."

We ordered room service afterwards, watching a movie together while curled up in bed. It was honestly the best night of my life. Domesticity was something I had dreamed about. Honestly, more than the sex.

I just wanted her. Just like this.

I didn't know what I did to deserve her, but having her in my arms, like this, made everything worth it.

Every single fucked-up thing.

28

MACKENZIE

The soft whirr of the air conditioning jolted me awake. I rolled onto my back, every muscle protesting. My hips throbbed, my skin tender where bruises bloomed. Max was draped over me, all limbs and heat, wrapped around me like an octopus.

We'd had sex all night, until exhaustion finally swallowed us both.

I was sticky, grimy, and downright gross. I rolled to my side, lifting his arm off my body as gently as I could. It fell back to the bed like a dead weight as soon as I moved it. Limb by limb, I detached myself, and I finally escaped and tiptoed to the bathroom.

I turned on the shower, letting the hot water hit the tile as I tried to shake off the stiffness and wake up.

A ping from Max's cell phone carved through the dark.

I froze.

Max didn't move. He lay in bed like something already emptied out—boneless, heavy, utterly still.

His phone pinged again.

And again.

Each chime sharpened, needling under my skin, echoing off the walls like it was coming from everywhere at once.

Ping.

Ping.

PING.

Curiosity and a flicker of unease compelled me to grab it. Flipping it over, my stomach clenched as I saw seven unread messages, all from an anonymous number. I couldn't read their contents, but his passcode was easy—my birthday. Of course. Typical Max. He had already changed his phone screen background to a picture of me in my wedding dress.

I opened his messages app.

UNKNOWN

You fucking married her?

I wondered how crazy you actually were. But I thought you were smarter than this.

You really think this changes anything? It doesn't.

The game started long before you decided she was yours. You just made it bloodier.

I was willing to wait before. The chase was kind of fun. But I'm done waiting.

You don't get to keep her.

I'm coming for her.

I paused, a cold shock racing through me as my heart thudded painfully in my chest. Who was this? Two more pings made me jump.

When they come for you, they won't be nice.

I hope you're already terrified.

I quickly deleted the thread with trembling fingers and silenced his phone. If he saw those, he'd blow up.

I didn't know if I was protecting him or protecting myself from his reaction.

Another ping made me look down.

TONY WEST

Max. Paperwork's in. Congrats. You're officially married.

The legal name change came this morning. Congrats to Mr. and Mrs. McKinnon.

I don't know what I expected, but the feeling I had now was… relief. Honestly? It felt right. I felt more like Mackenzie McKinnon than anyone else I had ever been.

The phone vibrated in my hand, and I looked back down.

You need to be on high alert from now on.

And keep what we discussed about her confidential. Delete these messages.

What was confidential? What had West and Max discussed behind my back? Anger bloomed low and mean in my stomach. Nurse Campbell's words from earlier echoed: "Never trust anyone. Not even Max."

He was my husband. I could trust him.

Right?

The word didn't feel like an answer. It felt like a lie I was telling myself.

I was about to text West back on Max's behalf when he stirred, shifting under the sheets. I slid his phone back onto the nightstand. His eyes cracked open slowly, groggily, and unfocused. But as soon as they fixed on me, a grin spread across his face.

"Hey," he murmured, voice rough from sleep. "Morning."

"Morning," I said, hunching over slightly, covering myself. I was still naked.

He didn't miss a beat. His arm snaked around my waist, careful not to touch my bandage, as he pulled me back onto the bed. He pressed me into him.

"Don't cover yourself," he groaned, pressing his chest to mine.

"Sorry… it just feels weird." My voice was small. "Being like this with you."

He brushed a strand of hair from my face, his fingers lingering.

"Why?"

"I don't know," I exhaled, looking away from him. "We've been friends forever. This is new to us. Exposing this side of me feels… strange."

He leaned back slightly, one brow raised, a mix of disbelief and amusement twisting his features.

"Are you kidding me?" His grin turned wicked. "You're my wife. Married, remember?" He pointed to his wedding ring. "I can see you naked anytime I want. And I saw a whole lot of you last night."

He squeezed my hip, and I flushed, heart hammering in my chest. His hand drifted downward, and I snatched it away.

"No," I whispered. "I'm too sore."

He groaned, stretching across the sheets, but his eyes darkened with that familiar, dangerous glint. The corner of his mouth twitched. "Fine."

Steam from the bathroom curled into the room, warm and inviting.

"Shower?" he asked, voice low.

I swallowed, nerves and desire twisting together. "I was going to, but, yeah, you're welcome to join."

The tension snapped, charged with heat.

He shut me up with a kiss—hot, wet, open-mouthed. I

wrapped my legs around his waist, and he got out of bed, walking me to the bathroom. He set me down right outside the glass doors, then pulled me into the shower by the wrist.

Water poured over us, soaking my hair as it traced the lines of his chest and abs, catching on the sharp dip of his hipbone. All I wanted was to taste every drop.

"We've got twenty minutes before we have to be back at camp," he murmured against my lips, backing me into the wall. "Plenty of time to make you cum twice."

"I don't want to go back," I breathed. "I'm scared. I just want to run away with you."

His skin was hot and slick beneath my palms, muscles flexing under my touch.

"I know, and same," he rasped, pulling his head back so he could look me in the eyes. His thumbs trailed over the side of my face. "You think we can rent a house at GCU?"

"What?" I asked against his lips.

He framed my face with his hands, dragging his tongue along my jaw.

"I'm going with you to GCU. No way in hell am I doing long-distance."

In the haze of everything, I hadn't really thought much about it.

"But—you've got a full scholarship to Vanderbilt."

His lips stilled. He pulled back just far enough to look at me.

"Yeah, I do. But I also have one at GCU, and I made the baseball team there." He kissed down my jaw again, pulling back to look me in the eye. "Surprise."

The shock must have been obvious on my face because he smirked, and then I felt him, hard against my stomach. The hunger in his eyes was undeniable.

"I can't fucking wait to come home to you every day, to be with you every morning. I've literally dreamt about it for years."

"I'm already moving into the dorms. I don't know how that's going to work."

"Yeah, that's not happening. We're married. We're getting a place off-campus, our own space. Just you, me, and whatever chaos we decide to create."

I laughed softly. "Chaos sounds about right."

"Yeah," he breathed, running a hand down my back. "And, uh, we'll need a plan for keeping our evenings interesting. I'm planning on fucking you every day for our first year of marriage, and then, if I didn't get you pregnant last night, I'm going to work hard to get you pregnant by Christmas. I want our own little *trouble.*"

I swallowed hard. "Max…"

"Yeah," he whispered, thumbs tracing circles over my hips. "I want to claim everything that's mine. I want it."

I shook my head, heart thudding. "You're insane. We're way too young for all of that."

"I'm in love with you," he said, dark and serious. "I don't care if it's crazy. You're mine, and I want a family with you. I don't care how old we are."

I smiled, half-exasperated, half-molten with desire. Max was leading with emotions again. Part of me melted. Another part wondered what happened to girls who belonged to men who never changed their minds.

"Fine. But you better not get lazy with those baseball practices because I was promised front row seats when you make it to the MLB."

He laughed. "Oh, baby, you won't be getting just front row seats. You'll be getting the suite."

He bent down, taking my right nipple in his mouth. My back arched as his tongue circled. I was already gasping, clutching at his shoulders, drowning in the feeling of him.

He bent down on his knees, running a hand through his wet hair and flipping it away from his face. He grabbed my hips, steadying me, and pressed his tongue flat against my center. I cried out. He gently inserted one finger as he circled me with his tongue.

"This is my favorite thing," he said against me.

I placed a hand on the side of the shower to keep myself balanced, and he grabbed my hips tighter, pulling me in closer to his face. He was licking me up and down, thrusting his tongue inside me, with such ferocious energy that I couldn't hold back any of the sounds I was making. I closed my eyes, my legs trembling.

The pressure built inside of me. So fast. He made me cum so fast. He grabbed me even tighter, and I saw stars as I came undone. I think I had shouted his full name, Max Alexander McKinnon, because he shuddered with laughter.

He looked up at me, his hands still on my hips, his hair soaking wet, his lips wet from my arousal, and his body glistening under the steam. I grabbed a fistful of his hair and pulled his head back.

"Never have I ever cum on someone's face," I teased.

"You're fucking with me, right?" He said, his mouth opened wide. I leaned down and kissed him.

"You know, you've been on your knees a lot the past few hours," I stated. "You haven't allowed me to be on mine."

His eyes darkened, and I could see his control starting to falter. His fingers drummed against my hips, and I could feel him holding back. He was waiting for me to take control.

"Never have I ever given head to my best friend at camp," I whispered, pulling him up and pushing him against the shower wall. I dropped to my knees before him.

He closed his eyes as I took him in my mouth. I was only able to get half of it in before I started gagging. I hadn't actually done this before. But I didn't want him to know that, so I forced myself to take him deeper.

"Fuck," he growled, his fingers tangling in my hair as he

gently guided me deeper into him. "And, I'm *not* just a best friend. Oh, *shit*. I'm your Hus—s… husband," he stammered.

He gently guided my head, helping me get to where he wanted me. I ran my tongue slowly along the underside of his shaft, and he let out a sound so deep it vibrated through me. His muscles flexed beneath my hands. I opened my mouth again, taking him inch by inch, learning the rhythm, letting instinct guide me.

My throat burned, eyes watering, and Max's grip loosened just enough to let me find my own pace. He was patient, letting me explore. I felt his body begin to tense when I found the perfect rhythm. I heard it in the way his breathing changed. His hand dropped to my jaw, thumb stroking across my cheekbone.

"Shit, Trouble," he panted, voice breaking. "I'm gonna, *fuck*, I'm gonna cum."

He swatted at me. He didn't want to cum in my mouth, despite all that dirty talk last night about how many times he was going to fill my sweet mouth with his release.

Too bad I wasn't sweet.

I shook my head *no* and kept going. His voice went ragged, deep and desperate, his hips jerking just slightly as he tried not to lose control. I looked up at him, my cheeks flushed, my lashes wet, my lips wrapped around him, and he stared down at me.

I pulled off him for a second, continuing to look up at him.

"You taste so good," I whined, and then wrapped my lips around his cock again.

He sighed.

"Keep those fucking beautiful eyes open while I cum inside that pretty mouth," he groaned.

We stared at each other until his body tensed, he closed his eyes, and came in my mouth with a groan.

I swallowed, trying not to gag, and slowly lifted my gaze to meet his as he leaned against the shower wall, chest rising and falling, breath ragged. He looked wrecked, in a beautiful, destroyed way.

Not going to lie, I was proud of myself. Powerful, even. Like I'd just unlocked a new, dangerous little superpower.

"If I had known you had that in you," Max said between breaths, smirking. "I would've tried to hook up with you earlier."

I rolled my eyes and smacked his chest. "Shut up."

"I'm serious," he said, still dazed. "Best head I've ever gotten."

"Better than the head you got at the party?" I scoffed.

He bent down and kissed me, slow and soft, his dick still pulsing from the aftershocks. He lingered there, his forehead against mine, water trickling down between us like we had all the time in the world.

"Way better," he said. His hands started roaming again.

"Max," I whined, playful and breathless. "I need to wash my hair and my actual body."

"I'm helping," he said innocently, grabbing the soap with a cocky grin.

Helping, my ass.

He lathered the soap in his hands and started gliding it over my body, down my arms, cupping my breasts like they were too fragile not to give full attention to. His fingers slowed when they reached between my thighs, lingering far longer than necessary.

"I just want to make sure you're really clean," he said, voice low and teasing in my ear.

I returned the favor, dragging my soapy hands along the slope of his shoulders, across the curve of his chest, the lines of his abs, down his hips, and over his perfect ass. He hissed through his teeth.

Then I glanced up and froze. He was staring down at me, his mouth slightly parted, his jaw flexing. Like he could *see* every version of me at once. The guarded best friend. The scared girl.

The messy girl. The girl in the tattoo shop. His wife. Because if this wasn't a look of true love, then I didn't know what it was.

His expression was so intense, but for the first time, I felt a sense of freedom. Because he knew everything about me, and I no longer had to hide.

I felt safe. I felt protected. He was my family. I was excited to start a new life with him, one where I didn't have to hide.

Finally, I didn't have to run.

Or so I told myself.

29

MAX

I hadn't wanted to return to camp.

Mackenzie was scared, even though Jackson was no longer there. I also felt uncomfortable, thinking about what had happened and what could have happened.

But we only had one week left, and Mackenzie still had no idea that the camp was being watched. I knew we had protection, and all eyes were on us.

I'd tried to get us moved into our own cabin, but the camp shot me down. I bitched about it to West, but he just said simply, "I'm a ghost here, Max. I can't pull any strings."

Privacy was a fantasy. Counselors complained about us taking over the back room, saying they could hear us fucking. Now that we were married, it apparently became a big problem for everyone. I didn't give a damn. I fucked Mackenzie every single minute, every single second of the day.

I couldn't get enough of her.

We couldn't keep our hands off each other. It was like an addiction, how badly we wanted each other. We were pulled to each other, like moths to a flame. We tried not to circle each other, but it didn't matter. We always ended up back in bed together.

I never took my ring off. I showered, swam, even slept with it on, and every time Mackenzie's hand brushed mine, I'd catch a glint of her ring and feel that possessive burn in my chest. It was like a low, violent itch. The band wasn't just proof she belonged to me. It was a warning. A promise that if anyone tried to take her away, I'd tear the world apart with my bare hands.

At night, I watched her sleep, memorizing the way the band circled her finger; proof she belonged to me.

When her new driver's license came in, and she changed her name to **Mackenzie McKinnon** on her counselor badge, it was honestly the happiest day of my life.

She was mine. *Fucking mine.*

Max and Mackenzie McKinnon. Forever. Heart eye emoji or whatever the fuck it was. I wanted to shout it from the rooftops.

We were reckless. Brushing fingers under the table in the dining hall. My hand slid under her shirt during movie night. Stealing kisses in the woods and pinning her against a tree when the kids weren't looking. Every chance I had, I pulled her back into bed with me. We'd moved our mattresses from our twin bunks to the floor to make one big bed for the two of us. She immediately started birth control, to my chagrin. I wanted to throw her birth control pills out the window to stake my claim deeper.

But it wasn't just the sex. She was different now—wild, unfiltered. She let me see all of her. Her fears. Her secrets. Her darkness. She told me everything that she could remember.

About *him*. The "Butcher." To my dismay, there was a lot she remembered.

We laughed until our stomachs hurt. I carried her across the lake dock on my back. I changed her bandage and cleaned her wound. She was my best friend and the love of my life, all wrapped up in one beautiful, dangerous girl. I didn't know what I'd done to deserve her, but I knew I never wanted to go back to the way things were before her.

We were perfect. *She* was perfect.

Fortunately, we managed to get Mackenzie out of her dorm at GCU and rent a house off campus with a fenced-in backyard. I was so excited thinking about our future.

"We'll get a dog. Two. There's plenty of space in the backyard to set up a soccer net for you to practice and for me to practice throws. And at night, we'll fuck in our own bedroom," I had told her one night. I kissed her hard, "and make lots and lots of babies."

"Max… what is your obsession with babies?"

"I'm serious," I cut her off. "I want to put a baby in you. Right now. So you're mine forever."

"You're not ready for a baby. We need to grow up a bit."

"I'm ready." I blinked, pulling back just far enough to hide my face.

Truth was, the more I thought about getting her pregnant, the more sense it made. She couldn't get hurt if she were pregnant. People don't drag a woman with a swollen belly into the line of fire. They don't put a gun to the head of someone carrying a baby. And if she were home with me, heavy with my kid, she wouldn't be running off to places I couldn't follow.

Mackenzie didn't know, but West had told me something that chewed at me every night: the Agency had pulled her and her mother out of the witness-protection program.

Whatever perimeter of protection they had surrounded them was gone. I was it now.

West didn't sugarcoat it. He'd come to me with an option I couldn't refuse the first day we had gotten back to camp, and he had pulled Mackenzie's protection team.

TONY WEST

We're going to run you through a security vet —nothing public, a shadow clearance.

Keep an eye out for a secure message in the next 24 hours.

When it hits, answer via the encrypted channel I set up. Don't forward it. Don't talk about it.

ME

What do I tell Mackenzie?

TONY WEST

Lie to her.

I could justify what I was doing a thousand ways. Protection. Duty. Love. But the truth was smaller and uglier: the line between protecting her and owning her was razor-thin. And I walked it every day, bleeding for it and loving the sting.

My size, my presence, I was a shield, sure. But I was also a threat. Even if I never used that threat on her, she felt it: the way her body curled into mine, the way she leaned on my chest like it was the only safe place left.

I told myself I was doing all of this—the control, the guarding, the possessiveness–to keep her alive.

But I was paranoid as fuck.

Jackson wasn't just some asshole with a grudge. His threats had teeth. He knew things about her father, shit nobody should ever have known, and that made him dangerous in a way we couldn't map. The problem was he'd vanished after the stabbing. Gone dark. No trail. No pattern. Nothing for the FBI to lock onto.

"That's the worst kind," West said one night when I called him in a pure panic. "When someone disappears, you don't know where to push. Keep an eye out. We don't know his plan, but your marriage to Mackenzie will likely prompt him to act. Don't trust him. Don't let her out of your sight."

West meant every word. We scoured every camera feed, every thread he might have left online. We pulled every lead. Every time we thought we'd pinned him—an ATM camera, a traffic cam—the footage would smear at the exact frame his face should've been in, a digital blind spot like he'd reached through the wires and erased himself. The bureau flailed at the edges. Jackson had gone off the grid on purpose.

Every noise in the dark, every stranger on the trail, felt like him. I watched the tree line until my eyes blurred. I listened to every voicemail, every dropped call, like a code only I could break.

But that wasn't all.

Heather had started acting strange, stranger than usual. The jealousy wasn't subtle anymore. It *oozed* out of her. One afternoon in the dining hall, I had my hand on Mackenzie's knee, feeding her strawberries off my plate, when Heather leaned in close.

"Ever wonder what would happen if we all switched roles for a day? I think Max would finally see what it's like being with a *real* woman. We'd look good together."

The strawberry slipped from my fingers, hitting the plate with a soft, wet thud.

"What the fuck?" I muttered.

Heather didn't flinch. She just smiled, slow and knowing, like she was letting me in on a secret only she understood. Then she picked up her tray and walked away, humming under her breath like nothing had happened. I pictured her hands, the way she gripped her tray. Strong. Too strong. For a split second, I saw those fingers on Mackenzie's throat instead, and bile climbed in my throat.

But my stomach turned. It wasn't a joke. Not with the way

she looked at Mackenzie, like a rival to be erased. I felt it in my bones. We were on a collision course, and everyone was becoming a predator.

Some of them just hadn't decided who to eat yet.

MACKENZIE

The next morning, sunlight streamed through the cabin window, hot against my skin. I blinked against the brightness. My hand shot out from under the covers, fumbling for my phone.

8:30 a.m.

Shit!

I scrambled, quickly remembering it was Saturday. No campers today, thank God. I hadn't slept this late all summer.

Max was still out cold beside me, face buried in the pillow, one arm locked tight around my waist. He was snoring softly, lips parted, hair sticking up in a thousand directions. Unfairly gorgeous, even like this. Usually, he was already up by now, halfway through his workout. But last night had drained both of us. Honestly, *every* night had. He couldn't keep his hands off me.

I rolled up out of the covers and swung my feet to the floor, half-asleep. I was heading for the bathroom when a ping from Max's phone stopped me. Three more pings chimed in quick succession.

I told myself not to look. The last time I invaded his privacy like this, I had read those text messages that continued to haunt me. But the nosy part of me, the one who'd always wanted to know, reached out and touched the screen.

He was my husband, after all, I rationalized. I needed to see who he was messaging. There was no harm in that, right?

He was still asleep, chest rising and falling, hair stuck to his forehead. I watched him for a few moments before I entered his passcode, and the phone silently unlocked.

The messages filled the screen.

UNKNOWN

Mr. McKinnon. Congratulations. You've been personally invited to an initiation hosted by The Alliance.

2300 South Clearing, 13:00 Sunday.

No weapons. No phones.

Good luck.

There was an image attached. A circle enclosing a jagged starburst, thirteen uneven points like cracked glass. Tiny harsh marks rimmed the circle, not letters, just scratches that felt coded.

The moment I saw it, I could almost smell it again—cigarette smoke, metal, and that bitter incense my father burned until it choked the house.

"I drew you a picture, Kenz," my father had said once, his voice soft. "This is our emblem. The star is our legacy. Keep it close." He'd press the paper into my little hands so hard the edges bit into my palms.

I clamped my hand over my mouth because the panic threatened to spill out loud. How did Max have this? What was this?

I yanked on shorts, turning off the shower faucet. I was barely a few feet out when the cabin door creaked open, and Max stepped out barefoot, tugging a white t-shirt over his head. His hair was wild, his eyes half-closed, until he saw me. I must've looked devastated because he was next to me in one heartbeat.

"What's wrong? Why did you run out so fast? You woke me up," he said, rough, his voice still layered with sleep.

My knees threatened to buckle just by looking at him. He knew something. He was part of something.

His hands were soft and steady as he cupped mine.

"Are you okay? Trouble, talk to me."

I nodded too quickly. "Yeah... I..." I started hyperventilating.

"No, actually, I'm not okay. I'm not okay, Max," I cried, the words ripping out of me.

He didn't hesitate. His arms closed around me, crushing me to his chest. He glanced over my head, scanning the trees, his jaw set. Then, in a low, clipped tone, he said, "Come on."

I followed him deep into the woods. He didn't stop until we were swallowed by shadows, far from the others. The air felt wrong here. It was too still, like the trees were holding their breath to listen. Every rustle of leaves sounded sharp, close, like something was circling just beyond the trunks.

I looked into his eyes, his perfectly blue eyes, which were full of genuine concern for me. He had no idea I knew. What was this initiation? What was he hiding from me? The betrayal was so intense that it roared through my bones, and I almost felt like I might vomit.

"Hey, hey," he said, running his hands down my arms. "You're scaring me. What's wrong?"

"I'm scaring you?" I seethed.

His brows twitched in confusion. He spread his legs wide to be nose to nose with me, his hands stopping me from my panicked pacing.

The cold metal of his wedding band scraped my wrist as he grabbed me, and for a heartbeat, it didn't feel like a promise. It felt like a shackle, a piece of him welded to my skin.

What would he do if I cut it off?

"I saw it. I saw everything. I read it," I said coldly. The look of confusion returned to his face, and he licked his lips.

"Saw what?"

"The text message on your phone. The initiation. There was a picture. How… how do you have that picture? That's my dad's—that's my family crest."

There was something in his eyes then, something heavy and shadowed, a secret crouching behind the blue.

"What do you know?" My voice came out brittle. He broke eye contact, staring at the ground like it might open and swallow him.

"Nothing."

It was a lie. A blatant, soul-deep lie.

"Max." I stepped closer, heat rising in my throat. "Tell me. The fuck. Now. What do you know?"

He dropped his gaze to the ground again. "It's… nothing."

He scrubbed his hands over his face. For a second, I thought he was going to say it. His mouth opened, and his throat worked as if the words were crawling out. My heart hammered as I waited for the truth.

But then he shut his eyes, shook his head, and said, "I can't."

The word tasted like my childhood. Doors locked from the outside. Voices behind them. My father's hands are on my shoulders, squeezing too tightly. The blood. So much blood.

My heart broke into a million pieces. "You can't, or you won't?" My voice cracked, anger mixing with fear.

"Mackenzie…"

"Don't you dare lie to me. Not you."

His throat bobbed, like the truth was trying to escape. His mouth even opened, but then he closed it again. A wall of tension fell between us.

"Don't do this." His voice was quiet. "Not now."

He scanned the woods around us, as if searching for something.

"What do you mean?" I pushed him hard, right in the chest.

"Are you saying I should pretend I don't know you're hiding something from me? You think keeping secrets is the same as protecting me? You think being in the dark makes me safer?"

His fingers tightened just a little too much around my wrists, enough for the bones to throb. Part of me knew he'd never hurt me. Another part knew he didn't have to. His size was its own kind of threat.

"You just don't get it. I can't tell you. If I do, it all falls apart. I made a promise to keep you safe, and this is how I'm doing it."

"You're not keeping me safe!" My voice cracked. "You're supposed to be the one person I can trust, and you won't even look me in the eye and tell me the truth."

For a moment, I caught a glimpse of it, the confession struggling to get out. His jaw clenched, his chest rose and fell. But then he kept silent.

"I'm coming with you, Max. You're not going alone. I won't let you!" I yelled.

He paused before speaking in a hushed tone.

"If I've been initiated, I have to go. I have no choice. But you can't come with me. This is *my* initiation. It's too dangerous."

"Who are you talking to? Who's messaging you? What the hell is going on?"

Tears spilled from my eyes.

"I can't tell you, Mackenzie. I'm so sorry, but I wish I could. There is some real scary shit happening. And there are people out to get you, and I have to keep you in the dark. I have to. I'm so sorry."

He was begging me to trust him, but how could I trust someone who was keeping such a huge secret from me?

"Why are you even involved? Huh?"

"I… I'm your husband."

"That doesn't mean shit. You're not the FBI. What are you doing?"

His mouth closed, and I saw the hardness in his eyes settle. He was shutting me out, so I couldn't read him.

I pulled myself away from his arms, tears clouding my vision.

"Fine. Keep your secrets. And when they get me killed, you can put your ring on someone else and pretend she was yours all along."

30

MAX

If she wanted to break my heart, she'd already done it. She shot out of my reach so fast I couldn't catch her. I knew myself well enough. If I didn't give her space, I'd be in her face in three… two… one.

"Trouble! Wait!" I yelled, but she kept running. I wanted to chase after her and drag the truth out into the light between us. I wanted to tell her everything. I hated hiding this from her, hated the way the secrets sat between us like a loaded weapon.

West's warning echoed in my mind like a curse: "You tell her, and you're putting her in even more danger."

Part of me wanted to hack in and see what I could find, to peel back the code and expose whoever was watching us, but I felt almost guilty now. It was as if, because we were married, I shouldn't do it. I didn't know where this sudden moral compass was coming from, but she made me want to be a better person. A better man. Less monster.

I also knew they were coming for me—the group of people who were hunting Mackenzie. I didn't have many details, but I knew enough to realize that whatever game we were in had already started. We were already pieces on someone else's board.

The characters changed often, and I was fucking terrified of that. You can't protect someone if you don't even know who the enemy is.

Yesterday, I heard her phone ping when she stepped into the shower. I told myself not to look, but temptation has never been something I'm good at resisting, especially when it comes to her safety. I picked up her phone from the nightstand and swiped my thumb up the screen to unlock it.

When I saw the text messages, everything around me came to a halt. The room seemed to narrow, the air getting thick and cold. I knew this was Jackson, even though it was an unknown number. This was the first time we had heard from him since her stabbing.

My paranoia escalated with every word I read.

UNKNOWN

They're coming for him first, then you. Be ready. 😈

The devil emoji stared back at me, stupid and cartoonish, but it made my stomach drop. I could almost feel him in the room, breathing down our necks, laughing.

I had stopped tracking her messages as soon as we got back to camp because I thought we were done with Jackson. He was gone, untraceable, and I thought our search was a bust. I was a fucking idiot to think he wasn't still watching us.

I quickly took a screenshot of the messages, my thumbs shaking, and forwarded the images to my email. Then I tried to trace the number, typed it into every search bar, and checked every handle I could think of. The profiles were gone. When I tried to ping one account, a block notification popped up like a door slamming in my face.

Typical. Ghosts in the machine.

I wanted to tear the phone in half.

"Fuck!" I yelled.

I deleted the messages from her phone before she came out. While I was in settings, I set up a passcode for her.

She walked out of the bathroom, towel twisted in her hair, steam ghosting around her like a halo. She was smiling like we were about to go to dinner or out to a movie, like we lived in some normal world where people didn't send death threats and stab girls in the dark.

Inside, I was exploding.

"Hey—whatcha doing?" Her voice was so sweet it was almost cruel. She had no idea what I was holding back.

I stared at her. I should've said something soft, something true, like you're so beautiful, but the words burned in my throat. Instead, I swallowed them and said,

"I saw your phone wasn't password-protected. I set it up for you. It's our anniversary."

"Thanks," she said. She gave me the sweetest kiss, and I clung to her like a drowning man, like if I held her tight enough, nothing could pry her away from me. Not Jackson. Not this game. Not fate.

"I love you. You know that, right?" I looked right into her eyes. They were moss on clover tonight—green on green, deep and wild.

"Yeah, I know," she said. "I love you, too."

"You can tell me anything." It came out more like a demand, more like a 'please fucking tell me before I lose my mind', but she just shook her head and stepped back.

"I know, and I do… tell you everything," she said, smiling coquettishly.

I sat back. She had just lied to my face, and she had done it so well that it felt practiced. That didn't sit well with me. My chest tightened.

She wasn't the only one capable of lying.

I HADN'T SPOKEN TO MACKENZIE FOR A FEW HOURS, EVER SINCE she ran off after our fight. I'd been texting her nonstop. She wasn't in her usual spots. The cabin, the dining hall, and the lake were all empty. Everywhere that usually held some trace of her felt hollow.

I couldn't find her, and it was making me panic.

> Where are u?
>
> Trouble, please text me back.
>
> Mackenzie.
>
> I'm not going to ask you again.
>
> Text me back now. Please turn your location back on.
>
> Please, please, please, stop ignoring me. I'm sry.
>
> I love u. I love u so much.
>
> Please. Please don't do this to me.

The longer Mackenzie ignored me, the longer my thoughts simmered. There was a two-week break before we headed to GCU for baseball and soccer training. I still hadn't told my parents that Mackenzie and I had gotten married. They expected me to come home, but not with a wife. Not with this kind of chaos stitched to my side.

The thought of her being alone without me made me want to gag. The world felt full of sharp edges and shadows, and she was walking through it without armor. I was a complete mess. I'd already lost my mind and kept imagining different scenarios of what might have happened to her. Her body in the lake, blood on the dock, Jackson's smile in the dark.

I checked my phone every five minutes for a text message from her and ended up draining my battery. I stopped by the cabin to grab my charger, and I also wanted to hack into her phone's location settings from my computer. If she wouldn't let me in, I'd force my way in another way.

As I blew through the cabin, I heard Megan say, "Did you see Jackson earlier?"

I stopped cold in my tracks.

"What?"

"Yeah." She was sitting on her bunk, scrolling on her phone. The click of her turning off her screen startled me more than it should have in the quiet room. "He stormed by Heather and me earlier with all his stuff. He mumbled a bunch of weird shit."

"Wait—he was here?" My voice was high-pitched, unlike anything I had ever heard from myself. I sounded like some other guy, like one who'd already watched everything he loved bleed out.

"Yeah, I was shocked to see him after everything that happened. I cannot believe he showed his face after stabbing Mackenzie. He should be in prison."

"Where the hell did he go?" I asked, my voice dropping, sounding strangely deep now. The rage pulled it lower, made it rougher.

"I have no clue. He said Mackenzie was his, that they had a history, and then he just took off into the woods. It was really weird."

The words "Mackenzie was his" scraped down my spine like claws.

It was hard not to react, but something in my expression must have given me away, because inside I was detonating. There was a hollow, echoing space in my chest where logic used to be.

Megan's frown deepened. "Do you have any idea what he meant by that?"

I just shook my head. "Probably just more of his twisted bull-shit. He hurt my wife, and I'm going to fucking kill him."

She stared at me for a moment but didn't press.

"He's creepy," she said, her voice dropping to a whisper, like even saying his name too loud might summon him. "I can't believe they've been sleeping together."

I spun around, surprised.

"Who?"

"Heather and Jackson. They've been hooking up all summer. It's not serious—that's just what Heather does. She loves psychotic guys," she sighed. "Jackson's into some weird shit, too."

I nodded absentmindedly, wrapping the cord around my charger. My mind was racing. Did Jackson have something to do with the initiation I received? I had tried to trace the source of the text, but couldn't get through. Was this part of my game? Part of hers?

"Hey, I think Heather and Jackson are up to something," Megan warned. "I really think you and Mackenzie should leave."

"What?" I asked, shoving the charger into my shorts pocket.

"Heather likes you," Megan said, throwing her legs off the bed and sitting up on the edge.

"Okay?" I replied coldly. I was being a total dick now, but I didn't understand what she was getting at.

"Heather always gets what she wants. She won't stop 'til she does. You need to be careful."

I leaned in close to Megan, my voice dropping a few octaves, the threat threading through it. "Tell Heather she can dream as much as she wants, but she doesn't have a fucking chance. I'm a married man."

I walked out, heading toward mine and Mackenzie's room in the cabin, my nerve endings buzzing. I couldn't wait to get out of here and start over with Mackenzie. We'd go somewhere no one knew us. Somewhere, the woods didn't feel like they were listening. California, maybe. This place felt too small, and everything felt wrong now.

I started shoving our clothes into my duffel bag, my hands shaking. Mackenzie was going to bitch about the way I was packing our shit, but I didn't give a fuck. She could deal with it.

We were leaving tonight.

I shot West a quick text.

> Something is wrong. Jackson was seen at camp today. I'm packing our shit. Send safe coordinates.

I waited a few minutes and got no reply.

That was not like West. The panic settled even deeper in my chest, thick and heavy, like someone was pressing a boot down on my ribs.

LATER THAT AFTERNOON, THE SCREEN DOOR CREAKED BEFORE I saw her. The sound sliced through the cabin's silence. The place seemed to inhale with me when she stepped in, as if even the walls were waiting to see what she'd do.

I was a nervous wreck. I didn't know what to do without her. I'd been staring up at the ceiling, tossing a baseball, waiting and pretending that we were a normal married couple, that our lives weren't a fucking disaster stitched together with secrets and fear.

I wanted to rage, burn the camp down, drag her out of here by her hair, and lock her somewhere only I could reach. Instead, I told myself to breathe, to save the Jackson bomb until I could regain my composure.

She needed a husband, a protector—not some broken, sobbing mess.

I didn't trust myself not to say too much, not to grab her and demand answers she wasn't ready to give. My chest was tight with all the things I wanted to say and all the things I knew I couldn't.

But then she stepped beside me, and I felt her before she spoke, like gravity shifting, like the only part of the world I cared about had drifted back into my orbit.

"Max," she said softly.

My heart fucking cracked.

She looked wrecked. Damaged in a way that made me want to hold her forever and lock the rest of the world outside.

"I'm sorry," she whispered, her eyes filling with something between guilt and fear. "For earlier. For everything. I didn't mean to push you away."

Relief hit me so fast I almost staggered back. I didn't realize how much I'd needed to hear her say that until she did. It was like someone loosening a tourniquet too suddenly. There was pain first, then numbness, then the rush.

"What have you been doing?" I said, my voice rough. "You were gone for two hours and I—"

She cut me off with a small shake of her head. "I've been thinking. I don't think we should keep doing this. You and me."

"What?" My voice was strangled.

She couldn't meet my eyes. "It's not fair to you. I'm dealing with too much. I'm dragging you into it, and I'm ruining your life."

"You're not ruining my life," I snapped.

"If something happens to you because of me... I can't live with that."

The knot in my chest tightened until it hurt to breathe. I could not believe she was doing this right now, when I could practically feel something closing in on us from the tree line.

I wanted her in my truck, now, so I could take her away from whatever was about to swallow us whole.

"You don't get to make that call for me," I said. "We're married. We do everything together. Listen, we aren't doing this right now. Something is off here. I don't feel safe, and we need to leave. Get your bag."

Tears pooled at the rim of her lids. She stepped back, and for a second, I thought she was going to bolt again.

"I'm not letting you walk away," I said, my voice softer. I grabbed her arm, steering her to the bedroom door, and she ripped her arm out of my grip.

"What?"

"I'm serious, Max. This summer… it was beautiful. But it needs to end before someone gets hurt."

The harsh edges of heartbreak rippled through me, like bare tree branches scraping down a window in winter.

"Stop being so dramatic," I said, grabbing her arm again. "Let's go."

Tears filled her eyes as she ground her feet into the floor. I wasn't in the mood to be soft. I was shaking, rage simmering just beneath my skin, hot enough to burn through my restraint.

"You don't get to throw me away because you're scared," I growled. "We're fucking married. Married. This isn't just a high school fling; we are legally bound to each other. Your business is my business. End of story."

Her voice cracked, barely above a whisper. "I'm doing this because I love you. Because you're my best friend. I can't lose you."

My whole body trembled. A pathetic sob ripped out of me before I could choke it down. Raw and humiliating. I was losing control. I needed to get her ass in the damn truck so we could leave this place before she was killed.

My fists were clenched at my sides. I didn't even realize it until the tears burned down my cheeks.

"No," I said, voice breaking. "I'm not accepting this. Stop it. We're fucking leaving right now."

Her eyes were red now, and they met mine. "You can't tell me what to do."

"Yes, I can!" I exploded. "Stop this fucking drama and get your ass in the fucking truck!"

She shook her head, tears falling faster now.

I knew I was being a jerk, but a cruel part of me wanted her to feel as guilty and desperate as I did. If fear was going to rip us apart, I'd rather she hate me than vanish from my life in a body bag.

She just stared, lips trembling.

"I'm not getting a divorce, okay?" I muttered, wiping at my face. "Just know this—wherever you go, I'm going too. I'll play ball, keep my head down, blend in, whatever the fuck you need. But I'm not letting you walk away from me. And I will continue to do whatever I can to protect you. Now stop being difficult and get in the fucking truck."

Her entire body stiffened.

"Okay, okay," she said quickly. "Let me just go get my toothbrush."

"I already got it. You're packed. Let's go."

I grabbed her hand, and as we were making our way out of the cabin, Graham stopped us.

"Hey, Mr. and Mrs. McKinnon! I was wondering if you could both lead the final campfire tonight? It's kind of a celebration, and since you're our longest-standing camp counselors, it would mean so much," he said with a smile.

I froze. I felt Mackenzie's hand twitch in mine. Her nails dug into my palm, and I silently gripped her fingers tighter, telling her without words: *Don't blow this. Don't show them we're prey.*

"Uh…" My throat worked uselessly. The duffel bag's strap cut into my shoulder, suddenly ten times heavier. It felt like a weight dragging us down.

Graham grinned at us, completely oblivious to our thundering heart rates. "It'd mean a lot to the kids; they love you both. Parents will be here too. It's your last summer. It would mean a lot to me and the camp."

I gave him a fake smile. I wanted to shove past him, drag her to my truck, and keep running. But every instinct in me screamed that if we bolted now, it would be obvious. Like jerking a rabbit out of a snare while the hunter was still watching.

Mackenzie's voice came out smoothly as she answered for us, but I felt the tremor in her hand. "Of course. We'd love to."

Graham clapped his hands. "Perfect! Sundown. Don't be late."

The woods creaked and whispered around us.

"We can't leave, Max," she whispered.

From the corner of my vision, I swore I saw a shadow move at the tree line. I turned sharply, heart slamming into my ribs, but only saw the empty forest. No one there. Nothing.

My pulse roared in my ears anyway.

We were trapped.

31

MAX

The campfire flames burned bright, casting a flickering light across our faces like the glow of a lightbulb just about to go out. The red and orange flames danced and sputtered, revealing secrets I was trying to keep locked away.

Mackenzie and I had just shared our experiences with kids, parents, and other counselors about why Camp Blackshear was one of the most amazing places we had ever been. How it had changed our lives.

But inside, I was screaming. Because every time I turned, I heard whispers coming from the woods..

My grip on Mackenzie's hand tightened as I struggled to shake off the fear and paranoia, but it was no use. Something was off; everything felt off. I was paralyzed with terror, convinced this might be the last time I ever saw her.

Losing her was my greatest fear. She was the love of my life, my addiction, my obsession. She was the part of me I didn't realize I needed, and the thought of losing her made me feel like all my limbs were being severed.

I wasn't interested in staying here and entertaining families when I just wanted to grab Mackenzie and run. I could tell she felt the same because her eyes kept drifting toward the edge of the woods.

"Let's go," I whispered to her, placing my hand behind my back and extending it toward her. I flexed my fingers to signal I wanted her to take my hand, and she responded by slipping her hand into mine. Just as we were about to leave, Graham boasted to the group.

"Tonight, we are excited to introduce our first-ever camp-wide scavenger hunt! This is a fun chance for team building, as we will divide you into groups. Each group will have a team captain to lead them through their course. Throughout the camp, clues will guide you to the final prize! Only one group will win!"

What the fuck?

In all the years we had been coming to this camp, we had never done something like this, not even on the last night.

The crowd erupted in cheers, with kids clapping and parents laughing as if it were all some big joke. But my stomach tightened.

We were being pushed straight into the woods. An eerie feeling of walking into the unknown cycled through me. We should've left earlier. We shouldn't be here.

Mackenzie's nails dug into my hand, sharp enough to draw blood. I glanced at her. Her face was pale, her eyes locked on the tree line like she already knew what waited out there.

I wanted to drag her away, but Graham was already herding groups, handing out little lanterns and cheap flashlights. His smile was too broad, too eager, like he couldn't wait to throw us into the dark.

"Max..." Mackenzie whispered, barely audible over the crowd's voices.

I leaned close, breathing her in like it might be the last time. "Don't let go of my hand."

She nodded, but then Graham came over and said, "I'm going to split you up for a bit."

"No," I ordered.

Graham didn't even flinch at my tone of voice. He just gave me the creepiest smile I had ever seen from him. For a second, I thought his gaze flicked past me, toward the black mouth of the woods, like someone was waiting there.

"Come on, Max, it's for maybe an hour at most. We need the groups to be with veteran counselors, and Mackenzie knows the woods like the back of her hand. Rhett will keep an eye on her."

I looked over at the douchebag. He was checking her out and wasn't being subtle about it. His eyes dragged up her legs, stopping at her hips, and then back up to her chest. When they landed on her face, he smiled.

Rhett pushed off the tree and sauntered over like he'd been waiting for this moment for weeks.

He pulled something from his back pocket—a cheap, plastic tiara, silver with rhinestones that caught the firelight.

He didn't even hesitate. He reached forward, brushing Mackenzie's hair back, and set the tiara on her head.

"There," he said, grinning. "Every queen needs her crown. Fit for our leader."

Mackenzie laughed; it was an awkward little giggle, but it still made me fucking jealous as hell. My chest went hot with rage. She looked so fucking beautiful, and Rhett was eating it up. He was trying to stake some claim on her right in front of me. I listened to the compliments she received about her crown and nearly gagged when I heard her say, "It does look good, doesn't it?"

I needed to calm down. But when I watched her laugh with him, touch his arm as he leaned forward, all I could see was red.

No. Fuck this. She wasn't going with him.

"I don't feel comfortable separating from my wife. I'm not going to allow this."

Graham looked over at me with a vicious stare.

"It's going to be okay, Max. You need to chill out."

I felt Heather next to me then, and I tensed.

"Ready… partner?" she said with a flirtatious grin, but when I looked at her, her eyes were cold. Over her shoulder, at the edge of the firelight, something pale and tall shifted between the trees. Antlers, or branches. I blinked, and it was gone.

I watched Mackenzie snap her head over, and a look of pure anger flashed in her eyes.

I sighed in frustration. "Fine, let's go."

I kept my eyes glued on Mackenzie as we descended into the woods. Her group was a few steps ahead of mine as we made our way into the clearing, but as the trees narrowed, I heard Rhett call out, "Sharp left, everyone!"

In a matter of seconds, her group was gone, swallowed by the trees. I pulled out my cell phone to text her, but I had no service.

"I'm going to fucking lose it," I whispered.

"Max… you're only going to be separated from her for maybe an hour. You need to calm down. There are kids here."

I looked back at the excited group of kids and parents and let out a frustrated breath.

"Okay, okay, I'll try," I whispered.

Heather pulled her backpack around to the front and unzipped the front pocket.

"Here," she told me, handing me a small blue and white capsule.

I opened my palm, and she dropped the pill into my hand.

"What is this?"

"It's an anxiety medication. I take it all the time. It will help calm your nerves so you can get through this game."

It looked too bright in my hand, wrong against my skin. But my heart was racing, my thoughts clawing, and she was smiling like she had the answer to all of it.

I took the pill dry, knocking my head back and swallowing it. The chalky taste clung to my tongue. By the time we moved deeper into the trees, the world felt a beat too slow, like someone had pressed a thumb against time and smeared it. My limbs were heavy, my thoughts slipping through my fingers.

Heather smiled, a slow, flirtatious smile, and then said, "You're going to feel a lot better here soon."

For about twenty minutes, we kept walking, following clue after clue, the kids' voices bouncing ahead of us through the trees. But slowly, the sound thinned until I realized it was just Heather and me.

"We've been following these stupid clues for what feels like forever," I shouted. My voice sounded so fucking weird. "Where is everyone?"

I peered into the dark line of the woods. The trees blurred at the edges, smearing into each other. From somewhere deeper in, I heard the faint scrape of something hard against bark. Like hooves.

"Did you hear that?" I called out to Heather. When I turned toward her, my body didn't turn with me. The ground tilted, and I had to throw my hand out to catch myself before I went down on my ass.

"Are you okay?" Heather asked, her voice suddenly sing-songy and sweet. She looked too bright in my vision, her long blonde hair haloed in the flashlight beam. My eyes kept losing focus, pulling her in, and then pushing her away.

I pressed a hand to my stomach. "Fuck, I feel like I'm about to puke."

Heat rushed up my throat. I lurched toward the nearest tree, shoulder slamming into the bark, and then bent over and spewed my guts.

MACKENZIE

THE GROUP OF CHILDREN WAS EXCITED, CHATTING LOUDLY AS WE moved further into the woods.

A few steps in, and we found our first clue pinned to a tree. I pulled it off and read it out loud to the group.

"Okay! We have our first clue. I wave when I'm happy, I wave when I'm proud, find me by the water, where the loons call loud. I'm rolled up tight, but I love to fly, look near the dock, and I reach for the sky!"

"It's a flag!" one of the kids called out.

We descended back to the dock, where, sure enough, the camp flag was rolled up with a second note attached.

Rhett grabbed the note from the flag and read out loud:

"Some friends are furry, with tails that swish, they hide in the forest and leap for a fish. Follow the trail where the trees grow tall, look for the sign of paw prints small!"

The kids rushed forward, heading back deep into the woods. Flashlights reflected off the ground, forming distorted orbs of light in front of us.

I followed, feeling Rhett slow down to walk next to me.

"You look good in a crown," he murmured, so quietly the kids couldn't hear.

I rolled my eyes, clutching the folded clue card. "Thanks."

"Max doesn't realize how good he has it," he continued. "You're so fucking beautiful."

I sucked in a breath, becoming uncomfortable.

"Sorry if that was too forward," he said, stopping right in front of me.

"It's okay, Rhett, but I'm married, and this conversation is inappropriate."

"I'm sorry. I'll stop. But know"—he stepped forward, closing the gap between us—"when he fucks up, there are others out here waiting for their shot. You have a full lineup."

He smiled, angled his flashlight low, and jogged to catch up with the group. I furrowed my brow at his comment. Full lineup? What did he mean?

My heart was racing as I followed the trail, which split in two. I turned right, hearing their voices echo through the trees, but as I moved forward, their voices grew fainter and fainter. I realized I'd taken a wrong turn.

"Wait… guys?" I called, picking up my pace. The rasp of leaves catching in the wind was the only sound that kept me company, along with the quickening of my heart rate.

My flashlight flickered, the light barely cutting through the trees. Every trunk looked the same. Every shadow bent toward me like dark arms outstretched.

I heard giggling, but it was faint, too far away. I followed the sound anyway.

The sounds intensified as I rounded the corner. And then I stopped.

My entire body felt as if it were being swallowed by quicksand. I couldn't move. I couldn't function. My brain went blank as I watched what was happening in front of me. I blinked hard, rubbing my eyes, desperate to erase the image.

Heather was shoving a tall, dark-haired boy against a tree.

Max.

She was plastered against him, fingers knotted in his hair as she yanked his face toward hers. His head wrenched away at the last second, her mouth crashing against his cheek instead of his lips. His hands weren't pulling her closer. They were on her shoulders, shoving, trying to force space between them. He looked… drunk. Sluggish. Like his body wasn't listening to what his hands were trying to do.

"Stop," he murmured. His voice was slurred, dazed. "I l… lov…love my wife."

"What the fuck?! What the fuck!! Oh my God, Max. What is

going on?" The scream ripped out of me. It almost didn't sound like me at all.

He pulled back from Heather and met my gaze, but his eyes were unfocused. His pupils were blown wide. He looked intoxicated, unnatural, like a ghost inhabiting his body.

He remained silent. There was no remorse, no tears, no flinching. He wasn't exhibiting any of his natural cues when he was in trouble. He just stared at me like he had no idea who I was while my screams shook the air. Then, he covered his ears with both hands and squeezed his eyes shut, like the sound of my pain was too much for him to bear.

"Mackenzie?" he whispered, his voice slurred and empty, like he didn't even know what he'd done or how he'd gotten there. "Run."

I stood there, shaking, my sobs punched back into my chest, about ready to run, until a new sound sliced through the clearing. Hooves scraping against wood.

Trembling, I turned toward the noise, my heart pounding against my ribs.

A man wearing a deer head stood in the gap between two trees. Antlers shimmered silver in the moonlight, grotesque and surreal. Broad shoulders. That lazy, confident stance. Even under the mask, I knew. He shuffled his feet from left to right, and he flicked his fingers at his side.

A habit I knew so well.

Jackson.

My lungs locked. I opened my mouth to scream, but Heather turned and smirked.

"Hey, baby."

The deer-headed man slowly tilted his head as he acknowledged her, then pulled out a long hatchet. The sharp blade caught the moonlight.

His gaze slid from Heather to me and stayed there, possessive and calm, as he lifted the weapon. When he finally spoke, his voice was low and warped under the mask.

"I told you you were always going to be mine."

I screamed, the sound shredding my throat, as he flipped the hatchet so the blunt side faced out and swung it sideways.

The wooden handle slammed into the side of Max's head with a sickening crack.

His knees buckled, and he crumpled face-first into the dirt.

Was he dead? Was he fucking dead?!

"MAX!"

He wasn't dead. His chest still rose and fell—barely—but he wasn't moving.

Please, God, let him be okay.

Something heavy shifted in the dirt behind me.

I didn't have time to turn before fingers closed around my arm.

32

MACKENZIE

I stumbled back, branches clawing at my arms like hooked fingers, moss slick beneath my shoes. My palms slapped against rough, wet bark, splinters biting into my skin as I fought not to go down.

Then something yanked me off balance.

I didn't even have time to scream.

I kept my eyes fixed on Max's lifeless form until I was dragged through the underbrush, my nails gouging furrows in the forest floor, scrabbling for anything to hold onto. Rotting leaves filled my mouth and nose, damp earth grinding against my teeth. Every instinct in my body shouted to fight, to run, but Jackson's monster dragged me along as if I weighed nothing at all—like I was already dead weight.

My legs slammed into rocks as he dragged me, each jagged edge tearing into my skin. Hot lines of pain burned down my calves. I tried to scream, but more leaves muffled me, forcing the sound back down my throat until it tasted like blood and dirt.

I twisted and thrashed, nails tearing at his arm, heels scraping uselessly against the earth. My muscles spasmed with panic. I could feel myself weakening, every pull stealing another piece of my strength. I was losing this fight, and he knew it.

Jackson grunted in irritation. His fingers clamped tighter around my ankles, the pressure so fierce I heard a tiny, horrible crack.

"Stop," I choked, the word scraping out of my bruised throat. "Let me go."

He stopped.

For a heartbeat, the world went silent. No wind. No insects. Just the pound of my pulse roaring in my ears. Then his fingers slid into my hair, slow and deliberate, before he yanked my head back so hard a white flash exploded behind my eyes.

"Shut the fuck up," he hissed, his voice so close I could feel every word vibrate against my skull.

Terror flared through me. My vision blurred. The trees around us seemed to lean in, their branches skeletal, watching me.

"Help!" I screamed, the sound tearing my throat raw. "Someone HELP ME!"

The words echoed into the dark, swallowed almost instantly, as if the night itself didn't want anyone to hear me.

Somewhere behind us, something moved. I heard the soft crunch of leaves, a low creak, like wood bending. For one wild second, hope clawed its way up my chest.

"Please!" I sobbed. "Over here!"

Jackson went still, his grip tightening around my wrists now until my fingers went numb. Slowly, he lifted his head, listening.

The sound came again. It was closer this time. A wet drag across the ground, like something heavy being pulled.

He leaned down, his lips brushing my ear.

"No one's coming for you," he hissed. "You hear that? The woods are leaning in to listen."

My heart pounded so hard it felt like it was trying to punch its way out of my chest. Jackson's fingers dug into my scalp, nails biting into my skin. I could feel a slow, hot trickle where he'd broken the skin, blood snaking down the back of my neck.

"Please," I whispered, the word barely more than a tremble.

He jerked my head to the side so violently my jaw clicked, a shiver of pain ripping through my skull. His other hand slid from my wrists to my throat, two fingers resting lightly over my pulse, like he was feeling the rhythm of my fear.

"No one," he laughed, maniacally. "Do you hear someone coming for you?"

I forced myself to listen. But I did hear something. A faint, irregular tapping, like bone against bone.

My mouth went dry. The cold crept inward until I could barely feel my own body anymore. Just the hurt. Just the terror.

"HELP!" I screamed again, every last shred of air ripping out of me.

This time, the echo didn't come back. The sound of my own voice seemed to hit something just beyond the treeline and die, snuffed out by the darkness' gaping mouth.

But I knew someone—*something* was out there listening to us. Breathing. Waiting.

Jackson shifted, and for the first time, I felt a twitch of unease in him.

"Shit," he muttered.

His hand fell from my throat. I took sweet, shallow, little gulps of air that felt like they might be my last.

I screamed again. He gripped my throat, harder this time.

"If you fucking scream again…" he whispered into my ear, "I'll kill you right here."

My body locked. It wasn't the threat that broke me; it was the way he touched me. His hands moved with the easy precision of someone who had rehearsed this, not just on me, but in his head, over and over, until my body was more blueprint than flesh.

He adjusted his hold on my wrist, thumb pressing down on a nerve that sent a lightning bolt of pain up my arm.

"Jackson," I said, the name flat, stripped of the question.

The deer mask tilted, those glassy black eyes catching the moonlight.

Then he ripped the mask off.

His grin was already waiting, stretched too wide, the skin at the corners of his mouth cracked and raw. His eyes were blown wide, fever-bright, skittering over my face as if he were checking items off a list.

"See?" he panted. "You *do* know me. So well, Kenz."

My mouth suddenly felt dry and metallic, like I'd been sucking on a battery.

"What… what the fuck is going on?" I forced out the words, clumsy, tripping over each other. "What are you doing?"

For a second, something in his expression faltered. The grin slipped, his jaw tightening like the question hit a seam he'd been trying to hide.

He didn't answer.

He just hit me.

The backhand came too fast to brace for. My head snapped sideways; my jaw popped, a bright spike of pain detonating behind my eyes. Sound thinned to a high ringing tone.

"I'm doing *my job,* " he spat, the words ragged, as if he were repeating something he'd been told. "I'm doing what I'm supposed to do."

He yanked me upward by my arms, slamming my back against the tree. Bark dug into my shoulders. His fingers locked around my forearms like restraints.

"Why are you doing this?" I gasped, copper spilling over my tongue. "Jackson, why?"

His breath hit my face in harsh, irregular bursts. His eyes kept flicking—not just to me, but past me. To the dark. To the trees. To nothing. Like he was looking into a portal to another dimension.

"No, no," he muttered, shaking his head once, sharply, like

he was correcting himself. "You're asking the wrong question. You always ask the wrong fucking questions."

"Then what's the right one?" The words scraped my throat on the way out.

He smiled again.

"Who I'm doing this *for,*" he whispered. "You need to learn. You need to fucking learn."

"Learn what?" I pushed, even as my chest tightened. "What did I do?"

His gaze snapped to mine, pupils almost swallowing the irises. For the briefest second, I saw a naked terror there.

"You fucked him!" he exploded, the word ripping out of him, going through the trees like a shot. "You gave him everything. You married him!"

Each accusation sounded rehearsed.

"You think he knows you?" His laugh came out jagged, too high, cracking in the middle. "He doesn't see you, Mackenzie. Not like I do. He never has."

Up close, the truth was impossible to miss.

The sweat beading along his hairline. A tiny muscle jumped in his cheek. The tremor in his fingers. His eyes kept darting to the side, to the tree line, to the sky. Someone was watching us.

This wasn't just about me.

This was a performance.

"You've been watching us," I said.

The words came out flat and heavy. A verdict.

His entire body jerked in a small, involuntary flinch. Then he straightened, forcing his shoulders back, rearranging his face into something like composure.

"Of course I have," he murmured, and now his voice softened, almost reverent. "That's the point. That's… that's the work."

"The work," I repeated, numb. "What work?"

"They picked me," he said, barely breathing the words. "Out

of everyone, they picked me. Because I see you. Because I see all of you. The lies. The pretending."

His grip tightened on my arms, not in anger this time, but in excitement.

"You think it's an accident?" His voice shook with a kind of wild pride. "That I'm here? That I know where you are, what you do, what you say when you think no one's listening? This is bigger than you and him and your stupid little vows." His lip curled.

Something icy opened in my chest.

"Jackson… who are 'they'?" I asked.

His smile turned inward, distant, as if he was hearing someone else speak just behind his own thoughts.

"The one's paying attention," he whispered. "The *Alliance*. The ones who actually give a shit about what's rotting this place from the inside."

The world *Alliance* sat between us like a third presence.

His eyes snapped back to mine.

"I finally matter, Mackenzie," he said. "I finally get to do something that counts. You don't have to understand. You just have to go through it."

His fingers dug deeper into my arms, almost shaking with conviction now.

He wasn't just unraveling. He thought this was him coming together, piece by piece, into exactly what they wanted him to be.

And I realized, with a nausea that hollowed me out, that somewhere in his head, this wasn't cruelty.

It was devotion.

He gripped my throat again, breathing in my scent at the base of my neck.

"God, you always smelled so good," he whined. He removed his hand from my throat.

I dropped to the ground, wheezing. My hands clawed at the dirt, useless and shaking as I tried to drag air back into my lungs.

"What do you want from me?" I spat, my voice raw.

"What I want doesn't matter," Jackson said, almost calmly. "What I'm *meant* to do does."

He stepped closer, boots grinding into the earth inches from my hand. That sick pride twisted his features. He'd finally become the thing he'd been practicing in the mirror.

A monster.

"You're 'Legacy Thirteen'," he went on, voice tightening with a horrible kind of excitement. "The endgame. I've got to keep you alive."

Thirteen. The word landed on my chest like a bomb. Like the prongs on the star. My family crest. A crown and a curse.

He leaned in with a calm, sinister smile.

"But that doesn't mean we can't have some fun."

I shook my head. The words didn't make sense; he didn't make sense.

"Legacy what?" My voice barely made it out.

He crouched, close enough that I could see the vein fluttering in his neck.

"You really don't know, do you?" he whispered, almost tender. "About your dad?" His eyes blazed. "The newspaper calls him 'The Butcher'. But really, he's 'The Alchemist'. The *Alliance* worships him. You're their queen, Mackenzie. The heir. Every legacy has to claim its place."

My stomach lurched so hard I thought I'd be sick.

"You're sick," I hissed. "You're so fucking sick."

He tilted his head, considering.

"I used to think I was sick. Until I met you. Then it made sense. I saw it in your eyes. I felt it. You're sick too. That's why we're meant to be together."

He leaned in and spat on the ground beside me, just close enough that I could feel the fleck of it on my cheek.

"You think this ends with you hiding in a dorm room and playing house with Max?" he grinned, the expression snagging at the edges. "He's an unmarked—a stray. Not blooded like me."

What the fuck was he talking about? He was talking in riddles.

"What? This is fucking insane, Jackson," I whispered.

His hands twitched at his sides, a constant, restless flex when he needed to feel steady. I could see the war in his eyes, a mix of devotion and rage. He wanted to worship me and destroy me in the same breath.

He stepped in closer.

"Time's up. All you've got to do is *scream,*" he said.

But I didn't scream.

I moved.

My fingers brushed against something solid just beneath the leaves. For a second, I thought I was imagining it. Then my thumb found the notch.

The hatchet.

He didn't see. His eyes were on my face, drinking in every flinch.

He straightened, looming. My hand tightened around the hatchet's handle, inch by inch, keeping my movements buried in the tremble of my body.

"I should have marked you first," he hissed. "I should've claimed you before you forgot who you belong to. But I was too busy following the fucking rules."

"I don't belong to anyone," I whispered, hoarsely, tears mixing with grime and blood on my face. "Max belongs to me. He always will belong to me."

My head snapped sideways as he backhanded me again; the world flared white.

"You don't get to choose your game," he whispered, breath hot and sour against my ear. "They choose for you."

He bent low, lips brushing my ear. The intimacy of it made my skin crawl.

"He'd be proud of me," Jackson breathed. "Daddy dearest. My future father-in-law."

He reached into his pocket with one hand. The other hovered above me, ready to strike if I moved wrong.

Something glinted in the pale moonlight. He was holding a small blade.

He pulled out a picture of Max, folded and worn at the edges. He lifted it up between us like an offering, then drove the blade straight through the paper. The metal punched through Max's printed face.

"I'll kill him for you," Jackson said softly. "Maybe then you'll see how much I love you."

The world narrowed.

I stopped seeing the trees, the sky, the blur of his face.

All I saw was the knife pinning Max's picture, and the hatchet in my hand.

"I hope he buries you," I spat, blood on my tongue.

He smiled, white teeth shining in the moonlight.

"Oh, baby. He ain't coming for you. Heather has a nice pussy. Super fucking tight. Max ain't gonna come for you once he gets his hands on her."

Something in me snapped.

I surged upward, driving my forehead into his nose with everything I had. The dull crack of bone-on-bone shuddered through my skull.

He roared, staggering back, hands flying to his face. The knife and photo dropped, forgotten, into the dirt.

I rolled, clutching the hatchet to my chest, and scrambled to my knees. My body screamed in protest, my leg on fire, blood soaking down into my shoe. The world tilted, but rage held me steady.

Jackson lunged.

I swung.

The hatchet's weight pulled my arm wide; I wasn't clean or precise. But the blade still caught his forearm with a sick, meaty thunk. He howled, stumbling sideways, clutching the sudden blossom of red.

"You fucking *bitch,*" he gasped, staring at the blood on his hand like it was a betrayal.

"Yeah, I'm a bitch," I panted. "And you still can't handle me."

My vision tunnelled in and out as I ripped the hatchet out of his arm. I could feel how much blood I'd already lost from the gash in my leg. My hands were slick on the handle, and I accidentally dropped it into the wet moss.

"You should've killed me when you had the chance," I said, my voice shaking but loud. "Because if I'm really the Alchemist's daughter, you better fucking run."

The hatchet lay in the dirt between us now, a dark, blood-slick shape beside the torn photo. We both saw it and lunged.

I was slower. My injured leg buckled. But I grabbed the hatchet in one swift motion.

He crashed into me, shoving me back into the tree. A strangled sound ripped from his throat. The massive gash along his forearm tore wider; fresh blood spilled, spattering onto the leaves.

For a split second, his grip faltered.

The hatchet slipped from my fingers.

Jackson's hand clamped down on the handle instead, knuckles whitening around it even as blood poured down his wrist, his arm, dripping from his elbow in thick streams. His face tightened in pain, lips peeling back from his teeth—but beneath it, something like exhilaration flickered.

We were nose-to-nose, blood streaming down his face from

his broken nose, his expression twisted, ecstatic. The hatchet's blade gleamed between us, flecks of red already drying along the edge.

"You think this ends here?" he panted, every breath hitching over the pain in his arm. "The *Alliance* doesn't stop. You'll play this game for years, until you're finally ready to move to the next stage." He grinned through a grimace, a wet, shaky smile. "And guess what? I'll be there every step of the way."

He grabbed me by the shoulders with his good hand and what was left of the other, and slammed my skull against the tree. A sharp, shrill ringing burst through my ears. The world wavered, then tilted sideways.

I slid down the trunk and hit the ground. The sky above was a smear of twilight and branches, blurring as my vision wobbled.

I let it blur.

I let my mind split open.

For just a second, I wasn't here. I wasn't in the dirt with Jackson's shadow looming over me and a hatchet in his hand. I was at the lake. Max's heartbeat under my cheek. His voice. His eyes when he thought I wasn't watching.

"I love you," I whispered into the ringing, to no one and to him. "I love you so much."

But clinging to Max wasn't enough. Not now. Not with the hatchet in Jackson's grip and blood screaming through his veins like fuel.

I wasn't the broken girl.

I was the storm.

A small white moth fluttered just above my face, its wings catching the faint light. I fixated on it. I focused on the softness of its movement, the impossible calm in its flight.

And then I twisted my body and got up.

Summoning everything left in me, I drove my elbow back, hard, into Jackson's temple as he reached down for me. He snarled, reeling sideways. His injured arm spasmed; he nearly dropped the hatchet.

I pushed off the tree, shoving my knee into his gut. Pain screamed up my own leg, but he folded with a wheeze, breath exploding out of him.

I clawed, shoved, and kicked. I fought like someone who had already died once and refused to do it again.

I scrambled to my feet, dragging myself upright on the tree trunk. Every nerve screamed.

He was already pushing up too, unsteady but grinning, teeth red. Blood poured from his arm in sick, rhythmic pulses, running over his wrist to slick the hatchet's handle again. His fingers trembled just to keep hold of it. I couldn't believe he was still fighting.

"You can't outrun what you are," he rasped, staggering toward me. Each step was a lurch, his wounded arm hanging a little lower, the hatchet wobbling in his grip.

He lunged.

I braced myself, lifting my arms—but then he jerked.

His entire body seized.

His mouth opened in a small, stunned O.

And then he slumped forward.

A wet, choking gurgle tore from his throat as he crashed into me and drove me back to the ground. Hot, sudden weight pinned me. Something warm and thick soaked through my shirt, my skin.

Blood.

His.

I froze.

The hatchet was sticking out of his back. It was buried to the hilt, the handle jutting up at a crooked angle.

Behind him, a shadow in black. A presence I recognized before my mind could form the word.

I didn't scream.

I didn't need to.

The shadow stepped past Jackson's sagging body, into the strip of moonlight.

My father.

The man who once cradled me in the dark, whispered lullabies, and taught me how to draw monsters—and how to become them.

He pulled Jackson's body off me like it was trash that offended him, one hand on the ruined shoulder, heedless of the torn arm and the hatchet still lodged deep.

"Failure," he said, almost bored, flicking his gaze over Jackson's twitching body.

Then my father knelt beside me.

"Get up," he said, voice low, almost tender.

I didn't move. Couldn't.

"I'm not here for you," he added. "Not tonight. It's not your game—yet. You need to run. They will take you if you don't."

My heart stuttered. He sounded almost protective of me. Like he was trying to shield me from the people who worshipped him.

He reached out and tucked a blood-matted strand of hair behind my ear with a touch too gentle for a killer.

"What about Max?" I croaked. My head swam.

He shook his head, almost fond.

"It's his turn now. Run, little one," he whispered.

I held my breath, staring into his green eyes. Exact replicas of my own.

"Who is coming for me? Tell me what all of this means," I rasped. "Are you the Butcher or the Alchemist?"

He didn't answer.

He rose, his silhouette dissolving into the trees, leaving only the rustle of leaves and the stench of blood.

I pushed myself up, raw, shaking.

I could hear it, my father's voice, echoing in my skull: *Run.*

The trees blurred into streaks of black and forest green as I staggered forward, then ran.

Jackson's words beat against my skull: *Legacy Thirteen. Your father. Max. Game.*

And beneath them, colder and calmer:

I'm not here for you. Not tonight. It's not your game—yet. It's his turn now.

33

MACKENZIE

I stumbled out of the woods, lungs burning, ribs aching, the cabins glowing in the distance like dying stars. My knees gave out, and I collapsed into the dirt, clutching the earth like it could anchor me to Max, to life, to anything except this fucking game.

"Mackenzie!"

The voice hit me like a jolt. Deep. Calm. Midwestern. Not at all what I expected.

I dragged my head up. The world tilted and slid, then snapped back into place around a single face.

He looked tired, shadows carved under his eyes, but it was him.

Jeremy. West's son. FBI, like his dad. He was supposed to be in Chicago. I hadn't seen him in five years, not since he went into the academy.

His dark skin and sharp Italian features contrasted with the black shirt clinging to his broader frame. New tattoos crawled up his neck. I saw black swirls and a spider, its legs stretching behind his ear like they were trying to burrow into his brain.

"Kenzie," he breathed, relief flickering across his face as he closed the distance.

Before I understood what was happening, I was on him, crashing into his chest. My fingers knotted in his shirt, clawing like I could peel him open and find Max underneath. My body shook so hard my teeth rattled.

"I've got you," he murmured, arms wrapping around me, strong and steady. "You're okay. You're out."

"Jackson… my dad…. they're—"

"I know," he cut in a low voice. "I've been… watching you. The cameras cut out and—" He stopped dead, jaw clenching, eyes skittering away for a second. "I need to get you out of here. Now." His tone snapped tight. "Where the fuck is Max?"

Max.

The name tore straight through me like a live wire.

I jerked back just enough to see his face, fingers still fisted in his shirt. "You don't know?" My voice came out shredded. "You said you were watching—tell me where he is. Jeremy, tell me. Is he in the woods? Is he still hurt? I have to get to him. I have to—"

"Mackenzie…" His voice was low.

A warning.

"I'm not leaving him!" The words exploded out of me. Everything else vanished. There was only the space between me and the trees. "He's still out there, isn't he? He wouldn't just disappear. He wouldn't leave me. He needs me. I know he needs me. He's hurt."

I tried to twist out of Jeremy's hold and turn back toward the woods, but Jeremy's arms locked around me like iron.

"Let me go!" I thrashed, nails digging into his chest, his arms, whatever I could reach. "Jere, let me go, I'm serious. I have to go back. I have to find him. You don't understand, he's not like them, he's not—"

"Kenzie, stop." His voice sharpened, grip tightening, dragging me closer when I tried to lunge past him. "You're not going back in there."

"You can't keep me here!" The words came out in a half-sob, half-scream. My lungs burned; my vision tunneled. "If you've seen anything, you have to tell me. You owe me that. Did he go deeper into the woods? Did he go to the cabins? Is he okay?"

He just stared at me, with a look on his face like he hated seeing me like this, but I could see the secrets behind his eyes. He was lying to me.

"I don't care what they told you to do. I don't care about your orders. Take me to him, Jere. Right now."

His expression sharpened. The guilt there was fast, sharp, and then gone.

"I can't," he said.

My hands shook so badly I could barely keep hold of him.

"What are you hiding from me? What happened to him? Tell me what the fuck happened, or I swear to God I will walk back in there myself—"

He caught my wrists as I tried to wrench free, pinning them gently but firmly between us.

"Mackenzie. Listen to me." His eyes locked onto mine. "You can't go back to Max."

The world went quiet for a second as I absorbed what he said.

"That's not funny," I said, but it came out thin, detached. "Don't say that to me. Don't you ever say that to me."

"I'm not joking." His voice dropped even lower. "You can't go back to him. It's not safe. Not for you."

"I don't care if it's safe." My laugh was too sharp. I felt wild, enraged, psychotic even. "Do you hear yourself? You think I care about being safe? He's my husband. Get out of my way." I shoved at him, tried to duck under his arm. He just shifted, blocking me, his body a wall between me and the tree line.

He wasn't as big as Max and not nearly as tall, but he was still about 6'1" with lean muscle.

"Move, Jere! I swear to God, I will scream this entire place down and shoot you with your own fucking gun. Move out of my fucking way!"

"We don't have time for this," he snapped, for the first time sounding like he might actually lose his grip. "You're in shock. You're not thinking clearly. I need to get you to med."

"I'm thinking fine." I could still taste dirt and blood and something dry that might've been panic. "Max is out there. He's alone. He thinks I'm dead or gone or—" My voice broke.

His jaw flexed. For a heartbeat, I thought I saw something like agreement flash in his eyes.

"Kenzie," he said quietly. "He's in the game now."

I stared at him. The words didn't land. They just hung there between us.

"What? How do you know about that?"

Jeremy swallowed, eyes flicking briefly toward the cabins, the trees, somewhere I couldn't see. When he looked back at me, his gaze was colder, more controlled.

"Max is in the game," he repeated. "He went all the way in."

I shook my head, hard, like I could rattle his voice out of my ears. "No. No, he wouldn't. He wants to protect me, but he would be looking for me first... he would."

"You saw what he did," Jeremy cut in, softer but somehow worse. "You saw what he chose."

"He didn't choose it!" My scream tore my throat raw. "They made him, or they tricked him, or they did something to him. He wasn't himself. He didn't choose this. You don't know him like I do. He wouldn't just—he wouldn't leave me. They attacked him. He wouldn't stay in there without me."

I tried again to twist free, to throw myself back toward the trees, and again Jeremy hauled me back, his grip unyielding.

"You're hurting me," I gasped, not sure if it was true or if everything just hurt.

"I'd rather you hate me than die," he said, voice flat. "You go back in after him, you don't come out. That's not a theory, Mackenzie. That's a fact."

"How do you know that?" My eyes burned; I blinked hard, tears smearing the world. "What do you know that you're not telling me?"

His mouth pressed into a thin line.

"Jeremy," I pleaded, the fight in my body turning frantic. "If you know something—if you've seen something—you have to tell me. Is he hurt? Is he alive? Is he—"

"Stop." His voice cut clean through my spiral. "There are things I can't tell you."

"No. No, you don't get to do that." I jerked against his hold until my muscles screamed. "You don't get to stand here and talk about 'the game' like it's some rulebook and then tell me there are things you can't say. That's Max. That's my…" The word caught in my throat, choking me. "That's Max."

His eyes flicked away again, for just a second.

"All I can tell you," he said carefully, "is that he's in too deep. And if you go after him, you'll be pulled in with him. And then we lose you both."

"Then lose us both," I shot back, instantly. The thought didn't even have to form. It was just there. Solid. True. "I don't care. I don't want to live without him. Do you get that? I don't want to live if he's still in there."

His hands tightened on my arms like he could physically hold that sentence back.

"That's not your call to make," he said.

"The hell it isn't."

"Mackenzie." My name sounded like a warning now. "This isn't just about you. Or him."

"Then who the hell is it about?" I demanded. "Your case?

Your fucking operation? Is that it? Is he just evidence now? A piece on your board?"

His face went still, the muscle in his jaw ticking.

"There's more going on than you know," he said finally. "More than I'm allowed to say. If I tell you, I put you in more danger than you already are, and you are already—" He broke off, biting the words back.

"I don't care about danger," I hissed. "I care about Max."

"I know." His voice softened for a fraction of a second. "That's why I can't let you go back to him."

I stared at him, chest heaving, everything inside me shaking apart. My mind raced, clawing for an angle, a weakness in his grip, a lie in his eyes, any way to get past him and into the dark where Max was.

"Let me go," I whispered. Then louder. "Let me go. Please. Jeremy, please. I'm begging you. I can't just leave him there. I can't."

His answer was final, brutal in its certainty.

"You're not going back to Max," he said. "Not tonight. Not like this. Not at all, if I can help it."

The words hit like a physical blow. The world dimmed around the edges, sound rushing back in a distorted roar. My body sagged against him even as my mind clawed and clawed, searching for a way to undo what he'd just said.

"When can I see him?" I rasped automatically. My thoughts raced in circles. I needed to figure out how to enter the game with Max.

Jeremy didn't flinch, didn't loosen his hold.

"I don't know. They don't tell us. If Max survives, he'll come for you."

I stopped breathing.

He'd said too much. I saw it in the way his eyes shuttered, the way his mouth snapped shut.

There was more. So much more. And he wasn't going to tell me.

Fine.

If he wouldn't take me to Max, I'd find my own way back to him.

JEREMY HALF-DRAGGED, HALF-GUIDED ME TOWARD THE GRAVEL road. Someone's SUV idled there, headlights cutting through the trees like interrogation lamps. Red and blue strobes from a distant cruiser painted the cabins.

Hands reached for me. They were all over the place—paramedics, uniforms, I didn't know. They talked over me, not to me.

"BP's elevated."

"Shock—"

"Get her seated…"

"I'm fine," I snapped, even though I couldn't feel my fingers. "Where's Max? Did anyone see him leave the woods? Did he—"

"We're handling it," one of them said smoothly, already turning away. "Just sit tight, okay?"

I grabbed his sleeve. "Handling what?"

He smiled the way people smile at scared kids. "We've got people on it."

On what. No one would say the word *Max* back to me.

Jeremy's hand closed around my arm again, gentler this time but no less firm. "Come on, Mackenzie. I'm taking you in."

"In where?"

"Someplace safe," he said.

I stared at him.

Nowhere was safe.

Jeremy put me on the back of his bike instead. It was the

same model he used to brag about back when we were kids, only darker now, sleeker, more government issue than reckless.

"Helmet," he said, holding it out.

"I don't need—"

"I know you're a fucking bad bitch and all, but sis, humor me."

I snatched it from him and shoved it on, fingers clumsy. I swung my bandaged leg over the bike, the wrap on my leg now pulling tight enough to make my eyes water. The engine roared to life beneath us. The first jolt sent a dull ache pulsing through my leg. The woods, the cabins, the screaming in my head started to peel away behind us in a blur of dark and cold air as we hit the road.

I pressed my forehead against his back, eyes open, watching the road rush by under the edge of the visor. Every bump in the asphalt jarred my ribs and sent a slow, mean throb through my bandaged leg, but it felt distant, as if it were happening to someone else.

Over the wind, I shouted, "You didn't answer me. Is he alive?"

Jeremy didn't look back. "Hold on."

"That's not an answer."

"I know."

The way he said it made my stomach drop.

Streetlights flicked past. A gas station. A closed diner. Normal life lined up along the road like a movie set someone had forgotten to shut down. No one was screaming. No one was bleeding. No one was playing a game with people's lives.

It didn't feel real.

I replayed every word Jeremy had said.

He's in the game. He went all the way in. There are things I can't tell you.

Couldn't, or wouldn't?

Everyone I'd talked to since I stumbled out of the trees had said the same kind of nothing, just dressed in different uniforms.

We're handling it.

We're taking care of it.

You need to focus on yourself right now.

No one had said: *Max is here. Max is gone. Max is dead. Max is alive.*

It felt less like they didn't know and more like they were all reading lines from the same shitty script.

By the time we rolled through the gates of the field office, my legs had gone numb. Fluorescent lights hummed overhead. Gray walls. Security glass. The kind of place that was supposed to make you feel safe.

It just made me feel trapped.

Jeremy killed the engine and swung off the bike. He offered me a hand; I ignored it and climbed off on my own, knees wobbling.

"They're waiting," he said.

My heart stuttered. "You mean, Tony?"

He didn't answer, which was answer enough.

Inside, the air smelled like coffee and toner and something metallic underneath. Agents moved through the corridors in dark jackets, glancing at me, then away, like they'd been told not to stare.

I caught snippets as we passed:

"—she's the one from the cabin—"

"—they said he stayed—"

"—don't mention the—"

Voices dropped when I looked at them. Smiles flickered on, bright and fake.

Jeremy led me into an interview room. There was no mirror, just a table, two chairs, and a box of tissues. I could hear the click of the camera in the corner of the ceiling.

I was being recorded.

Agent West came in stoically. Same suit as always, tie a little looser, hair grayer at the temples. His face carried that practiced mix of concern and authority I remembered too well.

"Mackenzie," he said. "I'm glad you're safe."

I didn't wait.

"Where's Max?" I asked. No hello, no pleasantries. "Don't tell me you're glad I'm safe until you tell me where he is."

A quick glance passed between him and Jeremy. It was over in a flash. If I'd blinked, I would've missed it.

West gestured to the chair. "Sit down. You've been through—"

"Don't." I stayed standing. "Don't talk to me like I'm a victim on a pamphlet. Tell me where he is."

He exhaled through his nose, slowly. "We're doing everything we can to locate him."

My jaw clenched. "That's not an answer."

"It's the only one I can give you right now."

"Funny," I said. "Jeremy said almost the exact same thing."

West's eyes flicked to his son again. "He did?"

Jeremy's expression didn't change. "I told her he's in the game," he said quietly.

My head snapped toward him. "You told him you told me?"

West's mouth tightened. I thought he might actually deny it.

"Given what you experienced," West said carefully, turning back to me, "it made more sense to be honest about certain aspects of the situation."

"Certain aspects," I repeated. "Not all of them, apparently."

He didn't argue.

"Okay," I said, my voice starting to shake for a whole new reason. "Then tell me the rest. How long have you known about this? How long have you been watching us?"

"I understand you're upset," West said.

I laughed, loud and sharp. "You have no idea."

"We've been investigating the group behind this game for some time." His words were smooth, practiced. "When we received information that you and Max might be targeted, we—"

"Might be?" I cut in. "You had cameras in the woods. You had Jeremy 'watching' us. That doesn't sound like *might*."

He paused. "We had reason to believe there was a high probability of an incident," he corrected.

"That's what you call it?" I asked. "An incident?"

His gaze stayed steady. "Mackenzie, I need you to understand that there are operational details I simply can't share with you."

"There it is," I said softly. "The line."

West frowned. "What line?"

"The one you all keep reading from. *We can't say more. We're doing everything we can. You're safe now.*" My hands balled into fists at my sides. "None of you will tell me where he is."

"Because," West said, the faintest edge creeping into his tone, "we don't know his exact location."

I stared at him. "Do you know if he's alive?"

Silence.

It lasted a second too long.

"We have no confirmation of his death," West said finally.

"That's not what I asked."

"It's the most accurate answer I can give you," he said.

Accurate. Not honest. Noted.

"You're lying to me," I said.

"I'm not," he replied calmly.

"Then Jeremy is," I shot back. "Because he told me if I go after Max, I don't come out. That sounds like more than 'no confirmation of death.' That sounds like you know exactly what the game does to people. To him. To me."

West's eyes cooled. "My son may have spoken out of turn."

"But not incorrectly," I pressed.

He didn't answer. Another one of those tiny, calculated silences he did so well.

Everything in me went icy.

They weren't just withholding. They were coordinating.

"Max is in the game," I said slowly. "You know what that means. You know where that puts him. You know what it would do to me if I tried to follow."

"Mackenzie," West said, leaning forward slightly, voice softening into what I recognized as his *interview mode*, "our priority right now is your safety. You've been through significant trauma. Your perception of events may be—"

"Don't you dare." My voice came out like broken glass. "Don't you dare tell me I didn't see what I saw just because it's not convenient for your report."

He sat back, studying me.

"I'm not your suspect," I said. "It's me. Mackenzie. I've grown up with you."

Behind me, Jeremy shifted his weight. I could feel his eyes on the back of my neck.

"We are not giving up on Max," West said at last.

"That's another line," I said.

"It's the truth."

My laugh came out thin and ugly. "You keep saying that word like it means something here."

He folded his hands on the table, perfectly composed. "Whether you believe us or not, we're working to dismantle the organization behind this and to recover everyone we can."

"Everyone," I echoed. "Not him."

"Everyone," he repeated.

But when he said it, his eyes slid just slightly away from mine.

Everyone was lying. Or if they weren't, they were lying by omission, which felt worse.

Either way, they were never going to tell me what I needed to know.

Which meant, like always, I'd have to figure out on my own.

34

MAX

24 HOURS EARLIER

A slight nibble from a rabbit on my fingers snapped me out of a deep sleep.

Or what felt like sleep.

I must have lost consciousness. Or blacked out? My brain wouldn't land on a word that felt right.

The sun shone brightly through the trees. It was fucking bright. I squinted, shielding my eyes as I looked up. Had the sky always looked like that? It looked like someone had pulled a fake sky down over the real one.

Heat bounced off my skin in thick, sticky waves. I was soaked in sweat. Damn. I felt hungover. My fingers rustled through the leaves as I hurried to find my phone.

It was cracked and lying on the ground beside me. I didn't remember dropping it. I didn't remember lying down. I didn't remember anything after Heather's face leaned in too close.

I tapped my phone's screen three times until the light pierced the shadowed corners of my surroundings.

1 p.m.

Holy shit.

Camp check-out was in an hour. It should've been loud—

cars, kids, counselors, parents—but the woods around me felt padded and far away.

I knew these woods so well. I had grown up around them. But today, I felt like a stranger in a new world.

I felt so dehydrated that I could have drunk a lake. I sat up and almost fell backward. My head was pounding, but not in a normal hangover way. It felt like pieces were missing. Every time I tried to grab a memory, it slipped through my fingers and left this raw, empty ache behind. A heavy wave of depression rolled over me from nowhere, like I'd just gotten the worst news of my life and forgotten what it was.

Fuck, fuck, fuck, fuck.

Something had happened, but my brain was mush. The last thing I remembered was talking to Heather. She'd slipped me something, right? A drink? A pill?

Panic struck me when I thought about Mackenzie. Shit. She must be so worried about me. Actually, she was probably furious and planning to make me pay. She was plotting my death right now. I could just see her furrowed brow as she bent over her journal, jotting down all the ways she was going to kill me.

I stood up too fast. The world lurched sideways. I staggered, catching myself on a tree. My steps felt delayed. Like, there was a half-second between my brain telling them to move and them actually doing it.

The walk to the cabins felt eerie. It was almost silent. Usually, the camp buzzed with kids' chatter as they waited to be picked up.

By the time I stepped out of the trees, my shirt was damp with sweat, and my hands were shaking.

As I returned to my cabin, most of the counselors had already left. The only person remaining was Heather, passed out in her bunk with her blonde hair splayed across her face.

I ignored her and headed straight back to my room to find Mackenzie and apologize. But it was empty.

At first, I didn't panic. Perhaps she was in the dining hall or in the bathroom. Maybe I'd walk in, and she'd be there, sitting on the counter, rolling her eyes, calling me an idiot.

I opened the bathroom door and was met with darkness. The air was stale, like no one had been in there for days. I flicked the light, just to be sure. The harsh yellow glow fell on the tile and an empty trash can.

I looked around. Her bags and belongings were gone.

I tried to rationalize with myself that I wasn't seeing what I was seeing.

My ears started ringing, a high, thin whine that drowned out my own breath.

No, no, no, no.

I grabbed my phone and shot her a text.

> Trouble, where are you? I'm so sorry to worry you. I dk what happened last night.
>
> I'm at the cabin. Please txt me as soon as u get this.

The bile rose in my throat as a distant alarm sounded. I stared at the text after I hit send, half-expecting it to disappear, for the words to rearrange themselves into something I hadn't typed.

Nothing was making sense.

I ran to the front of the cabin and poked Heather's shoulder. I used more force than I would've used for a girl, but I was freaking the fuck out. My fingers felt clumsy, too strong, and too weak at the same time.

She opened her eyes, rubbing them.

The look she gave me told me that something bad had happened, something really bad. It stirred a paranoia inside me I hadn't felt before.

"What the *fuck* happened?" I croaked.

Heather flinched but didn't answer. Her lips trembled.

"Say it, Heather," I growled, struggling to stand on wobbly legs. I had to grab the side of her bed to keep from falling over. "What did you give me?'

Her arms tightened around her chest.

"Just something to help you calm down," she whispered. "You were spiraling, and I didn't think you'd take it if I told you what it really was."

"What. Was. It." My voice dropped to a dangerous octave.

"GHB," she said quietly. "The date rape drug. It was just… it was supposed to help. I swear, Max, I swear."

The room spun. Not just the room—my thoughts. My memories.

"You drugged me?" I snapped, stepping forward. She recoiled. "You gave me that shit? Why?"

"I… I just wanted to know what it was like to be with you."

I stared at her like she was something rotten.

Images tried to push their way into my head. Memories of her hand on my chest, her breath on my neck, her body pressed against mine, rolled to the front of my brain. But they kept slipping, cutting in and out like a bad signal. Every time I reached for one, it broke apart.

"You fucking bitch." The words came out hoarse. Something flickered at the edge of my mind: her touching me, her kissing me, her trying to climb on top of me. My stomach rolled.

"You knew exactly what you were doing," I said through clenched teeth. "You touched me when I couldn't even think straight."

I paced the room, my hands pulling at my hair like a madman. The cabin felt too small, the walls too close, like they were inching in. The floor seemed to tilt under my feet, then snap back.

"You've been fucking waiting for this moment all summer, huh, Heather?"

Heather's eyes welled with tears, but it didn't move me.

"Did we fuck?" I asked.

If she said yes, I'd probably kill her.

"No," she said quietly. "You told me no."

At least I knew that even in my drugged-fueled state, I wasn't a complete fuck-up, and was still faithful to Mackenzie. It was always going to be her.

A jagged flash hit me, the memory of me shoving Heather off, slapping her hand away, my voice slurred, saying no, crying, telling her *I love my wife.*

"So you tried to rape me then," I said flatly. The words hung in the air like a guillotine.

She got up, legs unsteady.

"Please, Max, please don't say that."

"Why not?" I asked. "Because if I had done this to you, I'd be in jail already. If I had drugged you and tried to rape you, everyone would burn me alive. Why is it okay for you to do it?"

Heather was crying now, messy, choked sobs. She collapsed onto the mattress and curled in on herself.

I shoved my duffel bag onto my shoulder. It felt lighter than it should have. Or maybe I was going numb.

"Now, where the fuck is she, by the way?"

"Who?" Heather asked, voice thin.

"My wife." The word scraped my throat. "Mackenzie."

Heather shook her head, not meeting my eyes.

"She… she came in this morning. I mean, she saw us last night."

My lungs squeezed so tight I couldn't breathe. Had she seen? What had she seen? A loop of her voice sounded in my head.

What the fuck? Oh, my God, Max?

I couldn't tell if it was a real memory or something my guilty conscience made up. I didn't do anything, I kept telling myself. So why did I feel like I did?

I hadn't protected her.

"Did she… did she say where she was going?" I asked, my voice trembling.

Heather shook her head again. "No, but she was crying. She looked… rough. Like she'd been through hell. She was barely dressed… you know, she had been with Rhett."

My vision blurred at the edges. A red haze crawled in. I almost punched a hole through the goddamn wall.

I huffed, grabbing my phone out of my pocket. My fingers didn't feel like mine.

"Max, please. I'm so sorry. I just wanted to see what it would be like," she cried.

"Go fuck yourself," I said, coldly.

Heather's jaw settled, and then she went in for one last attack.

"She moved on, you know." She looked at me so matter-of-factly that it stopped me in my tracks.

"Shut the fuck up, Heather," I warned.

"After she fucked Rhett, she hooked up with another guy—older. Black hair, dark skin. He had his hands all over her. Her hair was a mess, his hair was a mess. She was wearing his clothes. He was shirtless."

The picture formed in my head instantly, too vivid, like it had been waiting there. Like I'd already seen it somewhere. Like someone was feeding it to me.

She wouldn't do that to me, would she?

I stopped, staring at Heather, and then walked over to her dresser, ripped one of the drawers out, and threw it. It landed with a loud bang next to the bunk. I grabbed another drawer and threw it.

I screamed so loud, so deep, so fucking primal that my throat was raw. Heather shrieked.

"Max! Stop! You're scaring me!" She had her hands over her ears.

Good, I thought, for one sick second. Then even that thought scared me.

I grabbed my phone again and found Mackenzie's number in my favorites.

MRS. MCKINNON ☺

As the phone began to ring, I looked over at Heather and said, "Have a great life, you fucking cunt," before walking out of the cabin.

The phone rang and rang and rang, then flipped to voicemail.

"Hi, it's Mackenzie! Leave me a message—"

The sound hit me like a physical punch. For half a second, I felt like I was glitching. I stuttered into her voicemail like a scratched CD.

"Trouble… where are you? Please, please call me back." My voice was shaking so badly I could barely get through the message. "I'm sorry. I don't—I don't know what happened. Please just call me."

I ended the call and immediately opened my messages app. My previous message was unread.

I started typing as fast as my fingers would allow.

> Trouble, please call me. Please.

> I am so sorry. So sorry. So fucking sorry.

> I love you.

I swallowed the lump in my throat. I couldn't imagine how she was feeling right now. The empty pit in my stomach was enough to make me want to climb into my grave. I had failed her.

Heather's voice rang through my head.

She's moved on, you know. Some guy was with her. She was wearing his clothes.

The image sharpened again, uninvited. The guy's face still

wouldn't come into focus. Like the game in my head was buffering.

I wanted to know who the fuck this guy was. I called her again.

"Trouble, please answer. I love you. Nothing happened, Mackenzie. Please let me explain. Heather gave me drugs. Please just answer."

I hung up feeling like my world had just exploded. I sent her off a few more texts. I couldn't remember exactly what I typed minutes after sending them. My brain felt like it was skipping frames.

As soon as I reached the checkout line outside the dining hall, I was a nervous wreck and felt as if I would collapse at any moment. I was hungover with confusion, guilt, and heartbreak. My skin buzzed. My hand instinctively went up to my shoulder —to *our* tattoo.

I held it while listening to the birds chirp in the trees. Everything felt normal now. I closed my eyes, listening to the wind, feeling the sun on my back, and hearing Mackenzie's laugh in my ears. She couldn't be gone.

Laughter from a group of kids nearby jolted me out of my thoughts. No one around me knew my entire life had just fallen apart. All the smiles from parents picking up their kids and the laughs from the counselors made me want to stab myself in the eye.

"Max! I can't believe this is it," said Graham.

I stopped, watching him.

For the first time, I was seeing him for what he was. An intruder. A snake. I had seen the look in his eyes last night when he split us up. He had wanted us to hurt.

But was that what actually happened? Or was that just how my brain remembered it now?

"Yeah, man, can't believe it," I said half-heartedly. I gave him my badge and quickly scanned the crowds for Mackenzie.

Graham noticed and started typing something on the computer.

"Mackenzie left already."

"What?" My voice sounded small, warped in my own ears. He gave me a cold look of sympathy.

"Yeah, I'm sorry, man. Some guy came and checked her out early this morning, like 5 a.m."

Graham handed me my sign-out papers.

"What guy?" My voice was possessive, and he noticed.

"Tall dude. Older, maybe like twenty-five? Dark hair, dark skin. Serious as hell. I don't know the details. You know him?"

I blinked.

The description matched what Heather had said. Too perfectly.

A chill ran down my spine.

"Did he say something to you?"

"He… uh… he said he was her brother, came into town for the weekend, was here to check her out. Kind of weird, right?"

The word brother was not something I had expected to hear.

"Are you fucking kidding me?" I barked. "Did you see her?"

"No. Just him."

I practically ran to my truck. As soon as I got in, I let out the most resounding scream I could muster, punching the steering wheel until my knuckles cracked.

"FUCK!" I screamed.

Something had fucking happened. I had let something happen on my watch. I was so confused. Fuck, was I confused.

I had fucked up so badly that I would never be able to live with myself if she had been hurt. Not just by me, but by anyone else.

Who the fuck was this guy everyone was talking about?

A small part of my brain went to the intrusive worst thoughts: that maybe she hadn't been faithful, that maybe there was a part of her life she still hid from me. But even those thoughts felt planted, like someone had set them in front of me and waited to see which one I'd pick up.

I pushed them down.

I had to make this right. I had to make sense of what was going on. I loved her so fucking much. I needed to fix this.

Driving home to Atlanta, I dialed her every five minutes, but I kept getting the same voicemail.

"Hi, it's Mackenzie! Leave a message!"

Her voice seared itself into my brain as I listened to it repeatedly. Sometimes I was sure the message was a little different. I'd hear an extra breath, a different lilt in her voice, only as soon as I replayed it, I'd realize it was exactly the same.

After about the 30th call, I was done.

"Fuck this."

I pulled over to the side of the road. My heart was about to cave in, and my chest felt like it had been ripped out. I pulled out my phone, found her contact card, and then typed her address into Google Maps.

I turned around.

Three hours and fifty-one minutes later, I was pulling up in front of her house. This was the first time I had ever been here. I should've made more of an effort with our friendship. As soon as I got my license, I should've visited. I had fucked up more than I thought. I was a shitty friend and an even shittier husband.

I fingered my wedding ring, as if maybe the touch would make her appear.

Her house was nice. It had a large wraparound porch and two rocking chairs in front. The welcome mat in front of the door had a dog on it that looked like her dog, Abby, and read, "WEL-COME FRIENDS."

The porch boards creaked under my feet in a slow, even rhythm. Too even. Like I was walking on a loop.

I was so nervous. I felt like I was going to be sick again, and whatever side effects that shit Heather gave me caused, I was still feeling them.

I rang the doorbell and waited.

And waited.

And waited.

No one ever came.

I rang the doorbell again.

Still, no one.

I looked through the front window and saw a large dining table in the front room, with what appeared to be a piano nearby. The house was dark, with no signs of activity. No dust either. Nothing out of place. Like a model home waiting for someone to move in.

I moved to the side and checked the windows there; still nothing. They weren't inside.

I came back to the porch and sank into a rocking chair, thumb hovering over the screen of my phone. I would sit here all day until she came home.

My phone rang.

I snatched it up. "Hello?"

"It's Dad." His voice was low; there was a steadiness to it that made my chest tighten. I let out a disappointed sigh, and then anger rolled through me at hearing his voice.

"Where is she?" I cut straight to it. My voice was calm by force, but I wanted to rip his fucking head off.

There was a long inhale. I could hear movements on his end, fabric rubbing. He was walking away from someone.

"She's safe," he said finally. "I can't tell you anything else."

"You're not my operator, you're my father," I said. "Tell me where my wife is."

"I told you, she's safe." He sounded tired, like he'd been up all night. "I can't—"

"Don't lie to me." The words came out sharper than I meant. Panic was a hard thing to hide. "If you know…"

"You don't get to ask about this," he snapped, then softened. "You failed."

The word went straight through me, clean and cold.

"I know," I interjected. "I know I failed to protect her. But you know how much I love her. I've loved her forever."

He let out an exasperated sigh.

"I know you wouldn't hurt her. But you took the pill, and now you've fucked everything up."

"Fucked what up?" I snapped.

"You went in," he said, like it was obvious. He let out an exasperated sigh. "You're in the game now, son."

An electric jolt ran through me.

"That secret society bullshit?"

"Max. You are aware of what is happening, right?"

I shivered. He was in on it.

"I know that camp is bugged. You can't fucking tell me you missed everything," I seethed, grabbing onto the only thing that felt solid. "You saw what happened. I know we've been watched."

"Max…" he warned.

"You work with them, Dad. You're CIA. You can help her, right?"

"That's not how this works," he hissed. "You agreed to it. You knew there were risks. You were briefed—"

"I wasn't briefed on anything," I cut in. "I took a pill 24 hours ago in the woods and woke up to whatever fucking nightmare this is. Dad—what the fuck is happening?"

"Max…" he warned.

"You keep saying I 'went in.' In where? Into what?"

He paused and then said, "That's classified."

A bitter laugh punched out of me. "So now my brain is classified?"

"Max, you signed—"

"I didn't sign anything." My heart pounded so loud it hurt. I dropped my voice just one octave before saying, "And I don't appreciate you taking my wife away and becoming a CIA lab rat."

"That's not what this is," he said quickly.

"Then what is it? "I asked. "Because from where I'm standing, this is all a bunch of bullshit. You took my FUCKING WIFE away from me."

On the line, the air thinned. I heard my mom's voice in the background, and his tone changed.

He laughed easily, calmly into the receiver.

"Listen—don't take too long. We've got your gear ready. Mom needs you to check your boxes to make sure she got all your stuff packed."

It was scary how fast he had switched personalities. Like flipping a channel.

"Dad," I said quietly. "Don't do that. Don't pretend this is normal. You knew, didn't you? When you sent me to camp. You knew there was more going on."

"Max, not now…"

"Is it your people running this?" I pressed. "CIA? You knew this was happening to kids, and you still let me go."

Static picked up on his end, like he'd covered the phone for a second. When he came back, his voice was low.

"Max, you can't follow her. You cannot hack in and try to find her. They are watching you closely now, and you need to do whatever you can to not draw attention to yourself."

"Who is watching me?" I asked, already knowing the answer.

"Your game started last night. Don't ask me about it again."

He hung up.

I stared at the dead screen as if it might split open and give me answers.

Your game started last night.

My hands went numb.

I had been an idiot to think that my father would protect us. Something was seriously fucking wrong.

✳

I waited two more hours, calling her over and over, until finally I decided enough was enough. The knots in my stomach morphed into one giant ball of panic.

Shit.

Heather had blown up my socials all night. I blocked her from everything. Fuck her. But I knew it didn't matter. What had been done was done, and now I was going to have to do whatever I could to persuade Mackenzie to take me back.

I checked Mackenzie's Instagram. The last picture was three days ago, our hands together in front of the lake.

I missed her so much I could barely breathe.

The next morning, I came up with some bullshit excuse about needing to go back early for baseball. My mom was disappointed but let me go, reminding me to bring Mackenzie by when I could.

I had told them last night that we were married. My mom noticed my ring right away. She was thrilled because she had always loved Mackenzie, but furious that we had done it without them knowing, and reminded me how young we were. My dad pretended to be shocked, and it took everything in me not to pin him to the wall and demand answers about Mackenzie.

He knew something. He was hiding. It drove me insane to know that I couldn't interrogate him.

This was my wife. This was Mackenzie. She had disappeared. I needed to know where she was. I needed to know what my game was. I was going insane.

As soon as I was on the road, I found myself obsessing over her in my thoughts. I hadn't called her since last night, and all my texts were still unread. She wasn't checking her phone, but I had to try.

I expected to hear her voicemail message, but instead got an automatic one:

"We're sorry. Your call can't be completed as dialed. Try again later."

When the three beeping sounds of the call being dropped rang through my ear, I nearly drove off the road.

SHE CHANGED HER FUCKING NUMBER?!

I dry heaved. I swerved into a gas station, not giving a fuck that I was driving like a maniac. I called her again.

"We're sorry. Your call can't be completed as dialed. Try again later."

FUCK.

She had. She had disconnected her phone. She had cut me off.

I immediately went to Instagram to message her. I typed in her handle @soccershotsmacmckinnon and went cross-eyed when it said NO USER FOUND.

No. Fuck, no. Had she deleted her Instagram?

Had she blocked me?

Had someone erased her?

I fucking burst into tears. I was… heartbroken. I was pathetic. I deserved this, but the pain was unbearable.

I felt my chest crack open, my ribs splinter apart, my breath stagnant and rabid. I was dying. Had to be. That was the only explanation for this feeling.

This overwhelming feeling of pure, terrifying sadness. I didn't know how to get in touch with her. I was losing my mind, even becoming psychotic. I hadn't gone a single day without talking to this girl since I was twelve years old. She was the goddamn center of my entire life. She was my whole fucking soul.

And in the blink of an eye, she was gone.

Like someone had cut her out of the world and left me in the empty space where she used to be.

35

MAX

I slammed my fists into the steering wheel again and again until my knuckles split open. Blood smeared across the leather, the metallic scent filling the car. My breath came in ragged bursts, hot and shallow.

I couldn't see straight. Couldn't think. The world narrowed to red.

Grief blurred into fury, and I hit harder, until the wheel rattled like it might tear loose from the column.

This wasn't anger anymore. It was torture.

I didn't hear it, not at first.

The screech of the tires beside me.

By the time my head snapped up, it was too late. Glass exploded across my face, shards slicing into my arms as my hands flew up on instinct. Two men in black masks were already there, swinging golf clubs at the car. Metal screamed against metal.

The door was yanked open. Rough hands grabbed me, dragging me out and slamming me onto the pavement. The air shot from my lungs as my shoulder hit the ground.

I shot up to my feet in a blur of rage. My fist collided with the first man's jaw. Bone cracked beneath my knuckles. He went down, but the second was faster. An arm snaked around my chest, yanking me back before slamming me into the side of the truck. Metal groaned. My skull bounced off the frame, and for a split second, the world went white.

I listened to my heart beating as I regained clarity of the world around me.

Ba-dump.

Ba-dump.

Ba-dump, ba-dump, ba-dump, ba-dump, ba-dump.

I tried to push myself up, but I could feel pieces of glass biting into my skin. Blood trickled down my arm, my leg, my side. Every nerve screamed, but my body wouldn't move.

I opened one eye, and the first thing I noticed was my wedding ring on my left hand. I looked at it intently, as it was my anchor to her, the only thing that could help me stay calm amid this chaos. I was fighting for *her*.

I could do this.

I wanted to yell for her. I wanted her to hear me. Hear my voice. I wanted *her*.

I pushed myself up, wobbling on shaky legs as I blinked at the world around me.

Two gas pumps.

A whispering fog curling low over the asphalt.

Glass at my feet.

And then—

A hand seized my wrist.

I tried to twist free, but I was too slow.

I felt the needle in my neck before I could react. Fire spread under my skin. The parking lot spun, colors bleeding together. The masked men blurred into silhouettes. Through the static roaring in my ears, a voice slipped closed.

"Congratulations, Mr. McKinnon," it murmured. "It's initiation day."

Darkness swallowed me, and I went down.

✦

MY HEAD WAS FUCKING POUNDING, LIKE A HANGOVER AND A concussion had joined forces behind my eyes.

Everything hurt—the back of my neck, my jaw, even my teeth.

I blinked slowly, as light flickered against the metal surfaces. The air smelled strongly of gasoline, rubber, and a sterile scent reminiscent of bleach and latex gloves.

My wrists were restrained with zip ties, the plastic cutting into my skin as I moved. My mouth was parched, coppery with blood. My temple was sticky.

I tried to sit up, only to realize I couldn't. My ankles were zip-tied as well. I was on the floor of a moving cargo van, the lack of seats and rattling steel walls giving it away.

What. The. Fuck.

I dragged myself across the floor, clawing for the wall until my fingers found cold metal. Pain tore through me as I forced my body upright, a raw scream ripping from my throat. Shards of glass jutted from my hands, arms, and legs, blood sliding down in slow, sticky streaks.

I pressed my back to the wall, fighting to steady my breath.

This wasn't random.

This was calculated retribution because of her.

Mackenzie.

Maybe she hadn't really left me. Maybe they had taken her, too. The thought of it made my fists clench until the zip ties cut in deeper.

A voice crackled from the front seat, muffled and faint. I couldn't catch the words. Suddenly, the van slowed, swerved, and hit a gravel road. I was thrown forward by the sudden movement.

They were taking me somewhere remote, off the grid. To do what? Kill me?

A shiver ran down my spine as a disturbing thought surfaced: had they already killed Mackenzie?

The van suddenly lurched to a stop, and I fell forward, hitting my chin on the floor. Pain sliced through my brain, and a shrill ringing filled my ears, like someone had jammed a live wire into my skull.

The engine from the van cut out, replaced by an unsettling silence. A loud clang sounded as the back doors swung open, letting cold, fresh night air flood inside.

I peered through the gap. The sky was filled with stars, and in the distance, the tall pines rose up in that shape I knew too well.

Camp Blackshear.

I was back.

A low buzzing from above made me flinch.

"Max McKinnon," a woman's voice crackled through the speakers, clear and Australian. "Welcome to your initiation."

I froze.

The doors at the back of the van opened with a sharp scrape of metal, and a masked man dressed in black stepped forward to free me from my restraints.

"Stand up, straight, please," the unknown woman said through the speakers. "I want to see you."

I felt like a prized cow about to be exhibited.

I saw a shadow just beyond the van's light, but I couldn't make out a face. I stood, wincing from the pain everywhere, but straightened my shoulders as much as I could to look strong.

"Very good," she said. "You'll do nicely."

"For what?" My voice was shaky. I hated that she could hear my fear.

Pain lanced through my body, every movement sending sparks of agony up my spine. My mind struggled to focus on what was happening.

"We have an outfit for you. Put it on," she said.

I turned and nearly laughed. The masked man was holding out a black, tactical FBI vest, thick and padded, with a matching mask that would completely hide my face. It was a matte black skull mask with mirrored eyes. Military issue, cool as hell, but I wasn't going to admit that to them.

Gloves, boots, and a utility belt completed the ensemble.

"Really?" I said, sarcastically.

"Put it on, Mr. McKinnon," the voice commanded.

"Fuck no." I crossed my arms and pressed my back against the cold metal of the cargo van.

A sharp *BANG* shattered the air as a gunshot tore into the ceiling above me. My heart slammed against my ribs, every nerve screaming.

"Put it on, Mr. McKinnon. This is an order."

I snatched the clothes from the man, every nerve on fire.

"Fine. *Fuck,* fine." My hands shook violently as I peeled off my shirt, then my shorts, the cold metal of the van biting at my bloody skin.

"I can see why Mackenzie chose you," the voice hissed through the speakers, satisfaction laced with malice.

"Close your greedy fucking eyes, you bitch," I growled, voice low, teeth clenched. "I'm married."

I dug my fingers into my skin, pulling out the jagged shards embedded in my arms. I winced as each piece tore through tender flesh. Blood welled and slicked my skin, dripping down in thin rivulets.

One by one, I worked the shards free from my legs, gritting my teeth as each pull sent fire through my muscles.

Then I felt it, a long, cruel piece buried deep in my side. My stomach clenched as I felt the sharp stab of pain that stole my breath. I yanked the glass shard out, the world tilting as crimson stained my hands, slick and sticky, a stark contrast against the cold metal floor beneath me.

Every movement made the blood run faster, every heartbeat a reminder of how raw and fragile my body had become.

"Where is she?" I snarled, yanking the clothes from the man's hands. The fabric felt heavy, alien in my hands, and my chest hammered so hard I thought it might crack my ribs.

I shoved my arms into the long-sleeved black shirt, then jammed them into the vest. The straps dug into my skin. I slammed the velcro shut and fixed the masked man with a glare I hoped could pierce through the hollow mask he wore.

"I said, where the fuck is my wife?"

I swore I could see the curl of a smile beneath the cotton, but a ticking sound, like a clock counting down, snapped my focus away.

"Your time is almost here, Mr. McKinnon," the voice said, smooth and detached. "You'd better get moving."

I huffed out a breath of frustration but kept going, swaying a bit from the amount of blood I was now losing.

I put on the black cargo pants, then the mask. It slipped over my face, feeling hot and suffocating, pressing against my jaw. The eyes of the mask slightly fogged from my breath. My visibility was almost zero. I could only perceive muffled sounds and faint shadows.

How many eyes were on me right now?

The air felt too still, too intentional.

There had to be cameras, hidden somewhere in the corners, maybe even behind the vents. Knowing how the Alliance operated, this wasn't just an initiation. It was entertainment.

I could almost *feel* them. Men in tailored suits, watching from the dark, placing bets on me like I was a horse in their private race.

How far until he breaks? They were saying.

How much pain before he taps out?

They were betting on me. For what? To prove I deserved Mackenzie?

She doesn't even want you, my brain sneered.

She left you.

I hammered the top of my skull with my knuckles until the van echoed with dull, hollow thuds. The masked man tilted his head, watching me. Maybe I was losing it. Maybe a little. I didn't know what the fuck I was doing.

The minute I slipped on that mask, something changed. I wasn't Max anymore. I was a different animal: a psycho, a killer. Exactly what they wanted me to be.

"Good," the woman's voice purred through the speakers, amused and predatory. "You'll look perfect for the task."

I flexed, testing the vest. The ring under my gloves was a tiny, hot reminder of Mackenzie. Of what we had been just hours before.

Did she still wear hers? Was she even alive?

A single tear tracked down my cheek, and I almost let myself break. I didn't want this. I didn't want whatever came next. I only wanted my wife.

But they had her name on their tongues. They would hurt her if she were even still alive. I was so stupid. So fucking stupid. I should've never let Graham split us up. I should've protected her more.

"Exit the vehicle," the voice snapped.

My feet moved on their own. The door slammed shut behind me, and I was immersed in total darkness.

I couldn't see a fucking thing. It was dark, darker than I remembered. I had been here just a few hours before. But it all felt different, now.

A gloved hand shoved something into my palm. I lifted the mask and found an earpiece clipped to a radio. My hands shook as I jammed the earpiece in and secured the radio to my waistband. I slid the mask back down, my breath fogging the inside.

The woman's voice was right in my ear. "Good job. Time to choose your weapon."

The illumination from an overhead floodlight stabbed down through the trees. I blinked against the glare and peered through the skull's eyeholes. A table sat in the clearing: a knife, a pistol, and a battered wooden bat.

"Notably, the gun only holds one bullet. Choose wisely." Her tone was clinical, patient.

Something rustled at the tree line.

A snap of twigs.

A footstep on rocks.

The forest sounded alive with teeth.

I was about to enter a game of catch-or-die.

A flicker of shock burned through me.

I stared at the weapons. The bat was honest, brute force I could handle. The gun was quick and final. The knife was close, personal, but it reminded me too much of Mackenzie, and my hand shook thinking of grabbing it.

My fingers itched. I wanted the bat. I grabbed it, spun it, felt the steady weight in my hands.

"Good," the voice said. "If you fail, you will never leave these woods."

"What?" My voice cracked.

"Tick tock. One hour, or she dies."

My heart detonated. My fingers tightened on the bat until I could feel my knuckles whiten under the gloves.

"You're threatening my wife?" I shouted into the dark, turning in a slow circle. "You think that scares me? I'll kill for her. Including *you.*"

"That's what we hope for," she replied.

"What about the FBI? This is federally protected territory.

Someone will save me." I tried to sound defiant, but the words tasted hollow.

I was scared.

Really fucking scared.

But I didn't want them to know that.

A soft laugh came through the speaker. "Camp Blackshear is Alliance territory now."

The world dropped out from under me. Panic hit like ice. My throat closed, and beads of sweat began to slick the inside of the mask.

"Good luck," she said, and the crackle of the channel closing echoed in my ear.

The floodlight snapped off.

Darkness swallowed me whole. The forest pressed in tightly, thick with silence. My pulse roared in my ears.

But I knew these woods. I could outsmart them. *Could I?*

I forced myself forward, one step at a time. The bat was heavy in my grip, slick with sweat. Every sound, the crunch of dead leaves, the rasp of my breath, felt too loud. Blood squished in my shoes.

Then, there was light.

A red flare hissed in the distance. Then another. Then a third.

They were leading me somewhere.

I followed the trail, muscles coiled and ready. The air grew colder the deeper I went, the scent of lake water sharp in my lungs.

Halfway there, a distorted scream exploded through my earpiece.

"Max! Max, please! Save me!"

I froze. My heart stopped.

"Mackenzie?"

"Max, please! He's coming! Please save me!"

I started running. Branches tore at my arms, shadows bleeding into motion around me.

"Trouble!" I shouted. "Trouble! Where are you?!"

Her voice looped in my ear.

"Max, help me! Please help me!"

Over and over, louder, and closer, her voice tortured me. She was right ahead, and everywhere.

Each scream splintered deeper under my skin until I couldn't tell what was real anymore. Had they taken her? Was this a trick?

Her voice hit another pitch. It was raw, broken, and pleading.

And it shattered me.

It was torture. I wasn't running anymore; I was sprinting through hell to get to her.

I stumbled into the clearing. Moonlight skated across the lake. In the center, strapped to a chair, was Jackson.

He looked like someone had used his face as a punching bag. There were purple and black bruises mottled on his skin, one eye swollen shut. His white shirt was dark with blood; red grooves marked his wrists where zip ties had bitten in. His left arm was fucked. A deep, jagged gash split through his forearm, crudely wrapped in blood-soaked gauze. It looked like someone had taken a chainsaw to it. He was pale as a ghost, sweat beading across his brow.

The voice in my ear came cold and clinical. I flinched.

"This is your trial, Mr. McKinnon. Kill him, or she dies."

I went rigid, then began to pace the bank, the bat a heavy metronome in my hands. Jackson lay slumped, out cold, until the voice cut in again.

"What are you waiting for? Eliminate the target!"

My hands trembled around the bat.

"Oh, fuck," I breathed.

The voice started counting. "Ten… nine… eight…"

I had thought about killing Jackson several times, but now that the opportunity was here, I couldn't do it.

On the last syllable, *one*, Jackson's head lolled up.

He blinked, then stared into the eyes of my mask, as if he

could see straight through it. He knew it was me. I could see the recognition all over his face.

A slow, ugly grin crawled across his blood-streaked mouth.

"Max… I told you, you couldn't handle her."

He spat blood all over the ground, giving me a smug smile. The anger pulsed through me.

"By the way, I was worried she would feel used up by the time I got her back. But she felt awfully nice in the woods. Still so fucking tight."

I nearly dropped the bat when I heard that.

"What did you say?" My voice trembled, my legs shaking.

"She didn't fight me after I hurt her. I loved every minute of it."

I pulled my mask off, wind rushing through my hair. All hesitation was gone now. A darkness spread through my body, and a heavy feeling of hatred pulsed through my veins.

I wanted him to see my face when I killed him. I lifted the bat, my hands shaking with rage, my heart hammering against my ribs. Time slowed. The world narrowed to the swing, to him, to the choice I had to make.

"This is for her."

I swung.

The bat felt like thunder in my hands. The first hit folded him. Jackson's smug face contorted as if surprised I did it. Blood splattered all over my vest as he let out a yelp that was swallowed by the pounding in my ears.

From that moment on, my mind went blank. I only felt. I could feel her. Crying. Smiling. Laughing.

His head was slumped over as he tried to gather his breath.

The second hit was uglier. Wood met jaw, and Jackson's knees buckled as he fell forward out of the chair. His hands clawed for the ground as if he could sink into the dirt and hide. There were sounds I'd never heard from him—raw, animal noises—until I drove the bat against his kneecaps, and he stiffened with a loud groan.

Around us, the world narrowed. I wasn't Max anymore. I was someone else.

The man behind the mask.

I was him.

When Jackson tried to push up, his face smeared with blood, his eyes wild and unfocused, I hit him one more time. The bat cracked against his temple, and the sneer drained from his face as I beat it in like a pulp.

The screams I made echoed through the trees. He folded like old paper as I beat him.

I stood over him, chest heaving, the taste of adrenaline metallic in my mouth. Jackson wasn't breathing.

Had I killed him?

Someone grabbed my arm, tearing the bat down, pulling me back, but I was already somewhere else. My mind was in a place where only anger lived. My vision tunneled; the edges of sound stretched thin and distant. Mackenzie's voice cut through the haze like a knife, and it was the only thing I had left to hold onto as the darkness rolled over me like a wave.

Everything went black.

✦

WHEN I WOKE UP, I WAS IN MY HOUSE AT GCU, THE ONE I HAD rented for Mackenzie and me. I was completely clean. Not a single speck of blood.

I groaned as I tried to sit up.

"What the fuck happened?" I groaned. My eyes fluttered open and closed as I tried to regain some sense of composure.

My whole body felt like it was about to shatter. I looked

around the room. Everything was in its place—my sheets on the bed, my things on the dresser.

Baseballs. Awards. Stacks of textbooks. It was exactly the way I would've set it up. If I had actually done it.

When the hell did this happen?

I tried to pull the covers off me, but a soft ping from my phone on the nightstand made me freeze. That sould shouldn't have been the scariest thing, but it was. I stiffened and snatched up the phone, my thumb clumsy on the screen.

I checked the date.

August 15.

My birthday.

Amazing.

One week had passed since Blackshear.

I had been out for a whole week. Gone. I had no one to call. No one to talk to about this. There were days missing in my head. Days ripped out like paper. My injuries were still all over my body from the glass, but I was bandaged and healing.

Somebody had patched me up.

Did the Alliance heal my wounds? Had they carried me in here, stepped over my shit, and tucked me into bed like a joke? I hadn't even moved in yet. How did all my stuff get here in the first place?

A cold feeling slid down my spine. They'd been in my house. In my room. They knew exactly how I would set things up.

Another ping from my phone jolted me out of my thoughts.

The message lit my screen.

You've survived. The real game begins soon.

My stomach dropped. Before I could even breathe, another notification hit. A photo downloaded, filling the screen.

Mackenzie.

She was on the back of a motorcycle, arms wrapped tight

around some guy's middle. Helmet on. No face I could see. Just her body pressed into his. I knew it was her. The way her shoulders were hunched forward, the way she held onto him.

Was this the guy who had checked her out from camp? Her *brother?*

I screamed.

The sound bounced off the walls. My hands shook so hard I almost dropped my phone.

I looked down at my other hand, at my wedding ring. My fingers trembled. My chest burned with jealousy and fear and something darker, something that felt a lot like the man in the mask back in the woods.

They had her.

They were using her.

I didn't care who got in my way; I would find her.

Even if it meant dying to get her back.

I just didn't realize the price wasn't my life.

It was Max McKinnon.

EPILOGUE

Max
Three Years Later

Max McKinnon was dead.

At least, the version of me that went on romantic kayak rides and shot arrows for fun. That version of me lurked in the shadows of Blackshear's trees.

These days, I was the new Max.

A killer.

A lethal weapon.

A psychopath.

A monster.

All because of a girl. All because of her. My fucking wife.

"Hypnotize" boomed in my ears from the nano, the bass rattling my skull.

Tap, tap, tap.

"Fuck off!" I groaned, mainly to myself, my hand trembling as I wiped it over my mask. I was high out of my fucking mind. Was I really hearing those taps, or was I creating them again?

Tap, tap, tap.

"What!" I screamed, pushing myself up off the floor.

The cargo van lurched violently, tires screeching against the asphalt as we raced toward my new target.

"Shut the fucking music off," Kate whispered in my ear through the headpiece. Her voice was a venomous hiss, cold and threatening, controlling my every move.

"Fine." I ripped the nano's earbuds out of my ears, a shudder running through me as silence slammed into my skull with oppressive weight.

"On my count," Kate hissed in my ear. The van jerked to a stop. "Door. Out. Execute."

By the time the van door slid open, the high had settled into a vicious, buzzing calm. Rain slapped the pavement.

The masked men shoved the bat into my hand, pointed toward the alley, and closed me out.

My target hunched over, his hands and feet zip-tied, soaked in sweat, whimpering in terror. He was primed for me, a broken figure.

Fuck.

I wanted a cigarette. I wasn't really a smoker, mainly because it wrecked my body for baseball. But now, I did things the old Max would have never dared.

Like, kill people.

I raised the bat and slammed it into his face.

My target spit out a mixture of blood and, I think, a tooth, but it was hard to tell behind my mask. My breath fogged the inside of the lenses. If I hadn't been so goddamn drugged up, I probably would've made more of an effort to cover my tracks.

But I was a twenty-two-year-old killer now. Four kills under my belt. I did what I was told, no questions asked.

I was born and bred a warrior for the Alliance.

I was so deep in this world, I didn't know how to claw myself out. I had tried a couple of times. They beat the shit out of me. They electrocuted me once. That was fun. I pissed myself.

Not my finest moment.

But they always threatened to kill her every time I tried to run.

Again. And again. And again.

So, I took it. The pain. I obeyed. I listened. I executed.

They sent me the coordinates. I followed the orders. I was a perfect little serial killer. I hadn't been Max in three years. I was just a conduit for a world of darkness, killing unknown men I knew nothing about because they told me they would hurt her.

Some would say I'd gone mad. Maybe I had.

"What are you fucking laughing at, you psychopath?" the man screamed from behind thick gurgles of blood.

Had I been laughing? Shit, I had.

My laughter died instantly. The only sound left in the alley was the dull pitter-patter of the rain.

"Are you going to kill me?" he sobbed.

I lifted the bat, rubbing the blood-soaked wood against my FBI jacket. They had upgraded me over the years. It was tactical now, bulletproof, knife-proof.

Everything I needed to be an actual psychopathic war animal.

The skull mask was the same, though. It helped me disappear. It helped me become the man behind it.

The Executioner.

That's what they called me in the news, anyway. I was an A-list celebrity in Athens.

I had no idea who this guy was. The only thing I was given was a picture of him touching Mackenzie. He had forced himself on her at a club in Florida.

So naturally, he was a dead man to me.

"Please. Please! I haven't done anything wrong. I'm a good guy!"

I lowered the bat and tapped it against the pavement.

Tap. Tap. Tap.

Most days, I didn't feel right in the head. If I wasn't hallucinating Mackenzie, I was killing. I liked the feeling of swinging my bat and hitting a target.

Every guy I killed was a predator anyway. After Blackshear, it felt like the only way to bleed out the trauma. I had held back too much then. I knew better now.

Did I hate that I had somehow become the very thing Mackenzie was terrified of? Her *dad.*

Yeah. It stung to think about. I'd spent years trying to protect her, and it turned out it was a complete waste of my time. In the end, she was always going to hate me, and I was always going to become a monster.

For the first two years after I was taken, after I lost Mackenzie, I obsessed over her. I checked the news. Hacked accounts. Drove past places we had been together, hoping maybe, just maybe, she'd be there.

I memorized every conversation. Every kiss. Every breath she ever gave. And I bled them into my nightmares. Every single fucking day.

After Jackson's death, everything changed. I only remember flashes. The swing. His blood. Then, I woke up in my room with no real memory of how far I had gone.

They told me she would be killed. My parents would be killed.

So, I played along.

Until I didn't want to anymore.

One afternoon, they cornered me on campus, dragged me into a van, and took me to a warehouse with barred windows on the outskirts of town. It happened so fast I barely felt it, but the pain seared my skin for weeks afterward.

They had branded me with a cattle prod—a deep, thirteen-pronged star. Right over my heart.

They had claimed me.

I was an Alliance creation now.

The cold band of my wedding ring scraped against my chest

beneath the tactical vest. It was the last tether to the man I used to be.

I'd tried to get rid of it. Believe me, I had.

But even buried in a drawer, it mocked me. I still couldn't let her go, even though I fucking hated Mackenzie McKinnon.

My wife.

The fucking bane of my existence.

I didn't want her dead. I wasn't a total sociopath.

But I wanted her to hurt.

I hated her for not saying goodbye. For moving on without me. For breaking me. For leaving me alive with a heart that wouldn't stop beating her name.

It took me three years. Three fucking years to cage the love that owned me.

And I did it.

Or at least, I thought I had.

I could still feel the love for her locked deep inside me, buried by the hatred that now consumed me. The fucking rage.

She was the only thing that kept me moving through those years.

But grief has a way of rotting you.

And I was coming for her.

I looked down at the coughing mess at my feet. Rain blurred my vision, burning as it slid into my eyes. He was nearly blind from the blood in his eyes, so he wouldn't notice who I was. Right?

I slid the mask off my face and exhaled into the heavy, wet air. It clung to my lungs like it didn't want to leave. I forced myself to really look at my victim.

Was I as high as I thought, or did I actually know this guy?

I looked again. Through the blood and spit smeared across his face, past the swelling and the streaks of red, I still knew him.

"Rhett?"

ACKNOWLEDGMENTS

The night I met Max McKinnon, I had no idea he would consume my entire soul.

I've spoken openly about my journey to Blackshear, but for those new here, Max visited me in a dream back in February 2019. In this dream, he candidly told me all about his best friend, Mackenzie, and a place called Camp Blackshear. The dream was so vivid I could smell the sunscreen and the pine trees.

I wrote the initial outline of the book on the back of my nursing log in the hospital, as I was about 24 hours postpartum when Max visited me. Was I having some sort of manic episode? Possibly.

However, shortly afterwards, I discovered my favorite band, Sleep Token, and their music propelled me to continue writing. I was heavy in postpartum depression, navigating life as a mom of two children, very close in age, working full-time, and living miles away from the closest family. At the time, I was living in upstate New York.

It took me seven years to get Blackshear to where it is today, but I'm so proud I kept going. Every time I felt like giving up, I could hear Max tell me to continue, that I could do it, that he was proud of me.

Sounds like Max, huh?

I'm so thankful for everyone who has helped me, and supported me in this journey. Never in my wildest dreams did I think I would be a published author, not even all those years I studied literature in college! But here I am.

Special thanks to my editor, Nicole, who brought Blackshear from debut level to where it is today. Also, special thanks to my artists who helped shape Blackshear's visual identity. I'm still so blown away by my cover art by Ashlee O'Brien. When I told her I wrote a dark romance with slasher vibes, she basically said, "Say no more," and came up with the coolest cover.

Thank you so much to my beta readers who helped shape Blackshear in its early format. I absolutely loved the ideas you brought to the table and how obsessed you all became with the world I created.

And to everyone who has sent me messages of encouragement, I love you.

ABOUT M.E. MASON

M.E.Mason is an award-winning former journalist with over 15 years of experience in marketing, public relations, and writing for television, film, and nonprofit communications.

She spent years covering crime stories, which gave her a front-row view of the darker sides of human nature. These experiences now inspire her dark, twisty romances.

She lives on the outskirts of Houston, Texas, in an area that she calls "suburban country." When she's not chasing deadlines or wrangling her busy household, she's crafting stories of obsession, betrayal, and love that burns.

instagram.com/authormemason
facebook.com/authormemason
tiktok.com/@immemason

A SHATTER IN THE WOODS SERIES

BLACKSHEAR

M.E. MASON